MORE PRAISE FOR JADE LEE!

HUNGRY TIGRESS

"A highly sensual, titillating read."

—*Romantic Times BOOKreviews*

"*Hungry Tigress* is unusual and provocative...[and it] delivers a love story that all romance readers can appreciate."

—Romance Reviews Today

"Jade Lee is quickly on her way to becoming a unique and powerful voice in this industry."　—A Romance Review

WHITE TIGRESS

"An erotic romance for those seeking a heated love story."

—*Romantic Times BOOKreviews*

"Jade Lee has written a complex, highly erotic story... extremely sensual."　　　　　—*Affaire de Coeur*

"This exotic, erotic and spiritual historical romance is unique."　　　　　—Harriet Klausner

DEVIL'S BARGAIN

"Jade Lee has written a dark and smoldering story...full of sensuality and heart-pounding sex scenes."

—*Affaire de Coeur*

"A luscious bonbon of a sensual read—the education of an innocent: hot, sensual, romantic, and fun!"

—Thea Devine, *USA Today* bestselling author of *Satisfaction*

"A spicy new debut...."　　　—*Romantic Times BOOKreviews*

*A NEW HISTORICAL ROMANCE FROM THE
CREATOR OF THE TIGRESS SERIES*

BRAVING THE STORM

Evelyn was drawn to fierce power. It was her one wild trait. Thunderstorms always found her outside, soaked to the skin, daring the heavens to strike her down. Perhaps that was why she walked directly toward Jie Ke now, into his dance of fists and feet that was just like a storm. He did not stop. She'd known he wouldn't.

His blows continued. With his eyes firmly fixed on her, he began a series of furious punches and jumping kicks, assaulting the air around her. She was safe; so long as she stayed absolutely still, he would not touch her. But one breath, one hair out of place, and she knew she could be knocked unconscious. It was his silent dare. How steady were her nerves when eight stone of weight was aimed right between her eyes?

Evelyn smiled. Part of her wanted to close her eyes and lift her face to the sky as she did in a thunderstorm, but she could not break the hold he had on her gaze. His breath touched her; she felt and gloried in its force. She smelled his scent then, too—strong, with alien spices, but not in the least bit rank. He was simply different...and wholly compelling.

Own me. Possess me. She cried those words to thunderstorms. She screamed them silently as she danced in the rain. She'd never before thought that about a man. Not until now.

JADE LEE

THE DRAGON EARL

LEISURE BOOKS NEW YORK CITY

A LEISURE BOOK®

September 2008

Published by

Dorchester Publishing Co., Inc.
200 Madison Avenue
New York, NY 10016

ISBN 10: 0-8439-6046-9
ISBN 13: 978-0-8439-6046-4

Printed in the United States of America.

10 9 8 7 6 5 4 3 2 1

Visit us on the web at www.dorchesterpub.com.

THE
DRAGON EARL

Chapter One

A Chinese monk was walking up the aisle at her wedding. Evelyn blinked to make the apparition go away, but there he was, bright yellow robes billowing out behind him as he strode the length of the Norman church. Right toward her.

Evelyn hadn't heard the commotion at first. She'd been waiting breathlessly for her moment to say, "I do." But a minute beyond "Dearly beloved," her bridesmaid sister had giggled nervously. Maddie often giggled inappropriately, so Evelyn ignored it. Moments later she'd heard at least four whispers, two creaks from the pews, and one gasp. The final blow had come when the Reverend Smythe-Jones faltered. His words stumbled and his mouth fell slack. That had been too much. She'd had to see what was behind her, no matter that it was her wedding and brides did not turn around in the middle of their ceremonies. So she'd turned her back on cleric and future husband, shot a warning look at her sister Madeline, then glared all the interruptions into silence.

That's when she'd seen him: the Chinaman. There were three of them, actually—two men and a boy—but the first seemed to dominate, with his ground-eating stride and his bright yellow robe.

This simply would not do. Evelyn shifted her gaze to her father and arched her brow. She could already see the Earl of Warhaven, her fiancé Christopher's father, rising to his feet on the other side of the aisle. But the earl was choleric in temperament; he'd likely make a bad scene worse. Thankfully, her father felt the same. He would get to the disruption before her future father-in-law. It would take only a moment.

Except, it did not take a moment. Her father had barely found his feet when the Chinaman reached the front pew. Evelyn expected that the twin form of both fathers would at least make the man pause, but it didn't. He neatly and almost magically sidestepped them. One moment the fathers blocked the man's path; the next moment, he had somehow left them behind and was continuing up to the dais.

And still, all Evelyn could do was stare. The man wore yellow robes that wrapped him from head to foot. At her wedding?

"Now see here!" Christopher exclaimed as he stepped forward, his outrage a palpable force. He sounded just as an indignant viscount and future earl should, and Evelyn felt the tension in her shoulders ease a bit. Christopher would handle this disturbance.

But the Chinaman completely ignored him. He bowed once respectfully to the reverend, then threw back his cowl to focus on her.

"My God, you're white!" she gasped. And he was, with bright blue eyes, a Roman nose, and ruddy, stubbled skin. If he hadn't obviously been in robust health, she would have thought he resembled Christopher's great-grandfather before the poor man died at the age of ninety-eight.

The white Chinaman arched an eyebrow at her. It was an aristocratic expression and completely at odds with his clothing. Then he spoke in a commanding voice that was strangely accented. "You are Evelyn Stanton? Of twenty-four years age today?"

Evelyn swallowed and forcibly reminded herself that she would one day be a countess. Lifting her chin, she responded as haughtily as possible, "I am, and you, sir, belong outside." She should turn her back on him, she decided. It was the best way, according to Christopher's mother, to dismiss someone in regal fashion.

But before she could even start to move, his arm shot out. He grabbed her elbow and held her fast. She squeaked in alarm, but fortunately Christopher intervened. He'd been too slow to prevent the Chinaman from touching her, but managed to grab hold of the man's rather massive biceps, clearly outlined by the folds of his robe. And there they stood, Christopher holding the bizarre Chinaman, who held her.

"Release her, sirrah," Christopher growled.

Again the Chinaman ignored her fiancé, and he boldly scanned Evelyn from head to toe. From the tight compression of his lips, he was none too pleased with what he saw. "You are to wed the Earl of Warhaven on this date? In this church?"

"Yes!" she snapped. "Now go away!" She glanced over his shoulder—no easy feat given his height—in the hope that the fathers would be able to help. But what she saw made her grimace with disgust. Trust the men to be having a furious whispered debate with two other gentlemen while completely ignoring the Chinamen interrupting her wedding. What was going on?

Meanwhile, Christopher leaned forward and spoke clearly and directly into the Chinaman's face. "If you have something to say to my wife, you can do so after the ceremony." He jerked his head sideways at his groomsmen. "These are my brothers. They will escort you outside where you will await our pleasure."

The Chinaman's gaze abruptly sharpened, but was not on Christopher or his bristling brothers. Instead, he pinned the Reverend Smythe-Jones with his intense stare. "The ceremony is accomplished? They are wed?"

Was there a note of hope in his voice?

"Er . . . no . . . n-not yet," stammered the cleric. "We'd just begun." Then the reverend abruptly straightened and peered down his bulbous nose. "If you would please leave the altar area, I will proceed."

"Then I am in time." The Chinaman's tone was almost dull, but still clearly heard. He turned to Christopher, and with every word, his voice became clearer and more authoritative. "You are not wed. And she is promised to me—the earl."

"Sirrah—"

"And now I am here." He turned to look at the reverend. "You may marry us. I am the Earl of Warhaven."

Once again, the words did not fit into Evelyn's consciousness. She heard him, of course. Everyone likely heard him, with that booming voice of his. But the meaning would not settle in her thoughts, and she simply gaped at him.

Not so Christopher, who snorted one word—"Madman!"—then waved to his two brothers. As one, they sprang into action to drag the disrupter out of the way. Evelyn did her part, shying sideways to stand protectively in front of the elderly cleric. She also kept a watchful eye on her sister. Madeline was more likely to join the mayhem than avoid it.

Unfortunately, this Chinaman who was not Chinese refused to release her. He held her fast in one hand while—quick as lightning—the other shot forward in two chops: one to Christopher's forearm, the other to his shoulder. Evelyn's fiancé gasped and stumbled backwards, his arm dropping uselessly to his side. Evelyn reached out instinctively, trying to steady him, but he was too far away and she was held fast.

Then it was the brothers' turn. They rushed forward, but the Chinaman lashed out with his soft brown boots from beneath his yellow robe. Truthfully, the footwear did not look all that solid—designed more for warmth than fighting—but Evelyn distinctly heard the impact of each kick. Alcott took two blows, one to his chest, then his face, and dropped on his bottom beside Christopher. Stephen's arms were raised to protect his face, but his knees were vulnerable. Two kicks to his legs and he dropped away.

"This is ungodly!" cried the reverend as he charged around Evelyn to attack the Chinaman. The madman did not react. He simply stood his ground. His hands remained lowered as the elderly cleric rushed forward. Evelyn had a moment of irrational hope that a man in his sixties could accomplish with fisticuffs what three brothers in their twenties could not. She was wrong. At the last possible second, the madman stepped back and away, easily avoiding the reverend's fists. The cleric swung anyway, missing by a mile as the madman arched backwards. Then the reverend's momentum carried him farther to stumble down the dais steps and into the arms of the other Chinaman, the one wearing orange-saffron robes.

"Don't hurt him!" Evelyn cried.

The other Chinaman—a real Chinaman this time—didn't need the warning. He gently guided the cleric to a seat—on top of the countess—and then returned to his place between the madman and everyone else.

Evelyn hurriedly scanned the crowd for more assistance. But the people in the pews remained rooted in place, their mouths hanging open like an audience at a bizarre show. To one side, Christopher and his brothers were regrouping, but it would take them a moment. On the other, Madeline had dropped her bouquet and raised her fists.

"Don't you dare!" Evelyn hissed, effectively stopping her miscreant sister long enough for their cousin, who was the other bridesmaid, to grab Maddie's skirt and hold her back. Which left Evelyn at the top of the dais with a madman. It was up to her to end this.

Using her bouquet as a weapon, she roundly smacked the intruder on the back of his head just as she would an errant child. "Why are you ruining my wedding?" she demanded. It was a ridiculous question. Madmen did not respond well to reason, but it did at least bring his attention to her. Perhaps that would give Christopher enough time to coordinate an attack.

"My apologizes for my tardiness," was the man's response,

and it came in surprisingly cultured tones. "I wish no one harm," he said as he tossed a glare at Christopher and his brothers. "But I am the earl, and you are my intended bride."

"Don't be ridiculous," Evelyn returned. "You are nothing of the sort."

"But I'm afraid he is!" came another voice, a young voice tremulous with apology. It took a moment for Evelyn to find the speaker. He was older than his voice suggested: twenty-six, she guessed. He was standing next to the arguing fathers, his pale skin slick, his expression anxious.

"What are you talking about?" she demanded.

He didn't answer, because the madman spoke up. "Nearly twenty years ago, my father took me, my mother and sister, and a few servants on his travels to China. He wanted us to be together as a family." He said those last words with a negligent wave of his free hand. "We were attacked by bandits. None survived except me, his son." He turned back to her, and she was struck by the raw intensity in his pale blue eyes. "My parents promised us to one another when we were children. I have returned now to honor that vow." His shoulders sank somewhat as he grimaced up at the altar. "I am here to wed you."

"Like bloody hell!" bellowed Christopher as he barreled forward.

Evelyn squeaked in alarm. She knew what would happen, even if she thought Christopher terribly gallant for trying. But without the support of his brothers, who were a step behind as usual, Christopher would not fare better against the madman this time than he had the last.

She tried to help. She jerked her immobilized arm backwards as hard as she could while slipping sideways to interpose her body between the two men. It didn't work. The madman easily moved with her, allowing her to step between him and her fiancé, and then follow all the way through until she stood on his other side. That gave ample room for his booted foot to connect with the center of Christopher's chest, and again her fiancé went flying backwards. The madman, of course, was not even breathing hard.

"This is outside of enough!" cried Evelyn. "This is my *wedding*!" She glared at Christopher's brothers before they could attack and fail again. "Do not be foolish. And you!" She turned to the madman. "You are not the current earl!" She looked out to her father for confirmation. She even tried to get the attention of the real earl, but it was useless. The fathers plus an older gentleman were hissing and blustering to one another, completely oblivious.

Or perhaps *not* completely oblivious, because at that moment Evelyn finally placed the graying man, who was nervously wringing his handkerchief as he cringed in the pew. It was the Honorable Mr. Grayson, the earl's family's London solicitor. Which meant the sweating young man who had spoken up in support of the madman was the solicitor's grandson and a solicitor in his own right. Evelyn blinked and tried to understand what could possibly be happening here.

"Solicitors argue like chickens," said the madman in a strangely reasonable tone. "But the truth does not change. I am my father's son. I am the current earl, and you were promised to me."

She focused back on him because, honestly, how could she not? He had that commanding tone that captured one's attention even in whispers. Still, the situation simply didn't make sense. "You cannot possibly be the earl." She looked into his very blue eyes and pleaded. "This just isn't the way things are done."

His eyes narrowed. His gaze was so intense, so direct, she felt as if her skin sizzled. He looked at her nose and her mouth, her ears even, but eventually, his gaze returned to her eyes. "This is important to you? That things be done properly?"

She stiffened. Here was proof positive that the man was

mad, but she answered his question nevertheless. "Of course things must be done properly. Anything else is . . . improper!"

The tension in his grip eased, and she thought perhaps his face relaxed, but it was hard to tell as he dipped his head in a bow. "Very well then, my wife, I will accede to your wishes. We will do things correctly."

She breathed a sigh of relief. Except, he didn't move. He didn't release her arm, and he didn't step away from her. And most importantly, he didn't take his fellow Chinamen with him and leave so that things could return to order. He simply stood and looked at her.

"What?" she finally snapped.

He reared back slightly and arched an eyebrow. Then, with a sweeping gesture of his arm, he indicated Christopher, who was whispering to his injured brothers, the arguing fathers and solicitors, and the entire slack-jawed congregation. "How does one proceed correctly in such a situation?"

There was no earthly way to answer that question. And yet it was incumbent upon her to answer, since the only other ranking woman in the room was the countess, who was sobbing uncontrollably beside the reverend, who had managed to climb off her lap to sit rather awkwardly by her side.

Evelyn sighed then made her decision. "Father," she called. No response. So she raised her voice despite the fact that brides most certainly did not do such a thing. "Father!"

Her father jerked around to face her. "Dearest, there seems to be some question—" he began.

"So I understand," she interrupted. "Perhaps our guests could all adjourn to the breakfast? It appears that there will be no wedding today."

Her father glanced ruefully back at the earl and the solicitors—both young and old Mr. Grayson—as the three hissed and spat in their squabble. The madman had a point: they did seem rather animalistic, though more like snakes than chickens.

Her father grimaced. "Don't worry, Button, we'll get this all sorted out soon enough. Then you can have your wedding day just as everything ought to be."

She smiled at her father. Simple and even-tempered, he always knew just what to say. Putting his words into effect, however, took much more time. Evelyn turned and addressed her mother. "Mama, do you think you could help everyone find the wedding breakfast? I'm sure they must all be very hungry." It was a polite fiction. No one was hungry; everyone clearly wanted to stay and watch the unexpected show.

Mama blinked, then a martial gleam entered her eyes. "Of course! Excellent idea," she said. Then with quick words and pointed stares, she shamed the audience into leaving, enlisting the bridesmaids in getting the stragglers out the door. At Evelyn's insistence, the groomsmen left as well: Stephen with a limp, Alcott nursing a bloody lip. The earl was urged by the reverend to remain silent, at least until they had more privacy. Finally, Christopher ordered everyone remaining to sit down and conduct themselves as befitted their stations.

No one obeyed until the madman bowed politely to Evelyn, then settled in her father's seat in the front pew. He reclined there like a . . . well, like a Chinaman, she supposed. He sat with his back straight, his legs spread, and his hands on his thighs. But he was at least silent and no longer holding her prisoner, so that was progress.

She waited until the last guest was escorted out. A number of Christopher's family remained, for he had retained them. Evelyn's own family—except for her father—was gone. Mother and Evelyn together had marshaled every last one to "assist" at the wedding breakfast. The other two Chinamen— the orange-robed one and the boy—were standing respectfully off to the side.

"Well," Evelyn said as the door shut behind the last straggler, "I suppose it's time to hear from the . . . er, from Mr. Grayson."

She'd almost said "chickens," which was a clear indication of how upsetting this whole situation was.

"You may sit beside me, wife," the madman intoned. He nodded regally to indicate where.

"I think not," Evelyn responded, startled by her sudden urge to laugh. Fortunately, the exchange prompted Christopher to stop fussing at his mother and to turn to her. He was beside Evelyn in a moment, taking her hand and escorting her gently to a place beside the countess. Unfortunately, the woman's sobs made it rather hard to hear.

"I am terribly sorry about this, Miss Stanton," said the younger Mr. Grayson. He bowed deeply in front of her. "Terribly sorry, but we got here as fast as we could."

"My grandson is an idiot!" snapped the elder Mr. Grayson. "Interrupting a wedding like this! If you had just waited an hour, then this poor gel wouldn't be in the middle of it. Contract or no contract, she would have been wed!" He folded his arms and looked most put out.

"But . . . but she thought she'd be wedding an earl—or at least a future one!"

"She is!" bellowed the current earl.

Evelyn stood up, crossing to Christopher's side because she wanted to hear and because she did *not* want to become trapped into comforting the countess. "Please, please, forget my situation right now. You can't possibly suggest that this . . . this . . ." How did one refer to an Englishman in yellow robes? "That his claims are true." And why was he staring at her like that, steady eyed, without apparent emotion, completely focused upon her? It was disconcerting. She resolved to ignore him completely in favor of her husband-to-be.

"He is a charlatan!" bellowed the earl.

"I'm terribly, terribly sorry," babbled the younger Mr. Grayson, "but I believe this to be Jacob. I am so sorry."

Evelyn frowned at the man, wondering why he was apologizing to *her*. After all, Christopher's father was the one who would lose the title. But that was ridiculous, since this madman wasn't the rightful earl. Either way, her place was beside her fiancé, so she smiled reassuringly at Christopher. His face was pale and set, his lips compressed into a thin line. And his gray-blue eyes glinted with steel as he stared at the madman.

"What is the proof?" he demanded.

"There is no proof!" bellowed his father, stomping forward. "We have the signet ring." He lifted his hand to wave the item. "Reggie went off to China and was slaughtered. The only survivor . . ." He turned and glared at the madman. "The *only* survivor was his valet, who saw it all. Higgins told us everything. Everyone was slaughtered except him. He stayed hidden, sneaked back to get the ring, then made it here to me." He turned to the young Mr. Grayson. "That is what happened. I am the earl, and there will be a wedding!"

From his place in the front pew the Chinaman turned, his expression fierce. "Higgins *did* survive! We searched the bodies and couldn't find him. I thought he'd gone home. I thought he'd tell someone I was alive. Why didn't you send someone back for me?" His voice was rising in clear fury even though his body remained absolutely still. It was as if he restrained all muscles but couldn't control the emotion in his voice. Or the burning intensity in his eyes.

"Because Jacob died!" bellowed the earl. "And you are a miscreant thief!"

"I wish that were true, sir," the younger solicitor inserted. "But he remembers things. We played together as boys, you recall. He remembers me."

The earl spun around to glare at the older Mr. Grayson. "Control your man, sir, then fetch the reverend."

But it was Christopher who stepped forward to glare at the madman. "What was your horse's name?"

The madman's gaze turned abstract as he looked not at Christopher but over his shoulder. "Zeus," he answered.

"Where did you hide your toy soldiers?"

"Under my bed."

"Did you have a pet?"

"A dog named Apollo. And the barn cat Ginger."

The elder Mr. Grayson snorted. "That's hardly proof. Every boy has a dog and a barn cat. And toy soldiers are always under the bed!"

"Look at me, God damn it!"

Everyone abruptly stared at Christopher, Evelyn included. She had never heard him raise his voice before, much less bellow a curse in the middle of a church. His face was flushed, his eyes sparked like flint and tinder, and for the first time in her life Evelyn actually believed that Christopher was related to his choleric father.

One glance at the madman showed that he, too, was now looking at Christopher. No expression, no emotion, his was just a simple, steady stare.

Silence.

No one dared interrupt as Christopher continued to glare. For a madman, the Chinaman possessed remarkable composure. In truth, he was completely and totally calm, whereas Christopher's breath began to huff and his hands were tightening into fists.

Then Christopher abruptly relaxed. His fists opened, his shoulders dropped, and in a low, calm tone, he said five very distinct words: "I do not believe you."

"Well, of course not!" his father began, but Christopher raised his hand and silenced his father.

"I remember Jacob as wild and loud and"—he glanced apologetically at the earl—"very much like my father." His gaze returned to the madman. "You are not Jacob. You may leave before we call the constable."

"You are my cousin Christopher. You had freckles on your nose and talked about sheep manure. You wanted to go to sea and be a pirate, and when we played soldiers you always wanted to be the French. You said it would prove you were smarter than any frog when you beat me." He frowned and shifted his gaze to a spot in the air over Evelyn's shoulder. "That is all I remember of you."

It didn't matter. No one cared what a madman claimed to remember. But at the very moment Evelyn decided everything was settled, Christopher's grandmother let out a wail. It was loud, it echoed, and it sounded of equal parts joy and terror. She struggled to her feet, using her cane to hobble around the pew.

"It *is* you!" she sobbed. "It's James! I knew it! I knew it!" And she went to throw her arms around the startled madman.

"Nana! Stop that!" Christopher cried as he tried to restrain the elderly woman. Evelyn also leaped forward, but the dowager countess pushed them both away.

"James used to speak just like that!" she cried. "That was James—stiff and arrogant!"

"Mother," the earl ground out behind them, "James was your husband. James is dead."

She glared at him with watery eyes. "I know that, you idiot, but I raised this boy. I would remember. Besides, there's proof!" With surprisingly quick movements, she abruptly shoved down the edge of the madman's robe, baring his shoulder and chest all the way to his left nipple. Evelyn gasped and tried to force herself to look away. She . . . didn't. She couldn't. She'd never guessed that a man could have such a well-developed chest.

Meanwhile, Lady Warhaven pointed at a moon-shaped scar, half-faded but still obvious. "You did that to him! Don't you remember? You were riding too recklessly with him, and he fell right in those horrible bushes." She lifted her chin. "This is Jacob."

"Don't be ridiculous—" began the earl, but he was cut off as his mother turned directly to Evelyn.

"And you, young lady," she continued, "will marry the correct grandson!"

Chapter Two

His future wife was a liar. Jacob closed his eyes and reminded himself that his true name—his monastic name—was Jie Ke, and that Jie Ke did not care that Jacob's wife-to-be was beautiful, young, and sophisticated. It did not matter, because he was not Jacob. He was a monk of the Xi Lin Temple—or rather he would be if he ever got through this ridiculous sham. And Jie Ke had no interest whatsoever in Miss Evelyn Stanton.

Against his will, he opened his eyes and found himself looking at her face. The monks had taught him how to read a person's future from their face. It was a Chinese belief, but one he had studied because it was fun. It taught him how to spot falsehoods of the flesh, and if nothing else, it had told him what the Chinese looked at when they saw a person. For example, a Chinese person would see that her light blue eyes were like his own, suggesting that the two of them were the same. Obviously a lie. Perhaps they were once similar in race, social status, and family friendships. But he was nothing like the boy he'd been. Ergo, she was nothing like him.

He looked at her nose, which was sweet, just long enough to signify honesty but not too long. This indicated a beneficial middle life. This fortune was echoed in her ears, which were centrally placed on her head, and the lobes were elegantly long, smartly accented by pearl-drop earrings. Then, best of all, her mouth was large enough to show fortune—

and she kept it closed, showing that she knew her place among the men who dictated her fate.

He tried not to grimace. A Chinese man would see a perfect wife. An Englishman would likely see the same. But Jie Ke did not want her. Her aspect promised riches and a life spent free from want, but his spirit was above want, and his only joy came from solitude and his meditations on merging with the divine. This woman was a gift for a blessed *earthly* life. Something he did not want. She would make a good wife for anyone but him.

Anyone but him. He trapped that thought in his mind and held it fast. Fortunately, he had performed a more thorough perusal of the woman, which made such a conclusion easier. He noted her peaked breasts and willow waist—both attributes of beauty—but then his gaze had landed on her most terrible flaw: large feet. She had big feet like a peasant's, and yet he knew she did not have the peasant's primary virtue, being able to cook good rice. Here then was something he could revile in her, even if her feet were encased in pretty slippers that peeked out from beneath her gown and suggested—

Jacob abruptly pushed up from the pew, unwilling to spend another moment considering his future wife's beauty. "Enough squabbling for one day," he said in his holiest tone. It was a deep sound, filled with his chi energy, and it never failed to command attention. Even his flushed and angry uncle quieted.

"Oh yes," whispered Nana. "Just like James . . ."

Jacob looked away rather than into the fond eyes of his grandmother. She was his oldest living ancestor and the only human reason he had returned to this ignorant land. But looking at her set his mind to churning. He remembered cakes and toy soldiers, pipes and rose water, and jumping down the stairs from halfway up. He had felt so free then. . . .

He turned away from his memories to address his onetime

playmate, Tom. The boy was now a lawyer, and he did not show well next to his stately grandfather, but Jacob liked him the better for it. "What is the next task?" he asked. "When do I wed the girl?"

"When you have proof!" snapped the elder Grayson, before Tom could frame a response. "I told you before, you need proof. Or you might as well just go back to China." He turned to glare at his grandson. "And the gel would have been out of it if *you* had just let things be."

Jacob felt the muscles in his shoulders tighten. Even as a boy, he'd disliked the elder Grayson. The man smelled of old leather and dirty smoke. Maybe he knew who had killed his family. Weeks ago, Jacob had forced himself to see the man. Though his memories of England were often sketchy, he remembered many hours spent with Tom while their elders were closeted together. He'd remembered the name Grayson, and that the Graysons were his family's solicitors. Therefore, that was whom he'd sought out to assert his claim to the title and to set his legal affairs in order. In retrospect, he might have done better with somebody entirely new.

The elder Grayson had met with him, listened with barely restrained impatience, and promised to look into matters most thoroughly. But within a week, Jacob had guessed the sneering elder was delaying matters. All Jacob's inquiries were turned aside for one reason after another. With the date of the wedding approaching rapidly, Jacob had finally found Tom. The two had many shared memories, so it had been relatively easy to convince his childhood friend of his identity. And then Tom had brought him here.

"But he is the earl!" Tom asserted, his voice shaking only the tiniest bit. Jacob nodded encouragingly. Tom was a good fellow, passionate in the best possible way. That would serve him well if he could harness the strength.

"Ridiculous!" bellowed Jacob's Uncle Frank, the one who currently held Jacob's title. If Tom didn't contain his passion, he would end up similarly choleric. Maybe Uncle Frank had let his passions get away from him and killed his family. Jacob remembered one time when—

Jacob ground his teeth as his thoughts slipped again into memory and useless speculation. With an act of will, he suppressed them, only to have pain burn through his forehead and a sneeze tickle his nose. This was how it worked in England for him. Every step, every place reminded him of something. And with those memories came loss of focus and wandering thoughts. Every minute he lingered in England had him losing sight of his goals. He needed to leave this country soon. He needed to return to the temple and find peace—in mind and body. But first he had to deal with a wandering wife-to-be.

He straightened his shoulders and put power into his voice. "The wind howls," he intoned. "The waters crash against the rocks. . . ." He looked at his bride. "And women weep. But the mountain remains unchanged."

Everyone stared at him, completely dumbfounded. If he were them, he'd stare too. When the abbot of the Xi Lin Temple said things like that, everyone was impressed; when he tried, no one understood. That was because he was a failure at attaining the peak, at reaching Heaven, at everything.

"My scar is proof," he said to Tom. "If there are questions, I will answer them. But I am the earl!" Did he sound like a petulant child? "I will have my title and my bride."

I am the mountain, he reminded himself in his thoughts. *A mountain at peace. A mountain in silence. A mountain outside of this stifling, old church.* He glanced at his dearest friend Zhi Min. Why did the man look amused? Why did he *always* look amused? "We will go now," Jacob intoned. "We can stay at the dower house."

"The hell you say!" Christopher started forward, his anger a palpable force.

Jacob whirled around to face his cousin. The man's challenge echoed in the massive stone building, and Jacob's pain increased in direct proportion. He had to tense his back and lock his shoulders to keep from wincing. Then he had to extend his arms to keep his balance while facing the cousin who had once been his best friend. Was there any of the lighthearted boy left inside Chris? Was there any left inside Jacob? What if Christopher was the one who'd had his parents exterminated?

"You are not moving into my house!" bellowed Christopher.

Pain burst behind Jacob's eyes, but he had already frozen his expression. What a surprise, to see that kind of passion from cold Christopher! Obviously, underneath Chris's calm exterior roared an inferno of emotion like his father's.

"Where should I stay, then?" Jacob asked. Anger began to build along with his pain. Anger that could only be controlled by an act of will.

"Go back to your rathole in China," groused his uncle. "You'll never see one groat."

"This must be handled in London," inserted the elder Mr. Grayson.

"He hasn't the money," returned the younger.

"Then let him find a rat's nest—"

Pain fractured Jacob's vision. The men were squabbling like chickens again. Worse, in this place each pronouncement echoed, the sounds returning again and again to beat at his ears. He couldn't take much more. Soon, his anger and his thirst for revenge would win, and they would all be dead. Vengeance didn't really care who it hurt. He looked about him, stretching for calm, wishing for peace. All he saw was a cold, stone edifice. Wasn't there a warm wooden temple anywhere in England?

"He will stay at the manor house," interrupted Evelyn, her voice thankfully low enough that it didn't echo.

Christopher rounded on her, his eyes wide with betrayal. "No! I couldn't ask that of you. It's too much."

The young woman frowned, her eyes softening. Jacob might not have noticed, but his gaze was fixed on her, his body completely still as he fought the pain in his head and the bloodlust in his heart. He saw every twitch of her mobile lips, her rose-tinted skin, and the lift and lowering of her breasts as she spoke. Except, mountains didn't notice that sort of thing and he was at one with a mountain. He was at peace like a mountain. . . .

"Don't be ridiculous," she continued. "We have room for him."

"He can return to my home with—" Nana offered.

"I accept your offer, my wife," Jacob interrupted. In part, he was fleeing his grandmother's suggestion. The idea of staying in her house—so filled with memories—made his teeth ache.

"She's *my* wife!" snapped Chris.

"I'm no one's wife yet," said the woman in question.

Jacob focused on her creamy, white skin as a way to block out everything else. Maybe she knew who'd killed his parents. "It would be good for us to learn about one another," he said to her. She would feel better about the wedding if she knew him better.

The younger solicitor spoke up. "That is most generous of you," he inserted, his glance hopping uneasily between Evelyn and his grandfather. "But I'm sure it would be somewhat awkward. Perhaps there is a local inn?"

Evelyn's lips compressed. She'd done that a lot as a child; it was what Jacob most remembered. The way her lips pressed together or quivered or opened for sweets. But she hadn't eaten the sweets on the day they'd first met. He'd had—

"Look at him," she said to the group at large. "He is English. Of that we can all be sure."

"An English thief with a wild imagination," boomed Uncle Frank. "He will steal the silver the first time your back is turned."

Again, Evelyn's lips tightened, and the shoulder nearest

Uncle Frank lifted. She didn't like her fiancé's father, Jacob realized. Well, apparently no one did. But they thought him an earl, so they paid him a great deal of deference. Would they do that to him when he gained the title? But—

"In the name of Christian charity," she continued, "we cannot turn him out on the street."

Thomas shifted anxiously. "A resolution may take some time. He could be housed with you for weeks. Maybe months."

Jacob restrained a groan. These people would dicker for days on end! "No!" he snapped. He turned his glare on Thomas. "No, it will be accomplished as soon as possible. Within the week."

Both solicitors widened their eyes with shock. "Sir," they cried in unison. "You do not understand the nature—"

"I agree," inserted Christopher coldly. "A week, no more. I wish to be wed and done with this miscreant."

The lawyers began to wheedle, and Jacob's vision whitened at the edges as flashes of pain became more frequent, more insistent. And with the pain came anger, fury. Soon he would step into unreasoning violence. He had to leave before his control broke. He grabbed his bride's arm without being careful of his grip. He only recalled his strength when she cried out.

"My apologies," he murmured, softening his grip as quickly as he could. "Tell me where is your home."

Her eyes narrowed on his face. What did she see? Did she remember him? Thankfully, she didn't ask questions. "Straight up the lane. It is some distance—"

"My thanks." He turned and strode back up the aisle past everyone. He heard their gasps behind him, but didn't care. Would Zhi Min follow, he wondered. And Mei Li? Of course they would. But why was the aisle so damn long?

The doors were heavy, but he could push them open well enough. Bloody hell, the sunlight was bright. Not *so* bright really, but the pain was sinking its claws into his breath. Each inhalation cut brutally at his lungs. Was it the cold air? Yes, of course it was. Dry, cold air like bones, and his chest and arm were still exposed because he hadn't adjusted his robes. But he was outside. No more echoes.

Nausea churned in his gut. He would vomit soon. He had to reach for the Drastic Act. Lord, they would think him an idiot. He didn't care. Was it better to be an idiot or a vomiting monk? Maybe both? No, vomit . . . that was worse.

Stop the pain now! Stop the thoughts!

As best he could, he scanned the area. People loitered there. Women, men—all were staring at him with open-mouthed shock. Maybe one of them knew who had killed his family. There! What he needed was there! But in front of everybody?

He stumbled forward, headed straight for the stone trough.

Clothes! Keep the clothes dry!

His hands shook as he whipped his robe back. Deep breath. Take a deep breath. Ignore the pain. He plunged his head down into the horse trough.

The cold splintered through his consciousness, obliterating everything. The pain, his thoughts, even the image of his bride-to-be, all was lost in a seizing moment of total and absolute shock. He heard only the gurgle of muffled sound. He tasted brackish water. And he felt . . .

Silence.

Ahhhh. The fury slipped away. Frozen acceptance. It lasted only a split second, but it was so perfect in its silence. Soon his head would pound and his lungs scream. Soon his body would rebel and he would have to withdraw into a colder reality, a more-bitter present. But for this suspended moment, all was still.

He held his breath as long as he could, but already it was too late—he needed to breathe! Without meaning to, he shifted the placement of his head and banged it on the back of the stone trough. Pain returned with a blistering heat. How was he such a clumsy idiot? Careful! Come out carefully. Try to preserve some dignity.

Gingerly, he pulled his head out of the water, then stood dripping and blind against the weak English sun. He felt a cloth pressed to his head, delicately patted by tiny hands. Mei Li, of course. Using the stone for support, he dropped to his knees before his pretend servant and allowed her to dry him off. She had done this for him before, and he focused completely on her tiny movements, each light press of her fingertips, each tiny explosion of pain where she touched. It was perfect—or as perfect as such a thing could be—and he lost himself in the present pain. Soon, when she was done, he would have relief. Soon.

Now. He allowed the cold air to fill his lungs. A full breath taken with ease. The pain had receded enough for him to function.

"The English think you are crazy," Zhi Min said in Chinese, his tone casual. Jacob started, ashamed that he hadn't realized his friend had joined him on his left side. None of the masters at the temple were ever startled. Had he just betrayed himself? Would Zhi Min notice? Of course Zhi Min noticed. He noticed everything! But Jacob's body was frozen statue still, so maybe not. Still, the failure chipped away at his calm and his answer came out curter than he intended.

"Peasants always think the enlightened are crazy."

He heard Zhi Min lean against the stone trough. "At first I thought it was something all English did—plunge their heads in freezing water—but these people stared at you then whispered like fishwives. So . . . now I believe it was you all along. You *are* crazy."

Jacob refused to be baited. His body was still reacting to the cold; his belly quivered, his muscles jumped. But his mind was blessedly quiet, and so he could respond in a calm, emotionless tone.

"Perhaps I am crazy." He opened his eyes and pushed to his feet. A smile and a bow of thanks to Mei Li, then another full breath, and his mind centered on one thought: "I am only sane at the temple. I must return there soon."

His friend tilted his head, dark eyes reflecting the sunlight with a surprising brightness. "You plunge your head in water there, too." Then he shrugged. "No matter. I think I like you better crazy."

Jacob smiled. *No*, he corrected himself, he was not Jacob. He was Jie Ke. And as Jie Ke, he could easily punch his friend in the shoulder. "That is because you enjoy studying disease."

Zhi Min blocked the blow with a casual movement of his hand. If this had been ten years ago, they would quickly have descended into combat, testing each other's skills and speed. But at this moment they were men with a task, so Jie Ke simply grabbed his pack. His head was beginning to throb again, though the pain was manageable and his thoughts relatively quiet. Plus, they were outdoors and Zhi Min was here to distract him, so all was well—or as well as it could be in England.

"She said her home was up this road a long way," Jie Ke said.

Zhi Min sighed as they began walking. "You couldn't ask for a horse? This pack is heavy."

"Not if I wanted to live. My uncle wishes me at the bottom of the ocean, and I was in no condition to fight them all." It was a lie. If they had attacked him when his head pounded, he would have killed them all. He would not have been able to stop himself. He paused a moment, remembering each of their faces in turn. Evelyn's lingered longest. Nana's image appeared, and was immediately pushed away as too confusing.

"None of them remember me," he said.

"Your lawyer friend does."

"But my family doesn't." He tried to shrug it off. He tried to remind himself that Buddha had no family except everyone and no one. But for all his strength of will, Jie Ke still could not repress a wave of sadness.

"The grandmother remembers," his friend offered.

Jie Ke shook his head. "She sees my grandfather, not me."

"Such is the way with the old. As they gain wisdom, they see all time as one." He turned to look his friend in the eye. "That is enlightenment, not error."

Jie Ke grimaced. "This is the rambling of an old woman. It means nothing." He said the words, even tried to believe them, but in his heart he knew something else was at work. Something that made him despise his grandmother for no reason at all. Maybe she knew who had killed his family. Maybe she . . .

He sneezed. Pain banged through his forehead, dull but excruciatingly heavy. So he resolutely blanked his thoughts and his feelings. No thoughts, no emotion, and no ties—no speculation!—meant no pain. He would be a Buddha and lift himself away from all pain.

When he opened his eyes again, he was fully present in that moment without attachment to anything. He could walk beside his friend, look at the houses and the shops along the lane, and not think of anything beyond how different they appeared from those in China. He blanked his mind to the stares and whispers that followed them, and as usual, his friend kept up a running list of questions.

"Why is your temple so gray? Stone and wood with little color."

"Why do the men wear clothing so tight that they cannot breathe? And their pants—do they not hurt the ability to breed?"

"What kind of roof is that? What advantage does it give?"

Jie Ke did not know the answers to his friend's questions. He never did. He was trying to blank his thoughts, not add to them, and yet Zhi Min continued.

"Why are the women's dresses cut so low on their chests? Does that make feeding babies easier?"

Jie Ke spun around, irrational fury suddenly bursting from him. "Shut up! Shut up! You are ridiculous, asking me all this!"

Zhi Min simply smiled, his satisfaction clear. It took a moment for Jie Ke to realize that once again his friend had bested him. Once again, he had pushed Jie Ke to lose all control while Zhi Min maintained a calm, peaceful presence. Jie Ke turned around and stomped forward, a single curse on his lips. "You! You are pig snot."

Zhi Min laughed, as he always did when he won. But a moment later, he started up again. "I really do want to know if the men's clothing damages their ability to create babies. Do you think your church is so dark because your men's privates cannot breathe? Why give color to something when you can't inhale for fear of squeezing yourself to death? And the women . . ."

Jie Ke let the questions flow past him like water streaming down a mountain. In this way, he walked without pain, without anger, without violence. And if he tried very hard, he would stay in this peaceful place until he could return to the warmth of China.

Jie Ke was halfway up the mountain. His body rested in the cross-legged lotus form, his back was just starting to ache, but his mind was resolutely climbing the mountain to Heaven where all his earthly cares would cease. His neck tensed and pain lanced from the inside of one shoulder blade down across his middle back. He breathed into it and pushed the awareness away. His mind needed to be blank, empty . . . holy.

I am as still as a mountain. I am the mountain that I scale.

He strained. He reached. Almost . . .

"Goodness gracious!"

Someone had entered the room. Jie Ke did not open his eyes. This was a holy task and the external world was of no relevance.

He heard a rustle as the nameless woman left. English women had no understanding of how to be silent. Worse, she forgot to shut the door. That left space for lots of other sounds and more gawkers to interfere with his meditation. But, of course, that was of no relevance. He was climbing the mountain. He should be able to meditate in the middle of a busy marketplace.

I am the mountain that I climb.

"Yes, Aunt Betsy, I see him." His bride's voice blew like a hot fast wind through his mountain serenity. It took an act of will, but Jie Ke did not open his eyes. The woman's presence did not disturb him.

"He is sitting on the harpsichord!" The older woman's voice buzzed like a wasp. If he asked her, would she tell him about his family? About how and why they died?

"Yes, I see that." His bride-to-be had a kind voice, soothing and deeply patient. It was the type of voice the best mothers used with children: gentle, but still in control. He admired that. "Do go on and play some cards. I believe Mrs. Wilkins is most anxious to partner with you."

"But shouldn't I stay here?" The woman's voice dropped to a near whisper. "Just in case? I mean, he's *Chinese!*"

I am the mountain, unaffected by the moaning wind.

"No, he's not, Aunt Betsy. He's as white as you and I. He just . . . um . . . dresses Chinese. And sits in odd places."

"It's a harpsichord," the wasp woman snapped. "You're supposed to *play* it!"

"I know, Aunt. Let me talk to him in private."

A gasp of horror. "But what about a chaperone? I could—"

"I'll leave the door open. Go on. It will be fine."

The wasp woman would just spy from the doorway, thought Jie Ke, but that didn't matter. Let them all gawk so long as they did not speak. Of course, the two women continued their whispered squabble just low enough that it required all his attention to catch half the words. But he wasn't supposed to be listening. He was the mountain. He was . . .

His bride-to-be prevailed, thank Heaven! With a heavy sigh, the aunt left. Now, of course, he would have to deal with his bride. She would not know about meditation. He was lucky she understood the style in which he dressed. At least English women were given *some* education. He deplored that about the Chinese—how the women weren't allowed any. But then again, such things didn't matter. His path was as the mountain. No, it was to *climb* the mountain, to climb to Heaven where all earthly cares would cease.

To be honest, he'd never understood how he was supposed to *be* the mountain and *climb* the mountain at the same time. Why did he not understand? The abbot had said something about that, but he couldn't remember it right now because his bride was present.

She *was* here, wasn't she? Why wasn't she interrupting him? Had she left? Wouldn't he hear her breathing or the rustle of her skirt? She would speak soon. She would be unable to stop herself. Then he would be annoyed with her interruption.

I am the . . . I am climbing . . . Damn it!

He opened his eyes then nearly fell backwards from his seat. She was standing less than a foot from him, her expression completely calm, her gaze unnervingly direct—especially since it came from a woman.

"You wish to speak to me?" His voice was curt, his hands clenched into fists. Zhi Min would say his mountain looked remarkably like a frightened mouse.

"I am sorry if I disturbed you," she said quite pleasantly, "but yes, I would like to have a word with you if I may." She was dressed in a russet gown made of velvet. He hardly remembered what velvet was, except that his grandmother had favored the fabric. But his grandmother had liked her dresses plain. Evelyn had flowers painted on hers, bright dots of pink buds, strong strokes of rosy petals, and a long winding vine of stems and leaves along the trim. Quite beautiful, in a purely English way. He almost reached out to touch the garment, but restrained himself at the last moment. He had no interest in touching his bride, he reminded himself. He was a mountain.

"How much money do you want?"

He blinked and said the first thought that came to mind. "I am a monk."

Her lips compressed into a tight line. Odd, that he liked it when that happened. It showed she was not as calm as she appeared. But then, as he stared, the expression became a smile. It reminded him of another time, another place long ago. In fact, it was so long ago, that he wasn't even sure of his memory. Had that been her before he'd left for China? Was she the girl who'd danced in the rainstorm, a wild thing? Did she remember—

His thoughts were cut short as her expression became flat, almost serene. She said, "I can see that you are a monk. Your yellow robe makes that more than clear." She frowned for a moment at his naked shoulder. "Aren't you cold?"

There was a fire in the grate, but it wasn't enough to heat the room. Still, he didn't mind the chill. "Sometimes it helps. A comfortable body leads to comfort of mind."

She frowned at his intonation, and a tiny furrow appeared between her eyebrows. Odd, how he found that so appealing, if in a purely worldly sense. Which meant that it was of no interest at all. "Is that bad?" she asked. "Comfort of mind?"

"Only when it leads to sleep instead of meditation."

She nodded, as if she now understood. But then she asked, "What is meditation?"

He opened his mouth to answer but stopped. How did one answer so sweeping a question? Words failed.

Her expression tightened into a grimace. "That is what I thought: you don't really know."

He started to ask what she meant, but she didn't give him the chance.

"Christopher will fight you in the courts until we are all old and gray. The earl will . . . well, he will probably beat you to a bloody pulp, so I would be careful where you walk at night. Me, I am of a more practical mind."

He straightened his spine, feeling a familiar tightening in his lower back. It was easier to ignore the noise of the outside world when the inner one was equally demanding. He started to close his eyes to better focus on the pain, but she kept him from it.

"I want you gone."

Her voice was low and almost pleasant. That was what snapped his eyes back open: the dichotomy between her lilt-ingly sweet tone and her bitter words.

"If that means paying you, then so be it, but it will be once and no more. If I see you again, I will have you put in jail. Do I make myself clear?"

"Perfectly." He closed his eyes. The abbot had taught him this trick. Whenever the young Jacob had tried to be imperious, had demanded this thing or that, the abbot had agreed quite pleasantly, then had blithely gone on his way and completely ignored the conversation. Everything and anything that Jacob had demanded was merely the noise of wind and no more.

"I believe fifty pounds will be adequate?"

I am climbing the Mountain of Immortality. "Is that a large amount?" He was playing dumb. He had a general idea of exactly how much money she was offering. But money was not a monk's concern—large or small. He could not help it if she did not understand who or what he was.

"It's a huge amount. So, we are agreed? I will get you the money by morning."

He smiled. He would enjoy seeing her face tomorrow when she realized that her money meant nothing to him, even so large a sum as fifty pounds.

"Do you know that you are sitting on a harpsichord?"

He smiled without opening his eyes. "Yes."

"Do you know what a harpsichord is?"

He could not resist taunting her. "It is what I'm sitting on."

Silence. Then in a soft, rather gentle voice, she spoke. "It is a musical instrument. You sit at the bench here." She waited until he opened his eyes. "And you play notes here." She hit a few keys just to make her point, then straightened and folded her arms. "Jacob would have known that."

He nodded. "Marie used to play. Badly, I thought. Mama tried to teach me but I wouldn't sit still long enough. In fact, I tried to bribe Marie to practice for me, but she was too little." His gaze centered on his bride-to-be's blue eyes. "Evelyn would know that story. She heard it the day before we were betrothed. We sat in that room over there, and I ate all the tarts. Well, almost all of them."

"You tried to get me to sit on one, but I was too fast."

"For that trick, yes."

Her face abruptly tightened as she recalled. "Jacob was a horrible boy."

He did not argue.

She bit her lip, looking at him with an expression he couldn't read. Then she stepped closer and leaned against the edge of the harpsichord close enough that he could see the flecks of gold in her blue eyes. "What happened?" she asked.

He blinked, startled into stillness. "When?" In truth, he knew exactly what she asked, but he hoped to delay the inevitable questions.

"I heard almost nothing, all those years ago. My mother came into the nursery and told me that I was to wed a different boy. That was it. Christopher told me later that you had died."

He frowned. "You didn't ask your mother for the details?"

She shook her head. "Mama would not know them, and

Papa did not care." She grimaced. "He did not like you very much."

Jie Ke frowned and tried to remember, but his mind was blank. "Why?"

"I believe you tortured one of his dogs."

Jie Ke's eyes widened as a memory whispered back. "A spaniel. We were playing in the parlor, and he bit me."

"Papa said you tried to kill it."

"I did not!" The response was automatic, but he wasn't so sure. His memory was sketchy. "I held his mouth closed, I think. He whimpered. That was all I did. I held his mouth shut. That is how you teach dogs."

Evelyn shook her head. "That is not what my father said."

He had no answer, so he kept silent. If anything, this was the one thing the abbot had taught him: when to keep his mouth shut. It had taken him nearly a decade to learn.

"So if you know what a harpsichord is," she pressed, "why do you sit on top of it?"

He straightened his spine and assumed his most knowledgeable tone. "To meditate requires a loftiness of mind and body."

Her eyes sparkled as she scanned the room. "Somehow I doubt that was meant literally. Otherwise you would have monks climbing tables, ladders, even stone pillars just to sit and . . . and . . . What exactly do you *do*?"

We try not to fall asleep. "We quiet our minds for the difficult climb to Heaven and immortality. And to inform you of the truth, the temple monks are often found on top of pillars or tables."

His bride-to-be's head tilted sideways. "I cannot tell if you are making a joke at my expense or if you truly believe that." She leaned forward. "Do you even know what monks do?"

"You are back to thinking I am a liar." The idea depressed him much more than it should.

"I merely wish to understand."

"Why?" The word was startled out of him. He could hardly credit that any woman wanted to understand his religion. It was unusual enough in China, where monks were revered. He couldn't imagine it in a Christian Englishwoman.

"If you really are Jacob, then you will know why." She frowned. "Or perhaps not. Jacob was such a thoughtless boy."

Was I? "I am not Jacob. I am Jie Ke, and I . . . I don't remember a great deal from our first meeting. I was a boy and you were . . ." He looked to his hands trying to sort through his thoughts. "You were a girl who was too proper to be fun."

She laughed, but the sound had no humor. "Jacob called me stupid—too stupid to be a countess."

He stared, the memory not settling well in his spirit. "I do not recall that."

She looked at him for a long moment, then finally sighed as she pushed away from the harpsichord. "You are right. You are definitely not Jacob." And with that, she turned and walked away. But just before she left the room, she paused and looked over her shoulder. "You will have your money in the morning. Good-bye, Jie Ke."

He watched her disappear, watched the sway of her skirt as she moved and the proud tilt of her head. Then he closed his eyes and resolutely wiped her from his thoughts. Next he wiped the memory of her smile from his mind. He erased her sparkling eyes and the curve of her lips. He even pushed aside her trim waist and pleasant height. He spent the next twenty minutes repeatedly suppressing all thought of her, but it was like trying to suppress a landslide. He could not climb a mountain when the image of her beauty stole the ground right out from beneath his feet.

And so he gave up. Sometimes the body overwhelmed the mind and had to be indulged. Unfortunately, he was not alone—neither here nor in his bedroom, which he shared with Zhi Min and Mei Li. This meant there was nothing he could do to alleviate his body's lustful condition. He had to sit and hope the folds of his robe covered his ailment.

He sighed. A dispossessed English earl in saffron monk's robes sitting on top of a harpsichord trying to hide an erection? This was not the homecoming he had imagined.

Chapter Three 🐉

"What are you doing?!"

Evelyn hunched her shoulders over the lockbox, but she didn't jump. She had every right to be in here. Besides, Christopher wasn't her husband yet. It nonetheless took everything she had to straighten her spine and slowly turn to face her fiancé.

"Christopher," she said calmly. "I thought you had gone to London with all the other men."

"I had," he said as he shut the doors to her father's library. They now had total privacy, since everyone else in the house had gone to bed. The room abruptly felt intimate and a little confining, especially since Christopher was glaring at her as if she were stealing the family silver. Except she was in *her* home and it would be *her* silver.

Christopher crossed his arms over his chest. "I decided my father could adequately handle the legal side. I was not comfortable leaving you—or anyone—alone with that imposter."

She nodded slowly. "Sensible, I suppose, but I really don't feel in any danger from them. Foreign or not, they're still monks."

"They pretend to be monks," he said as he crossed the room to her side. "We have no idea what they really are."

True enough. She looked up as he joined her at her father's desk. This close, he towered over her. She had to tilt her head to look up—into his nose, which, frankly, wasn't an awe-inspiring sight. "Christopher, do you think you could sit down—"

"What are you doing with your father's strongbox?" He twisted and pushed at the metal lid. She hadn't had time to open it, so it didn't move.

She bristled inside at his presumption. How dare he intrude upon her family's financial affairs! But she swallowed the response. He was to be her husband, and this concerned him. So she put on a congenial smile and gestured to the box. "I intend to pay our Chinese monks to leave."

His head jerked back to look at her. Fortunately, he had just eased himself down on the desk, so she could now look him directly in the eye. "You believe he's a charlatan, then?"

She shrugged. "I don't know what to believe, but I have made a bargain with him. Fifty pounds, and he will leave forever."

"Fifty pounds!"

She tightened her grip around the key in her hand. "It is worth that much to be rid of him."

"But my father will handle this. I doubt it will even reach the courts."

"That will take time and money." She stepped forward, more at ease with him now that she could see his eyes without putting a crick in her neck. "It's much better to pay the monk off now and be done with it. We might even be able to get married before all the guests leave. We could still have a proper wedding." She couldn't disguise the note of longing in her voice. It galled her that Jacob or Jie Ke or whoever he was had already robbed her of a proper English wedding suitable to a future countess. Her mother-in-law would be *tsk-tsking* at her for the rest of their lives!

Christopher's eyes narrowed on the lockbox. "I don't like the idea of giving in to such tactics. Allow one charlatan to take advantage of us and a dozen more will appear in Chinese hats claiming something else."

She arched her eyebrow just as his mother had taught. "I hardly think that likely. Besides, we can tell everyone that things were settled in the proper fashion. Or that you frightened him away. Whatever you like, so long as he leaves."

He sighed, his back's rigidity slowly easing as he lowered his head toward her. "What if he returns for more?"

She shrugged and lifted her face to his. Would he kiss her? He frowned instead. Chris didn't like her to be so easy with him, so familiar. A countess had to be wooed, he said. "I have told him that this is it. If he returns, we will lock him in gaol. Besides, by that time we will be properly married."

Christopher nodded, his smile back in place. They were doing this dance a lot lately: his press to touch—not because he wanted her, but because he was testing her. The minute she tried to accept his advance, she failed as a future countess. It was infuriating. She knew that this was what happened between many men and women—that men should always want, and women should always resist—but it galled her nonetheless. Why was she always the one who had to maintain propriety? When did she get to escape from the constant vigilance of a countess-to-be?

Meanwhile, Christopher's expression became severe. "The title is tricky business. There can be no doubt. We wouldn't want our son to be in constant threat of being disinherited."

She actually giggled at that thought—a nervous whinny of anxiety which she abruptly cut off. They were having a difficult enough time getting through a wedding ceremony. The thought of having a son who worried about a title he wouldn't inherit for decades was just too much to contemplate. "You are looking a long way off, Christopher."

"That," he said soberly, "is a prospective earl's job. Something, I might add, that Uncle Reggie was woefully unable to do. Whoever heard of an earl wandering off to China, for God's sake? What a harebrained, irresponsible—"

"Yes, yes," Evelyn interrupted before Christopher got too

deeply into his rant. It was usually the earl, his father, that rambled on—and with a great deal of choler—about his brother's irresponsible, un-English pastimes. But Chris was known to follow his father's example on occasion, so she needed to distract him now. "Do you have any money? I would rather not dip into Mama's kitchen money, but if I need to—"

"Hmm?" He took hold of her hands, entwining her fingers with his. "Oh, the fifty pounds. Are you sure you need to give him that much?"

She nodded. "It is the amount we agreed upon."

"And you can be sure he knows how to count English money," he groused.

"Er, yes. Though he did ask if that was a large amount."

Christopher released a quick bark of laughter. "Playing dumb, no doubt. As if he were fooling anyone." He quieted, his gaze steady on her face as he tightened his grip, pulling her inevitably closer. "How much do you need?"

She swallowed. "I believe my pin money plus father's strongbox will leave me five short." She didn't know for sure because she hadn't opened it yet.

Christopher remained silent for a long moment. In the end, he dropped his forehead to hers. "Leave your pin money alone. And your father's strongbox. I will pay."

"But—"

He pressed a finger to her lips. "Didn't men once pay a price for their brides?"

She lifted her chin such that his finger slipped away. "It was called a bride price, and that's a Jewish custom, I believe."

He shifted his touch so that he could lift her face even higher. "Whatever it is called, I shall pay it and be grateful if it means we can finally be wed." And with that he kissed her.

Christopher's mother had made it clear that once they were affianced, Evelyn could allow him the occasional pressing of lips. But no more than that, and no more than once a week. Since they did not get their wedding kiss, Evelyn thought this would be allowable. Besides, she was tired of measuring out kisses like they were alms for the poor. She lifted her face to his and allowed a gentle meeting of mouths. But soon the pressure became harder, and his tongue teased at the seam of her lips.

A thrill of excitement slipped down her spine. They had kissed like this twice before, once on the ballroom terrace the evening their wedding date had been announced—after the party guests had departed, of course—and once again a few nights ago when he had arrived for the prewedding activities. Just as now, the pair had found themselves unexpectedly in private, and just as now, Chris had slowly pulled her into his embrace and possessed himself of her mouth.

She opened herself to him—clearly not what his mother had in mind—and she felt a quickening in her heartbeat, a secret thrill at this tiny bit of sexual daring. He thrust his tongue inside her mouth and wrapped a hand around her waist, drawing her even tighter to him. Her back arched, her head fell back, and her eyes fluttered closed. But she couldn't stop her gasping choke at the awkward position of her neck, and she pushed against his shoulders as she tried to straighten up.

"Chris—"

"Evie," he murmured against her lips, then kissed her again.

He sounded so passionate in his breathless exclamation that she almost smiled. He brought his free hand up to cradle the back of her head, so the gagging problem was eliminated and her neck muscles relaxed. Her own hands rolled across his shoulders, delineating their breadth from collarbone to the outside of his arms.

Her heartbeat was speeding up. Evelyn's own mother had warned her this might happen. There were no tingles like the ones Maddie whispered about, but there was a kind of warmth from where his hands touched her. Actually, it felt like a sweaty warmth in her hair. Christopher did have large hands, so he was covering a lot of her scalp; a certain warmth would stand to reason.

His mouth broke from hers and he seemed to hover for a moment over her lips. She felt him exhale, a slight huff that breezed across her lips before he touched his forehead to hers. "Are you afraid of passion, Evie? Afraid of our wedding night?"

Afraid? She almost laughed. The idea of finally allowing herself the freedom to explore her passions as a married woman was the secret dream of her heart. It was her night-time fantasy as she counted out the days to her wedding. But Christopher was a childhood friend. They had spent so much time together, he felt like a brother. The idea of becoming passionate with him seemed . . . improper. But she could hardly tell him that, especially since she longed for intimacy. It was much easier to focus on the difficult arch in her back and the way her neck strained in this position. "Christopher," she said. "Let me stand, please."

"Hmm? Oh yes." He pulled back and helped her attain her full height. Then they stood face-to-face while the silence stretched between them. He seemed to expect her to say something, but Evelyn had little idea what he wanted. What would a proper wife say?

"I have known you forever, Chris," she finally stated. "You were—are—the man I'm going to marry. The . . . um . . . details of our marriage weren't very . . . um . . ."

"Real?"

She nodded. "Yes, they weren't real until now. I just . . . I mean . . . It's all been so unsettling with Jacob returning and all."

His gaze abruptly sharpened. "You can't possibly believe that he's Jacob! I thought you said—"

"No, no," she cut in quickly, though in her heart she wondered why she'd said that. "It doesn't matter anyway. He's taking the money and disappearing." She frowned and shifted her stance so that there was another inch of separation between them. "Is that something Jacob would do, you think? Come here to get money, then leave?"

Christopher frowned. "Of course not. He was a wild boy, to be certain. Always moving, always with some plan about something. But he was honorable enough. Honest about . . . well, about the big things." A fond smile flitted across his features. "There were those cherry tarts we stole from Mrs. Littleton. And the cows we pushed over—you know, when they were sleeping. Boyish pranks, but certainly nothing like this. And he wouldn't take money to throw over his title." His gaze abruptly focused back on her. "Certainly not for a paltry fifty pounds. He was much smarter than that."

She smiled, her breath easing in her chest. "See? That proves it then. He can't be Jacob." Then she impulsively reached for Chris's hands, holding him so that they touched palm to palm. "But how do you think he knows all those details? Thomas said he remembered a great many details of their time together. And the things he said to us . . . Could Jacob really have survived an attack and then, injured or dying, told everything to his man?"

Christopher grimaced. "Well, that's an ugly thought. Quite depressing, really, that Jacob would have spent his last days with a charlatan."

"But that is what we're saying, isn't it? How else could this man know so much?"

Christopher locked eyes with her, and she could see his discomfort. In the end, he looked down at his lap. "I don't know how to find out the truth, Evie," he confessed in a muted whisper. "My father claims he will handle everything, and I'm sure the title is secure, so you needn't worry on that matter. It's just that . . ." He raised his eyes to her. "Ask me about sheep husbandry, about wheat crops and the repair of thatched roofs. I have answers galore. But how to make a man confess to a crime? How to make a Chinaman tell us what really happened to Jacob? Short of beating him to a bloody pulp, I haven't the foggiest."

"That is a task for a Bow Street Runner, not a future earl," she agreed.

He nodded. "I suggested as much to my father, but . . ." He shrugged. "You know my father. He has no interest in details, just results. The title will be secure, and this mad English Chinaman will be gone." He abruptly pressed a quick kiss to her lips. "You and my fifty pounds will see to that." Soberly he added, "*I* will give him the money, you know. I won't have you meeting that man alone. It's not safe."

She straightened and her tone hardened, but she kept her eyes soft. This at least was familiar ground between them. Just like his father, he could easily turn pompous and dictatorial. But Evelyn had spent a good deal of time watching the countess manage the earl. She knew just what to do. She smiled sweetly but did not waver in her stance. "This concerns me as much as you, Christopher."

He stiffened, as she knew he would, but she did not give him time to object.

"I will not have him coming to me claiming that you did not pay him." Then she softened her body, leaning toward him. "You will be there to keep me safe and to impress upon the man that he will not return. We will appear a united front against this pretender. Besides," she added as she pressed a quick kiss to his cheek, "it will be good practice for me. My first act as a countess-to-be." She straightened and beamed at him. "It is very important that I learn such things, you know."

He looked at her, his eyebrows arching to show that he was not in the least bit fooled. He knew she was attempting to manipulate him. "Evie, it is not safe."

"Christopher, you will be at my side."

"I was at your side this morning, and it did not help in the least."

She bit her lip. What could she say to that? He was right. Jie Ke had easily bested him in a fight. "I thought you were very brave," she pressed. Flattery was the surest way to divert the man.

Unfortunately, Christopher was not so easily distracted. He abruptly pushed away from the desk and began pacing in agitation. "Evie, I do not trust him. And I certainly don't want you in the same county with the madman!"

She leaned against the desk and put one hand on the strong-box. "Then let us pay him off together and be done with it."

He grimaced as he swung back to glare at her. She held his stare for a long time, remaining quiet, calm, and absolutely firm. In the end, he relented with a sigh.

"Very well. I shall meet with you here at dawn. Any later, and I will be gone."

Evelyn nodded. "Agreed." Then, again they stood looking at one another, this time from opposite sides of the library. He seemed to want something from her. She hovered on the tips of her toes, ready to do whatever it was that he desired. But she didn't know what, and he clearly had no idea how to tell her.

In the end, he simply shrugged. "Everything will be better when we are wed. This I promise, Evie."

"I know, Christopher. I swear I will be a proper wife to you. I have been well trained for it all my life."

He nodded and left, and she knew she had said exactly what he wanted. Unfortunately, her words left an increasingly cold place in her heart. She felt like a volcano slowly going dead inside, all warmth fading away. The exterior would remain—even flourish—but inside all would be cold and dead.

Evelyn pulled herself out of bed before dawn, knowing Christopher would hold to the letter of his decree. If she wasn't in the library by dawn, he would use that excuse to pay off Jie Ke himself. She wasn't quite sure why she wanted to be there. After all, Chris was right: this was more properly dealt with by men. But her future was at stake. She would see it through to the end.

She dressed for warmth. The cold wind that had been blowing on her wedding day had continued through the night. Her yawning maid helped her into another brown velvet gown, this one with bluebells painted on it. She wasn't sure why she liked it. Christopher had once said blue flowers on brown made him think of a women's frivolous garden and therefore were not appropriate to a countess. But she particularly liked that image, and so had developed a fondness for the dress.

She sent her maid back to bed and slipped downstairs to the library. No one was about. Even the servants were strangely absent. Then she heard two maids whispering in the dining room. She meant to resist. After all, a countess would have little interest in servants' gossip. But when they began to giggle, she couldn't stop herself from wandering over. Gliding with silent dignity—something she had practiced for years—she stepped into the formal dining area to find two maids and a groom peering out the window.

She moved closer, but couldn't see over their shoulders. Then the groom, a London import, whispered, "Blimey!"

"Mr. Foster, might I inquire as to what is so interesting in my back garden?"

All three spun around, red staining their cheeks. The maids immediately dropped into hurried curtsies and left the poor groom to answer.

"Er, it's the Chinamen, miss. I, uh, I was about to ask Mr. Thornley if he . . . if something should be done about it."

Evelyn stepped closer and stretched as tall as she could, but the three servants still blocked the view. "Perhaps I could make a determination if you would just step—"

"Oh no, miss," one of the maids gasped.

"Begging your pardon, miss," Mr. Foster said. "Perhaps if your mother were awake . . ."

"Really?" she drawled, her curiosity firmly piqued. "Unfortunately, she is *not* awake. Please, step aside."

They had no choice but to obey, and Evelyn finally got to see outside.

It was the Chinamen—or one of the Chinamen and Jie Ke—no doubt about that. Stripped naked and . . . dancing? She leaned forward, peering into the predawn gloom and trying to see past the bushes. They stood side by side, moving through motions that were clearly not a dance of any form she knew, and yet she recognized a beauty in everything they did. She could only see their upper bodies and their arms, which moved with lightning speed and absolute precision in quick jabs or sudden blocks. Then, to her complete frustration, the patterns of their dance took them behind the bushes; she could see nothing except the very tops of their shaved heads.

She straightened away from the window. "Yes, I can see the problem," she said stiffly. "I believe I shall have a word with them."

"But, miss—"

She waved the groom to silence and then gave all of the servants instructions for their days. Her mother had long since stopped directing any of the staff, so it was up to Evelyn to make sure that idle hands did not cause bigger problems. She sent the footman to remain at Aunt Betsy's beck and call. It was her aunt's most annoying foible that she needed to rearrange furniture wherever she was so that she could tell everyone where to stand and sit. One maid was dispatched to clean up the inevitable mess Aunt Betsy created, and the other was sent to learn every guest's favorite food. That had the added benefit of occupying some of the guests as well. Once all those tasks were assigned, Evelyn was free to proceed as quickly as possible out the door to the rear gardens.

As she feared, the air was extremely chill and the grass wet. Her slippers soaked through in minutes, but that didn't slow her as she maneuvered the path and finally stepped around the shrubbery.

Not naked. That was her first thought. They weren't naked. The two men wore a short kind of skirt about their loins. But that was all. Everything else was completely exposed, including their bare feet, which they lifted and lowered in a most immodest display. Evelyn saw their sculpted torsos, their muscular thighs, and the way their hips and rippling stomachs stayed perfectly balanced, almost still, especially compared to the sometimes lightning-fast movements of arms and legs. They were sparring, and yet she had never seen anything so beautiful.

Her plan had been to step right into the center of the small grassy area and confront them. Any display that caused servants to gape at windows was properly done in private. But once she'd moved past the shrubbery, she couldn't force herself to interfere. Their motions were like ballet, only with raw power and a masculine energy that made her sweat.

But then they stopped. She licked her lips to speak, but again she couldn't. The garden was so quiet in the predawn gray. Even their fighting had been done with reverence. While she watched, they bowed to one another then silently crossed to a stone bench where a large bowl rested. First the Chinaman, then Jie Ke lifted the plain wood bowl with both hands and drank with closed eyes. This close, she could see the physical differences between the two men. First off, despite the oddity of his behavior, Jie Ke was clearly an Englishman. His skin was white, though it held a golden tone that came from hours in the sun. She could clearly see the tan marks from when he'd worn his robe on one shoulder. Most especially, she saw he had chest hair, a gentle darkening that aimed steadily downward past his navel.

She swallowed as she studied that hair. She looked and she wondered and her palms itched to touch him. Then she remembered that she was a countess-to-be and jerked her gaze away.

The other man was wholly Chinese, thinner of chest, though taller, with hairless skin—more slender, but powerfully muscled in his own right. In this light, she saw how similar he was to an Englishman in all the basic anatomical ways. It was Jie Ke who seemed different, not because he was white, but because he had an energy about him. It was contained and yet elemental, electrifying the air even when he did nothing more than drink.

She had no idea how long she stood there, her gaze absorbing every tiny detail of Jie Ke's body, but eventually her eyes rose to his face to discover that he was watching her equally closely. Panic flared inside her hard enough to cut off her breath. He had seen her! He knew that she had been lusting after him like a low-class trollop. And yet, who was he to be parading about in such an unseemly display? How dare he look at her with such disdain when he had incited her reaction in the first place! How dare he . . .

She blinked. He was not looking at her with disdain. Neither was he preening. He simply stood unabashedly naked before her.

Everything about him was strangely silent, reverent even, and yet his eyes burned across the clearing toward her. His intensity seemed to cut right though her thoughts and defenses. She felt as if her soul was laid bare to him and—her mouth went slack and she took an unwilling step forward—he did not find her lacking!

She came back to herself in a moment, soon enough to stop herself from God-only-knew what thoughtless and improper action. Instead, she folded her arms to hide her hardened nipples and stood stiff in front of the shrubbery. A moment later, the water bowl was empty. The two men turned to face one another, bowed slightly, and then . . . battle!

She had seen men fight before. It was inevitable wherever there were males: fisticuffs or tussles on the ground. This was nothing like that. This was two men striking each other with open hands turned flat, with feet that shot out like snakes, or jumping whirling kicks. It was too fast for her eyes to follow. There were sounds too, grunts and slaps, the impact of flesh against bone, but none of the blustering curses or howls that came from boys when they fought. This was in earnest, or so it seemed. And yet, they did not have the look of two men who wanted to kill one another. There was a stillness between them, a quiet in the air even when they were both whirling, punching, kicking fiends. Seeing this was the first moment she truly believed they were monks—religious, holy monks.

Their fight took them across the entire grassy area, first one advancing, then the other. Neither seemed to dominate. Truly, they had the look of men who had fought often. Neither ever appeared surprised or off balance. And the longer they fought, the more she saw differences between them.

Jie Ke had a frenzied power. He fought with lightning speed and seemingly no end to his attacks. One such advance rained down dozens of blows without pause. During those moments, the Chinaman could do nothing but attempt to block the furious onslaught. Eventually Jie Ke slowed. His breath became labored and his step would slow, and then the other would attack.

The Chinaman's blows were slower, but more powerful. Three of his strikes took the time Jie Ke struck ten times, and yet the Chinaman's had more force. He did not land blows often, but when he did, Jie Ke shuddered from the impact.

On and on it went, with Evelyn breathless from the sight. She felt like she was watching a lightning storm. Jie Ke was the lightning, terribly fast and bright. His companion was the thunder, slower, rolling, but so incredible when that power crashed about her.

As always, Evelyn was drawn to fierce power. It was her one wild trait: thunderstorms always found her outside, soaked to the skin, daring the heavens to strike her down.

When she was a child, this had terrified her nanny and her mother. As an adult, she endured Christopher's stern frowns and her sister's teasing amusement. Only one person had ever shared her fierce desire for storms, but he had disappeared as quickly as the thunder that had once brought him. And now . . . now she once again felt powerless against the lure.

So, she walked into it. It was that simple and that unstoppable. She walked forward into the dance of fists and kicks. The Chinaman drew back, pulling himself sharply away, but Jie Ke did not. She knew he wouldn't. Perhaps that was why she walked directly toward him.

His blows continued beside her, then around her. He was still aiming at his companion, who had closed ranks to protect her. Evelyn was never touched, but the Chinaman was. He blocked blows that would have landed on her. But that left him open on other sides, and Jie Ke was lightning fast. In the end, the Chinaman simply stepped away. He left her unprotected against the force that was Jie Ke, and she reveled in her proximity to danger.

She thought then that Jie Ke would stop. She thought he would pull his arms together and bow as his companion did, but he did not. With his eyes firmly fixed on her, he began a series of furious punches and jumping kicks, assaulting the air around her. She was safe—so long as she stayed absolutely still, he would not touch her. But if even one hair were out of place, she knew she could be knocked unconscious. It was his silent dare to her. How steady were her nerves when fourteen stone of weight was aimed right between her eyes?

Evelyn smiled. Part of her wanted to close her eyes and lift her face to the sky as she did in a thunderstorm, but she could not break the hold he had on her gaze.

He made one last assault. He began with kicks thrown low by her knees, steadily rising until they landed in the space between her hip and wrist. Next came his hands, slamming back and forth near her chest, then by her face, while the breeze from his blows caressed her skin. Then, finally, he slammed his head forward, a furious plunge straight at her face. Without a conscious decision, she lifted her chin to meet him.

He stopped. A hair's breadth from her lips, he froze. His breath touched her, blowing in and out as he recovered his wind. She felt and gloried in its force. She smelled his scent then, too—strong, with alien spices, but not in the least bit rank. He was simply different . . . and wholly compelling.

Again, without conscious decision, she reached up a hand to touch his chest. She felt wet, springy hair and the steady lift and lowering of a man's lungs. His heartbeat thundered beneath her fingers—excited, fast, and so identical to her own.

Own me. Possess me. She'd cried those words to the thunderstorms. She'd screamed them silently as she danced in the rain. She'd never before thought that about a man.

He didn't hear her, he couldn't. But his eyes were so intense as they fixed on her, she could swear she saw the lightning flash in them.

She had to have him. She had to draw him inside herself, if only for this moment. So she did. She didn't move her head. She simply extended her tongue the tiniest bit, bridging the space between their mouths. She tasted him: salt, wetness, and the odd softness of flesh.

He shuddered in reaction. Perhaps she did, too, it was hard to tell. So she tasted him again.

This time his mouth opened a bit. Her tongue slipped inside for just a moment before withdrawing. But it wasn't enough. She returned to him on her next breath, this time with her lips. Deep in her heart, she began to laugh. Finally, she was kissing the storm!

Chapter Four

"Evelyn!" Christopher's bellow burst through her consciousness. He might have been yelling for a while, but she wasn't sure. In any event, he was impossible to ignore now as he gripped her arm and jerked her backward.

She blinked and stumbled just as she had the last time he'd dragged her out of a thunderstorm. The impression was so overpowering, she was surprised to find her clothing dry. It was ridiculous, of course. She was a rational woman who knew what she'd been doing. She'd been braving a mad Englishman who thought he was Jacob, her onetime fiancé. And she'd been kissing him!

The very idea shook her to the core. What had happened? She looked up at Jie Ke, terribly afraid to see a knowing smirk on his face. Instead, his expression was completely blank. Not holy, as one might hope for from a monk, but empty. Blank stone. Until she looked in his eyes. There she saw the flash of lightning, the turmoil of the storm that had so mesmerized her. It drew her even now. Then he looked down, shielding his eyes from her, and she felt completely bereft.

"You, sirrah, will be gone within the hour!" sputtered Christopher. He pulled a heavy purse from his pocket and threw it on the ground at Jie Ke's feet. "Within the hour!"

Jie Ke frowned for a moment at the purse, and Evelyn wondered at his confusion. He didn't seem to remember what the money was for. Then he abruptly straightened his body and slapped his left fist into his open right palm. It was such a violent gesture, she feared for Christopher's life. But then Jie Ke bowed in a gesture of respect completely at odds with his earlier movement.

Evelyn glanced at Christopher, seeing that he was equally wary. But Jie Ke did nothing more threatening than turn to his companion, who handed him a small, lumpy wooden bowl. Jie Ke accepted it with another bow, then lifted the bowl up with both hands, holding it high, right in front of Christopher's nose. Then Jie Ke froze with his head bowed and his bowl upraised.

Christopher stared. "What madness is this?"

It was the Chinese servant boy who answered. Evelyn hadn't even noticed him at the side of the clearing, but now he darted forward, carrying a folded mass of saffron fabric in his hands. "The alms walk is a sacred tradition in our temple," he said. Then he stepped over to Jie Ke, whom he gently wrapped in his outer monk's robe. This close, Evelyn could see that it was not actually made of one cloth, but of dozens of pieces of crude fabric sewn carefully together. The servant reverently wrapped the garment around Jie Ke's chest, then draped it over his shoulders. Except for his bare feet, Jie Ke was fully covered.

"Alms walk?" echoed Christopher. "What has that to do with anything?"

Again the servant dashed forward, bowing as he spoke. "Any who wish to give, do so as an act of virtue and contrition."

It took a moment for Evelyn to realize that Jie Ke meant for the purse to be placed in his bowl as if it held alms. It was a disgusting thought, and one that soured her on him. Christopher had the exact same reaction.

"This isn't a holy act!" he snorted. "It's highway robbery, and—"

"What does it matter," Evelyn interrupted softly, "so long as it means he leaves?"

Christopher turned to her, his body rigid and his eyes blazing. She could hardly bear to look at him, knowing that he was justified in every furious thought. She had been kissing the madman, and now she saw the effect of her betrayal. "I'm sorry, Chris," she whispered. "I'm so, so sorry."

Then she knelt down and picked the purse off the ground. It was heavier than she expected, but then she had never held fifty pounds in her hand. The weight indicated that there were probably golden guineas in there as well, and her guilt multiplied with every ounce she held. How had he gotten the money so fast? What sacrifices had he made to get this for her?

She glanced back at the men. Neither Jie Ke nor Christopher had moved, so it was up to her to quietly hand the purse over.

"Please forgive me," she whispered. She had no idea to whom she spoke. She had meant the words for Chris, but as she talked, Jie Ke's gaze abruptly jumped to hers. Their eyes met and held as she carefully dropped the purse into his bowl. His arms dipped for a fraction of a second before steadying, but that was his only reaction beyond the dizzying storm she still glimpsed behind his eyes.

Then his gaze dropped again, and she was left with the sickening sensation of falling back to earth. Her stomach clenched, and her body jerked as if from the impact. Then Christopher turned away.

"Evelyn," he said, his voice tight, "the Reverend Smythe-Jones is here to speak with us. He waits with your mother in the breakfast parlor."

She knew her duty. She quickly fell into line a half step behind him.

Christopher walked too fast, and the path was too narrow for her to stroll by his side. Worse, his every step was rigid with fury. To keep pace, she had to scurry to match his longer strides. She slowed only once. Right before she rounded the shrubbery, she had time for one last glance at Jie Ke before he left their lives forever.

He had not moved. He still held his bowl upraised before him. His servant was kneeling in front, slipping on his shoes. His Chinaman companion was lifting his own bowl in the same reverent attitude. There was no sound at all, not even the chirping of the morning birds, and Evelyn wondered at the templelike feel of the clearing. It was a ridiculous thought, she knew, since they'd just bribed a thief to leave them alone. But Jie Ke didn't feel to her like a thief, and she couldn't shake the sense that she was leaving holy ground.

She stepped inside the manor, and Christopher took a moment to wipe the morning dew off his feet. That gave her a chance to try to make amends. "Chris, I didn't mean . . . I'm so sorry . . . I don't know what came over me. I just didn't think . . ."

He held up his hand to silence her. The struggle to contain himself was visible in his closed eyes and a shudder that came before a slow exhalation. When he finally looked at her, his expression was calm and his eyes rather dull, especially when compared to the stormy gaze of Jie Ke.

"Swear to me," he said. "Swear that it won't happen again. Swear that you're the girl I've known since I was ten." He grabbed her shoulders and squeezed her painfully tight. "Evelyn, I won't be one of those pitiable fools who are cuckolded within hours of their wedding."

"Of course, I swear!" she cried. "I would never hurt you that way! It's just been so confusing—"

His mouth descended on hers. It was harsh, it was possessive, and it was completely unlike Christopher. Evelyn and her fiancé had shared kisses before, but not like this. Not with raw emotion and brutal strength. She barely had time to gasp in surprise before he thrust his tongue inside her mouth. Was this another one of his tests? Was she supposed to push him away with disgust? But she didn't want to. If things had gone as they should have, he would be allowed that and so much more. But when he pressed his hand to her breast, she found herself shrinking away. He had every right to touch her body. He had every right to take what he wanted from her . . . and yet as much as she longed for someone to touch her just like this, this caress felt hollow and empty, a mundane press of flesh without the raw power of . . . of Jie Ke.

She flinched away from the thought. She was meant for Christopher. She was going to be a countess. She had been trained for it since the day she was born.

As gently as she could, she pressed her hands to his shoulders. She didn't struggle. She simply allowed him to do as he would and waited for him to finish. Then, when he eased his passionate assault, she slowly pushed him back. "The reverend," she whispered, "and my mother, not to mention the servants. Anyone could see."

She could see a bitter retort forming on his lips. She hadn't much cared who would see out in the garden. But he didn't say this, and she was eternally grateful.

"He will leave today," she whispered. "We can have the wedding tomorrow, and a wedding night such as you want. Whatever you want, however you want." Those words, especially, were hard to say. Not because she didn't want to experience it, but she couldn't help but wonder what a night spent with Jie Ke would be like. Did Chinese monks know levels of passion well beyond what an Englishman was taught?

Christopher didn't answer her. He was scanning her face, searching for deceit. In the end, she said the words she knew he needed to hear.

"I will not shame my husband, Christopher. I swear."

He sighed in relief and dropped his forehead to hers. "I know," he said. "I know you, Evie . . . but I am afraid." He straightened, his heart in his eyes. "I have never said it before, but I do love you. You are everything I want in a woman. I can't let that slip away. I can't!" The words were like a vow, and they echoed deep inside her. She had never felt so loved or so wanted. Then he added one last push. "But you have to act the station, Evie. Always. A countess is watched even in her own home. Especially there."

She nodded, ashamed because the reproach was well deserved. She had been kissing another man.

"I will do better," she promised. Then she pressed her mouth to his—a brief touch that he accepted not with a fierce possession but with gentle understanding. It was sweet and kind, and she forced herself to feel grateful for his forgiveness. A moment later and the touch was done. He pulled back with a sigh of regret.

"Tomorrow night," he whispered. "Then we will explore at our leisure."

She nodded and gave him a trembling smile. They would rub along well together, she told herself. She only had to control her impulse to wildness. And she certainly would never wander in any more thunderstorms.

He answered with a smile of his own. Then he straightened just as a future earl should, and she placed her hand on his arm just as a future countess would. They walked together into the breakfast room.

Mama looked tired. That was Evelyn's first thought when she entered the room. Mama's skin looked pale, and her shoulders drooped. Clearly the last twenty-four hours had been quite a strain. While Evelyn supervised the servants, Mama orchestrated the conversations. And yesterday's conversations—beginning with the "wedding" breakfast, through "please have tea," on to after-dinner cards before bed—had all been a minefield of sneering speculation and outright ridicule. As the mother of a future countess, Mama had weathered it all with aplomb, but the strain showed on her face. Sitting next to Mama, Maddie also looked subdued. Given that the girl had the resilience of a young, very high-spirited horse, her current silence screamed as loud as the dark circles under Mama's eyes.

This whole wedding nonsense simply had to end. It was too great a strain on everyone.

By contrast, the Reverend Smythe-Jones looked positively bright-eyed. He had Mama's hands cupped between his as he exuded sympathy and concern, but Evelyn did not miss the selfish gleam in his eye. The reverend was a true gossip, and anything he heard here would make its way around the parish by noon.

As she and Christopher entered the room, the reverend released Mama's hand and pushed to his feet. "Dear Evelyn," he intoned, "I cannot express how worried I have been for you. Such a terrible happening on your day of days."

Evelyn experienced a moment's panic when she realized the reverend had been right here during her . . . well, during her moments in the garden. If anyone had seen her . . . If he had chanced to hear the servants gossiping about it . . . Oh heaven, the disaster would be monumental! And the shame to Christopher would be insupportable. She had to find a way to nip any possible gossip in the bud before it even began.

Disengaging from Christopher, she stepped forward into the reverend's fatherly embrace. "You are so kind," she murmured. Then she straightened and turned her most infatuated smile on her fiancé. "But I have faith that everything will work out just perfectly. I prayed, Father, I truly prayed hard all night long. And I know the earl is doing everything he can in London." She turned back to the reverend. "With God and country on my side, how can I fail?"

"Oh!" cried the cleric with true delight, "I knew you were a strong child. I knew . . ." His eyes widened and his voice faded away.

For the second time in as many days, Evelyn had that terrible feeling that something behind her was woefully out of place. To the side, her mother wore an equal expression of dumbfounded shock, and even worse, Maddie giggled. Nothing proper ever happened when Maddie started giggling. Steeling herself for the inevitable, Evelyn turned to look.

The monks were filing into the room. The Chinese monk was in the lead, followed by Jie Ke. Both had their bowls lifted high before them, both shuffled forward with their heads bowed, their attitudes reverent. Behind them came the servant, equally bowed, but without a bowl of his own. Stretching up on tiptoe, Evelyn could see that Christopher's purse was still in Jie Ke's bowl.

The monks shuffled forward like a glacier—slowly, and pushing everything in their path aside. They were only halfway in when a footman appeared. The poor man pulled up short, chafing dish in one hand, serving tongs in the other. Jie Ke stopped before him, bowl raised right in front of the man's eyes. Evelyn gasped and stepped forward, though what she intended to do she hadn't a clue. It didn't matter. Christopher's large hand wrapped around her upper arm and held her still.

The footman, of course, had no idea what to do either, but Jie Ke did not move. In the end, the servant shrugged. Carefully juggling his platter, he uncovered a dish of steaming sausage. With excruciating care, he dropped one, then two, then a third fat tube into the bowl right on top of the purse. Evelyn barely restrained herself from rolling her eyes. At least it wasn't kippers. Imagine the mess!

Apparently satisfied, Jie Ke turned away from the servant and once again the line of Chinese began moving . . . straight at the reverend. The elderly man's eyes bugged out and he began to look desperately at his half-eaten breakfast— poached eggs on toast with the yolks already broken and oozing about his plate.

Evelyn stepped forward. It was one thing to make sport of a servant, but to do so to an elderly cleric was beyond the pale. She would not allow it in her home. But Christopher did not release her. He held fast, and so she had no choice but to press her lips together and silently will her fiancé into stopping this farce.

Unfortunately, Christopher seemed all too willing to allow the monks to appear foolish before one of the biggest gossips in the county, no matter that it embarrassed the reverend at the same time. The monks lined up before the clergyman with their heads bowed and their bowls upraised. From this distance, Evelyn could see additional money in the Chinese monk's bowl. Then the Chinese servant slipped forward and spoke in high, melodic voice. His words were heavily accented and somewhat stilted, but they were clear enough.

"Beg pardon, sir," he said. "You are highest ranking abbot?"

The Reverend Smythe-Jones's gaze hopped about from the bowls to the monks to the servant, but in the end, he nodded. "I, um, yes. I'm not an abbot, so to speak. I'm called—"

"Beg pardon, sir. In our temple, alms walk is most sacred. Did I say correct? You understand giving of alms?"

The reverend cleared his throat, then nodded most sagely. "Of course, of course, I understand. Giving alms is a most sacred pillar of the Christian faith—"

"Beg pardon, sir, alms walk is silent. The monks do not speak. I must speak for them."

The reverend's head had begun to bob up and down. "Yes, yes. Um, am I supposed to give alms then? Right into their bowl?"

"Beg pardon, sir. We are long way from temple. Monks do not hold money. We give to temple abbot who gives to those in need. But we cannot hold alms for many month return. Monks give alms to local temple." The boy paused a long moment. "Alms give to you, English abbot."

It took a moment for the reverend to understand. Then his eyes abruptly widened. "You are giving *me* the alms? For the church?"

The boy bowed in the just same way that Jie Ke had: left

fist against open right palm. "Yes, yes, sir. Monks do not hold money. Alms for your temple."

The reverend looked down at the bowls. He didn't have the same height as the monks, but he was tall enough to see the money lying there. With shaking hands, the man began to pull out bills and coins, making a small pile on the linen tablecloth. To Evelyn's stunned amazement, Christopher's purse was the least of the wealth. Coins of every denomination fell on the table.

"There must be close to four hundred pounds here!" the cleric gasped. "How did they get so much?"

"Beg pardon, sir. Alms giving is . . . is . . . no name, sir."

"Anonymous? Yes, of course it would be." The man was still pulling coins from Jie Ke's bowl, though these were rather greasy from the sausage.

"Heaven knows names of people who give gifts. The monks do not speak."

"Of course, of course." The reverend was clearly distracted as he stacked up the coins. "This is most generous, most generous indeed." All waited in silence as the man finished his accounting, then poured it all back into Christopher's purse. It wasn't large enough, so Mama gestured to the slack-jawed footman. Within another minute, a napkin was produced. The reverend dropped the last of his pile on the cloth and tied it into a neat bundle.

At last he straightened, looking back at the Chinese servant, then to each monk. His eyes were still wide, but his attitude was of heartfelt gratitude. "I humbly accept your gift and promise that all will be spent for the glory of God." And with that he gave his own awkward version of a bow. But after he straightened, no one moved. The reverend paused, his chin quivering with confusion as his gaze hopped from monks to servant, then back. Flushing scarlet, he bowed again, this time to the servant. Still, the monks did not leave. They remained directly in front of him, their bowls still raised before them.

"Er, is there something else?" the reverend finally asked.

"Beg pardon, sir," the servant responded. "Temple abbot must take all alms. All given . . . to glory of God."

Smythe-Jones blinked. It was clear he didn't understand, and the monks weren't speaking. In the end, it was Maddie who piped up, an indecorous note of humor in her voice.

"The sausage, Reverend. I think you're supposed to take the sausage, too."

"Oh! Er, really?" he asked the servant.

The boy bowed. "Food is most glorious alms."

"Sausage? Oh, er yes, I suppose it is." Then with a rather wan smile, the reverend reached in two long fingers and picked up a sausage. It slipped right out of his grip, but he persevered and eventually lifted one out. Unfortunately, he didn't know where to put it and stood there holding the thing and looking confused.

Evelyn repressed a sigh and snatched up the saucer from beneath his teacup. She held it out while the reverend dropped one sausage, then the second, and finally the third upon it. At last Jie Ke's bowl was empty. In one motion, both monks and the servant bowed deeply before the reverend.

"Thank you, honored abbot," the servant said. Then he added something else in Chinese—a benediction perhaps, it was hard to tell—before all three resumed their shuffling walk to the door. But before they could leave, the servant gasped as if he had forgotten something. He quickly dashed back to bow once again before the reverend, who froze halfway down into his chair.

"Beg pardon, sir. Monks pray now." He glanced at the others in the room. "No one disturb."

"Yes, yes, of course," agreed the reverend. "I completely understand."

The servant bowed again and repeated his strange Chinese words. When he straightened, he flashed a quick grin and whispered, "I speak blessing on all." After one last bow, the boy dashed away.

No one spoke until the door swung shut behind the servant. All then released a collective sigh of relief. The reverend's was loudest, as he was finally able to drop into his chair. Mama shook her head as she stared at the purse and wrapped pile of money.

"Is it truly four hundred pounds?" asked Maddie.

"Four hundred ten pounds, six shillings, and thruppence," answered the reverend.

"But that's . . ." Mama apparently could not find an adequate descriptor. "That's . . ."

"A farce of the grandest order!" snapped Christopher, his glare centered straight on Evelyn.

"Chris . . . ," she began, but she had no idea what to say. He was right. She had made him find £50 as a bribe to monks who had just given it—plus another £360—all to the church. It made no sense.

"I am going out for a ride," he ground out. "They had best be gone by the time I return."

"But . . . but . . ." sputtered the reverend from the side. "They are praying!"

Christopher's gaze didn't so much as flicker toward the man. "By the time I return, Evelyn. Make sure of it." Then he spun on his heel and left.

How long did it take a pair of monks to pray?

Evelyn paced outside of the "Chinese bedroom," as the servants now called the room. She had been out here for two hours now, wearing holes in the carpet while every servant and guest made an excuse to visit the hallway. Everyone knew about Christopher's decree that the monks be gone, that he had left it to her to see to the impossible visitors, and that she would be the biggest ill-bred lout to interrupt clerics at prayer. Especially clerics who had just given over four hundred pounds to the church! Everyone knew and waited to see exactly what she would do next. She wouldn't have been surprised if the question were being printed on broadsheets in London.

CHINESE MONKS DISRUPT EARL'S WEDDING! ILLICIT KISSES!
FURIOUS BRIDEGROOM!
WHAT WILL THE BRIDE DO NEXT?

She closed her eyes and prayed that was not the case. But how could her quick-whispered plea to God hope to compete with two hours of Chinese monks' prayers? Oh bloody hell! She rubbed both fists against her eyes. She was tired and not thinking clearly. And she still did not have an answer to her most pressing question: why, oh why, had she kissed him?

Crash!

A noise! She rushed forward and pressed her ear to the door. She heard male voices speaking in Chinese—one was loud and clearly agitated, the other was lower, calmer, and little more than a low rumble of sound. Through the wood, she couldn't tell who owned which voice, but it didn't matter. They were not praying. Which meant she could interrupt.

She knocked on the door. When it wasn't immediately answered, she knocked again much more forcefully. Christopher would be returning any moment now, and she did not want him to find out she'd been pacing outside the room all morning. She was about to knock a third time when the door was jerked open by Jie Ke. He grimaced when he saw her.

She swallowed, her eyes absorbing every detail of his appearance. His body seemed tense, his face pulled tight, and his upper body was just as beautifully sculpted as she remembered. He wore his monk's robe, but only over one shoulder. That left a clearly defined triangle of muscled torso directly before her eyes. Lean and rippling right in front of her. No doubt about it, he was a beautiful man.

"Yes?" he said. His voice was short, clipped, and yet the

power of that one word sent a tingle of excitement down her spine.

"Er . . ." She blinked. "I heard a noise—a crash. Like something broke."

"It is nothing."

She looked over his shoulder to see the other monk grinning. He lifted up a wooden bowl. "His alms bowl," the Chinese monk said. "Nothing broken. We know better than to leave anything fragile around when Jie Ke meditates."

"Of course," she said, though she didn't understand at all. "But I thought you were praying."

"We are!" Jie Ke snapped.

"It is one and the same," answered the other man.

Evelyn nodded. "Oh, I see," she lied. A heavy door closed somewhere on the first floor. It could easily have been Christopher returning. She had to end this quickly. "I . . . um . . . I thought perhaps we could assist you with your bags, since you're leaving now."

Jie Ke arched an eyebrow. "Leaving? We are not leaving."

She felt her stomach clench, her worst fears confirmed. "But we made a bargain." Down the hall, one of the maids topped the stairs. A hurried glance to the side showed Evelyn that the girl was cleaning the railing as slowly as possible as she listened to every word. Evelyn dropped her voice to a forceful whisper. "Fifty pounds was our bargain! Fifty pounds and you would leave." She almost spit on his robes. "And you call yourself a monk. Haven't you any shame?"

She saw his face darken with color. "I told you," he repeated firmly. "I *am* a monk. I cannot help it that you do not understand what that means!"

"It means you don't steal people's money and lie to them!" she shot back, completely failing to moderate her tone.

"I stole nothing!" he shot back. "All our money has been given to your abbot."

"Reverend!"

"Reverend, then!"

"So, why aren't you leaving?"

He glared at her, his face the picture of a man completely incredulous. "We are monks!" he repeated firmly. "We do not barter. We take money as gifts to the temple. Or your church." Then he abruptly straightened, folding his arms across his chest. "And why would I leave? I am the earl. And your future husband!"

Her mouth dropped open. Her body trembled with fury. "Not yet, you're not! And you told me you would leave!"

"I told you I would take honorable prayer money. I said nothing of leaving. I have never, ever said I would leave."

She almost called him a liar and tore his lying tongue out right then and there, no matter how many maids were listening. She had never met anyone who could challenge her sense of propriety so quickly! Except, of course, honesty forced herself to think back. Had he actually said he was leaving? Or had she said it? "You lied," she persisted. "You made me think we had a bargain."

He sighed. The sound was heavy and loud. It actually echoed in the hallway, and she was sure the maid heard. "I am a monk," he said. "We do not bargain. Your ignorance of that may be excused, but you did not ask what I meant. You did not ask to learn, you merely told me what I would do without regard to who and what I am. That is willful blindness and stinking arrogance. Even the Christian God finds that sinful, and yet you ask if I have no shame." He shook his head, as if she were unworthy of even God's understanding.

"That's not true!" she cried, though in her heart she wondered.

Could he be right?

"I am a monk," he repeated. "I need to meditate." Then he shut the door, leaving her outside.

Chapter Five

Jie Ke shut the door a split second before his best friend began mocking him.

" 'I am a monk'!" chortled Zhi Min. "You are a loud and smelly fart!"

"Shut up. I *am* a monk." Jie Ke settled back onto his cushion and tried to compose his thoughts. *I am the mountain. I am a mountain.*

His friend's snort of laughter interrupted him. Jie Ke exploded off his cushion, his fists flying. "I am a goddamned monk!" he shouted.

Zhi Min defended himself. They were well matched in their skills, neither having truly bested the other in years. Provided Jie Ke never crossed that invisible line into madness. If that happened, he didn't know who would prevail. He didn't want to find out. Unfortunately, the furniture always suffered. By the time they fell apart in sputtering exhaustion, the nightstand was in splinters and the water bowl upended on them both. He would have to find some money to replace that, he realized. But they had just given up everything to the Reverend Smythe-Jones. Jie Ke sighed and wondered when he would next go into the ring to gain money. Though he didn't object to a monk's enforced poverty, it did make certain things awkward. Especially in England where no one had the ingrained reverence for a man in saffron robes.

Jie Ke let his dripping head fall back against the bed frame, his grin already fading. Normally a tussle like that buoyed his spirits for an hour at least. Not this time. It was another long moment before he realized he was staring at the shut bedroom door and thinking again of his wife-to-be.

"So the English boy has discovered girls."

Jie Ke's gaze cut hard back to his friend. "I have known women before. I have . . ."

"Watched and touched yourself? That is not the same thing as stopping dead in the midst of your morning training." Zhi Min leaned forward, his eyes narrowing in . . . laughter? In challenge? "We were right in the middle of a fight and you stopped to kiss her. How did that make you feel, English boy?"

"Shut up," Jie Ke shot back, doing his best to appear righteous. "I was doing what the abbot told me to do: honor my parents, marry the girl vowed to me. Besides, I had already beaten you and was bored," he lied.

Zhi Min wasn't fooled. He never was, but he also rarely argued when Jie Ke resorted to stupid lies. Without so much as a breath to compose himself, Zhi Min shut his eyes in meditation. When had he returned to his meditation pose? His hair was still sodden and yet there he was, legs folded, hands relaxed, body composed and at ease. Jie Ke, on the other hand, was still sprawled against the bed, water dripping into his eyes.

How did he do it? They were the same age, or near enough. How did Zhi Min manage to be serene, while Jie Ke merely faked it—and faked it badly? Was that part of the secret rite of transition? Was that the power that was bestowed when an apprentice monk ascended to full status? Was that the secret that Zhi Min had experienced a decade ago while the English boy Jie Ke stood outside and wondered? He *still* wondered, since the abbot refused to let him take full vows.

"Have you ever tupped a girl?" Jie Ke abruptly blurted. "I know you thought about it with that one. I don't remember her name, but you were with her many nights alone. I remember that. How did it feel? What was it like?"

Zhi Min didn't even open his eyes. "Tup your own woman and find out."

Jie Ke looked away. He *had* done it before, and it had been horrible. The first time had been a woman who'd wanted to experience a white man. She'd caught him behind a market stall, shoved him against the wall and begun opening his robes. It had been fast, brutal, and he'd felt like an idiot when she threw him onto his back then dropped herself on top of him. When it was done, she'd sniffed and declared that tupping a monkey would have been better. The shame had been like a black stain on his heart ever since.

Then there were the other women. He hadn't believed that his one experience was the reality, but with every streetwalker, every woman out for the novelty of a white man, his heart had grown colder, his humiliation more real. He'd seen Zhi Min with a woman. Jie Ke didn't know what they did, but he'd seen the glow that suffused the two of them for a time. He saw it sometimes in others, too, so sex had to be better than what he'd experienced. Unless something fundamental was lacking in him that made him unable to feel the total joy of man and woman. But he did not want to confess that to his friend, so he straightened his spine and spoke with a pompous air. "Monks do not tup."

"Husbands can," Zhi Min replied.

"I am a monk."

"You are a fraud." Jie Ke's friend opened his eyes, his gaze disturbingly calm as he sliced Jie Ke open with his words. "Neither English nor Chinese, neither a monk nor a husband. Find yourself and you will find your power."

Without thought, Jie Ke grabbed his alms bowl and hurled it at his friend with all his might. "I have plenty of power."

Zhi Min did not flinch. The bowl wasn't intended to hit him, anyway, but to zoom straight past his nose. Zhi Min remained statue still nonetheless, and the bowl clattered against the wall to land upside down on the floor. Zhi Min replied, "Imagine how much power you could have if you knew who you were."

Jie Ke huffed. "I am a monk of the Xi Lin Temple." Then he closed his eyes. *I am a mountain. I am mounting. I am mounting Evelyn, who spreads her thighs so sweetly. . . .* "God damn it!" he exploded in English. Then he folded his arms and glared at his friend. "I can't do this here. I need to be back at the temple."

"A monk's temple is his heart. No other thing is required."

Jie Ke shifted onto his knees as he crawled closer to his friend. "I need to be back at the temple so that I can take my vows. Come on, Zhi Min, I have done all I can here. Let us go back home."

His friend opened his eyes, but there was a strange look inside, one Jie Ke had never seen. Zhi Min's entire aura became abruptly mysterious, dark, and echoed with infinite power. As if he needed merely to reach out in order to cup the universe in his hand. "Is that an official request to be evaluated?" he said.

Jie Ke reared back. "What? Does it have to be recorded in a tablet? Reported to the abbot?"

"Yes, and yes."

Jei Ke blinked, his spirit completely stunned. Fortunately, his mind kept working, puzzling out all the hidden traps. Zhi Min loved to add traps. "Do I have a limit on the number of times I can ask to return home?"

"A limit? With you, always." Zhi Min's lips curved in to a shadow of a smile. "Else we are pestered to death. Remember what you did to Brother Xin Mao?"

"He doesn't count. He was already crazy." Jie Ke picked up his alms bowl and set it carefully, respectfully, aside. "Besides, you can't just decree a limit because you want to."

"Three requests. No less, no more."

His bowl put away, Jie Ke leaned back against the wall and allowed his bare feet to flop out in front of him. Then he shifted again, this time to push his back against the wall. "And if I ask a fourth time?"

"You will not ever be allowed to return to the temple."

Jie Ke sobered and stared hard at the other man. Even though they had lived most of their lives together—ever since that awful day when he was ten—there were times when Zhi Min seemed completely alien. Why would his best friend threaten to expel him from the temple? And it was a real threat, too. Zhi Min always followed through.

He would have to sort through the details to reason out what was required. Zhi Min was the abbot's official representative on this trip, and therefore had to be treated with all due reverence and a certain amount of pomp. Jie Ke gave an internal shrug. If Zhi Min wanted a bit of pomp, that was a small price to pay for freedom from this ridiculous task.

"Fine," he huffed, "you want to play at being powerful, so be it. Reverend monk, please bear witness that I have fulfilled my task as requested. I have returned to my homeland, done all that I could to reclaim my lost title, even attempted to claim my bride. I have disrupted the wedding, thrown their lives into chaos, and remembered my heritage. I have done all this because the abbot demanded it as my final task. It is done now, Brother Zhi Min. Please do not force me to hurt these people anymore. Therefore, I request . . ." He couldn't resist adding a slight sneer to his voice. "I most humbly beg your holy indulgence, permission, and company in the return to the Xi Lin Temple. Once there, I ask that you stand by my side as I take my holy vows."

Zhi Min's head dropped to his chest as though he was in deep contemplation. Jie Ke watched closely. He sensed no dishonesty in his friend, or even mischievousness. His pronouncement would be made in true holy character as befitted a Xi Lin monk. Which meant that Jie Ke could direct his attention to packing up their things and saying good-bye to this frigid English weather forever.

"Do you feel as if you have done all you can to embrace your English heritage?" Zhi Min intoned.

"Yes, Brother Zhi Min."

"That you have donned their garb, eaten their food, and reclaimed all that your parents would value? And having fully experienced what they might wish, you have made a man's choice in taking another path?"

"Yes, Brother Zhi Min," he returned solemnly. But then Zhi Min stared rather pointedly at his monk's robe. Jie Ke frowned and looked down, forced into deeper thought. "I have!" he snapped. "I grew up here, remember? I dressed and ate as one of them for ten years. Actually, eleven years, since I still wore my English clothes at the temple. Or I did, until you stole them."

"They smelled of dog piss," Zhi Min responded lightly.

"And it was the right thing to do," Jie Ke acknowledged. "I could not fully accept my new life without releasing the trappings of the old."

Zhi Min didn't respond, and Jie Ke sat there waiting. And waiting. In the end, he exhaled with frustration. "So, can we return to the temple now?"

"No, Apprentice Jie Ke, we cannot. You have not reclaimed any of what your ancestors value. You have not even tried."

Jie Ke exploded up from his place on the floor, turning to face his best friend. Games were all well and good, but he would not allow a boyish prank to keep him from his life's calling. "Zhi Min, what is the matter with you? I've come here. I've done all that I can."

"You have not—"

"I have *hurt* these people, all because you insisted." He leaned forward, fighting to keep the fury from his voice. "I've done all I can to reclaim the title, but Uncle Frank will fight to keep it. And he'll win because he has the friends and the solicitors on his side—and because I don't want it. Let them go on with their lives, Zhi Min. And let me continue on my path."

Zhi Min frowned, clearly as frustrated as Jie Ke. "What of the woman, Jie Ke? She is the one you were supposed to marry. Do you not long for her?"

Jie Ke straightened, pulling his arms down near his hips in a powerful stance. "I have kissed her, and I do not want her," he lied. Then he lifted his chin and focused on meeting his friend eye to eye, challenging him. If he wavered even the smallest bit, then Zhi Min would see. He kept his gaze steady even though it was hard to forget the texture of her mouth against his, the way she seemed to cling to him, her body taut with excitement.

Zhi Min grimaced as he pushed up to his feet. It was the first show of ill humor that Jie Ke had seen from him all morning, perhaps all week. And that awkward, saddened expression was aimed at Jie Ke. "The abbot gave specific instructions, Jie Ke. You must *be* English for a time. Then, when I am satisfied—"

"I have been English!" Jie Ke cried. "You still call me English boy!"

"Listen to me, Ja-cob." The name sounded strange and very wrong coming from his friend.

"I am Jie Ke!" He growled. "Out there I will be Jacob, but not here. Not between us!"

Zhi Min tilted his head to one side. It was a look that said he studied something foreign and strange. "Why not between us? Why not be Ja-cob now?"

Jie Ke sighed and struggled to explain. "I long for something of home. You and Mei Li are the only thing I have. Do not make me throw that away."

His friend shook his head. "You are always clinging to the past. In China, you longed for England—"

"Only as a child!"

"And in England, you long for China." Zhi Min reached out and grabbed Jie Ke's shoulders, tightening his grip as if he wished to press a message into his skin. "Be here now in this moment, in this place. You will not be allowed to take vows until you can release the past."

Jie Ke stared back at his friend, trying to hear, trying to learn, but it made no sense to him. Where was he, if not here? When was it, if not now? "Say it differently, master," he said in his most formal Chinese. "I do not understand."

"Be Ja-cob completely. What would he do now?"

Jie Ke shrugged his shoulders, dislodging his friend's grip. "I don't know. It's been almost two decades since I knew anything English."

"If I were a mandarin's son, I would want all the trappings of my status. The money and title—"

"I can't do anything about that! I told you, Uncle Frank will never allow it!" He almost threw his alms bowl again. They were going in circles.

"The title is less important than the respect. Do they see you as the earl?"

"Of course not! They think I'm some thieving interloper."

"Then make them see the earl. Wear his clothing, look at his possessions, demand his respect. And his woman."

And there it was: the one aspect that he most wanted to avoid thinking about, the woman. Money, land, even the title— all were just words written on paper. They meant less than nothing to him. Whether he took the title or not, the earl's money would land in the estate coffers. The earl's managers would handle that money. He had no intention of changing any of it. As for respect, who cared if someone called him "earl" or "my lord?" Words meant nothing.

But Evelyn was not nothing. The stiff, prissy girl in pigtails he remembered was now a beautiful woman. The feel of her mouth on his had been like sunlight on a mountain lake, blindingly bright and dazzling, shimmering in his thoughts. Just looking at her brought back a favorite memory of another girl, another time, and his very last English rainstorm. In short, Miss Evelyn Stanton was the one thing, the one part of England that tempted him.

"A monk does not need a woman," he said to himself.

"You are not a monk."

Jie Ke barely restrained his curse. This was an old argument between him and everyone else. "Yes, I'm white. Yes, I was born English. But that is no reason to keep me from becoming a monk! Why can't you see your own prejudice? God damn it, Zhi Min!" He whirled around, spinning uselessly because he was so angry he teetered on the edge of madness. "Why are you making this so hard?"

"I would release you from this task if I could, truly I would," Zhi Min replied. "But there is more to taking vows than simply saying the words. The ceremony splinters a man into shards of glass. If there is any doubt, anything left unresolved, then you cannot put yourself together again." He shook his head. "The process is very painful. Seeing you now, Jie Ke, I know you would not survive."

Jie Ke swallowed, stunned by the absolute certainty in his friend's expression. "But . . . why? What do I lack?"

Zhi Min sighed. "You run from your past."

Jie Ke tried to understand. He didn't—he never did. All he could do is obey, for now, and pray the answer would become clear.

"Very well," he finally said. "I will wear English clothing. I will eat English food. I will even appear in the House of Lords and demand my title. But do not ask me to woo the English wife; it is too cruel to her. Do I engage her affections only to leave her and become a monk? Disrupting her wedding was bad enough, but now you ask me to toy needlessly with her. That is neither honorable nor holy."

His friend simply shook his head. "You must dress, act,

and live as Ja-cob. Do all that your English parents would want."

"But she—"

"Your parents wished you to wed her, did they not? They betrothed you."

"Yes, of course, but that was years ago, and it had to do with property, not people."

Zhi Min shrugged. "A wedding between aristocrats is always about money. Surely she knows that. She merely fights because she thinks you are penniless. Once you claim the title, she will have everything she wants."

Jie Ke ground his teeth together. Why didn't his friend understand? "But I will not win the title; my uncle is too powerful. Even if I succeed, I will abdicate to Chris. That's who should have had the title from the beginning."

Zhi Min did not appear to care. "Then give her enough money before you leave and she will be satisfied." He leaned forward, his expression intense. "Your arguments are as straw—easily knocked aside. Ask yourself why you fight this process so much."

"I fight because it's cruel—"

"You fight because she tempts you. So explore your temptation. See if it is your true path."

"It isn't!"

Zhi Min didn't respond. He simply closed his eyes and resumed his meditations. Obviously the conversation was finished, which left Jie Ke to struggle on his own. And yet, no matter how he turned the task over in his mind, he could not find a way out. He wouldn't toy with a woman. It wasn't fair to either of them, especially since he feared she would prove the one temptation that England truly offered. But that was Zhi Min's whole point, wasn't it? Something had to tempt him to stay in England so that he could freely choose to leave.

"Fine," he snapped in English. "I will woo her." Then he stomped from the room.

A decade ago, he would have slammed the door or would have sat and pretended to meditate in sulking fury. But he was a man now, and he understood the workings of the universe better. He knew that enlightenment came at odd moments, often when one least expected it. One such moment had happened just a breath ago. He had not thought a new solution would appear in the space between one breath and the next, but one had. And with enlightenment came purpose. Finally, he had a viable plan.

Jie Ke walked too quickly down the stairs. If he were at the temple, monks young and old would have glared at his unseemly demeanor. But he was in England, where his very presence was an oddity. They would stare no matter how quickly he moved, and so he walked to please himself and to find Evelyn.

He found his grandmother instead. She was waiting in the central hallway, sitting in a chair usually occupied late at night by an exhausted butler or footman. Her eyes brightened the moment he rounded the bottom of the stairs, and she struggled to stand. "Jacob! Jacob!"

Common courtesy required that he stop and assist her. His monastic respect for all souls demanded that he give her reverence, especially considering her age. But the scent of the powder in her hair tickled his nose and he struggled not to sneeze. How strange that he simultaneously wanted to inhale deeply and shove her far, far away from him.

He didn't want to look her in the eye. He feared it would make his urge to sneeze that much worse. And his headache was coming back, too. So he shifted his gaze downward and ended up seeing her hands. They were frail, her skin like parchment as she gripped her cane. He did not want to see her skin looking so white and thin. He wanted to see Evelyn and set his new plan into motion, and yet his conscience required him to remain by his grandmother. So he locked his knees tight and remained exactly where he was.

"Are your prayers over then?" she wheezed. Well, it truly wasn't a wheeze. Monk Ming Hai wheezed. His grandmother spoke as he remembered, except without as much authority and with a thin whisper of air around her words.

"Jacob?" she said again.

"Hmm? Oh yes, my morning meditations are over for now."

"You didn't eat anything earlier."

How would she know that? Gossip, most likely. His every action was probably being dissected by everyone in the surrounding countryside, from servant to titled lord. Would his family's murderer hear the gossip? Would he laugh at how effectively he had destroyed everything Jacob loved? Would he—

"Would you care for tea?" she pressed. "Perhaps eggs? Porridge? You used to like Cook's Banbury buns, but I don't know how they are done here."

A maid came down the stairs, slowly dusting the stairway rail. Another woman peeked her head out of parlor along the hallway, then pulled back before reappearing with a man. Jie Ke had no idea who they were, except that they were obviously a married couple and interested in whatever he said. Had his grandmother said Banbury buns?

"Jacob, surely you wish for tea. You have been ever so long in those heathen lands—"

"My dog liked the Banbury buns." He remembered his dog, the feel of its large, lolling tongue slurping wetly about his fingers as he fed it.

"Yes, well, that dog liked everything. And you would feed him anything, you naughty boy." She smiled, and her face wrinkled. He saw little bits of powder stuck in the creases. When had Grandmother become this old?

Panic began to clog his throat. His breath shortened, and his mind splintered even more than usual. "I am looking for Evelyn. I need to see Evelyn," he said.

"Well, Evie is here somewhere, dear. She was most angry at you."

"I say," interrupted the parlor woman. Her voice was high-pitched and trilled falsely. He had not heard such a thing in China, perhaps ever. He stared at her, wondering if she had an ailment of the throat, but she continued, "I believe Miss Stanton took a turn with Mr. Wilkins."

"No, no, my dear," said her husband, his voice pitched nearly as high. "Mr. Wilkins went out, but she stayed inside to find me a newspaper. It was still being pressed, you see. And that footman was making a fuss about rearranging the parlor furniture or something."

"You and your newspaper, dear. Why, just the other day . . ."

There was more from the couple, but Jie Ke lost the sense of the English words. The voices were so strange, and why did the man's hair curl in such a way—in perfect rows like sausages? Did the murderer have curling hair like that, too?

He forced a breath into his lungs, but got a big whiff of his grandmother's powder instead. It irritated his nose and throat. Putting fist to palm, he bowed just as a fierce sneeze ripped through him. There wasn't room in the hallway to proceed forward, so he pushed his way backwards into a parlor. Was it a parlor? It didn't matter. . . .

"Jacob! Jacob, dear, what about tea?"

It was a parlor. White walls and light blue furniture. Blue like Evelyn's eyes. He needed to see her. He needed to not see his grandmother. But why? Why did he fear an old woman? It was indeed fear that pounded through his veins. He couldn't think. He sneezed again. A parlor maid spun around. She had been dusting and now was wide-eyed in terror at seeing him. He bowed to her with all reverence, but that only seemed to frighten her more.

How ridiculous was this? A panic-stricken monk facing a terrorized maid. He swallowed. She looked like she was about to scream. The duster was shaking in her hand like a wet dog. This was funny. He should be smiling. How could he make her relax?

He tried to laugh but hadn't the breath. Wet dog? He remembered wet dogs. There were dogs at the temple, too, but he remembered his wet dog from childhood. The one that liked Banbury buns. Why was he shaking?

"Evelyn. Miss Stanton." He forced the words out. Now *he* was wheezing, and sounded like an old man. "Where is she?"

"I'll find her, sir. Right away!" Then she sidled past as fast as she could.

Jie Ke backed against the window to give her space. In fact, he wedged himself between a settee and a table to give her room. What was wrong with him? His grandmother was coming in with the high-voiced couple. He needed to be calm. He needed to understand. He knew how to control himself.

Inhale. Straighten the body. Exhale. Bow the head. Inhale. Press the hands together. Exhale. Quiet the mind. Inhale—

"Jacob? Oh dear, you don't look well."

Outside. He needed to be outside.

"Lord Greenfield, I believe we need some tea. Do be so kind as to—"

"Yes, yes. Of course, of course." The man bobbed his head but didn't leave.

Jie Ke was shaking. Why was he shaking? Grandmother's powder tickled in his nose again. He backed farther away from the group, but they just pushed in closer. He barely avoided hitting his nose on a lampshade while turning away. There were now two more scents added to the powder. It came from the married couple, each of whom had a perfume of sorts. He sneezed again, and the force from that made his head pound.

"Oh, dear. I do hope you aren't catching ill."

Greenfield pressed farther forward, holding out a palm-sized ebony box. Snuff! That was the smell on the man.

"I say, chap, would you care for a pinch?"

Jie Ke shook his head, though he reached forward a finger anyway. His grandfather had taken snuff. He remembered snuff. *Aiee,* the pounding in his head made his vision quiver. He sneezed again, this time more violently. All three shrank back in horror. Jie Ke now held his hand suspended over nothing; the snuff box was now a foot away, removed to a safer spot.

"Please," he said. "I must go outside."

"What did he say?"

"Was that Chinese?"

Had he spoken in Mandarin? He took a breath. Not another sneeze. Don't sneeze!

"Lord and Lady Greenfield!" came a voice from the doorway. "I have been looking for you both! Thank goodness I have found you."

It was Evelyn. Jie Ke could see her, but he couldn't breathe enough yet to speak.

"Lady Greenfield, Cook most especially needs to talk to you about your diet request. I do understand about your difficult stomach. Mary here will show you to the kitchen."

Was the maid there, too? There she was, peering around Evelyn's hip like a frightened child.

"And Lord Greenfield," his wife-to-be continued, "I believe Mr. Wilkins wants to discuss your horses. Seems one of them is off his feed. You remember where the stables are, do you not? Davis!" She gestured to a footman. "Take Lord Greenfield to the stable and make sure he is well satisfied. Show him every inch of the stable, will you? We wish him to be completely sure of things. *Every single inch.*"

Evelyn linked arms with the husband and wife, resolutely pulling them out of the room, babbling all the way. The couple could not speak. She didn't give them time. And as they were pulled from the parlor, Grandmother came in even closer. Her powder . . .

He sneezed again.

His grandmother took his hand and tugged him out from behind the settee.

"Come along, dear. Do sit down."

He was a grown man and much stronger than she. He could shove her away with a single finger then dash out the door, but that was cowardly and disrespectful. He gritted his teeth. He would not sneeze again. He stepped away from the window, feeling like it was a Herculean task. He remembered who Hercules was—a Greek demigod. Hercules didn't sneeze.

"I think tea would be best," intoned Grandmother. He recognized her voice, but when he looked in her face, she was so very old. He sneezed.

"It's those clothes," she said with a *tsk*. "You need some proper English clothing."

He remembered her scolds. No one, not even the most pompous monks, scolded as she did: concerned, disappointed, and so very maternal. If he closed his eyes, he could remember his grandmother as she had been. But he couldn't keep his eyes closed—he wanted to see Evelyn.

And then there she was, his wife-to-be. She stood in the parlor door, firmly shutting it. Looking over her shoulder, he glimpsed other people in the hallway—another wedding guest and a footman, maybe more. Then the door closed and he remained with Evelyn and Grandmother. If only Grandmother would leave, too.

"The tea will be here in a moment," Evelyn said as she came back to the center of the room. She looked down at him, her eyes narrowed, her expression thoughtful. He stared back, wondering what she was thinking.

"You don't look well," she said flatly. "Your prayers go unanswered?"

"Always," he responded without thought. Then he blanched. That wasn't something he usually admitted.

"You must be a very bad monk, then," she said.

He shook his head. "That's just it, I'm not a monk at all. Not a full monk. Not like Zhi Min." He swallowed, forcing himself to focus. He had to get this done now. He needed to return to China where things made sense. He was a man. He did not cower next to settees. And he had something important to say. "I need your help."

Her eyebrows shot up. Grandmother leaned forward to touch his hand. He flinched away from her powdered hair and parchment-thin skin. "Of course, Jacob, we will do whatever you need."

"No," responded his bride-to-be. "No, we most certainly will not."

"Evelyn!" Grandmother's tone was sharp with censure, but Evelyn didn't appear to care. She had folded her arms across her chest, and her face was set in stubborn lines. Grandmother echoed the stance. *Aie-yah*, they were going to squabble. Women always squabbled.

"Stop!" he whispered. It was a quiet word, but he invested it with all his chi strength. Even whispered, the word echoed in the room. Both women jumped in surprise. Fortunately neither spoke. And in the silence, he was able to focus on Evelyn. "Do you know what it means to be a monk of Xi Lin?"

She shook her head.

"It means study, meditation, and serenity. Serenity of body, mind, and spirit. Most men pledge themselves to such a life at the age of eighteen. I would have done so, had I been allowed."

Evelyn arched her brow at him. "Not a very good student?"

"I'm an excellent student," he answered truthfully. "I mastered the physical forms by the time I was sixteen. I mastered the holy texts soon after. But I am white, and they look at me as if I were tainted."

"You *are* white, dear," said his grandmother. "You don't belong in some foreign temple." She tried to touch him again, but he slipped away to settle farther down the couch. It was an obvious movement and one that hurt her, but he couldn't bear to be touched. Not by her. It made no sense to

him, but he did not have the breath to argue. Her powder
clogged his throat and made his head pound.

Meanwhile, Evelyn slowly sat down in a chair opposite
him. "So you're . . . what? An apprentice monk?"

He nodded. "Exactly."

She leaned back, but he saw intense concentration on her
face. That alone gave him hope. She was a person who *thought*.
She didn't just feel, she used her brain. He took a deep breath,
feeling the tightness in his chest and between his shoulder
blades. He needed to do his fighting forms—that always
helped restore his serenity. And when he practiced, she would
watch him. He would like that.

"I want to return to the temple. I want to become a full
monk. But in order to do that, the abbot says I must put my
English past to rest. I must honor what my parents wanted of
me." He looked directly into her pale blue eyes, so like his own.
"To do that, I must reclaim my title and marry the woman
promised to me."

"No," said Evelyn.

"Of course," said Grandmother.

"Listen to me!" How to explain the complicated and often
mysterious commands of the abbot? "Zhi Min is my judge."

"I thought he was your friend," inserted Grandmother.

"He is that too, but he is my judge in this. He must see me
embrace everything English."

Evelyn's eyebrows rose. "And by English, you mean your
title. And me."

"More than that. English clothes. English food." He
shrugged. "Everything."

From the side, Grandmother beamed with delight. "Why,
that is most excellent. Your abbot sounds like a very smart
man."

"He is a blind man!" The words boomed out of him like
thunder, an unfortunate display of temper. Jie Ke tightened
his fists and mentally beat the emotion down, down, down

and away. "My abbot has been searching for an excuse to make me leave the temple. He does not wish to have a white monk."

Evelyn arched a brow. "So, he is not a very holy man."

"No," Jie Ke replied in a softer tone. "He is extremely holy." How odd that this woman had immediately figured out his dilemma. "In this one aspect, he seems prejudiced beyond reason. I have chosen my path: I want to be a monk. But he insists that I embrace my white heritage before I set it aside."

Again, Grandmother beamed her approval. "But that is exactly what you should do! You have been away from England so long, you have forgotten—"

"I have forgotten nothing!" He exploded off the settee and began to pace. Unfortunately, that brought him within her powdery sphere, and abruptly he began sneezing again. It was ridiculous! England and his own grandmother made him sneeze!

But it was what it was, and so he stepped away from his relative to kneel before his future wife. "I don't want to marry you. I don't want to be in England. And I certainly don't want a title or the responsibilities that come with it."

"Well, at least you acknowledge that there will be responsibilities," she drawled. Then she pressed her lips together as if to hold back the rest.

She needn't have bothered. He remembered the rest. "That is more than my father did," he finished for her. "Yes, young as I was, I still remember the arguments between Father and Uncle."

He watched her eyes widen in surprise. Apparently, she still didn't quite believe he'd once been Jacob.

"I don't care what you believe," he said with enough vehemence to surprise even himself. "All I care about is that Zhi Min see me try to become English."

"But—" began Grandmother.

Evelyn held up her hand, silencing the elderly woman.

"You want to pretend to be English so you can prove to your judge that you tried."

He smiled, excruciatingly relieved that she understood. "Yes."

"But you are doing it for real. You have ruined my wedding, challenged the earl for the title, and have thrown my life into chaos."

"All to show Zhi Min and the abbot. My final task, and then they will be forced to allow me to take vows." He tightened his hands. "It is for show, not for real."

She stared at him, her eyes narrowing into tiny blazing points of fury. "It is very real to me."

He sighed. "I know it is, and I am sorry. But if you want me gone, if you want this over, then you have to help me prove myself to Zhi Min."

"How?"

"Help me dress English. Help me be English." He took a deep breath. "Help me court you."

"No."

"We would not need to marry. I have told him how cruel that would be to you."

"No."

He grabbed her hands for fear that she would run. "I swear to you by all that is holy that I will not ruin you or the title. I will abdicate it so that Christopher will someday inherit. I will hand you over for the wedding and marriage you want. But I can only do that if I prove to Zhi Min that I have remembered everything it is to be English, and that I truly do not want it."

She shook her head, but her words said something entirely different. "And if I agree, what then? How long will it take?"

"I don't know, but it shouldn't be long. A fortnight. Enough for Thomas Grayson to fail in my petition to reclaim my title. Enough for Zhi Min to see that I have eaten boiled potato and compressed my neck with your ties." He tightened his grip on her hands. "That I have wooed and won my wife.

That is essential. That is most essential, because it will show that I have the one thing that tempts men away from the temple: a woman and a possible family. And once he believes that I have her—you—then I can tell him that I don't want any of it. Then I can leave and never return."

He took a deep breath, trying to impress upon her the importance of her answer. She had to know that without her help, neither of them could have what they wanted. But if she saw things his way, then everything was within reach. Everything.

She was silent a long moment as she searched his face. Long enough for Grandmother to huff in disgust. Long enough for the tea service to arrive with a discreet knock. Long enough for him to open the door to the servant and stand silently by as tea was laid out and poured.

Only after she had served both Jie Ke and Grandmother did she face him. "A clever scheme," she said softly. "A clever story to enlist my aid against my fiancé's family."

"It is no scheme!" he shot back.

"And after I help you, you will suddenly change your mind—"

"Never!"

"And then you will have everything you want: title, wife, and money."

"I have no need for money! I am a monk."

She slowly pushed to her feet, facing him from across the tea table, her eyes infinitely calm. "You are not a monk, and you are not an earl. You are not English and yet you are not Chinese, either. In short, sir, you are nothing but a clever thief, and I will never, ever help you."

And with that she stood and swept from the room.

Chapter Six

The nerve of the man! Evelyn fumed as she swept from the room, not really knowing where she was going, so long as it was away. Unfortunately, there were eyes everywhere.

She'd gotten rid of Lord Greenfield and his wife, but more guests were around every corner watching every move she made. The strain of this morning had sent Mama to bed, which left Evelyn alone to stem the tide of demands that came from their guests' gossip-hungry hearts.

She looked outside, thinking to escape into the middling-fair day. Just a few moments peace and she would be able to function again. She had just stepped through the doorway when she spotted a group of women walking up the lane. Mrs. Whitsun and her three daughters. More gossipmongers. Evelyn quickly spun around and shot back inside . . . only to run smack-dab into a hovering footman.

"So sorry, miss. Is there something—"

"Mrs. Whitsun and her girls appear to be walking up the lane. Show them in, give them tea, and then come looking for me."

"Of course, miss—"

"But don't you dare find me!" she added on a hissing whisper. "In fact, ask Lady Greenfield to fill in as I'm . . . I don't know, indisposed somehow. Think of something plausible."

"Of course, miss." Then he glanced significantly over her shoulder. "Better hurry. They're almost here."

She nodded and prepared to dash upstairs, only to be stopped short when the footman did some hissing of his own. "I wouldn't suggest your painting parlor, miss. The Countess of Warhaven is up there."

Bloody hell! She couldn't even retreat to her private storage room. She called it her painting parlor because she'd once claimed she would repaint the walls. She never had. Mostly it was a very cluttered top-floor retreat with light and books and all manner of furniture that couldn't be placed anywhere else. And yet, somehow, her future mother-in-law had discovered how very soothing silent clutter could be.

"How long has she been there?"

"All morning miss. Betty said she heard crying, and the lady wouldn't even open the door for her son."

"She wouldn't see Christopher? My goodness, he must be beside himself. . . ." Her voice faded away. Christopher's emotions were not something she wanted to dwell on just then. "She was crying, you say?" Guilt ate at her. As hostess and future daughter-in-law, Evelyn really should see what was the matter. And yet, another woman's dramatics were not what she wanted just then. Not when she felt besieged on all sides. There had to be somewhere else she could go. She glanced nervously outside. Mrs. Whitsun and company were moments away. "Very well," she abruptly decided. "I'll go to my room. Try to delay people from finding me too quickly."

She mounted the stairs, but one glance there showed two maids tidying her room while they giggled over something— her aborted wedding, no doubt. Unwilling to face yet more gossipers, even if they were her own servants, she turned and headed for the back stairs. But where would she go? Her thoughts returned to her painting parlor. Why was the countess so upset and closeted there? It wasn't *her* wedding in shambles. True, the possible loss of title would be upsetting, but the woman wasn't of a delicate nature. So why the waterworks?

Evelyn didn't really care. If the countess felt the need to hide herself away and sob, so be it. But did the woman really need to do it in Evelyn's private sanctuary? Without another choice, and with the sound of the front door knocker banging ponderously behind her, Evelyn dashed up the back stairs. Rounding the corner, she rushed down the hallway to stop short beside the tiny closet that she alone ruled.

No sound from inside. Perhaps the countess had left. Evelyn was about to knock when she heard footsteps. Someone was climbing the back staircase. Bloody hell, was there nowhere she could escape? She quickly reached in her pocket and pulled out her key chain. The lock was quickly undone, and Evelyn spared no time in pushing through, silently shutting the door behind her. Then she leaned against the frame and closed her eyes, breathing a full, deep inhalation of solitude.

"Evie, my dear! Oh Evie!"

The countess's words spun her around, and Evelyn peered through the shadows to find the woman. The room was sunny, filled with light from two windows, but there was furniture stacked every which way, and the countess had shrunk into the dark behind an armoire.

"Countess?" Evie said as she picked her way around four stacked chairs. "What are you doing in here?"

"Sitting, my dear. Just sitting." She didn't look at Evelyn when she spoke, but watched her hand where she stroked idle designs in the dust atop a small table. It was a game table, intimate enough for two, and had a shallow cabinet built into the sides for holding chess sets or children's toys. It had once been her favorite nursery table, but was now relegated to this upstairs repository of lost furniture. Odd, but the countess looked appropriate here. Though gowned in rich amber and perfectly coiffed, she still fit the shadows and dusty, lost pieces of another time.

"Evie, dear, how are you faring? When the maid came to clean my room, I tried to force myself to go downstairs and help you, but I wound up here instead."

"Why, thank you, my lady. You are so kind to think of me." The words came by rote, spoken sweetly, as all polite lies are. She sincerely doubted the countess had thought to help with any tasks involved with a household overflowing with guests. Something else weighed heavily on the woman, and it had nothing to do with whether Evelyn managed to duck away from the Misses Whitsun or not. "Is there something I can do to help you?"

In fact, her question was also insincere. She had no interest in helping the countess, and yet, as hostess, she felt obliged to offer. She actually resented the fact that the countess had made her worm through boxes of moldy linens and past an old hobbyhorse to get to the back of the room. There was space of a sort on the opposite side beneath the near window. Evelyn's private retreat was there, and it included a comfortable chair, a desk, and a stack of books set inside a cradle. But the countess had managed to maneuver her way to the back shadows where no one had been in years.

Evelyn pushed the boxes sideways, then sneezed at the dust. "I really need to do something about those," she murmured.

"Do you know that I used to gather round this very table with my two dearest friends? All three of us had children by then. You were too young, of course. I used to hold you on my lap. The boys would play at being horses or whatever around our feet. We would talk and watch the children and have such a wonderful time."

Evelyn nodded. She knew the story. The women had been the best of friends: Christopher's mother, Regina; Evelyn's mother, Jane; and Stephanie, Jacob's mother. Then Stephanie and Jacob's entire family was declared dead. Regina had become the new countess, and suddenly duties prevented her from visiting. That was the kindest interpretation. In Mama's darker moments, she claimed that Regina simply became too lofty to bother visiting less-titled old friends.

"I know Mama enjoyed your visits immensely. She missed them terribly when I grew older." That was as close as she could come to criticizing the countess. After all, the woman was supposed to be her new mother-in-law.

"I missed her too," the woman murmured, her gaze abstract. One finger continued to toy with the dust on the table. "I should have visited you here, but Frank insisted you come to us. He believed you would not learn your proper place when surrounded with less rigid society. And so you came to us in London and your mother stayed here in the country."

"You should tell that to my mother," Evelyn said. "Begin to mend fences—"

"Run to Gretna Green."

Evelyn blinked. "What did you say?"

"I have money. Hire a carriage, grab my son, and leave." She gathered her skirts and made to stand, but Evelyn stopped her.

"Countess—"

"Do not call me that!"

Evelyn reared back, stunned by the vehemence of those words. "Um . . ."

"I was your Aunt Gina once. Don't you remember? Frank hated it. He said we weren't related by blood and so you shouldn't call me 'Aunt.' But I liked it. Don't you remember it?"

Vaguely. Everything about this woman—memories included—seemed vaguer lately. Except for her fever-bright eyes.

"We are women," the countess continued. "We cannot control what men decide regarding the title. We can only snatch at what happiness there is."

"Please, calm yourself, Aunt Gina." How odd those words

felt in her mouth. The woman had been the countess for so long now that Aunt Gina was long gone.

"You will make Christopher an excellent wife. He is a good man who will be a good and steady husband." She abruptly leaned forward, grabbing Evelyn's hands in a clawlike grip. "You care for Chris, don't you? Maybe even love him?"

"Of course," she answered without thought. It was what one said to one's future mother-in-law.

"And I know you are dear to him. It is an excellent basis for a marriage, title or no."

"But . . ." She steeled herself to not shrink away from the woman's painful grasp.

"Listen to me!" The countess's face came alive, but in a way that was frightening in this place of dust and shadows. Her eyes burned bright, and her white lips pulled starkly back from her teeth. "Why do we rely so heavily on men to make decisions for us? Did they consult any of us when you were betrothed to Jacob? Of course not! It was about the dower property, and you were merely the means to absorb land into the title."

Evelyn knew it was true. She'd once even resented that fact with every fiber of her being. But as her mother had told her over and over again, there were worse things than becoming a countess. And even more, Evelyn had grown to love Christopher.

"Do not rely on men for your happiness!" the countess hissed. "Take what you want now while there is still time."

Evelyn hadn't wanted to think it was true. She had blocked the possibility from her thoughts, but it had remained there, a constant nagging fear. "You think this Chinaman really is Jacob, don't you?"

The countess dropped Evelyn's hands, denial in every part of her body. "He is dead. Jacob died with the rest, and there isn't a day that I don't mourn them all."

Evelyn tucked her hands into her skirts, surreptitiously

wiping the woman's touch away. "They why rush to Gretna Green? Why not wait until the men return from London?"

"Sssss." It was a hiss of disgust and disapproval. Evelyn had not heard the sound often, but when she did, she knew the countess was at the limits of her patience. "You are not listening! What do you want, girl? Do you want to be bartered like a bale of hay? Do you want other people to decide who you wed or why?"

Evelyn clenched, stunned to hear these words from the very woman who had drilled her on proper behavior. One month out of every three had been spent in London learning how to be a countess. And now she dared suggest the most improper act of all? "You want me to run away with complete disregard for my family's wishes? You suggest I incite gossip that would follow not only myself but my children for the rest of our lives?" Evelyn stepped forward, anger burning her throat. "From the moment I was born, I have been told who I would wed and why. This was decided for me long before—"

"Take it back! Decide for yourself!" The countess abruptly pulled out a heavy purse from the depths of her skirt. She half handed, half threw it at Evelyn, who caught it rather than allow the coins to spill wildly over the floor. "Do you want my son? Do you want happiness? Then take the money and go! Gretna Green is not so far away."

Evelyn stared at the purse. She didn't even want to open it, but she knew from the weight that it held a great deal of money. Enough, certainly, for an elopement to Scotland. "Christopher is too honorable to agree."

"Then convince him. Bed him, Evelyn! You are a strong girl, stronger than I ever was. Forget what you have been told. Forget the title, the money, and the life you have always lived. Think only of the man. You want Christopher, so take him. Seduce him!" She abruptly straightened then began pushing Evelyn to move for the door. "I will take care of your duties. Just go!"

The woman was in such agitation that Evelyn could not refuse. If only out of concern for the elderly woman's heart, Evelyn nodded her agreement and quickly wended her way out of the attic hideaway. But by the time they had stepped out of the room, Evelyn had found something to say. She turned around and took the woman's hand.

"Please, Aunt. You have been a second mother to me, showing me the duties and deportment required of a countess. Surely an unseemly dash to the border is too rash a move. You are just feeling unsettled."

The countess raised her hand. For a moment, Evelyn thought the woman was about to strike her, but in the end she simply touched Evelyn's cheek. "You have been taught from your first breath to obey. Your demeanor is that of a woman leader of England, your steady deportment as vital a trait as your beauty. But no one has ever told you to think for yourself."

"Not true!" Evelyn objected. She had been taught to think—of others, of duty, and of England. There had been moments for herself, for her education and her private thoughts. But they had come only when the others were seen to, when the crofters were supported, the servants overseen, and her myriad responsibilities fulfilled. "I will be a good countess. And you know as well as I do that that requires a great deal of discipline and intelligence."

The woman's face softened. "Of that, I have no doubt. It is the obedience that distresses me. You are so restricted you do not even think to object." She leaned forward and pressed a kiss to Evelyn's cheek. It was a tender press that was so rare from this usually cold woman. But then Evelyn began to withdraw, and the woman gripped her shoulder and held her close.

"They are playing with your life, girl," she whispered. "Go bed my son. Run to Gretna Green and propriety be damned." Then she abruptly straightened and swept past. Evelyn was still staring in dumbfounded shock when the countess stopped at the top of the stairs and shot her a steady, almost angry look. "I shall tell everyone that you have retired to your rooms to rest undisturbed for the rest of the day. Perhaps even until morning." Her eyes blazed with fury. "Now go!"

Evelyn didn't find Christopher for two more hours. She knew he was out looking at the renovations to the dower property. It was easy enough to slip into the stables and get a horse. Easy to ride to her bridal home. Not so easy to avoid the people who farmed her property and looked to her as the lady of the land.

She was forced to stop and talk to every soul on the road. Each had heard of her interrupted wedding. Each offered their support and a stern condemnation of those damned foreigners invading their land. Evelyn hardly thought two monks and a boy constituted an invasion, but these were the people who tilled her land. They loved her in their own way, and she could do no less than graciously accept their support in the way of a true countess. And on the way, she also learned of three illnesses, a broken rocking chair, two boys who had come to blows, and of a cow fallen ill. Little cares, little responsibilities, but it was up to her as lady of this land to remember and address each problem as best she could. Baskets of food would be sent to those who were ill, and a new chair if one could be found in her attic. Even the cow would be seen to by the man in her stable who specialized in sick animals.

By the time she made it to her future home, her face ached from smiling and her jaw burned from the way she gritted her teeth. She dismounted quickly and went in search of her fiancé. She found him sitting on a fence post and staring out across the vast farmland that would be his when they wed.

She stood at his side in silence, waiting for him to acknowledge her. He did so almost absently, with a slight tick of his eyes and a dip of his chin. It was so quick, she might have imagined it. But they had been friends for years. She knew what he was doing.

"Brooding, aren't you?"

He shook his head. "Counting sheep, actually."

She looked out over the plain. There had to be close to three hundred head out there. He could not expect to count them accurately from here.

"You know you are an heiress, don't you?" he said.

Yes, but only the crass discussed such things. "I know I have a vast number of families to care for, and they in turn give over some of their profits to me."

"A very learned response," he said absently. "You also know that the betrothal document could be broken. If you were determined, if your father helped you, it could be done."

She shifted around to lean against the fence. Near him, but not touching. "I had my Season in London. I wore pretty gowns, danced at the parties, flirted with all the gentlemen I could find. I did not find any man the match of you."

He turned to face her, a gentle smile on his face. "My father made it clear that we were to wed. I believe he would have called out any man who dared pay court to you."

She smiled. Yes, she knew the earl had threatened her suitors. But it didn't matter. "No man," she repeated, "was the match of you."

"And what of a monk?"

He was thinking of her kiss with Jie Ke. And here she had almost managed to forget her morning's aberration. She looked out over the plain and began counting sheep on her own. A dozen at least here. Another dozen there. "Your mother believes he is Jacob."

Though her gaze was on the sheep, her attention remained on Christopher. She saw him flinch in her peripheral vision. "Well," he finally drawled. "That is disappointing. Are you sure?"

"Why else would she beg me to seduce you then run away to Gretna Green before it was too late?"

This time his reaction was much more pronounced. He reared back enough to wobble on the fence post. "You're joking."

She lifted the heavy purse from her pocket and passed it to Christopher. "That must be an entire quarter's pin money for her."

"At least," he murmured as he weighed the bag in his hand.

She turned back to the sheep. "She thinks the title will revert to the monk. She called me too stupid to think on my own and too obedient to question the dictates of men."

Christopher snorted, and his hand took hers in a warm grip. "You are many things, Evie. Stupid is not one of them."

"And obedient?" She turned to face him, and kept his hand tight in hers. "Do you find me subservient, a slave to your commands?"

He shook his head, obviously at a loss as to how to answer. "I have always found you to behave exactly how you ought. Do you feel like my servant?"

"No," she admitted, bothered to realize that she was irritable and taking out her bad humor on the one person who shared her problem. His wedding and his future had been interrupted just as much as her own. "So," she said, rather than try to sort through her strange mood. "Do you want to elope? Shall we make a mad dash for Scotland and be wed?"

He arched his brow. "I hardly think it will be a mad dash. Who would try to stop us? Will the monk drag you away by your hair?"

She laughed at that thought, because he intended it to be funny. But she couldn't deny the elemental response the image evoked. She knew in her heart that she had no wish to be dragged anywhere, by her hair or otherwise . . . but Jie Ke had a power about him. And she could well believe he might drag her off into the darkness to ravish her. She knew such a thing would be awful. She *knew* that, and yet the thought was not horrible. Truth be told, she found herself excited.

"Let's go, Christopher. Let us off to Scotland where we can have our wedding night."

He stood slowly, pushing off the fence post to stand tall and dashing in front of her. Normally, he remained a respectful distance away. Normally, he did not push forward until a deep breath would have them touching breast to chest. But at this moment he towered over her, and when he brushed his finger across her chin, she tilted her face and her breath quieted in her chest.

Would he do it? Would he kiss her? Would he ravish her as she wanted to be ravished? As she *needed* to be ravished?

"I adore your impetuous side, my dear. It is charming and sweet. But a countess does not act—"

"Do not quote me platitudes about what a countess does and does not do," she snapped, wholly annoyed because he had not kissed her. "I know my responsibilities better than you."

He sighed. "Very well then, we shall not talk of appearances. But a mad dash anywhere would only support your monk's ridiculous claims."

"He is not *my* monk," she said as she stepped away from him. If he would not kiss her, he had no need to look down his nose at her. But he caught her arm and kept her close.

"Let me explain what my mother clearly doesn't understand. This monk will never gain the title."

She jerked her head back to look at him. "Have you heard from London then?"

He shook his head. "Not a word, but I don't need messages to know what will happen. Good God, can you possibly imagine Prinny—or any of the bon ton—allowing a man wearing foreign orange robes into the peerage?"

"If he is Jacob, then the ton will have no choice."

"Of course they have a choice!" he said with a laugh. "The entire situation is a choice. Let us pretend for a moment—and mind you, it is only pretend—that this monk is truly Jacob, somehow lost in China and now restored to us."

She nodded. That was indeed the question.

"The title has already passed to my father. Jacob would have to be acknowledged by the House of Lords in order for the earldom to be restored to him."

She bit her lip, seeing the sordid truth. "So the question is not whether Jie Ke is Jacob. The question is whether the peerage will acknowledge him as Jacob."

Christopher grinned. "You see, you are smart enough to be a countess." He slowly pulled her into his arms, wrapping her in his warmth. She went reluctantly at first, but her resistance was short-lived. It felt good to have a man's strength surrounding her. "No one will want a Chinese monk in the English peerage. They will not question my father when he says this man is an imposter."

She nodded against his chest, hearing the steady beat of his heart. She stood there, absorbing his calm assurance into her very bones. But in time, she grew bored with the experience. And soon after that, she felt restricted and rather crushed. She wanted to take a full breath on her own, and so she pushed away. Christopher did not release her. He held his arms rigid, iron bars that let her move only so far but no farther.

"Christopher," she said softly, but he did not hear her. "Chris!"

He pulled back far enough to stare down at her. "Hmmm?"

"You're crushing my dress."

"Oh? Sorry." He released her then, and she stepped away. It was cold without him holding her, but not so cold that she wanted to go back.

"Jie Ke says he has no wish for the title," she said. "He merely has to obtain it as some sort of trial before becoming a full monk."

Christopher frowned at her. "Of course he said that. You don't believe it, do you?"

She shook her head. "No, I don't. But he seemed sincere."

"Accomplished liars always do."

She looked at her hands. "He said if I helped him become English, helped him appear to win me as his bride, then his task will be complete and he can leave. Earl or not, he will go." She heard Christopher release a deep sigh. It was the sound of a man plagued by a woman's irrationality, and it annoyed her to no end. "I am merely repeating what he said to me."

He turned to her, his gaze steady, his lips pressed into a tight, thin line of disapproval. "Some part of you believes him."

She lifted her chin. "I do not know what to think. He could be Jacob, in which case the title is rightfully his."

"You wish to talk of rights? What of the rights of your tenants? Do you remember Uncle Reggie? Do you remember how irresponsible he was with the title? Crofters neglected, people starving, and not a thought in his head for appropriate management. Was that fair to them?"

"Of course not! But—"

"My father is an excellent steward."

"I never said he wasn't."

"And I will not neglect my duties. I have trained from birth to act responsibly, to take care of those over whom I have sway. I will not hare off to China on a whim! I will not allow the estates I manage to fall to rack and ruin. I will not—"

"Since when has this been about you?" she cried. "I speak only of Jie Ke. And Jacob."

"And you think he will be a good steward of his property? You think he will make a better earl than me?"

She snorted. "Of course not. He wants to become a monk in China."

"Then why do you come here pleading his case?"

She stared at him, her mouth dropping open in shock. She wasn't here for Jie Ke or Jacob or anyone else. She'd come here to speak to her fiancé. She'd come to suggest they run off to Scotland so that they could begin their life together as intended. The last thing she'd wanted was to plead the monk's case to Christopher.

All those things seethed in her thoughts, but not a word spilled from her lips. He had already made up his mind and would hear no more, reasonable or not. She merely shook her head in disappointment. "You are right," she said with just enough sarcasm in her tone to make his eyebrow arch. "Jie Ke will not win his suit no matter who his parents are. That makes what he wants completely irrelevant."

Christopher didn't respond. He never did when she turned waspish. He simply waited until her temper faded—or was tucked away—and they returned to their usual accord.

But then he surprised her. He turned sideways and looked out at her sheep, his gaze scanning the vast expanse of her lands. She was watching him closely so she knew what he saw, but not what he thought. "I think you should do it," he said.

"I beg your pardon?"

"I think you should help him. I think you should spend more time with him. Talk to him, find out about his life in the monastery, learn of his plans for the future."

She frowned. "Are you teasing me?"

He shook his head. "Not at all. Evie, listen to me. You are the smartest woman I know. And, if I recall correctly, you spent a great deal of time learning about every country in the world, including China."

She nodded. She had spent many long nights proving to herself that she was smart enough to be a countess. Jacob-the-Cruel-Boy had accused her of being too stupid to hold a title. Understanding the world his father studied so avidly had been paramount to proving herself.

"You can gain this blackguard's trust," Christopher continued. "Talk to him about China, ferret out his lies. Prove to yourself and everyone else that the man is nothing more than a clever thief."

She grimaced to cover the excitement that quivered in her belly. "What if I discover that he is really Jacob? What then?"

"It will not happen." His words were flat with certainty. "That man is not Jacob."

She lifted her chin. "But let us suppose he is."

He smiled. It wasn't a pleasant expression. It was devious, with a touch a cruelty, and it aped his father exactly. "Then I have faith that you will see the man beneath the title. You will see that he is unfit to be an earl, and that you want him out of England as much as I do."

"And right of patrimony be damned?"

He shrugged. "My uncle was not a good steward of his land. That is not how God and king intended the land be run. In time, we may develop a way of deposing unfit leaders from their place, but for now . . ."

"For now, you will be content to let Jie Ke remain a monk and nothing more." She shook her head, startled by this practical and rather ruthless side to her fiancé. But she could not deny that it made sense. Many a time she had deplored the irresponsibility of some aristocrats. How dare they take all the privilege of their name but none of the responsibilities?

"So, my girl, will you do it? Will you expose this fraud for all of us?"

She nodded slowly, reluctance eating at her. Her mind told her she was flirting with danger. *A countess is watched even in her home.* That's what he'd said just that morning. And yet heat shot through her belly at the thought of spending a great deal more time with Jie Ke. Desire burned through her in a heady rush. She wanted to explore it, and yet her entire future was at stake. Could she really wander that close to temptation when she was about to commit herself to another man?

"Make love to me, Chris," she said. His eyes widened in shock, but she did not give him time to answer. Pushing herself right up to his chest, she pressed her lips to his. He responded not as he had this morning, but with a firm pressure that quickly ended.

"Evelyn, what has gotten into you?" His tone was tight with disapproval. In his mind, she was failing to act as a countess ought. But she did not care.

She grabbed his lapels. She had never done anything so bold before, but panic drove her. "You want to throw me into another man's arms? Very well, Chris. I will push my familiarity with Jie Ke."

"I never said—"

"But be sure of me first, Chris. Make me your own as you would have already if those damned monks hadn't walked up the aisle at our wedding. If they had been delayed by a day or even an hour, I would already be your wife."

"Yes, I know, but—"

She pressed her mouth to his, cutting off his words. He would have none of it, setting her back on her heels.

"Evie!" There was no other word but that. He held her apart from him, and he searched her face as confusion filled his own.

"That is my house," she said, gesturing backwards as best she could. "Upstairs is the bed we would have shared last night. Make me yours, Christopher. Right here, right now."

He froze for a moment, a long eon where neither of them breathed, and then he crashed his mouth down upon hers. She opened for him as he thrust his tongue inside her mouth. He touched her in ways and places she had not experienced before. He filled her.

Or she wanted him to fill her.

Or she thought he *ought* to fill her.

She clutched him tighter, trying to draw him closer.

Weren't couples supposed to touch in other places? Shouldn't he be undressing her?

She broke away, confused by her thoughts. "We shouldn't be out here in the open. Come inside." She tugged on his arm, pulling him forward, but he didn't move. He stood immobile, his breath coming in deep gasps.

Shouldn't she be breathless too?

"Chris?"

"Not now, Evie. God help me, but when I bed you it won't be in some slapdash manner. I won't steal moments from our future." He looked at her, his eyes tortured. "You deserve better."

"I don't want better."

He gave her a rueful smile. "Nevertheless."

He was decided. She could see it in his eyes and in his rigid stance.

"You don't want me," she whispered, wondering why she felt a little relieved.

"Oh, I do," he said firmly. "I most certainly do." He shifted his stance as if in pain. "If you were less innocent, you would know that."

She *was* less innocent. Her gaze dropped to his crotch, and she swallowed. Perhaps he did want her. "But then . . ."

"No, Evie. I'll take you after we are wed, as is proper." Then he took her hand. "Come on. Let's walk a bit before I take you home."

"But—"

"Don't argue, Evie. Please let me keep my honor intact."

She sighed, not knowing what else to do. Christopher's sense of honor was a confusing and prickly thing: he could strip the rightful heir of his title, but he couldn't bed a willing woman who would soon be his wife. And they thought women were irrational creatures!

Chapter Seven

Evelyn couldn't sleep. There were too many thoughts spinning in her head. Mostly her mind kept returning to one question: what did she want? The answer was obvious. She wanted Christopher and the life she'd been born to live as a countess. Unless, of course, she wanted those things because she'd been told all her life that she did. How could she tell the difference? Was she so obedient to the dictates of society that she'd never actually learned what she wanted for herself?

But if she didn't want Christopher, then what did she want? Not Jie Ke. That much was a certainty. Though she couldn't forget how electric his kiss had felt or how her belly heated at the thought of kissing him again.

She glanced out her window. No storm tonight. She wished there were a booming, thundering, mind-splitting apocalypse out there right now. Only in the center of such a storm did all her thoughts disappear. She was wiped away during those, leaving just the crashing turbulence of the storm around her—huge, seething, so alive. That's what she wanted. But there was no storm tonight, and besides, she had promised Christopher she wouldn't wander in them anymore.

She sighed and got out of bed, dressing quickly in a warm gown. Without stays, it was large and loose on her, but she could button this one on without her maid. It was in the Chinese style, with clasps at the shoulders and down the side.

Then, as quietly as possible, she slipped out of her room, down and out of the house. There might not be a storm tonight, but there was the night as large and alive in its own way as a thunderstorm. One just had to quiet oneself long enough to feel the textures of the darkness, to be at one with the whispering world. And if she was very lucky, she'd meet the boy from her memory, the night sprite who had danced with her so many years ago.

She had several favorite paths for her nighttime wanderings, but only one brought her to the place she wanted, close enough to the house for safety but still sheltered by trees, and far enough away for silence. She found the open grove where Jie Ke and his friend had sparred. Her destination was the far side of the clearing, a place that could not be spied from the windows or doors.

She walked quickly along the path, rounded the shrubbery, and saw a figure sitting in the center of the clearing. It was he. Not the night sprite, the fond memory of her childhood, but Jie Ke. How odd that part of her knew he'd be there. She couldn't possibly be so attuned to him as to know where he would be in the middle of the night. And yet, she wasn't surprised to see him. His legs were crossed oddly, his body absolutely still. He was at one with the night, and so she quietly slipped around the edge of the copse to sit where she'd intended to sit all along.

Her back was not so strong that she could mimic his position. Her legs might contort like that, but her back would scream within moments. So she settled against a tree at the perfect angle to see but not disturb him. She tried to sit with her knees bent, but in the end she stretched them out before her, allowing her skirt to settle warmly about her bare legs. She closed her eyes and tried to breathe in the night. The wind rustled sweetly through the trees, and somewhere a dog barked before quieting. And soon she became part of the darkness, just another living thing taking her ease. If she kept at it long enough, she knew what would happen. She would remember every moment of a stormy night when she was eight. She would taste the wetness on her tongue, feel the crash of the thunder overhead, and know the playful touch of her sprite.

But she could not find that memory tonight. As much as she tried, she could not forget the man sitting less than five feet away. He was not simply part of the night. He was an entity all his own, and she could not force him to fade into the background or expand into nothingness. He was there, and he was watching her.

She opened her eyes. He was not watching her. The disappointment cut at her keenly. She closed her eyes.

Quiet. Calm. Would he be looking at her now? He was dressed in his bizarre robes again, but with bare feet. Was he cold? It was a chilly night. This was ridiculous. He was invading her private moments. She ought to leave. She could find another of her quiet spots. She huffed and opened her eyes.

His eyes were closed. She waited, irritated with him for no reason at all. She should leave. After all, he had been here first. Instead, she waited for his attention.

Eventually, he opened his eyes. They were so very white in the darkness. And he and she looked at each other.

"Christopher wants me to help you." Why in the world had she said that?

He arched a brow. "Why?"

"I am very smart and I have studied China. I could prove that you are a fake, that you are not Jacob."

He dipped his chin in a slow nod, then closed his eyes again. "I am not Jacob; I am Jie Ke. And you are not restful right now."

She frowned. What did that mean? It had not sounded like a criticism. And yet, it certainly wasn't a compliment. "Why are you out here?"

He didn't open his eyes. "Sometimes it is easier to lose oneself in darkness than in daylight."

"I know exactly what you mean." She took a deep breath. "Sometimes I come out and sit for hours. I have a favorite spot at the top of a rise that is perfect for that. My maid knows to find me before everyone else wakes. Mama says that future countesses sleep in beds; only peasants sleep on rocks."

He glanced about the clearing. "Is this your favorite night-time spot?"

"No. It is over that way."

"Then how will your maid find you in the morning?"

She shrugged. "Maybe I don't want to be found."

He didn't respond, but the air between them changed. Instead of simple quiet darkness, suddenly there was sexuality in the air. She had not intended to put it between them, and yet whenever she looked at him, it was there, an echo or a call to her most primal self. She did not want to hear it, but she could not deny how it thrummed in her blood.

"I should go inside," she said, but she didn't move. "This was a bad idea."

"Why?"

She heard no underlying current in his voice, but awareness sparked in his eyes. As she watched him, her nipples tightened, her belly shivered, and she swallowed in nervous excitement. She recognized the symptoms of flirtation, of beginning excitement, but with him in this dark place, she felt so much more. It was wrong of her to be here, and yet she didn't want to leave. To distract herself, she leaned back against her tree and switched topics.

"What is it like to be a monk? What is China like?"

"What is England like?" he countered. "There are too many answers to those questions, and each would be correct for someone different."

She leaned forward. "But I want to know how *you* answer."

"For me"—he closed his eyes and took a deep breath—

"China is quiet. The serenity of a cloud or a mountaintop. And that is my answer to both your questions—about being in China and being a monk."

She frowned. "Quiet? Truly?"

"Honestly? Not in the least." A smile pulled at his lips. He had a beautiful mouth: even teeth, full lips, and powerful jaw. "China is loud with animals and people squabbling, just as in any other country. But at the temple, it is quiet. Not a quiet of sound, but a quiet of spirit." He looked down at his lap. "I miss it."

"But if a soul is quiet, wouldn't it be silent wherever you are? I mean, your soul is inside. If it is still, then what does it matter if you're in England or China or America?"

His gaze sharpened on her. "That is exactly what Zhi Min would say." Then he grimaced like that wasn't a good thing.

She didn't care. She liked pricking him, forcing him to acknowledge her. "So, your soul isn't quiet in England. Why? What bothers it?"

Instead of answering, he lifted his chin in challenge. "Why do you come to the dark?" he asked. "What do you seek?"

A boy who danced with me. But even as she thought of her sprite, she knew she was lying to herself. She didn't seek the boy; he was long gone. She sought the happiness he'd shown her. "In the dark, I am only myself. In a storm, I am without trappings—not a countess-to-be or lady of this land or even Miss Stanton. I am free of everything but a darkness and a fury so wild that I am nothing beside it."

"You seek nothingness? That's very Buddhist." He sounded surprised and a little impressed.

She knew a small bit about Buddha. She had read about him, but knew nothing of his teachings. "If I asked, would you tell me about your religion?"

"Of course."

"Even though I am a girl? Even though it's not a proper thing for a woman to press into a monk's religion?"

"If you ask, I will teach. To do otherwise would be wrong."

She leaned forward, intrigued. "Then tell me, please! Tell me everything!"

So he did. Without preamble, he began speaking of what he'd been taught while she peppered him with questions comparing his faith with Christianity. He knew little of the Anglican Church beyond the holidays and basic forms. He had a child's understanding, she realized, something that might be remembered from a boyhood in England. But his knowledge of Buddhism was vast and complex. She struggled to comprehend it all. And then . . .

And then he fell silent.

"What?" she pressed. He had been speaking of the Chinese nine Immortals and trying to distinguish them from Buddha.

"You have a mind like Zhi Min," he said softly. "You question everything, explore the corners of thought that I once believed were unshakable until I wonder if I know anything."

She frowned, unsure whether he admired or reviled her. "Christopher doesn't like that I ask questions. He says that I'll learn more if I just listen. Eventually I'll hear whatever I need to know."

Her companion snorted. "Chris always had a lot more patience than I."

"Me, too," she said, laughing for the first time since her aborted wedding. Or perhaps it was longer than that. Since the last thunderstorm. Since the last time she had lost herself into the night. But she wasn't alone this time, and she certainly wasn't lost. She was here with an Englishman turned Chinese monk, and his very presence energized her as much as a thunderstorm.

Her laughter faded, and she looked at the dark figure across from her. She saw him as a man, and yet she felt so much more from him. Something elemental that called to her.

He noticed the change, of course. Perhaps he was the originator of it. Perhaps he created the sudden sexual awareness that seemed to fill the space between them. The darkness grew thick with their intimacy, and her breath quickened.

"Chris has given permission for me to woo you?" he asked. "And here you are in the middle of the night. Do you know what danger you face from me? I could overpower you in seconds."

She lifted her chin. "I thought you were a monk. Don't monks foreswear physical pleasure?"

"I have not taken my vow of celibacy yet."

His words were spoken softly. She felt the danger underlying his words, the certain knowledge that he wanted to bed her whether she wished it or not. Excitement shivered down her spine, and that far-off call of man to woman grew louder in her ears.

"If you attack me, then you will be exposed," she said. "I don't believe your Zhi Min will want a rapist in his temple. And one scream from me will bring the whole house running. You will be tarred and feathered by morning."

He inclined his head, acknowledging her point. But in his eyes, she still saw desire. She wanted him to kiss her again. She wanted him to lay her down and ravish her, if it meant that she would be as consumed as she had been this morning. If one kiss could obliterate all thought, if one touch could imprint itself on her mind as a thousand of Chris's kisses had not, then she wanted him to do it. She wanted to know—just once—what it was like to be consumed by the storm. But the damned man would not move. And she was not that bold.

"There is a technique whispered among boys at the temple," he suddenly said. "A game that only the masters play. It is a way of touching a woman without even coming near her."

She frowned. "How is that possible?"

"When a master meditates, he becomes one with all that is. There is no separation between him and the . . . the All."

She nodded, waiting for more. When he said nothing, she had to confess the one thing she hated to say above all else. "I don't understand."

"Are you not part of the All?"

"Of course."

"Then if I am one with the All, I will be one with you as well."

"And you could touch me then, without hands but with . . . your mind?"

He nodded. "Yes."

"I do not believe it!" She laughed, but it was a nervous giggle, because she was titillated by the idea.

"Perhaps I should prove it to you? Perhaps I should see if I am a master."

She leaned back against the tree and shut her eyes. "Perhaps you should." She waited, breathless with excitement. It wasn't possible, of course . . . but what if it was? What if he had powers of the mind unheard of in England? What if?

Nothing happened. She had been a fool to imagine it could. She exhaled her disappointment only to be startled by the stroke of a hand on her ankle. She jerked her eyes open to see him kneeling beside her. One hand stroked the inside of her ankle, then slipped slowly up her calf.

"It would appear that I am not a master."

She swallowed. "You are too familiar, sir!"

"And yet you want this." His hand drew higher to the inside of her knee and began stroking circles on her thigh.

"Stop!" she gasped.

He stilled his hand, but his mouth moved closer. Closer. Slowly, he touched his mouth to hers and then turned his head back and forth so that their lips brushed. "I am on fire," he whispered with awe. "I need to touch you. I *need* it. Do you feel it?"

"Yes," she answered, her heart pounding to the rhythm of his caress. It was the danger of the moment that excited her so, she thought. No one had ever dared boldly slip his hand up her skirt, fingers dancing along her thigh. Christopher never did. He wouldn't even if she begged. And she would scream if any other man tried.

But Jie Ke was different. Whenever he was near, she felt the pulse of the storm, a fire in her belly, and the blustering whirlwind of power that obliterated all thought. Her legs relaxed, slipping open, and his hand moved higher. She had no undergarments on. She hadn't wanted to bother wearing anything beyond her simple shift, so his path was clear of obstructions.

"Have you ever touched yourself, Evelyn?" he asked in a whisper. "In the seclusion of your bedchamber when the sameness of your days sets your mind to screaming, have you touched yourself and lost your mind to the sensations?"

"Yes," she answered, her mind completely absorbed by the feel of his hand on her thigh. She shouldn't let him. She couldn't. But oh how her breasts ached and her belly quivered. Blood roared in her ears like thunder.

"Boys at the temple are no different. I have touched myself, I have peered at the women doing laundry and stroked myself until the rush overcomes me."

She swallowed. She knew about the rush, and she knew how short-lived it was. Would it be different with a man? Would it be different with *this* man?

His voice was quiet as he admitted, "I watched Zhi Min with a woman once. I spied on him as he undressed her and put his mouth to her breasts." He looked down, and Evelyn felt his gaze as clearly as if he were touching her there, too. "How does it feel?" he asked. "How does it feel for a woman?"

She closed her eyes and imagined her breasts bared to the moonlight. She thought of his hands and his mouth on her nipples and her belly quivered. No man had ever touched her like that, but she had caressed herself. She imagined what it would feel like. "Lightning flashes through my blood," she answered. "Bright sharp explosions of light and color pulse behind my eyes."

"Spread your legs, Evelyn. I won't take your virginity, but I want to know what it feels like for you. Tell me what you feel." She opened her eyes and met his gaze. Now was the time to decide. She could step away from him, she could obey the dictates of society and flee these sensations. Or she could trust him to give her what she had desired for so many years now. Which would she choose?

She widened her thighs. "Show me what a monk can do."

She almost laughed at her boldness. She almost laughed the way she did when she stepped into a thunderstorm and let the buffeting winds sweep her away. Almost. Instead, she put her hands to her breasts and flicked her nipples. Bright flashes of sensation burst through her mind. But those flashes were nothing compared to her body's reaction to the exploration of his fingers. He pushed her most intimate flesh open, slid his thumb all around.

"Tell me what you feel," he ordered.

She gasped then nodded. "I feel you," she said. "Your finger is long and . . ." She swallowed. "And slow. I feel your calluses, your knuckle."

"But how does it make *you* feel?" he pressed.

"Wild," she answered. "Free."

He moved upward to where she was most sensitive. A knuckle that was too hard, too forceful, and she flinched backwards. She gasped and he stilled.

"Has anyone ever touched you like this before?"

She didn't want to answer. She didn't want to confess that this was unique, that he was special beyond reason. She did not want to give him that power.

"Tell me!" He used his other hand and pulled her legs as wide as her skirt would allow. With an impatient curse, he used his free hand to push the fabric higher. She felt the air kiss her thighs, but her most inner core was covered by his hand and she shuddered at how vulnerable she felt and how she loved it.

"A thousand men!" she burst out, her gaze trapped by his. "A thousand and one!"

"In your fantasies," he pressed.

"Yes."

"And in your dreams, did you ever once imagine a man would drink of your essence? The Chinese write poetry about the taste of a woman. They believe it is magic—that it will bring a man long life if he drinks it daily."

She arched her brows. "That is ridiculous. There is no magic there. Only . . . Only . . ." Her thoughts splintered as his fingers began moving, slipping in and out through her folds, dipping deep inside her only to withdraw in exquisitely long strokes.

"That is what I fantasize about. I dream of tasting a woman," he said as he shifted between her thighs. "May I taste your essence?"

She blinked, the sensual fog slowing her thoughts. "What?"

He shifted his hands, too fast for her to follow. He slid his hands beneath her buttocks and lifted her up. She gasped in alarm but retained enough sense not to cry out. She didn't dare risk someone hearing her.

Her body was dislodged from the tree trunk, and her head fell to the side and backwards. He lifted her up easily, drawing her center up to his mouth. She flailed with her hands, trying to keep her balance, but there was none. Her upper body dropped backwards to the grass and her chest arched to the sky.

She felt completely disconnected from the world. Her legs were high and open, her back flat on the ground. It was like the storm had upended her, as if the winds had tumbled her head over heels. How appropriate then that the rain began to kiss her inner thighs. How wonderful to feel the wetness of his mouth as he began to drink.

His mouth was large as it pressed to her center. His lips were wet, his tongue broad as he began long sweeps across her body. Each stroke built the thunder in her blood, each probe of his tongue shot lightning through her mind. She was adrift in the storm, unable to resist and completely consumed. And this was exactly what she wanted.

He lifted her up higher, and her legs felt spread so wide she thought she might split. Suction and stroke, thrust and caress, his mouth did all to her. Nothing was left untouched, and all of her was spread before him.

More. She tried to draw him closer. The deeper his touch, the more all-consuming his stroke, the better she liked it.

But he controlled the pressure of his mouth. Her arch meant nothing as he adjusted his grip. Then he began the rhythm of thrust and pull while she echoed with gasps and whimpers.

The tension built within her belly. She was familiar with this, but with him, it was so much more. And this too he controlled, slipping lower on her body to drink her essence while the higher spot throbbed and cooled. Then, switching, a quick circle or sudden thrust high and her legs would tremble, her mind blanked white in a lightning flash.

Yes! Oh yes!

He pulled back just a bit, only enough to murmur against her thigh, "I will drink all of you now. Be careful not to scream."

She pressed the back of one hand to her mouth as she sometimes did in bed. A whimper of hunger escaped anyway, but that only added to the storm.

His tongue was so perfect as it stroked her. Again and again—thick and hard—while her blood roared and her back arched. Again. One last . . .

Yes!

The storm claimed her. The buffeting contortions of body and breath combined into ecstasy. Oh yes . . . Oh! *Too much!*

In her bed she would have stopped. She would have ridden the waves of the storm to silence and blissful sleep. But he didn't stop. He continued to drink her, his tongue stroking and pulling and exciting her whenever the contractions began to fade. On and on he went, while her mind grappled with reality and lost. Her body convulsed while he drank. She wasn't a storm anymore, she was lightning—bright, electric, and wholly white.

Then he stopped.

Thank God, she thought. Then, *Oh no. It is ending.*

The sensations continued, but the steady stimulation of his tongue had ceased. He was lowering her gently to the ground.

"I am sorry," he said in a hushed and reverent tone. "I could not continue without you screaming."

He would have continued? The very thought of remaining longer in that blindingly bright place was both terrifying and so wonderful that she smiled. Her breath was returning to normal, her body lay boneless and sated on the ground. He adjusted her skirt, stretching the fabric out to cover her demurely. Or as demurely as it could, with her stretched out on the ground like a wanton.

"How do you feel?" he asked gently.

Wonderful. Expansive. Cold. The air was cold.

"The joy . . . it is fading, isn't it?"

She nodded, trying to hold on to the experience as long as she could.

"Search inside yourself, Evelyn, deep inside. Your body is content, but what of your mind? What of your heart?"

She frowned, irritated that he was pulling her away from that glorious blank place she had become.

"Does the bliss extend inside that deep? Or do you still know restlessness—a vague discontent that even the best experience of body cannot erase?"

She swallowed, slowly pushing up onto her elbows as she

stared at him. "How can you know that?" she whispered. Everything he said was absolutely true. Deep in her heart, she was still unhappy. And she hadn't even known it until this very moment.

"That is what it means to be a monk, Evie. To know deep inside that there is an emptiness and to search eternally for the way to fill it."

She shook her head. "It's not true," she whispered. "Monks are at peace. They are filled with . . . with God's holy presence, or something like that."

Jie Ke shrugged. "Perhaps that is so. I believe it is so for the masters. But for me . . ." His voice trailed away, and she saw a bleakness in his expression. "I am still searching."

"But . . ." She didn't know what she wanted to ask. She looked at him, at the bulge beneath his robes, and the sprawled openness of her own body. "But I was satisfied. For a moment . . ." For many incredible moments. "I felt wonderful."

He nodded, and his hand trembled on her thigh. "And I would feel it too, if I listened to the demands of my flesh. I could bury myself within you and find the same mindlessness. But in the morning . . ."

She shook her head, not wanting to think of the consequences she would face in the morning.

He continued, "The dictates of society would be difficult enough, but there would be something much worse: the emptiness in my heart. Physical bliss is all-consuming until it fades. And then what am I left with but a discontent all the more stark because the sex did not fill it? The pleasures of the body alone cannot ever fill the heart and mind."

The picture he painted was so bleak she almost cried out. "How can you stand it? To live in such emptiness?"

"We all live in it. We simply deny it, suppress it, throw ourselves into the body to hide from it. To be a monk . . ."

"Is to see the truth with clarity," she whispered, startled to realize that she understood.

"And to search for a better answer." Then he pushed to his feet, adjusting his robes with a rueful grimace. She pulled her knees tight to her chest, making sure her skirt covered all of her. He bowed before her, deeply and reverently. "Good night, Evelyn."

She nodded, too full of strange thoughts to respond, but the words came out automatically. "Good night, Jie Ke."

Then he left. She remained for hours later, her mind churning and twisting with all they had said and done. In the end, she had reached only one conclusion: being a monk was not so easy as putting on an orange robe and begging for alms. What shook her the most, however, was that she now believed him. Jie Ke was a monk.

Chapter Eight

"Your nighttime wanderings seem to have done you good."

Jie Ke blinked his eyes open and squinted at his friend. Zhi Min was squatting over his makeshift pallet on the floor, a grin on his face.

"What?" Jie Ke managed as he rubbed his eyes.

"You were smiling," Zhi Min said. He straightened.

"I was asleep," Jie Ke groused.

"Nevertheless."

Jie Ke shot him a glare but couldn't hold it. Within a moment he realized he was smiling. He sat up and stretched sore muscles. Then he felt the familiar ache of physical desire, remembered what had prompted his current state, and his smile grew.

"Who were you dreaming about?" Zhi Min asked. His gaze dropped to Jie Ke's crotch. "I don't have to ask what you were doing."

Jie Ke didn't answer. Instead, he hopped up and began his morning ablutions. The ache of desire did nothing to dim his good humor. Every boy from the age of twelve knew this particular ache. And if any woman were worthy of his discomfort, it was Evelyn.

"Have you thought about what we discussed yesterday?" Zhi Min asked.

Jie Ke grimaced, his mood abruptly dipping. "I will become more English this afternoon. My grandmother's doing."

He sighed. "We will need more money, though. I must pay the tailor, and the shoemaker, and heaven only knows whom else."

Zhi Min slowed as he wrapped his robe about his shoulders. "You wish to fight again. And to let the English bet against you."

Jie Ke shrugged. "Do you know a better way? Yes, I'd prefer it if they gave us alms to survive, but this is England not China. And you just gave away our entire purse yesterday." He could not keep the note of irritation from his voice.

His friend kept his gaze hooded. "It was important for you to understand the difference between a monk and—"

"And an English lord. I understand, Zhi Min, but we still have to pay for my clothes."

Zhi Min finished adjusting his robe, and his gaze seemed heavy and troubled. "Do you fight because you need money? Or because the anger is building inside you again?"

Hatred boiled up hot and hard inside Jie Ke, but he was prepared. He held it back, swallowed it, tamped it down so tight it was hidden from everyone, including himself. When he spoke, he kept his voice light and easy. "You gave away all our money, but I need to pay for my clothing somehow. That's why I fight." Then he flashed a saucy grin. "I can't help it if I enjoy winning."

"You enjoy the fight, Jie Ke. Why? Do you know why you are so very angry?"

He fury struggled to explode, but Jie Ke kept it tight inside. Instead, he rolled his eyes. "But it is so very, very easy to win in England! How many fights have I lost so far? Let me think . . ." He snapped his fingers. "None! And let us remember that without these fights and the money I win, we would never have made it halfway here."

Thankfully Zhi Min didn't challenge his answer, but his expression was still troubled. "I do not like this fighting for money. The mob gets very angry at losing so much."

Jie Ke shrugged. "I don't force them to bet. I merely collect their money when they lose."

"It is wrong to encourage their vices in such a way. Many of them cannot afford the loss."

"And many can. Those who cannot afford it will learn not to wager." He turned as Mei Li entered the room. "I only take the coin they have; I dun no one." Then he smiled at Zhi Min's younger sister. "Can you find us another fight?"

She looked up, her eyes sparkling. She loved taking the English money as much as he did. "I have heard of a fight to be held in two days. I shall make sure your name is among the warriors." She turned to her brother. "And you?"

Zhi Min held up his hands. "I am there merely to make sure you both stay alive. The last mob—"

"Stop whining," Jie Ke said with a grin. "We both know the real reason you won't fight. You know I'd put you to shame."

Zhi Min arched his eyebrow. "I believe you require a thrashing, young master. Maybe then you will remember that a man at peace inside is always the better fighter."

Jie Ke was laughing as they left the room. This was the best he had felt for many a morning. He was practically swaggering as he walked the path to the grove. He knew in his heart that today his martial arts skills would be at their finest.

Apparently, his heart was ill informed. He fought terribly. It was one thing to wake with an erection, dreams of lust reminding him that his body was alive and healthy and yearning for a beautiful woman. It was another thing entirely to fight with such a distraction. He kept waiting for Evelyn to step around the corner, to watch him as she had yesterday. Would she walk into his fighting pattern and dare him to kiss her again? His best friend took advantage of the situation.

"You have the concentration of a howling monkey. The English will take your money and laugh while they do it."

"It is what happens to a man when he is about to become English," Jie Ke lied. He gestured to where his grandmother had come onto the lawn to watch. "She is anxious to change me back into Jacob."

"She wants her family returned to her. It is understandable, if undesirable. Honor her as she deserves."

Jie Ke bowed, taking the admonishment as deserved. His grandmother was due a great deal of respect, though he could not bring himself to give it willingly. He even had to force himself to stand in her presence. "Her face powder makes me sneeze," he groused. They were speaking in Chinese so she would not understand.

"So, do not breathe deeply when standing beside her," Zhi Min responded. Then he turned to the elderly lady, bowing deeply. "Your grandson is most anxious to begin his day with you," he said in English.

The old woman immediately brightened, her pale cheeks turning pink with happiness. "Truly? I confess to a great deal of excitement as well." Her watery gaze turned to Jie Ke. "Are you ready then? Shall I send for the tailor?"

"A few moments longer, Grandmother. Please allow me to bathe."

"Oh, yes. Of course." She clapped her hands with the vigor he remembered. "Very well, but be quick about it!"

He bowed to her, holding his breath as he did. "Right away," he responded. And then he sneezed four times.

Exhausted! That's how he felt, completely exhausted. And all he had done was stand still while being pricked, prodded, and touched until he nearly screamed. And that was when he wasn't sneezing. Who would have guessed that the tailor favored cosmetic powder as well?

Thankfully, his grandmother and the fussy tailor had spent a great deal of time apart from him, deciding on the fabrics and styles. It was quite a discussion. Had he known that English men were as vain about their clothing as the women? He didn't think so. But then again, his mother and nanny had made all those decisions when he was a child. Thank Heaven he would never have to go through that torture again! A monk's robes were the height of simplicity, and they allowed a man's body to breathe. He hoped it took weeks for the clothing to be sewn. Perhaps he could be back in China by the time they were finished, and then he'd never have to wear—

"Excellent news, Jacob!" his grandmother crowed. "Mr. Barker has at least two pair of everything you need already made. You can get out of those robes immediately and be a proper English gentleman for dinner tonight! Well, except for the boots, of course. I'm afraid those will have to wait for tomorrow."

Thank God for small favors. That had been his mother's favorite expression. He'd never truly understood it until now.

"Oh!" she exclaimed as she clapped her hands together. "I can't wait until everyone sees you turned out as a proper English gentleman."

He didn't care about "everyone," though he wondered how Evelyn would react. And Zhi Min, of course. Would his judge see that he was adopting his birth country's attitudes? Or would Zhi Min see through to his core and know that Jie Ke was only faking it? He had no wish to embrace his heritage, he merely wanted to get through this last trial so that he could discard it all for vows and a full life as a monk. But either way, his path was clear, and after a few more sneezes he agreed to allow Mr. Barker's assistants to help him dress.

"Stop fidgeting. Even the young novices aren't so twitchy."

Jie Ke forced his body still even as he glared over his shoulder at Zhi Min. They were descending the stairs to the main parlor on this longest day of his life. After a morning spent with the tailor, his grandmother decided he needed to remember the basics of English deportment. He had relearned how to sit, how to stand, how to speak. All of it brought back childhood scolds with vivid clarity. Lord, no wonder he preferred the temple. Certainly the Xi Lin had their own rigid set of rules, but at least he hadn't been strapped up in too-tight clothing and choked to death with a necktie.

"Are you ready to eat the English food?" Zhi Min asked as they reached the main floor.

Jie Ke shrugged, then abruptly stopped as the movement pulled at his tie, which strangled him even further. He looked at the footman who stood before the closed parlor door. It was time to make his grand entrance. At least he still got to wear his soft Chinese boots.

With a smile and a flourish, the footman drew open the parlor door. Zhi Min stood behind and to the side, watching with a wide grin. Meanwhile, Jie Ke tried to block out his friend's humor while scanning the room for one person. He found her in the corner, being the gracious hostess as she entertained three girls barely into their adolescence and the high-voiced Lord Greenfield, who continued speaking, oblivious to Jie Ke's entrance. But everyone else stopped to stare. Titters began at the same moment Lord Greenfield realized he'd lost his audience. First came the not-so-discreet coughs, then the awkward throat clearing, and finally outright giggles.

"I say, dear boy," intoned Lord Greenfield as he finally turned toward the door, quizzing glass at the ready. "Lovely boots, there. Did you bring them in from the stable?"

It was meant as an insult, of course, but Jie Ke had lived as a foreign boy in China and knew how to handle insults. He'd learned from the street boys who came in to the temple for meals. Add to it a dash of his imperious grandfather, and he had the perfect response delivered in the most cultured English tones he could manage. "They're delightful. Cool in summer, warm in winter, and so soft inside that it's like being cradled in a willing woman." He paused. "In truth,

I cannot take a step without thinking of your charming mother."

The man sputtered in outrage. His wife and a few others gasped and turned their backs on Jie Ke. The young girls just stared, frowning in their innocence. But, what was Evelyn doing? His gaze centered on her face and the slight wrinkle between her brows. She noticed his attention, of course, and cut her gaze sharply across the room to his grandmother.

Jie Ke had a moment's guilt that he hadn't even noticed the elderly woman ensconced near the fire. But then he understood Evelyn's silent message, and a great deal more guilt weighted his spirit. His jab at Lord Greenfield was not the kind of thing said in front of ladies. And now he had embarrassed the poor woman who just this morning had been brimming with joy.

With true contrition, he moved forward to address the older woman—remembering to hold his breath when he came near—and bowed in his best English manner. He belatedly remembered to take her hand and kiss it. The whole affair was awkward, but she didn't seem to mind. In fact, her eyes shone with unshed tears as she looked at him from head to toe.

"Grandmother, you look radiant this evening," he remarked.

"And you, Jacob," she said as she patted his hand. "You look just as you ought." She turned her gaze to Evelyn. "Evie, dear, doesn't my grandson look most handsome?"

Evelyn had no choice but to glide forward. "I would say that he looks quite English, but I believe that he is still very Chinese inside."

In other words, she had made a decision: she had no intention of helping him fool Zhi Min into thinking he had embraced England.

He was just trying to form a reply when Christopher joined their group from the other side. "Nonsense," the man drawled in a smooth and urbane manner. "I would say he looks quite dapper. Almost as if he had been wearing our clothing for years. Your cravat has been . . . most expertly executed."

Jie Ke grimaced. He heard clearly the other man's implication—that he was a fraud who was only faking being Chinese. Did these people not tire of calling him a liar? Did they know that there was a murderer among them?

"After four hours closeted with Mr. Barker," he replied, "I should hope I learned how to dress." Then he sighed. "But I confess that my servant is the one who tied the neckcloth. I believe Mei Li learned it from your valet." He turned to the group in general. "The truth is the same the world over: we gentlemen are nothing without our servants."

It was an innocuous comment thrown out in the hope of peace. He did it for his grandmother's sake—and Evelyn's too, he supposed. Both women had reasons to want this evening to go smoothly. Unfortunately, the assembled elite had no interest in welcoming him, no matter what he wore. His comment was greeted with vague disapproval. One lady even sniffed and turned her head away.

Jie Ke suppressed his sigh and turned back to Evelyn. What now? He wanted to ask her, but her eyes were trained on Christopher, who had folded his arms and regarded him as one would a stray dog.

"It isn't so often that we get Chinese travelers in our little corner of the world," his cousin drawled. "I might say never, not since the last time I saw Uncle Reggie." He toyed with the drink in his hand, but his gaze remained razor sharp. "Tell me about my uncle's studies. Was he able to complete any more? Do you have any copies of his notes?"

Jie Ke throttled his urge to punch his cousin unconscious. He had known he would be questioned about what happened to his family; he just hadn't expected the moment—the memories themselves—to be so painful. Fortunately, he had an answer ready. Not so fortunately, he took a breath before speaking, and immediately began sneezing.

It was a violent fit, explosion after explosion. Most people drew away from him in horror, or so it seemed through his watery gaze. His grandmother, of course, exclaimed loudly and moved even closer, which simply made the powder's effect even worse and caused more sneezing.

"Bloody hell!" someone cursed.

"English pig snot!" laughed Zhi Min in Chinese.

Jie Ke straightened enough to glare at his friend, and at that moment, the fit eased a bit. Then Evelyn came close, offering a handkerchief in one hand and a glass of water in the other. Jie Ke focused on her face, released one last horrible sneeze, and then stopped.

He used her handkerchief, he drank her water, and only then did his breath return. "It's this horrible English clothing," he groused. "How do you stand having such itchy cloth wrapped tight around everything? If I were to fight, I'd rip my pants from belly to ass."

A gasp of horror met his comment. He only belatedly realized that he'd spoken in English. He'd meant that last comment for Zhi Min alone, but the horrified looks of the others told him he had erred, and erred badly.

"If you think starched linen is difficult," Evelyn said into the silence, "you ought to try stays. Sneezing against whalebone is nigh on impossible."

He gave her a weak grin, then looked down at her now-disgusting handkerchief. With a shrug, he casually tossed it into the fire. "Given my current affliction, stays might well be required."

Her answering smile was warm and genuine, and Jie Ke spent a long moment basking in her beauty. But before long he felt the dark, assessing gaze of his cousin. Without even looking, he answered Christopher's question.

"My father's notes were not in the wreckage. I don't know what happened to them. We went back to . . ." He swallowed. "We went back and . . . and . . ." He sneezed again.

This time it was Zhi Min who provided a handkerchief, and then answered on Jie Ke's behalf. "We went back later to bury the bodies. Everything was gone, stripped away by the bandits."

Christopher arched a brow. "Surely the papers were there. No bandit would want English papers and a sketchbook."

Jie Ke took a breath and mercifully did not sneeze. "We didn't find Mr. Higgins's body, so I assumed—I hoped—he had survived. As Papa's valet, he would have recognized what was important. I thought he took everything he could back home. And that he would send someone for me."

"He did," Evelyn inserted. "He brought back the signet ring and some notes . . . but not all of them." She paused for a significant moment. "But he told us everyone died. Everyone but himself."

Jie Ke's eyes drifted to the fire. He remembered white ash drifting on the air and clogging his throat. The urge to sneeze pressed down on him, but he fought it by blanking his memories. In the end, he could speak—softly, but very clearly. "I didn't die. I grew up in the monastery and waited for someone to come get me."

"We thought you were dead," whispered his grandmother.

"I waited," he repeated. "With no money, all I could do was send letters. I never received a response. There was a time I would have worked my way back to England. I was willing to do anything to join a caravan, so long as it was headed west."

"Why didn't you?" Christopher pressed.

Jie Ke looked at his grandmother then. It wasn't an easy thing to do, but he forced himself. She needed to know the truth, needed to understand. "At first I thought Higgins would send for me. I had no money, no way to travel, and I was a boy and an earl. I waited for someone to come get me."

"But we didn't know," whispered his grandmother. "We thought you were dead."

Jie Ke looked down at her frail hands because he could not

look her in the eye. "I guessed as much, but only years later. And in that time, the temple became my home. I had lost my first family. Why would I abandon my second to come back here?"

"But we are your family!" the old woman cried. "We were always here!"

He shrugged. "I am happy there, and I thought you had abandoned me."

No one responded to that. There was nothing to say in the face of his grandmother's grief. And into that awkward silence came the mellow note of the dinner bell.

The response was immediate. Everyone pushed to their feet and began the dance of finding the appropriate place in line. Except, where was Jie Ke to go? The highest-titled man would escort his grandmother—the dowager countess—into the dining room. That man was either Christopher or Jacob, depending upon the veracity of the monk's claims. Of course, even if Jie Ke did not want such status, his grandmother definitely wanted him beside her. That, of course, left Christopher out in the cold.

Evelyn wanted to intercede—Jie Ke could see it in her face. To him, she was the embodiment of the best of England, a gracious, beautiful woman who would see to everyone's comfort and happiness, no matter the cost to herself. Even in the middle of a disrupted wedding, she and her mother had handled themselves and everyone else smoothly, seemingly without effort. He admired that. He recognized the skill in her every breath and movement, knew that she was as much a master of her domain as the abbot was of his temple in China.

He yearned for that himself, he realized, the ease with which she brought all into peaceful harmony. He smiled at her and would happily have allowed Christopher the preeminent position if it meant he could stand by her. He even made a start toward Evelyn, but his grandmother would have none of it.

"I want both my grandsons by my side," she declared. Then she held out her arms to each of them.

The matter was settled. Jie Ke and Christopher took her arms with as much grace as possible—which in Christopher's case was quite a lot—and Evelyn disappeared somewhere toward the back of the line. It was even possible that Zhi Min escorted her in, but Jie Ke wasn't sure. His attention was caught by Christopher, who spoke in a low tone to his grandmother.

"Grandmama, this is all well and good for now, but you know only one of us can have the title. You must choose sides, and one of us will lose."

Jie Ke felt the tremble that shook the elderly lady, and anger surfaced. Without thinking to moderate his tone, he snapped at his cousin. "It is an evil system that forces a woman to choose between children."

"It is the system we have," returned Christopher, his gaze hard and burning into his nemesis over their grandmother's head.

"And does her view carry so much weight in the English courts that her pick will determine the course of the title? Of course not. Let her have us on both sides. She is the only reason I came back." He hadn't meant to speak so honestly. It was ridiculous in any event, since just standing in her presence made him sneeze. But hers had been the face he remembered on the long trek back to England.

"Oh, Jacob," his grandmother whispered.

"What kind of man are you?" hissed Christopher. "To hurt an old woman so? You are not Jacob. Cease this charade, for you will get nothing."

There was no chance to answer, for they had made it to the dining room and both fought to pull out Grandmother's chair. It was mere posturing, masculine drama with insignificant stakes. Even the youngest initiates in the temple would recognize the futility of fighting over these things. These were the idiotic things over which men went to war. Jie Ke felt the same, but he could not stop his shoulders from tensing or the hatred from burning up through his mind.

His gaze caught and held Christopher's in a silent battle of will. He could flatten his cousin with one punch. He could likely best his cousin in any physical contest, but this was a drawing-room war, a social battle that could not be won in any way he knew except with courage and discipline.

Grandmother ceased to exist. All other guests, as well. Silence reigned as the two men stared. And in Jie Ke's thoughts, the questions boiled. Did you kill my parents? Did your father? Your solicitor? Your friends? How did you arrange it? Why did you do it? Why? *Why?*

At last, Evelyn intervened. "Christopher, dear, I know you should by rights sit by your grandmother, but I would adore it if you could come down here by me. Do you think we could break with propriety enough to do that?"

It was the necessary solution, but Jie Ke cursed it with every fiber of his being. If anyone would give up in favor of Evelyn, it was he. But Christopher was faster and had the invitation.

His cousin bowed deeply to his grandmother, then smiled warmly. "Of course, Evie. I think our guests understand how an affianced couple long for any moment they might have together." Then he sent such a look of moony-eyed calf love toward Evelyn that two of the trio of girls giggled. The third sighed in delight.

Jie Ke kept silent, his eyes following his cousin, who crossed the room and took Evie's hand. The memory of how she had come apart against his mouth lingered on his lips. The sound of her muffled cries, the taste of her on his tongue. And yet there she was, smiling urbanely at his cousin, the man she clearly intended to marry. And at that moment, Jie Ke's world changed.

The revelation came quietly, in the space between one breath and the next, but the knowledge hit him with more power than a lightning strike. If he hadn't been holding on to the back of a chair he would have stumbled.

He had come back to England because of the abbot's requirement. He had traveled back to this cold, gray country thinking only of how to end things quickly and perhaps learn a little of his grandmother and whether she'd survived. But now another face supplanted hers, another person vied with the abbot for dominance in his thoughts. Evelyn. Her beauty and skill brought harmony to everyone around her. She created that peace he knew in the temple and the quietness he experienced only in the best meditations.

Was it possible? Could he possibly want to woo her in earnest? Could he actually want to remain in England as her husband, as the father of her children?

His gaze leaped to Zhi Min in shock. He felt lost in this holy revelation, adrift without anchor or support. Did he truly wish to become English again? For Evelyn?

Of course not! And yet, for such a woman, how could he resist?

This was a nightmare! Evelyn forced herself to smile at her fiancé who held out a chair for her. Of all the places to have a stare-down with Jie Ke! Didn't the two men realize that everyone was watching their every move? Didn't they know that every second of this evening would be dissected and resurrected for gossip?

Of course they did! Or at least Christopher did. But he had to have his staring contest with Jie Ke nonetheless. And every moment of their power struggle only hurt the dowager countess more. The poor woman just wanted her grandchild back. She didn't care about politics or the machinations required to obtain the title. Let her have her precious Jacob and allow the courts to decide about the earldom!

She glanced up the table to where Jie Ke was paying court to his grandmother. Or rather he should have been. Instead, he looked dumbstruck—pale, sweaty, and with mouth hanging ajar as he stared at her.

She squirmed in her seat, acutely uncomfortable at his blatant attention. It was hard enough to be in the same room with him without remembering last night. Lord, she ached in places she hadn't even realized existed. Her every breath reminded her what she had done was sinful and a horrible betrayal to Christopher. And yet, she longed to do it again. She wanted . . .

But now wasn't the time! And Jie Ke's obvious staring was going to be remarked upon by everyone!

She tried to glare him into behaving, but he didn't seem to notice. It was as though he looked at her and through her at the same time. What did he see with that unbreakable stare? What was he thinking?

"You look divine, as usual," murmured Christopher as he took his seat beside her. "You seem to be bearing up well, unlike my mother." Upon learning that her son and Evelyn had not run off to Scotland, the countess had retired to her rooms and had not been seen since.

"Your mother has a delicate constitution," Evelyn murmured as she reluctantly directed her attention back to Christopher. "Whereas I—"

"You are perfect," pressed Christopher, obviously playing the lovesick swain for all the assembled guests. The Misses Whitsun were halfway to swooning at the romance of it all. "I could not be happier unless this entire farce were over and we were already wed." He clasped her hand. "I begin to regret certain earlier, more responsible decisions."

There was no mistaking his meaning. He referred to his

refusal to bed her yesterday, and she felt her face heat in embarrassment. If he ever found out what she had done last night . . . She swallowed and forced herself to smile.

"It seems I must rely on wiser, more rational minds," she whispered. "My composure seems to be severely lacking of late."

"Nonsense," he returned. "You would have come to your senses eventually. You have always behaved exactly as you ought, Evie, and of that you can be extremely proud. I know I am."

Then there was no more time to speak about it, for the first course arrived and regular dinner conversation took over. And then the next course arrived. And then the next. All went as smoothly as could be expected. By the time the women rose to withdraw, Evelyn's mother was beaming.

Evelyn managed to state quietly to Christopher that there could be no more theatrics or she would never forgive him. In response, he lifted his glass and turned toward Lord Greenfield—the only other ranking male in the company, since he would not acknowledge Jie Ke.

"I, for one," he said, "much prefer my lady fiancée's presence over any of you lot. So might I suggest that we retire to the parlor together?"

The perfect response from a perfect fiancé. Evelyn smiled in gratitude. Lord Greenfield of course nodded, and everyone filed out of the room in perfect accord. But Evelyn knew her pleasant expression was forced and would fade the moment she was alone. Truthfully, she had been looking forward to a few moments without the aggravating presence of either man. With everyone still together, now in the parlor, she would remain on pins and needles until bedtime.

"Evie, dear, come sit by the fire with me." It was the dowager countess, looking sweet as she manipulated Evelyn to sit down next to Jie Ke, or Jacob, or whoever the man was. It was all getting rather confused in her head.

"Of course," Evelyn responded, because that was what she was expected to say. "Would you like me to bring you some tea?"

"No, no, dear. Just come sit with me and my grandson."

Was it possible for a face to freeze in place? Would her muscles lock in this farce of a smile if she wasn't able to escape? "It would be my pleasure, my lady."

"Oh, nonsense, Evie. You must call me Grandmama like everyone else. You are, after all, about to be one of the family."

"Of course, Grandmama." Evelyn settled onto a stool directly across from the dowager countess. Jie Ke stood to the side, obviously uncomfortable and apparently trying not to breathe. His face was turned resolutely toward the fire, which only seemed to highlight his sallow skin. Truly, the man did not look well.

"I have been discussing things with Jacob," the dowager countess said. "I believe it would be best if he retired with me to my home. It is not that far, and"—her voice dropped to a conspiratorial whisper—"I believe he could use the time to fully adapt to an English life."

One glance at Jie Ke's wan face told Evelyn that this was the last thing he wanted. But it would solve certain problems. She wouldn't be so afraid of pistols at dawn, for example, between Christopher and Jie Ke. But then she imagined Jie Ke in his monk's robe taking his twenty paces, gun in hand, and a nervous giggle leapt from her lips.

"Evie?"

"Um, I'm sorry, Countess . . . er, Grandmama, but I believe choice of residence is entirely up to him, don't you think?"

The elderly lady released a huff of disgust. "Well, of course it is, but I don't think he understands that everyone here is watching him. Or that they judge him unfairly."

"Oh, I think he does understand," drawled Christopher from directly behind Evelyn, and she had to restrain herself from squeaking in alarm at his sudden presence. As it was, she shot him a glare over her shoulder. He didn't see. His eyes were trained on Jie Ke, who had suddenly straightened and turned to face him.

Good Lord, another male argument was coming, and just when she thought the evening couldn't get worse. "The room is so close in here," she said, making a valiant attempt to steer the men apart. "Chris, do you think we should open a window?"

"Grandmama," he answered, completely ignoring Evelyn, "you have already taken upon yourself the expense of an entire new wardrobe for this—"

"If you say 'charlatan' one more time, young man, I swear I shall box your ears!"

Christopher sighed, dropping to his knees before his grandmother. "Do not let this man into your heart. It will only lead to—"

"She will not pay for my clothing," Jie Ke said, his voice loud enough to carry in the now silent room.

Christopher leaned back on his heels enough to stare at his nemesis. "And where would a monk—"

"Have close to five hundred pounds for Father Smythe-Jones?" He gestured to the man in question on the opposite side of the room. "And more yet to pay for English clothing?" He shook his head. "You are so used to seeing money in one way—on quarter day from crofters and the like. You cannot imagine that a man could have resources beyond his land and his country."

Evelyn frowned, not understanding what he was trying to say. "You have funds all the way from China?"

He shook his head, his intense attention warming her face like the rays of the sun. "I am a monk. We have the skills to survive."

"Of course you do, Jacob dear," inserted the dowager countess. "But I don't think you realize that you need time.

You cannot remember what it is like to be English all in a day." She gripped his hand, her eyes pleading. "You must gain some polish, dear, away from prying eyes."

Evelyn saw the struggle within Jie Ke. She doubted anyone else did, but she'd had cause to study him. She watched him swallow, and his too-steady gaze focused on the elderly woman.

"I cannot go to your home, Grandmother," he said gently. "It would be too far away." Then his sights lifted to pin Evelyn.

Her breath froze in her chest. Was he declaring that he intended to court her? Was this part of his ruse to fool his friend, the other monk? Or was it as real as it felt?

She had no breath to speak and no thought as to what she would say anyway. She wanted to look to Christopher, to seek solid anchor in him, but she couldn't force herself to do it. When had she ever been able to flee a storm?

"I believe you are correct, Evie," Christopher drawled from somewhere far, far away. "The room has become quite stuffy. Shall we open one window or two?"

It was too much. All three of them wanted to stake a claim on her: Jie Ke, Christopher, his—their?—grandmother. Four, if she added the still-echoing pressure from Christopher's mother not to be blindly obedient. Could any of them simply allow her to be herself?

Abruptly disgusted, Evelyn pushed to her feet.

"Well, Evie?" Christopher drawled, obviously pleased because he thought she responded to him. "What shall it be? One window or two?"

"Open them all, Christopher—the windows, the doors, even the flue. I intend to escape." And so she did. She flung open the parlor door and went directly to the back of the house. With a footman's help, she pushed open the back double doors and walked calmly, confidently out into the night. She walked mindlessly, her feet knowing the path she wanted.

She didn't pause, didn't stop, didn't even breathe until she came to her destination.

But once there, she didn't know what to do. In the end, she simply collapsed. She crumpled to the ground, pressed her head to her knees, and began to sob.

Chapter Nine

"I knew you'd be here."

Evelyn jerked upright, her eyes adjusting slowly to the suddenly dark sky. Had she fallen asleep? She couldn't orient herself fast enough to respond. But that never really mattered with her sister. Maddie would talk whether or not anyone listened.

"You always come here when you've had too much. Something about the wind, I think." The girl dropped to the ground beside her. She'd brought a lantern that illuminated her rumpled dress and undone hair ribbons. "You like being buffeted by the wind here. What is this strange fascination you have with weather?"

"How long have I been gone?" Evelyn's voice came out as a croak.

"Long enough for Chris to start blathering on about calling out the dogs to search."

Evelyn gasped and started to stand, but her feet were numb and she stumbled. Then she froze because her sister was laughing at her.

"No, no! Don't go. I was only teasing. Christopher and Mama have everything well in hand. Chris handles the servants almost as well as you do. Jacob or Jie Ke—whatever his name is—has retired from the field. Something about prayers. The rest have remained to slash his reputation to shreds." Maddie sighed and shook her head. "I fear he will not regain his title no matter who his parents were."

Evelyn stared at her sister, momentarily stunned by the girl's perception. "I forget that you are much older than you act." Then she winced. She had not meant it to sound like that.

Maddie reacted as usual, simply laughed off the criticism with a wave. "But it's all to the good, right? Without his title, you get to marry Christopher and everything will be as it should be—the viscount and his viscountess making proper little babies in their proper little home."

Evelyn rolled her eyes, taking comfort from this familiar sisterly argument. "Only you could make such a good life sound like a curse. What is wrong with being a viscountess?"

"Nothing at all," Maddie answered absently. Her agile mind had hopped off somewhere else, and Evelyn could only wait to see where it landed. "It's just so clearly everything you want, one wonders why you ran here."

Evelyn blinked and took in the vast, windswept plain before her. Or she would have if she could see it; right now it was a black pit of shadows. All she could really sense was the wind. "Here? Why *not* here?"

"Because here is where you went when Mama told you it didn't matter whom you met during your Season, you would marry Chris."

Had she? It was so long ago, she didn't remember.

"And here is where you ran when that child got trampled and you had to spend all night with her mother."

"I did not," Evelyn said firmly. "I arranged for the funeral and sent Gus to fetch Mary's sister."

"You did all that"—Maddie agreed with a nod—"and then right after the sister arrived and the funeral was finished, you came here. Fell asleep then, too. Mama was frantic with worry."

The memory returned. "You found me then, too."

Maddie grinned. "That time I remembered to bring a picnic. Wish I'd thought of it tonight. Some of Cook's apple tarts would be perfect right now."

Evelyn smiled, her thoughts settling into a comfortable rhythm. The wind pushed hard at her chest, the darkness surrounded her, but she was here with her sister. For this moment in time, at least, everything was perfect.

"So, why are you here?" Maddie pressed.

Evelyn released a snort that was half laughter and half disgust. "Don't I have enough reason? My wedding was interrupted by Chinese monks! Good God, who would ever have thought that?"

"Hmmm," returned Maddie as she flopped backwards onto the ground. "Yes, that probably was pretty upsetting. I mean, what do you do about the next wedding? Do you order a new dress? Everyone's seen this one. And Cook worked so hard on that menu. She made all her specialties. She's frantic trying to learn new recipes good enough for the next ceremony."

Evelyn spared a moment's thought for her dress, then shrugged and relaxed backwards onto the ground next to her sister. The sky was overcast tonight, so there was little moon and no starlight. And yet, the blackness was even better this way. No shadows, even with the lantern light. Total emptiness.

"The countess gave me nearly two hundred pounds to take Chris to Gretna Green."

Maddie bolted upright. "Never you say! Chris's mother did that?"

"It would solve the problem of what dress to wear. And Cook would not have to think of a new menu."

"Hmmm." Maddie's head fell back and she stared up at the sky with a murmur of disgust. "Chris refused, didn't he? Not proper. Would support Jacob's cause, and all that." She spoke in a dry mockery of Chris's rigidity.

"He's right. Why invite the scandal when everything will be sorted out soon enough?"

Maddie rolled onto her side and peered at her sister.

"Which brings us back to the primary question: why did you run here?"

Evelyn let the wind wash over her. It wasn't as strong when she lay flat. "Hmm?"

Maddie popped up onto her elbow. The wind played havoc with her hair, sending curling tendrils into her face. It didn't stop her words, though. "If everything is going to work out, why did you run here?"

Evelyn closed her eyes. That created total blackness. A void. Safety. "Maybe I'm just feeling impatient. Maybe I want to get on with my life. Get married, have children, do every-thing—"

"That a countess should." Maddie's tone was mocking. "Or maybe it's because you were very uncountesslike last night with a certain monk."

Evelyn's eyes popped open in horror. Maddie couldn't know, couldn't have seen! "Oh my God," she whispered. Her sister *had* seen. She knew! "Oh my God, Maddie, you can't tell!"

Her sister reared back, obviously insulted. "Of course I won't tell! I wouldn't do that to you!"

"But sometimes you just say things. Sometimes they just slip out." Panic clutched at Evelyn's throat. Lord, it would kill Chris.

"I can keep a secret," Maddie huffed. "I have a few of my own, you know. None quite so salacious, mind you, but—"

"Maddie!"

Her sister grabbed her hands and smiled. It was an impish smile full of her good heart and quick mind. It was Maddie through and through—and not in the least bit reassuring. "I won't tell. I swear! But I do wonder what my oh-so-proper sister was doing kissing a man who isn't Chris."

Evelyn blinked. "Kissing? You thought we were kissing?" Maddie *hadn't* seen. Thank God!

Her sister shrugged and tried to look coy. "Well, I assume that was what you were doing. I mean, I only saw you when you came back in. And I know it wasn't Chris who made you look all rumpled like that."

Evelyn released a breath of relief. "One kiss," she lied. "One gloriously fabulous kiss. And I don't know why!" she added with a wail. "I have been sick with the thought of it all night and all day."

"Well, truth be told, it was your *second* kiss, the first being in the morning—"

"Maddie!"

"Sorry."

Evelyn flopped onto her belly and glared at her sister. "This isn't funny. This isn't like me."

"Are you sure?" Maddie asked, her voice strangely sober. "I mean, you can't be absolutely perfect all the time, can you? Perhaps last night you were the Evie who isn't going to be a countess."

"But I am going to be a countess. And I am Evie. And you are making no sense whatsoever!"

"And you went to be with the wrong man. On the lawn." Maddie released a nervous giggle. "I still can't believe . . . I mean, Evie, you looked . . . I don't know how you looked, but you were happy! Is that what kissing is like? Is that why you couldn't stop yourself?"

"That's just it," Evelyn whispered in reply, her eyes drifting up and out over the dark field below. "It was wonderful. And it was awful, too." She rolled onto her side. "Maddie . . . it wasn't enough."

"You mean, you want to do it again?"

Evelyn nodded. "No. I mean, yes, but no. It faded so quickly."

"It was the middle of the night," Maddie drawled. "I doubt it was quick at all!"

"My God, what were you doing out of bed at that hour anyway?"

Maddie bit her lip and looked guilty. "I couldn't sleep and

went to the kitchen for some milk. And then you came wandering in."

Evelyn rolled away, unable to bear the sight of her baby sister thinking she was little better than a whore. "It wasn't enough, Maddie, because I still feel empty. How did I get to feel so empty?"

She heard Maddie sit up to look down at her. "But you've always seemed so content."

"I thought I was."

"And you're not now?"

A deep voice slipped out of the shadows behind them. "She doesn't know how she feels now."

Both women spun around, but only Maddie gasped in surprise. Evelyn had known he would come eventually, that she would have to face him again. Jie Ke was back to wearing his monk's robes, these a bright saffron that absorbed the lantern light.

"How did you find us?" she asked.

"I followed your sister." Then he settled down on the ground near them. "That is the problem, isn't it? You have never questioned your future or your life, and then suddenly, here I am and everything is different."

"Is that how *you* feel?" she whispered.

"No. That is how I felt at the temple."

Maddie shifted uncomfortably beside them. "I don't think you should be here," she said, a bristling protectiveness in her tone.

"No, it's all right," Evelyn replied, already mentally surrendering to the inevitable. "I think I need to talk to him. I need to sort all this out."

Maddie looked uncertain. Jie Ke simply sat, waiting for a decision.

"I am of age, Maddie. Let me make my decisions as an adult." Then she glanced back toward the house. "Tell everyone I've gone to bed."

"Mama will check. They're all worried about you."

Evelyn smiled. "Then tell them I'm walking and will be home by morning. They should be used to that. I do it often enough."

"Evie—"

Another figure melted out of the shadows. It was the other monk, his robe so bright that Evelyn was surprised she hadn't noticed him before.

"May I escort you back, Miss Madeline Stanton?"

Maddie shook her head, her gaze hopping between her sister and both monks. "This really isn't a good idea."

"Sometimes," the other monk said, "a man and a woman must find their truths in their own way. They cannot do that except in private."

Maddie still did not move. She sat there in a half crouch, uncertainty in every line of her body.

"What do you fear?" the monk asked.

"I will not harm her," Jie Ke said. "I swear that by all that I hold holy."

"It's true," put in Evelyn. "He'd never hurt me." She wasn't sure why she believed such a thing, but she did.

In the end, Maddie nodded. She straightened slowly, then crossed to the other monk. He offered her his arm in a very English gesture, and she took it shyly, almost girlishly. But then she turned, her voice strong in the darkness.

"Come home soon," she said firmly. "I'll be watching for you."

Evelyn nodded. "Of course," she lied. It did no good to tell Maddie the truth, that whatever was between her and Jie Ke wasn't going to be resolved in a few minutes. So she smiled warmly at her sister and waved her away. A few breaths later, Maddie and the monk disappeared into the night. That left just herself and Jie Ke alone on a remote bluff.

"We're going to make love now, aren't we?" she asked him.

His eyes widened in surprise. "What? Is that what you wish?"

"Of course not!" she snapped. "I am not a beast driven only by lust." But she was lying.

"Why ask the question?" he responded. "I had not thought— I did not mean to—" He swallowed. "That is not why I came here. Is it truly what you want?"

Was it? Why was she pushing for something so completely disastrous? It was too fast, and yet she had been longing for someone to come ravish her for so long. Christopher always refused, and no one else had been allowed near. "Last night was not enough," she said.

"But it was the best you have ever felt? The most full, the most alive, the most anything ever?"

She nodded. "For that brief moment, it was everything." She looked at him, pushing up to her feet. She was insane, she realized, completely insane even to contemplate this. And yet, her blood was already pounding, her hands were slick and her mouth dry. She was moments away from the storm and she wanted it with every fiber of her being. She already had one hand to her bodice, ready to pull open the buttons.

"Christopher will never forgive me," she said, "but I want this so much. I have *always* wanted this."

"I will not tell Christopher. He need never know."

She released a short laugh, in some ways mocking herself as much as him. "You don't sound like a very holy monk."

He grimaced. "Yes, I know."

"Is this . . . is what goes on here part of the lie? Is this so you can convince the other monk—"

"Zhi Min."

"Zhi Min," she echoed. "So you can convince him you have won me?"

He shook his head. "This is for me. And for you. So we can see what we choose between."

"Married life or your monastery?"

He nodded. "For me, yes."

"And for me?" He still hadn't moved. She tugged at her dress, pulling open the buttons on the back as best she could.

"Only you can say why you do this."

"Because . . ." She grimaced as the first of the buttons finally came free. "Because I can't stop myself," she lied. "Because you have mesmerized me and I can think of nothing more than letting you have me. Because I must have you or die."

Chapter Ten

She was lying. Jie Ke knew it. Knew as well that the lie was more for herself than for him. He was well familiar with the stories one told oneself. The question was, did he allow her the illusion?

"Do you want me to ravish you?" His body throbbed at the idea. It took all his willpower to remain still on the ground with just a few feet separating them. "Should I throw you down to the ground and overpower you?"

Her eyes widened and her lips parted. Almost breathlessly she nodded. He wondered if she realized what she was saying.

"You would wish to be overpowered? Why?"

Her gaze skittered about, suddenly uncertain and anxious. With an angry jerk, she pulled more of her buttons free and her dress slipped down enough to reveal white lace and corset. "It is what women do, isn't it? Men take, order, command. And we obey."

"And you want this from your lover?' "

She shook her head even as she shimmied out of her dress. The wind whipped her hair about her face, flattening the delicate lace against the pink blush of her skin. There was little moonlight here, but the lantern glow cast her in softer tones— golds and the flickering grays of shadow. She appeared more spectral than real, but her need throbbed in the air between them, a physical presence. Or perhaps it was Jie Ke's own hunger.

She kicked her dress away and stood before him, tall and proud in a corset and no shift. Her stockings outlined long legs, and the rosy ribbon at her thighs taunted him. The wind carried her scent. Even now, his mouth watered for another taste. If he moved one finger, he would be upon her like a beast. But no matter what she claimed, he knew she did not want that.

"Why me?" he whispered. That was the real reason for his restraint. Not out of some noble desire to let her truly choose this path. It was his pride that needed to know. "Why me, when you could have any man you want?"

"There are no limits with you." She closed her eyes and turned her face to the wind. As she spoke, it snatched away her words almost as if she had never said them. But he heard and understood.

"It's not real with you, either," she said to the darkness. "If you told everyone what we do, no one would believe you." She turned an impish smile in his direction. "They might even kill you for saying it."

"Christopher will know. On your wedding night, he will know if you are not a virgin."

She released a nervous giggle. "No, he won't. There are ways to fake such things. I have asked and learned from those who have done it."

"You have thought of this, then."

She nodded, then raised her arms to the sky and spun around and around, her hair flying, the ribbons pulling ever so slightly apart. "I learned. Not on purpose, but a lady listens— to her family, to servants, to crofters. And sometimes she hears things that are not appropriate for her ears." Her spinning stopped, and she stood there swaying before him. "Once I'd heard, I could not stop thinking or imagining or wondering. But I never dared . . ." She abruptly dropped to the ground in front of him. "Touch me," she whispered. "Fill me."

He could not resist. He raised his hand to stroke the top of one breast. It was round and full such as he'd seen only with white women, especially when amplified by a corset. Her skin was cool from the wind, but so beautifully soft. He meant to brush only lightly then withdraw, but once he'd begun he could not pull away.

"I have been with women before," he confessed. "There are women who pride themselves on making monks fall. And a white devil is a novelty to them." He shook his head. "They were quick and hurried affairs, meetings of the body without the mind."

She shivered at his caress. "No thought at all," she murmured. "That is exactly what I want."

"It can leave one emptier than before."

"But during that moment, in that short time during . . ." She tugged on the ribbons in the front of her corset, which opened wider and wider with each breath.

"It is just a short moment," he said.

Her eyes opened, but he barely noticed; the rosy tips of her nipples had appeared. They were tightened from the cold, but so beautiful.

"Did you feel free?" she asked. "Did you fly like never before?"

Jie Ke's hand that had been stroking her breast dipped lower. His fingers outlined her nipple and tugged it. She shivered in response.

"Did you feel free?" she asked again. "In that moment of release, when pleasure consumes everything . . . were you free?"

He leaned forward, needing to kiss the cool expanse of skin she had just bared. Once touched, he needed to taste it. He extended his tongue, brushing a long stroke across her breast. She arched into him, lifting herself more fully. He didn't even need to move. He coiled his tongue around her nipple and drew it into his mouth.

Her hands came to his shoulders to steady her. His hands

fell to her hips to grasp and hold. But his mouth was on her breast and his tongue toyed with her nipple, sucking, drawing, and even biting enough to make her quiver. Then he pulled back just enough to look her in the eye.

"There are other ways to expand beyond the body, other ways to feel free."

She shook her head. "This is the one I know."

He stilled, the thought of other men in his place a sour burn of intrusion. "You have done this with others?"

She shook her head. "Alone. In my bed. But last night . . ." Her eyes took on a dreamy cast. "You showed me how much better it can be. I never . . . I never dared before." She touched his head, stroking her fingers from his temple to the nape of his neck, and then she tugged him forward. "Kiss me like that again."

"I do not know how to unbind your corset."

She smiled and with one powerful movement pushed the edges together, unhooked the bindings, and then pulled the garment totally free. She was naked except for her stockings. Then she took Jie Ke's hands, lifted them up, and put them on her breasts.

"Touch me," she ordered.

He did. It was heaven, and he worshipped at the altar of her breasts. He coiled his tongue around her nipples and drew them each individually into his mouth. While one hand stroked and shaped on the right, his mouth pulled and teased on the left.

He had never seen a woman so well-endowed. The Chinese women he'd been with were smaller proportioned, stingy in their attributes and their emotions. Her breasts overflowed his hands and his mouth. Even better, the slightest touch, the smallest nip of teeth produced a rewarding response from her. Evelyn's body quivered, her breath came in stuttering gasps, and whenever he abraded her nipple with fingernail or teeth she moaned with abandon. Never had he heard so many erotic sounds, felt such total physical absorption.

With every breath, every caress, he wanted more of her, more of this. *More.* He pushed her down into the grass. She went easily, stretching her arms out wide. He didn't follow, being too intent on stripping off his robes. As he stripped out of his clothing, she put her hands in her hair and pulled out pin after pin, tossing them over the edge of the bluff. Her hair spilled down and free, pale strands of shimmering gold that blew across her face and fluttered in the wind.

His breath caught in his throat. The last twenty years he had spent with dark-haired people of different skin and slanted eyes, many of whom had reviled him for the difference. Here was a woman more physically like himself, a lush white goddess with pink skin, full breasts, and a golden halo of hair. If ever there were an angel in this land, it would be she, and he was breathless with the thought of making love to her.

"Come closer," she said as she lifted up onto one elbow. He moved as though in a trance, his eyes feasting on the curve of her shoulder down to waist, then up again for hip and leg. Her pale stockings looked even more shocking now, especially contrasted to the dark shadows at the juncture of her thighs.

"I have never seen a man before," she murmured. She reached out and touched him with the flat of two fingers. There was no apology in her touch as she outlined the full shaft of his organ from tip to base. The pounding in his veins beat louder, harder, and his organ thrust forward in that primal tempo.

She gripped him. His eyes nearly rolled back in his head. To be surrounded by her was glorious, but the pressure—her strength—was too much. Pleasure and pain, he could not sort the one from the other.

"Evie!" he gasped.

"Oh!" She immediately gentled her grip, but she did not release him. Instead, she levered herself up onto her knees to look at him more directly. "I've seen babies, of course. And sometimes the older boys when they went swimming," she said. "But never a man. Never this."

She opened her hand to stroke him. Sensations piled on top of one another. She fluttered her fingers from tip to base. Her thumb rolled around the head and through the bead of moisture at the tip. Then her other hand cupped his sac. He was fully supported by her hands as she tugged him closer.

"Evie," he gasped through the pounding beat. "Do you know what you are doing?"

"The wives—they talk sometimes. I'm not supposed to hear, but I do. And I've thought a lot about it." She looked up at him, her eyes luminous in the darkness. "I want to know, Jie Ke. I want to understand it all!"

She leaned forward and put her mouth to his organ. Her lips touched first, a perfect circle of sweet pressure. She started off-center, but rapidly adjusted. Then her tongue swirled and swept across him. He groaned at the overpowering wetness, the wondrous heat. His buttocks tightened and his hips spasmed forward, but she held him tight—oh yes, so tight—and his thrust went only as far as she allowed.

He tried to control himself. He tried to keep his legs taut, his body under his mastery. He failed. In this moment, he was hers. The beat in his blood, the contraction of his buttocks, the thrust of his body—it all happened whether he willed it or not. It happened because she willed it.

She opened her mouth and engulfed him. Her movement was tentative, her timing exquisite. She moved with his thrusts and allowed him to push past her lips. His hands tightened where he gripped her shoulders. He didn't even remember touching her, but she was all he had to ground himself in reality, and his reality was her.

She began to toy with him. Her movements were random—a caress of her tongue, the suction of her mouth, or the sudden tightening of her fingers around his balls—all came at her pleasure, with her timing. He could do no more than surrender. And the pounding in his blood beat stronger, louder, and ever wilder, until it was all he knew.

His eruption came as a total release of all that he was. His mind, his body—it all poured into her, and still she continued to suck. He thrust, he pulsed, he gave until his legs buckled under him. He collapsed onto his knees, his consciousness gone except as an awareness of her.

He was hers. The enormity of that truth overwhelmed him. He fell forward, his head dipping to the ground in boneless worship. And in his soul, he felt . . .

Awe.

Evelyn stroked a hand across Jie Ke's back, watching her fingers flow over the wide expanse of muscle and bone. How broad he was, and how beautiful.

Without closing her eyes, she could see how he looked when he sparred with his monk friend. She could see the explosion in each punch, the brute force in every kick. The sound of impact, of flesh hitting flesh, had echoed in the clearing. She remembered it so clearly.

And yet here he was, collapsed before her on his knees as if in worship. She had brought him to this state. She had touched him and stroked him and brought him not only to his knees, but completely spent before her.

Her body still simmered with desire, her blood still thrummed with its hunger, but this was something beyond the demands of her body. This was more incredible than anything she had felt before. Not freedom, exactly. Power, perhaps. Was this what it was like to be a fully mature woman?

She let her fingers trail across his head, then skate again over his back. She brushed over the ridges of his spine, lengthening her arm as far as it would go down toward his narrow waist and tight behind. She could not see it clearly in the shadows, but she didn't need to. She remembered. Hadn't she just cupped him a moment ago and felt the immense strength of his thrust?

"Are you still breathing?" she asked, startled to hear the note of joy in her voice. She was happy?

She watched his back expand as he inhaled and heard a low groan as he pushed himself upright before her. He went slowly, his face pale, his eyes huge.

"I breathe," he said.

She almost laughed, he looked so . . . so young. All of his masculine power, all of the harsh angles of face and jaw were gone. "Tell me how you feel," she said. She wanted to understand everything he had experienced.

He breathed again, his chest expanding as his eyes drifted shut. "My body is sated, my mind is silent. I feel as though I could sleep for a thousand years or that I could conquer a thousand worlds." He smiled, a soft curve of his lips. "I feel at peace."

"Does that always happen? Did you feel that way with . . . with those other women?"

He shook his head. "Only with you."

She grinned, startled and immensely pleased. She had brought this strange, intense man peace. "It was like that for me last night. A beautiful, wonderful peace, but only for a moment. It didn't last long enough."

"To yearn for the past, to plan for the future—these are useless activities. We have only now. And now . . ." He grinned. "Right now, I feel at peace."

She frowned, trying to understand his words. She couldn't imagine a lifetime spent without past or future, without thinking of what she had to do or ought to be doing or would soon be told to do. "Is that what it is like in China?"

He shook his head. "That is what it is like at the temple."

She closed her eyes and breathed, just as he had done a moment ago. She lifted her face to the night sky and spread her arms wide, lifted and arched, feeling the wind on her naked breasts and glorying in the sensations of a body unfettered by clothing. "How wonderful that sounds," she said to the sky. "To feel like this always."

"Not always, Evie. Just now."

On his lips, her name sounded like a prayer. She liked that. So she straightened back to face him. "Tell me about the temple. Tell me everything!"

He laughed, then gestured at her body. "I can tell you all that you want, but aren't you cold? Do you want . . ." Was he blushing? "Do you want what you had last night?"

Yes, she did. But no, it wasn't preeminent in her thoughts. Her desire was a physical call, but this other thing—the demands of her mind—seemed so much louder now. "Will you help me dress?" was what she replied.

He nodded and immediately went to gather her gown. She stood, taking one last moment to appreciate her nakedness. It felt like sacrilege to cover herself again, but now that he had mentioned it, she was cold. Her skin felt tight from the biting wind and she shivered.

She reached for her dress. He handed her the corset instead. "No." She couldn't go that far, couldn't don that thing again tonight. She wanted to toss the garment off the bluff, but knew that some shepherd would find it, and then the whispers would begin. The material was too fine, the whalebone too expensive for it to be anyone else's. It would not be hard to track it back to her.

With a sigh, she resigned herself to keeping the damn thing. And once kept, she might as well wear it. With another sigh, she wrapped it around her chest and hooked herself in. Then she knotted the ties loosely. She was restricted, but not completely bound. Jie Ke held out her dress, and she stepped into the skirt.

"You have lost some buttons," he said. "But I believe I can fasten it adequately."

She nodded and felt the familiar tug of propriety settle around her. The loss was so acute that she almost cried.

Then she felt him, a press of lips at the base of her neck. It was tender, though she felt the gentle abrasion of his beard on her skin as she shivered in delight. Sensual hunger rumbled through her body like thunder in the distance. It was there and it was powerful, but it was an echo of what was. Or maybe, hopefully, it was a precursor to what could be. Then it was gone and her dress settled firmly, tightly into place.

"Do you want to stay here? Or should we walk?"

"Let us head back to the house. Maddie will be watching for us. Is my hair too wild?"

He smiled. "Just wild enough, I would say."

She nodded, but she smoothed it anyway and then quickly plaited it down her back. While she worked on her hair, he grabbed his robes and began dressing. Her fingers slowed as she watched him don fabric that didn't appear to have any fastenings at all. Three pieces, all wrapped and tucked, under-skirt then overwrap, then a heavier, fuller robe on top.

She frowned at the flash of fabric. "Is it the light, or does that have different colors?"

He smiled. "All one color, but different pieces of cloth. We make our robes from discarded scraps."

Her eyes widened at the thought of him stitching together rags. "But why? Surely one piece of cloth is easier." She brought the lantern closer to examine stitching done in a neat even hand. "You sewed this?"

"My first efforts were not so fine. It took me many years and many robes before I made this."

"But . . ." How to phrase her question. If he were truly Jacob, the son and heir of an earl, he would not have known how to sew. Certainly not this neatly. Although she supposed he could be taught.

He must have understood her confusion, because he shrugged. "My first years at the temple were angry ones. I was not kind to anyone about anything. The abbot made me first collect the rags, then wash them. You cannot imagine how furious I was. I, an earl's son, walking the streets looking for rags? Disgraceful!"

"It is a wonder that you did not run away." They were both dressed now and so began the slow walk toward the manor.

"I did a few times, but where would I go? I was not stupid. I saw what happened to the street boys. The lucky ones were used as slaves. At temple I had a bed and food. Not the kind I liked, and certainly nothing I was used to, but it was food and rest in safety. Plus, I believed that eventually someone from England would come for me."

She looked at him, trying to see the angry, frightened boy somewhere within the man. She didn't see him. Whatever had happened to the boy, this man had made peace with it. Assuming it was all true, that is, and not some elaborate fiction.

"How long did you hold out hope? For someone from England?"

"A long, long time." He shrugged. "My pride needed to believe that someone would look for me. I was the son of an earl. Surely I was important enough to come find."

"But what if Higgins had died? You couldn't have known he came back to England."

Jie Ke shook his head. "It didn't matter. Someone would need to talk to my father eventually. Matters of the title, perhaps, or a simple demand that he come home. Whatever messenger came would look for a white man in China. He would have found me—or so I believed."

"So you waited at the temple?" She tried to imagine a decade spent waiting for a messenger that never came.

"After what happened to my family, I was too afraid to

travel back on my own. Certainly not until I was much, much bigger. And by then, I didn't want to go."

He spoke so casually of the past, but it couldn't possibly have been that easy. Not after the slaughter of his entire family. Not for a ten-year-old boy in a foreign land. "What happened to that angry boy? How did he change?"

He smiled and readjusted the shoulder of his garment. "You will laugh when you hear. It was my robe."

She stopped walking, turning enough so that she could study his face. Was he teasing her?

"I was so angry at being sent to find rags that I found the worst pieces possible, horrible bits of cloth that the rats didn't even want. Half of them disintegrated when boiled. You should have seen the water! Gray scum clogged with string. Oh, it was terrible!"

"You boiled them yourself?"

"Zhi Min's mother watched to be sure I didn't boil myself alive by mistake."

"I thought you lived at the temple. Why would—"

"Zhi Min's father was our guide through that part of China. When the bandits came . . ." His voice trailed off and she saw a dark fury settle on his features. But then he noticed her watching, and he slowly tucked it away. For the first time, she realized that his anger was not gone, just merely pressed deep inside.

"The bandits killed both your fathers."

He nodded. "Zhi Min's mother had no way to survive except to attach herself to the temple. It is a large complex that needs many hands. She helps with the washing and cooking, played mother to the street children who would come and go."

"To you?"

He nodded, a soft smile playing about his lips. "And she loves watching the novitiates wash their own clothing. With me, she watched and pointed and laughed the whole time. It's a good thing I didn't understand the language very well.

I don't think my pride could have withstood the humiliation."

"But she made you do everything yourself?"

"Every last bit. And when half the rags fell apart, I had to go out and get more. Oh, I was angry. Ordered about by a washing woman? The great son of the Earl of Warhaven?"

"Did you ever refuse?"

He laughed, the sound light and whole as it filled their tiny corner of the night. "Many times. But if I didn't do the work to her satisfaction, I would not get dinner. Nothing to eat until the next night."

"Night?"

He nodded. "The monks do not eat before sundown."

"But you must have been starving!"

"I certainly thought I was. But then I saw real starvation: beggars who had not eaten for days, girls abandoned because the family could not afford them."

Evelyn shuddered. How strange was this place he called home. "But that's horrible! How can families be so cruel?"

He paused, his face a dark shadow. "Have you seen the rookeries in London? Do you know of the children there?"

She bit her lip and looked away. "I was never allowed in such areas."

He nodded. When he spoke, there was no condemnation in his tone. "Of course not. But places like that exist the world over, even right here in England."

She didn't respond, her thoughts too caught up in what he was saying. In the end it became too much. A world of starving children was beyond her ability to help. The best she could do was care for the crofters who relied on her, and that alone took up the better part of her time. Everyone thought that the men cared for the people who tilled their land, but it was the women who watched the children and helped the ill. Few understood how much work went into women's days.

And it was the responsibility of the lady of the manor to be sure that it all got done, or so she had been taught. But then perhaps here was a man who did know, who did understand the labors of women.

"We were speaking of you," she prompted. "Of the rags and the washing."

"In time, I had gathered and washed enough material. Fortunately for me, Zhi Min's mother made sure the rags were clean."

"What would have happened if they were not?" she asked, thinking of beatings or other fearsome reprisals.

"It would have been a disgusting, smelly mess when I began to sew. A worse disaster than what I already had."

"Had you ever even seen a needle and thread? Did you know the basics of what to do?"

He shook his head. "Not a thing. But I learned between cuffs to the head."

"No!" She knew it was ridiculous, but she couldn't shake her shock that anyone would dare cuff an earl or the son of an earl. But of course, no one in China would care who Jie Ke's parents were.

"She never hit hard and it certainly was no more than I deserved. I had a foul mouth on me then, and Wen Xia was not a woman to accept disrespect calmly."

"This is the laundry woman? Zhi Min's mother?"

He nodded, and his gaze grew abstract with a tender smile.

"You care for her," she said.

He grinned. "She was more of a mother to me than my own. But in truth, she was mother to all the orphan boys at the temple. I was simply more stubborn than the others, so I required more of her attention."

"I cannot imagine what you must have lived through."

He stopped, turning to face her completely, his expression sober and terrible. "Do you not understand? It is not what I faced at the temple that was so terrible. It is that I had been raised so ignorant in the first place."

She frowned. "But you were an earl's son. Of course you wouldn't be expected to know how to sew or boil clothing."

"Do your crofters' boys know such things?"

She nodded. "Of course. They all have their tasks, but every child helps as they can."

"And why was I spared these basic skills in life? Because I had a title? It did not help me survive. I was woefully unprepared, and too stupid to see that a name—Earl of Warhaven—did not make me any more or less worthy than anyone else. I was simply luckier."

She had no response except fascination. She had never heard anyone speak as he did. So she guided him to a bench in the garden near the house. He set the lantern on a sundial, and in the flickering light, his yellow robes seemed to glow.

"What happened then?" she asked.

He leaned back against the bench and laughed. "I sewed the most horrible, misshapen, threadbare, saddest-looking robe ever. Only to discover that I had been making my own clothing."

She blinked. "You didn't know they were to be your own robes?"

"The abbot hadn't told me, though if I had paid attention, if I had spoken to the other boys, I would have guessed. But I was too arrogant to speak to orphans, and too poor at the language to eavesdrop."

"So you made a terrible robe. Did you wear it?"

"Not at first. But my English clothing was in rags as well. One night Zhi Min stole them and told me he'd burned them. Oh, I was angrier at that moment than I'd ever been in my entire life. He'd been my only friend at the temple, and I called him horrible names. Thank God he was a better fighter or I might have killed him." He shook his head, his eyes focused on his memory. "I thought he had taken away my whole life."

"Of course you did! Those clothes were your last tie to England."

He shook his head. "That is what I thought, too. But they were only clothes, Evie. And I was no longer English."

"To yearn for the past, to plan for the future . . ." she said, remembering his words. "But you were just a boy very far away from home. I am surprised you didn't walk around naked."

"I thought about it. Truly, I intended to. But do you know what? I had made those robes with my own hands. I climbed through garbage piles and sweated over boiling water for them. I pricked my fingers a thousand times as I stitched and restitched that thing together. Then I sweated again as I dyed them."

She heard the pride in his voice and knew it was honest.

"I wore those robes with my head held high. It was the first thing I had ever done on my own, from beginning to end without servants, completely on my own. Except for the instruction, that is."

"What an amazing story," she breathed.

He looked at her a long moment, and it was as if all the joy leached from his face. "It's not a story, Evie," he said softly. "It happened."

She blinked. She had not meant to imply that the tale was a lie. Merely that it was almost too fantastical for her to comprehend. Like a tale from the colonies of Indians with face paint. Or of Australia and long wood tubes that played music. "I did not mean to imply differently," she said softly.

"I changed, Evelyn. I am not that arrogant little boy anymore."

"Of course not."

"I would not be here at all except it is the only way to

become a full monk. If the abbot had not set me to this last ridiculous task—"

"You would never have returned to England? Never?"

"Never." Then he pushed up from the bench and read-justed his clothes so that they fell smoothly from shoulder to ground. "I learned the lesson of my robe very well. All the abbot's tasks have a purpose. I may not understand at first. Those purposes may be difficult—some are perhaps more terrible than I could possibly imagine—but I know that I have to try to fulfill them. And that one day I will under-stand."

She stood, rising up to face him though she was uncertain how to stem the anger she felt rolling off him. She thought perhaps that here was that lost boy again, that maybe Jie Ke had not quite buried Jacob as much as he believed.

"I did not mean to upset you," she said.

He was silent a long moment. She heard his respiration at first harsh and angry through his nose. But then his breaths lengthened, growing softer and more controlled. He was tucking away his fury, compressing it into a tiny part of his heart and then closing the door. His anger did not control his actions, she realized, but it also wasn't truly gone.

"Jie Ke," she said. She had only his name. She tried to touch him. She lifted her hand and extended it toward him, but he remained too aloof for her to reach. She let her hand fall back to her side.

"Your sister will be waiting for you. I can escort you in-side."

She nodded because she had no words. They fell into step beside one another. Within moments they had entered the house and mounted the stairs. A light shone beneath her bed-room door, and she knew that Maddie waited there for her.

Back now in the close atmosphere of the house, Evelyn's thoughts turned more toward propriety and convention. Without her willing the change, she became excruciatingly aware of how improper his presence was in her wing of the manor. So she stopped at the top of the stairs.

"Thank you," she whispered. "Thank you for . . ." How to finish that sentence? "For sharing this evening with me."

He pressed his right fist against his open left palm and bowed to her in the way of his fellow monks. She hesitated, but then gave him a quick curtsy in return. It seemed the only thing to do. Then she reluctantly turned and headed toward her room.

He waited without moving as she stepped through pools of light cast by the candles in the hall. She didn't hear another sound until she placed her hand on her door.

"I never wanted to come back here, Evie," he whispered. "I'm so sorry for all the problems I have brought you. I will leave as soon as I can."

It was like a slap across the face, a repudiation of all that she had lived and breathed for her entire life. Even understanding what he meant—even knowing that he had found a life in China and had no wish to leave it—it was still a horrible insult.

She spun around, meaning to tell him that she had no wish for him to be here either. That everything had been perfect before he walked down the aisle at her wedding. And why didn't he just leave now, if England was such a trial? But by the time she had formed the words, there was no one behind her at whom to throw them. He was gone, and that made her feel even worse.

Chapter Eleven

Jie Ke did not appear for his normal morning sparring. Evelyn didn't care. She was too busy sorting out her emotions from the previous night to want to face him again so soon. Except his grandmother had obviously been hoping to see him, and the elderly woman's disappointment exuded a quiet grayness that echoed through all the guests. If nothing else, the Chinamen certainly added color—and fodder for gossip—to all their lives. At least half her guests had risen early to watch.

Evelyn was staring morosely down at her morning tea when Christopher joined her at the table. She gave him a polite smile, saw that he had adequate food to break his fast, and then returned to idly stirring cream into her tepid tea. Then he spoke in an undertone audible only to her.

"I think I have discovered what our mysterious Chinamen do on their wanderings."

She counted it a success that she did not spill her tea. "Truly?" she asked sotto voce. Or at least she tried. Her voice came out high and strained, and Lord Greenfield lifted his head to look directly at her.

Christopher pushed up from his breakfast. "I believe I shall go for a walk," he said to the table at large. "If you will please excuse me." Then, with a dashing kiss on the back of her hand, he bowed and left.

She smiled blandly at the other four people in the room, all eying her curiously. She prayed that they could not see how her heart beat painfully in her throat. Then, when she judged it an appropriate amount of time, she pushed aside food that she'd barely touched. "If you will all excuse me, I have to meet with Cook about the menu." With a nod, she made her escape through the kitchen.

Fortunately, she'd already done the meal planning for the day. Not quite so fortunate, Cook's assistant—another huge gossip—waylaid her. "Begging your pardon, miss. I didn't want to bother you as such a time. . . ." The woman's round face beamed hopefully up at her.

"Of course, Gladys, is there something I need to know?" Gladys was a robust woman with a sister and a score of nieces and nephews who were all in service to one house or another. She was a shrewd buyer of market goods, and better yet, knew all the servants' gossip this side of London. She was an invaluable asset to Evelyn, and not a woman to ignore.

"Aye, miss. It's Ben Brown. He cut himself real bad yesterday. Gashed his palm all the way up his arm. Nan is beside herself with worry."

"Has a doctor been called?"

"Yes, miss. I already sent for the surgeon in your name. I knew you'd want it."

"Excellent work. Thank you." As she tried to edge past the woman, Gladys slipped sideways to block her. "Was there more?"

"Well, miss, like I said. Nan's beside herself with worry, what with the baby coming an' all."

"Do you think a basket is in order?"

"Actually, miss, I was thinking of a basket and money for a cradle. Ben . . . well, he hurt himself while he was trying to make one. There ain't no way he could do it now. Not in time."

Evelyn mentally calculated the kitchen money. They had set aside extra for the wedding guests. "Has all of the food been purchased for tomorrow night?"

Gladys shook her head. "No, miss, I was going to market this afternoon."

"Fine. Take some of that and . . ." She grimaced and pulled out the purse that she always carried in case Gladys found her. She counted out coins. "Here. That should be enough to pay Mr. Daniels for a proper cradle. Tell them it is my gift to the new baby."

Gladys beamed. "Oh thank ye, miss. I know they'll be right grateful." But when Evelyn tried to move, the woman remained solidly in her way.

"Was there more?" she asked, wondering just how long Christopher would wait. And worse, exactly what he would say once she got there.

"Aye, miss. Ben won't be able to work for a few weeks at least. An' with the surgeon's bill . . ."

"Oh yes," she said with a sigh. She'd forgotten that part of the story. "Yes, well, you can tell Ben and Nan that I'll take care of that. Will you arrange that with the good doctor?"

Gladys beamed even brighter, dropping another curtsy before stepping aside.

Evelyn didn't waste any time as she rushed outside. She found Christopher quickly, thank Heaven. He was pacing in the near garden right by the sundial. She paused a moment, flashing on last night and the way an entirely different man had stood there with her. Oh, her life was becoming excruciatingly complicated. Here she was with Christopher by day and Jie Ke by night. This could not continue. But she couldn't focus on that right now.

She rushed over to his side. "I am so sorry. Gladys stopped me."

He frowned. "Someone hurt?"

She smiled. Of course Christopher would instantly understand Glady's function in the household. "Ben Brown cut himself making a cradle for the baby. I've sent over a basket and . . . things."

"Excellent," he said, his attention already back on his own matters. "So it's taken care of."

Well, no it wasn't. She still needed to visit to make sure both the man and the cradle were coming along as they ought. And the entire family would need more support with the husband out of work. But that was a care for another day. Today's problem was something else entirely.

"Come take a turn with me," Chris suggested.

She took his arm and they began a companionable stroll. The ease with which she slipped into stride with him was both reassuring and disturbing. Easy camaraderie was wonderful. But she'd also noticed that during their whole exchange, he never once looked directly at her. Or perhaps he had, but he never truly saw her. Certainly not in that direct, focused way that Jie Ke—

"Have you noticed how those monks disappear for long stretches of time?" he abruptly asked. "I mean, they don't spend much time among the guests, do they?"

"I rather think it is uncomfortable for them," she inserted. "Besides, aren't they praying?"

"That's what they tell us," he drawled. "And of course, you are busy managing all the guests." He glanced sideways. "You are doing wonderfully, by the way. I can't imagine this has been easy for you. No surprise that you wandered off last night."

"I just needed a moment's respite. I keep feeling like—"

"Of course you did. But don't you see? I think I've discovered the truth behind them." He grinned at her, his expression almost boyish. "I've been following them. Spying on them, so to speak. Truly, it's been rather exciting."

She forced herself to give him a wan smile, though panic set her heart to pounding. What had he seen?

"The truth was to be found with their servant," he continued. "It always is, you know. But of course you do. You manage the servants better than anyone. A true master at it!"

he said as he once again lifted her hands to plant a warm kiss on the back of one. "So I suppose it is to you that I owe the inspiration."

She looked at him, her thoughts spinning in anxious circles. "I don't believe I have ever seen you this giddy. Christopher, what have you discovered?"

"Ah. Well, as to that . . ." He coughed and turned his head. "You understand that I am not completely certain yet. I shall know for sure this afternoon."

"Chris! You cannot mean to keep this from me!"

He turned back to her. "They are boxers, Evie! Common boxers. They have traveled throughout England earning money by fighting."

She nodded, but she couldn't quite understand his glee. "Well, I suppose that explains why they had so much money. But I don't see how that solves our problem."

"Ah, but that is because you are not a man!" He turned, walking backwards as he spoke so that he could face her directly. "These men, these boxers, gain a reputation, and then the money dries up."

She frowned. "I'm sorry?"

"Well, if you are known for never losing, then who will be against you? No one! The big money comes from being a nobody and winning. Everyone bets against you. Then when you win, you can collect a king's ransom. But only if no one knows who you are." He spoke so rapidly that she had trouble following. "Especially if you are good, but not great. I mean, the great will go on to make history and the real money in London. The merely good must find other ways to survive."

"I suppose that makes sense. But how does that help us?"

He stopped walking to clasp both her hands together between his. He was so giddy that she couldn't help but smile. She didn't think she had ever seen him this excited about anything—their marriage included.

"Don't you see?" he asked. "Our Jie Ke is nothing more

than a common boxer who had to reinvent himself. But fighting styles are like a signature. They can be traced. I will bet that a little digging will reveal our Jie Ke has been around England and Europe all his life making money from fighting." He leaned forward. "That means he is not Jacob. He never was!"

Evelyn nodded, but her smile was strained. "How soon will you know? How soon will you have proof?"

He grinned. "That is the greatest laugh of all! This afternoon, Evie! There is a fight this very afternoon."

"I had forgotten that," she said with a frown. Of course she'd known there would be a fight. One could hardly miss the local talk about it, though such a thing was generally not for her ears. In fact, she believed it had been planned specifically for after her wedding so that the men could enjoy themselves a bit while the women gossiped. This was the way things went in the country.

Meanwhile, Christopher guided her to sit at a stone bench. "I have a friend who is mad for boxing," he said. "Never misses a fight. Even went to them all across the Continent during his grand tour. If anyone would recognize the man, it would be he."

"And he will be here this afternoon?"

"I can't imagine he would miss a fight this close to London." He leaned forward and dropped his forehead against hers. "Never you worry, Evie. We will have this monk exposed by evening, and then everything can return to normal."

It was a good thing that Evie was looking down, because she couldn't bring herself to grin. For the first time in her life, her normal, everyday life didn't seem so exciting. She told herself that she was being ridiculous. Of course she wanted all this confusion to end as quickly as possible. Finding out certainly that Jie Ke was a liar would accomplish that. But she couldn't bring herself to believe it.

"Are you sure?" she said as she pulled away from her fiancé. "I mean, he doesn't seem like a liar. The stories he tells seem so real."

Christopher's eyes brightened. "So, you have been talking to him? You have been ferreting out his Chinese make-believe?"

She looked at her fiancé. She stared into his green eyes and saw a lifelong friend before her. He was a good man who deserved to know the truth about the woman he was marrying. And so she formed the words that would confess her sins. She would tell him everything she had done with Jie Ke and pray that he could forgive her. "I've spoken with him several times, Chris—"

"But it doesn't really matter, does it?" he interrupted. "I mean, how would you know if he lied to you?" he returned. "A man who is well traveled could easily make up stories about China. Certainly if he had a good imagination and a gift for pretending. You wouldn't really know the truth, would you?"

She swallowed her words of explanation. He was too giddy right now to listen.

"Don't worry, my dear," he said as he caressed her cheek. "I will sort this all out and then we can be married just as we planned."

She smiled because that was clearly what he wanted. But she couldn't keep completely quiet. "What do you see in our future, Chris?"

"What?"

"What do you think our lives will be like?"

"Well, exactly how they ought to be!" He frowned, obviously not understanding her question. When she didn't reply, he squatted down before her, his gaze, full and troubled, on her face. "You are truly upset, aren't you? You manage so well—the house, the crofters, and the guests—I forget that this must be a horrible strain on you."

"I . . . yes, I suppose." This wasn't what she wanted to talk about. "I have been acting so unlike myself lately. I went out last night."

"Yes, I know. But that is really not so unlike you. You have always mucked about in thunderstorms and the like. I sometimes think you would prefer the Irish moors—all that dark, spooky wind . . ." He smiled and tweaked her cheek. "I think of it as your charming eccentricity."

She did not like the direction this conversation had taken. Did he not understand that she had done more than just walk? Of course he couldn't know that, perhaps must never know that, but this was Christopher, the man she was to marry. She would bear his children! Could she really keep such secrets from him?

"I am wandering with no purpose," she said. "There is no future in what I do, and yet I cannot stop myself."

He laughed, the sound carefree and rather condescending. "But, my dear, that is the point of wandering, isn't it? As I said, it is your eccentricity. All the best countesses have one, you know. Much better in my book than a predilection for dogs. So long as you keep to the near grounds, I shall know you are safe. And, of course, don't teach it to the children. The boys will wander because that is what boys do. But we can't have the girls haring off. Who knows where they might get to?"

He waggled his eyebrows at her. He was making a joke of sorts, and at one time she would have laughed. Girls, after all, couldn't be trusted to know their own minds. And hadn't her nighttime exploits proved exactly that? She could not be trusted beyond supervision.

"So that is what you see?" she pressed. "Marriage. Children. And I shall be doing, well, exactly what I have been doing all my life," she realized with shock.

"Well, of course, except there will be more of it. More property to supervise means more peasants to watch. Eventually

I shall take my seat in the House of Lords, and you will have our children. I understand that takes up a great deal of time, even with a nanny."

She watched his expression closely. Was he teasing her? Did he truly have no idea how much time it took to raise a child? Even with a nanny?

"Chris, do you know how to sew?"

He drew back slightly in disgust. "I beg your pardon?"

"Do you know how to use needle and thread? I mean, if you needed to, would you be able to sew something?"

"Of course I know how to sew!" he said, humor dancing in his eyes.

"You do?"

"Why, yes! You bring your purse to the tailor and tell him what you want!" Then he laughed fully and heartily at his own joke. When she didn't join him, he slowly sobered. "Why is this important? Why ever would I need to know such a thing?"

She shook her head, then pressed her hands to her heated cheeks. "Oh, I am being silly, aren't I?" She released a laugh that was too high-pitched to be natural, but he didn't notice. "Truthfully, I could not do a neat stitch if my life depended upon it. We are completely dependent upon our servants, aren't we?"

Why had that thought never rankled before? It certainly bothered her now. It made her want to run upstairs and immediately practice darning. Except, of course, such a thing was ridiculous. She had plenty to do without adding darning.

"Don't worry, my dear," Christopher said fondly. He held out his arm and she obediently rose to take it. "I shall have it all worked out this afternoon."

"The fight, yes. Christopher . . ." Her voice trailed away on a hopeful note. He was in such a happy mood, perhaps he would be indulgent.

"Yes?"

"I should very much like to go to this fight."

He didn't even hitch in his step. "I wondered when that would come up."

"Well, it is my life as much as it is yours. I should like to be there when we are set back on track."

"Mm-hm."

She turned, hope sparkling in her eyes. "Does that mean you will take me?"

"No, my dear, it does not." He smiled at her, but she was not fooled. There was a core of strength behind his eyes. She did not see it often, but she would have been a fool not to recognize it when it was there. "Fights are not so tame a thing as you imagine. The very worst element gathers for such events."

"But you will be there. And your friend."

"It is not a place for a countess."

"I am not a countess yet!"

"Neither are you going." He patted her hand. "I swear I shall tell you all about it when I return."

"No, Christopher." She didn't know why she was being so stubborn. Usually the argument would have ended long before this point. She knew he would not change his mind; she could read it in his body language and the tone of his voice. And yet, she could not stop herself. "I wish to go," she said firmly. "I will go in disguise if I must, but I will be there."

He laughed. Truly, he laughed with full good humor. "No, my dear, that will not fadge. I know you. You have too much sense to go without a chaperone, and I will not take you, no matter how much you beg."

She stopped, suddenly pulling her arm away from his, and planted her hands on her hips. "Christopher, I am not teasing. I intend to go."

He frowned, his eyes growing stormy. "Evie, I do not know what has gotten into you. It is this whole monk nonsense, I know, but do not give me reason to doubt your sense. You are to be a countess and must—"

"And must at all times act as such. I know! I was raised from the cradle on such words. But what if I want to choose how a countess acts? What if I want . . . I don't know . . . to go to the rookeries and help impoverished children?"

"Whatever are you talking about? Where did you hear of the rookeries?"

She threw her hands up in the air. "Does it matter where I learned of them? I learned. And I know. You called me the smartest girl you knew. What if I want to travel to all those places I have read about? To the colonies, maybe, to see an Indian?"

"They just had a war over there!" he snapped.

"Fine, then what about Africa? Or China?"

"Now you sound like my uncle! Haring off to God knows where and getting himself killed. Really, Evie, I had not thought you so irresponsible."

And right there was the death knell of her argument. The moment Uncle Reginald's name was invoked, the word *irresponsible* reared its ugly head and all was lost to the holy altar of what one ought to do. "Chris," she whispered, "can you not understand? I merely want more from my life."

"More?" he scoffed. "More than children? More than becoming a countess? My goodness, one would think that would be enough for any woman!"

She swallowed. Put like that, she did sound ungrateful and horribly greedy. "How much land does the earldom hold?"

"A great deal. All told, there will be five times the land to supervise now."

Five times the numbers of crofters. Five times the Ben and Nan Browns. Five times the baskets to make, cradles to order, and surgeons to pay.

"And don't forget the children," he reminded her.

Ah yes. Five times the number of babies too, plus her own. "I will have no time to travel, will I? We won't ever go anywhere but London and here and the family seat." She didn't know where this sudden urge came from, but it reared up so abruptly that she almost thought it belonged to a different person, a different Evelyn altogether.

"Well," he said slowly, his face lifting into a sly smile. "I suppose there will be time for a party or two." He winked at her. "Or many more. After all, a new countess must be celebrated."

"But I won't be a countess yet."

"A future countess, then. A grand ball, I should think, in the London town house." He lifted her hand and set it on his arm. Then he began walking them toward the house. "That should keep you busy, I should think."

"I don't need more things to do!" she snapped. "I need . . ." What *did* she need? "I need different things to do."

He laughed. "Ah, now I see what the problem is. You are feeling your oats."

She pulled back, a little startled that he would compare her to a horse. "Christopher—"

"Hear me out. The horses—usually the young ones, but sometimes the older ones too—have a moment when they cannot wait to begin the day. They have eaten their food and feel strong and powerful. It's quite a fun time, actually. They prance around and act extremely foolish and are said to be feeling their oats."

"I know the expression," she said dryly.

"You are offended, my dear. My apologies, but hear me out. You see, you just have to let them dance for a bit, maybe ride them hard for a time, and eventually they settle down and become excellent goers."

She sighed, wondering if perhaps there was some merit in what he said, much though it hurt her pride to admit it. "You think I am merely anxious to begin my . . . our future and am—"

"Fighting the bit, so to speak."

Evelyn grimaced. "Well, if that is true and I will settle

down in a bit, then there is nothing wrong with letting me, er, dance now, right?" She stopped to challenge him directly. "Take me to the fight, Chris. I shall obey your dictates completely, but I simply must see this fight."

He smiled and chucked her under the chin. "Ah, but you see, it is the stable master's job during these times to watch the filly in question—to let her dance in a safe place and not hurt herself."

Her shoulders dropped and she glared at him. "I am not a horse, Chris. And I am not helpless." She lifted her chin. "I will go to that fight."

He smiled, then suddenly leaned forward to plant a swift kiss on her lips. "No, my dear, you will not."

She would have argued more, but she could see the steel in his eyes. He would not budge on this no matter how much she pleaded. In short, he acted exactly as she had known he would from the very beginning.

She was not going to that fight.

She was going to that fight.

The determination did not take long to surface. The same undeniable drive that pushed her outdoors last night became overwhelming within moments of being away from Christopher. She wasn't sure what was happening to her. She'd had a lifetime of ingrained proper behavior that included following Christopher's dictates. After all, he was older, male, and her future husband. Furthermore, his orders usually made sense. Therefore, she had been following his direction—or his mother's—since the very beginning.

Until now.

Now she was calmly, methodically setting up a disguise so that she could go safely to the fight. It turned out to be relatively easy. Even discounting her brother's vast wardrobe, she had men's clothing for emergencies, for times when she had traveled to one crofter's hut or another's in the dead of night.

At those times, it was best to dress in pants and ride astride. At those times, she pinned her hair up beneath a cap, darkened her face, and wore a heavy greatcoat. It worked beautifully so long as no one looked too closely at her face.

The next problem was finding the fight itself. There were miles of possibilities for such an event, and she really hadn't the foggiest idea where it might be. After all, she was supposed to be on her honeymoon. She hadn't cared what the men did while she was away. Fortunately, she knew just the woman to ask.

Evelyn wandered into the kitchen, found Gladys within moments and inquired about her brother and what the man was doing this afternoon. The whole story came tumbling out, location and all. And how funny that it was a place quite well known to her: the large grassy area behind the smithy. Horse fairs were sometimes held there, as well as the yearly county fair. They even had stands: crude planks built up in a dozen rows for people to sit upon. According to Gladys, the men had a raised square platform and put rope around the edges. The fighters would fight, the men would bet, and a great bloody time would be had by all. She and Gladys shared a womanly moment of disgust at men's need for blood sport, then it was over. Evelyn commented that she intended to go riding for a bit and disappeared to her room to change.

Planning stage complete.

Slipping down the back stairs was tricky but not impossible. The stable was harder, but all the hands were used to her odd behavior. She grabbed the youngest stableman and paid him a penny to distract everyone else. When she added that she was off to see Ben Brown about his poor hand, all was accomplished. She managed her own tack and saddle, then rode off within minutes.

Execution of plan complete.

It wasn't until she arrived on the outskirts of the fight area that she realized there might be a problem. First of all, it was day. That made it a lot harder to disguise her identity in the full afternoon sunlight. Second, there were a lot of people at these fights. A *lot* of people. Carriages and horses crowed together for half a mile at least. And that was nothing compared to the area nearest the ring. The crush of people was quite daunting.

But having begun on this mad course, she was determined to see it through. Her only hope of getting close to the action was to tether her horse and wander forward on foot. Within moments, she would be within spitting distance of dozens of people who would recognize her. A few minutes later, she would be shoulder to shoulder with some of them, even as-suming she did not try to venture up into the hastily con-structed stands—which hardly bode well for anonymity. On the other hand, everyone was looking at the raised platform. No one would expect to see a woman—much less Evie herself—wearing a young man's attire and attending a fight. People tended to see only what they expected. At least she prayed that was true.

With one last pat for her poor abandoned horse—more for her own encouragement than his—she pulled her cap farther down over her face and began a casual walk forward into the crowd.

Chapter Twelve

It ended up being easier than she expected. Everyone was busy doing things—either discussing the fights with their friends, counting money, or pointing at a spot at the side of the ring. She didn't think they noticed her at all. They also didn't let her through as was normal, either.

She hadn't realized that people just naturally gave her space when she walked—she being Miss Evelyn Stanton. But now she was nobody, and no one gave her the least bit of breathing room. She was hedged in on all sides, assaulted with smells that were better left in the stables or worse, and buffeted on all sides. It was unnerving, especially since she couldn't push her way through with her usual future-countess stare.

Then she heard him. She wasn't sure why Christopher's voice would carry so distinctly to her ears. Perhaps it was simply the fact that it was familiar, but she saw and heard his cultured tones and then, a moment later, spotted him about midway up the stands.

He wore casual clothes, for him. Always neat, always perfect, his dark pants and tight-fitting jacket silently proclaimed him better than much of the crowd. He sat next to another man—a Corinthian by the cut of his clothes and slightly bulldog-aggressive look to his face. There were others around the pair—young bucks, older men, all obviously moneyed.

She recognized many of the men from her trips to London, and knew, in fact, that some of them actively despised one other; yet the entire group congregated together. They occupied the center section of the near stand, speaking in their cultured tones and relegating all the others to the periphery.

She moved in the opposite direction. The last thing she needed was for one of them to recognize her, but that put her even more among the poor and dirty. She felt a little guilty for her thoughts. After all, not everyone had the luxury of a full staff that could draw bathwater whenever it was wanted. And she began to understand some of the choices Jie Ke had faced his first years at temple. What a decision: to live as an indentured servant on a trip across the world or in a temple with food and water and an entirely different way of life. Such a choice for a little boy to make! Assuming, of course, that everything Jie Ke had told her was true.

And with that thought, she finally spotted him. His saffron robes shouldn't have been hard to see, but he was surrounded on all sides. Now that she pushed up on her toes, she could see a bit more. It looked like Zhi Min was there, too, as well as their servant boy.

She tried to edge nearer, but couldn't get far. There appeared to be a furious amount of betting going on by the ring. And then a bell rang out. Someone leapt into the center ring—was that the butcher from the village a little ways north?—and said a bunch of words to much cheering and jeering, none of which Evelyn understood.

What she saw instead was Jie Ke, stripping off his robe and his underrobe until all he wore was a kind of faded yellow diaper. She had seen him so dressed before, on that first morning when he and Zhi Min sparred. The crowd, of course, had never seen this, and the jeers quickly became deafening.

Evelyn shook her head. Didn't they know? Couldn't they see that there was unimaginable power beneath that smooth skin? That he was lightning fast and amazingly flexible? Of course not. All these people saw was that he wore a faded yellow diaper and bowed in the reverent way of a monk. Or an idiot. After all, what holy man stepped into a boxing ring while hundreds of men bet on the outcome? What could possibly be religious about that?

Then another man stepped into the ring. Oh sweet Heaven, he was huge! It was the blacksmith from the same village as the butcher. From the response of the crowd, he was clearly a local favorite. He was dressed the way she would expect: open breeches cut short to mid thigh, no shirt, and light shoes. And he looked like he could crush Jie Ke between his two massive fists.

She struggled to remember the rules of this event. She'd never really cared to know, but her brothers enjoyed these fights. What had they said? She rapidly reviewed everything she could remember and came to a single horrifying conclusion: there were no rules. The two men fought however they wanted—hands, feet, head—as long as they were without weapons. They fought until one could not get up again.

She looked again at Jie Ke's opponent. He was huge! Would he kill Jie Ke? Would Jie Ke be forced to kill him? The very idea was barbaric! And then it began.

Without preamble, the butcher stepped away from the ring. Jie Ke bowed in his usual manner, fist in open palm, a slight bend at the waist. The blacksmith arched a brow, playing to the crowd, then turned to face Jie Ke.

Everyone—the people in the stands, the bettors up close, even Evelyn—collectively drew a breath. She desperately wanted to look to Zhi Min, to see what he thought of the coming disaster. Did he know that his friend was about to die? One look at the crowd told her they would accept no less than blood. Probably a lot of blood! But she couldn't tear her eyes away from Jie Ke standing there so calm. His eyes weren't even fully open. Was the man falling asleep? Didn't he—

The blacksmith lunged, his massive fists descending like two hammers. She didn't even see Jie Ke move. He swerved around the fists somehow, then spun around and kicked the blacksmith once beneath the arm, then again in the face. The huge man's breath went out of him with a burst of spittle, then he spun and dropped. He hadn't even landed one of his fists.

The whole thing was over that fast, and was shocking. The crowd went dead silent as everyone waited for the blacksmith to move. Jie Ke took a step back, repeated his characteristic bow, then retreated to the side to wait in absolute stillness. Still the blacksmith didn't move.

Was the man dead? Everyone strained forward, anxious to know. Did his chest tremble? Was he breathing? Yes. Small movement at first, then larger, fuller. He released a groan. The crowd roared in approval. Evelyn felt almost bowled over by the roll of sound urging the man to stand up and fight again. Many hands reached through the rope to help him sit up. He wobbled drunkenly, shook his head to clear it, then blinked at Jie Ke.

"Git up! Git up!" screamed a hundred voices.

The blacksmith tried. He pushed unsteadily to his feet. The crowd roared their encouragement. Evelyn winced, feeling sorry for the man. He was clearly no match for Jie Ke, and yet he didn't want to let down his fans.

The blacksmith tightened his hands into fists again, and the crowd began howling with glee, but Jie Ke didn't move. Evelyn was watching him closely, wishing she were in a better position to see his face. All she could see was a leashed potential in his beautifully sculpted body, and a silent question to the blacksmith as to whether they would fight again.

The smith took a deep breath, his chest expanding to huge proportions, and he lunged. Jie Ke didn't fight back, he simply sidestepped. Even Evelyn could see he had many opportunities to strike the blacksmith, but he didn't. He simply avoided the man's blows again and again.

The crowd began growling in fury. At first she didn't understand why. Then she began focusing on the words. "Hit him! Hit him! Knock him down!"

She thought they were encouraging the blacksmith to strike Jie Ke down. Many of them were. But it soon became clear that the blacksmith would never lay a finger on Jie Ke, so the crowd was demanding his blood. Anyone's blood would satisfy—if it couldn't be the monk's, then make it the blacksmith's.

The very thought sickened Evelyn, but she couldn't deny the excitement the crowd generated. There was a power in the collective demand of so many people. She began to share their frustration when pass after pass from the blacksmith brought no resolution.

In the end, the big man chose to finish it. After one last futile attempt to grab Jie Ke, he simply stood and faced his opponent, giving him an awkward bow of his own. Jie Ke returned it with reverence and, Evelyn thought, a kind of respect.

The crowd was having none of it. The blacksmith retired from the ring amidst the most vehement sneers and insults that Evelyn had ever heard. No wonder females did not generally attend these things. A proper lady would be blushing for at least a month!

Of course, now that she looked, there were indeed a few women. None of them were aristocrats, and many were screaming viler insults than the men. Just the sight of them sent Evelyn into a bit of a quandary. Was she becoming one of those women, those foulmouthed harridans screeching imprecations at the blacksmith's manhood?

Of course not, she told herself. Then again, she was again beginning to feel the excitement that ran through the crowd, for the next man stepped into the ring.

Now that she knew Jie Ke would not be killed, she felt a tingling thrill at seeing his sleek body facing off against a thicker, more muscled man. Jie Ke would surely win, and she loved being here to see it.

She was right: he did win. Every match. Two hours later, Jie Ke was still in the ring fighting. He'd beaten every comer with relative ease, though as time went on, Jie Ke began to show signs of exhaustion. His punches were slower, his kicks less high. He worked as efficiently as possible, ending fights in amazingly short time, but his opponents were also getting better.

And worse, the mood of the crowd was getting ugly. As the locals lost more and more money, their curses became more vicious, their fury all the more bloodthirsty. How long could Jie Ke keep this up before the crowd lost control?

Without even realizing it, she pushed forward until she was nearly on top of the ring. Her cap had been restricting her view, so she tilted it back, confident now that no one would recognize her. After all, everyone was watching the ring.

It never once occurred to her that Jie Ke would look out and see her. She never once thought that he would stop in the middle of a fight, his body obviously jerking in surprise as he stared right at her. And in that moment of frozen shock, when their gazes locked and held, the very first opponent of the afternoon managed to connect.

Wham! It was a blow to his face, and Evelyn cried out in alarm.

The crowd drowned her out. Finally, someone had drawn blood from the saffron-robed interloper! And as Jie Ke struggled to his feet, blood dripping from his mouth, Evelyn realized that everything up to this point had been just child's play. Now the bloodletting would really begin.

She could not be here. That was Jie Ke's only thought before the anvil-fisted butcher or shepherd or carpenter or whomever he was fighting took him completely unaware. The blow caught him high on the cheekbone, snapped his head around, and threw him into the ropes.

If he were back at the temple, the monks would be roaring

with laughter and his instructor would be shaking his head muttering about white devils who could not keep one thought in their heads. Jie Ke *had* one thought in his head. Unfortunately, it didn't have anything to do with fighting. It was all about Evelyn standing there for all the world to see.

What was she wearing? That dirt on her face wouldn't fool anyone! Even absent so long from England, he knew that women of her sort were not supposed to be here. And given that this particular day of fighting was looking to end up—

Another blow across the face reminded him to return to the here and now. His head bounced painfully against the ground, but not so hard that he lost consciousness. In truth, this was the moment in every fight that he both awaited and feared: that breath when pain and adrenaline combined with raw power. When all his world shrank down to the fight, and he released all practice, all thoughts, to simply become Fighter.

It was not what they taught at the temple. It was not what monks were supposed to do, but Jie Ke did it anyway; he stepped from calm restraint into sublime violence. He let all his fury and his hatred boil up through his body. Assuming he kept one part of his mind rational, he could stop himself from killing. That was the plan, and part of Jie Ke relished the knife's edge of control that existed in this place.

He lay nearly still, allowing his opponent to believe that he was whipped, but still stupidly willing to fight for bravado's sake. He rolled awkwardly to one knee and watched for glee in his opponent's eyes. It came quickly. Jie Ke blanked his mind in preparation. His eyelids even drooped as he cut out all external sights and pretended to semiconsciousness.

The man swung. Jie Ke reacted with a speed he only had in this place. He allowed the punch to connect with the top of his shoulder. There was no pain—there often wasn't in these moments, especially since his shoulder was already prepared to give way to the punch. Then he slipped beneath the man and rolled, using his feet to lift and launch the fighter head over heels into the crowd.

He had a split second to think of Evelyn. She wasn't in that part of the crowd, was she? She wouldn't be hurt, would she? Oh hell. She was, and she would be! The woman had no skill in self-preservation.

He shifted his throw, but his timing was off, his balance incorrect for what he now wanted to do. Both he and his opponent landed in a sprawling heap of tangled limbs.

This was not where Jie Ke fought best, not with legs and arms entangled. Brute strength always overcame defensive flow here. He took blow after blow on his face, on his arms. The man holding him gripped him with massive thighs, and his body weight kept Jie Ke from scrambling away. The crowd was screaming in the background, but all Jie Ke heard was her voice, her high-pitched wail. "Stop it! Stop it!"

Was she insane? Didn't she realize that if he could hear her, others would too? How would she explain her presence here? Alone and dressed like that she was completely vulnerable to any number of disasters. The danger to her reputation was the least of her problems. Theft, rape, murder—all happened from time to time at these fights. That's why ladies didn't come.

He had to end this. He had to get out of here so that he could get *her* out of here. He shifted his grip and his knee to throw the man off him. It meant that he exposed his face and jaw, but only for a moment.

He shifted, taking the hit, then tensed to throw. But then he stopped.

He couldn't win this. There were at least a dozen more men waiting to fight him. They never allowed a man to leave the ring until he had either beat all comers or lost. If he won now, then the fighting would continue on and on with the risk to Evelyn multiplying every minute. Which meant he had to lose.

The violence that boiled up inside him at the thought took

him by surprise. His rational mind struggled for control while raw hatred screamed inside him. This was why he fought! So he could destroy all opponents. So he could beat those who attacked, defend himself from all disasters, and make a pile of money while doing it. To lose on purpose would be like exposing one's throat to the bandit—on purpose! He couldn't do it.

He began to fight with blind fury. Even from his back, he could hit with frenzied speed, impacting his opponent's eyes, his nose, his jaw. Blood scented the air and dripped into his eyes, while inside his anger churned all the darker because of it. He wanted to kill!

Her voice brought him back. Her scream—high and keening. He heard it and froze. What did he do now? How did he—

His opponent slammed forward again, and a fist detonated across his temple. Hatred boiled up, but he needed control. He needed to think! He needed . . .

To save Evelyn.

He relaxed his grip, not needing to feign light-headedness. The rain of blows continued. He managed to lift his arms enough to protect his face, but that only exposed his belly.

He tensed his muscles, biting back a groan. His head was swimming with pain, and he kicked without conscious intent. The man fell sideways, momentarily winded from the blow. Now was the moment when Jie Ke would surge upwards. Now was the time when he would finish the beating, finish his opponent. His body screamed with the need to kill this man who had hurt him so badly.

His mind reeled. He could hear Evelyn screaming—one voice among hundreds, but he heard her nonetheless. His hands tightened into fists and his vision narrowed onto his opponent. There was blood on the man's face, blood on his fists. Whose blood? And why? Why did he fight? Why was he so angry? Questions! Questions!

He surged upwards, his control shattering under the on-slaught of pain, anger, and those damnable questions! To stay sane, he had to narrow his focus down to one thing: the bloody bastard who had hurt him. Jie Ke could end this man. He knew just how. His feet were free, his hands lightning fast. The clarity with which he could accomplish the task sparkled before him with such beauty—and it was even possible to finish the fight without killing the bastard. Possible. Even probable.

But what of Evelyn? How would he protect her?

He froze in indecision. That gave his opponent time to re-cover his breath. The bastard surged forward, murderous in-tent in his eyes.

Don't fight, he told himself. For Evelyn, take the blows, lose the fight. For Evelyn.

The force of will it took to restrain himself was more in-tense than he had ever imagined. From moment to moment, he thought he would break. With every breath, every blow, he saw ways to escape, ways to break the man's attack. But he couldn't. For Evelyn, he couldn't.

He didn't.

He lost consciousness.

He woke to the sound of Zhi Min praying over him. He heard the familiar Chinese sounds and felt his whole body re-lax. How many times had he woken just like this after losing a bout on the temple grounds? The familiar Chinese prayer reassured him that he was safe. But then other noises in-truded. English gloating, laughter, and a few jeers. He was still in England. He must have lost a fight, but to whom? And why?

The memory rushed back with a vague kind of horror. He had lost on purpose? Evelyn! Her image popped into his mind, and his eyes flew open.

"You are alive then," Zhi Min said.

"My bride-to-be," he said in Chinese. He could not risk saying her name aloud in English. "She was here, watching."

"I should have known you lost your mind over a woman," Zhi Min said, his voice tight with disapproval. "Before or after he hit you in the face a thousand and one times?"

"Before," he groused. "And during. And after. But where is she?" His face was swelling, probably to the point of being unrecognizable. But he still had eyes enough to see. There! She was moving against the crowd toward him. It reassured him a bit that her face was tight with anxiety. Good. She ought to feel worried. Unfortunately, her concern was obviously misplaced. She set it on him rather than on the fact that anyone with eyes would know who she was.

"Over there!" he said, gesturing vaguely to Zhi Min. He didn't dare risk pointing directly.

Then Jie Ke looked in the opposite direction. He had to know if anyone was staring and pointing at Evelyn. Even knowing her less than a week, Jie Ke knew how devastating it would be if the scandal were revealed. He didn't much mind the scandal in and of itself, assuming she was not in any danger, but he knew she would feel hurt by it. So he searched anxiously for signs that she'd been recognized.

No one was looking at Evelyn. Everyone was crowding around Mei Li, gathering their winnings. Damn. He'd lost all of Mei Li's money now too. She was the one who'd kept enough coinage to stake him at the fight. Zhi Min had insisted that they give up all their money to the Reverend Smythe-Jones since monks did not carry money. Well, Zhi Min got his wish. Now all three of them had nothing. He had no money to pay back his grandmother or even to leave this wretched country. Bloody hell.

His gaze traveled back to Evelyn. Why had he done something so stupid for her? Was Mei Li's survival less important than Evelyn's? Was his grandmother's money less important than Evelyn's reputation? And was it all for naught if she didn't leave? Didn't she see that the crowd was thinning? She was risking more and more exposure! He murmured instructions to Zhi Min. His friend immediately understood.

"You there! Boy!" Zhi Min cried, pointing at Evelyn.

Her eyes widened in shock at being selected. Good! Let her be frightened by the risk she took.

"Do you have a horse?" Zhi Min demanded.

Evelyn didn't speak. Smart girl. She simply nodded and pointed behind her.

"Get it!" ordered Zhi Min. "He cannot move by himself." A lie, but a good one. Then Zhi Min paused as if reconsidering. "Better yet, we will walk to it with you. I think we can manage."

Damn right he could manage. Jie Ke pushed to his feet—or he tried to. Bloody hell, his ribs were on fire! Were they broken? Zhi Min gathered his arm on the other side. Jie Ke gratefully took the support and then he glanced behind them.

"You cannot leave Mei Li," he said in Chinese. Zhi Min had to stay and protect his sister.

His friend shrugged and answered, "You cannot defend this white woman by yourself. And you are certainly in no condition to fight if someone decides to punch you in revenge."

Jie Ke straightened, though it produced an eon of searing agony. When he could breathe, he pushed Zhi Min away. "I am stronger than you think," he lied. "I can certainly protect one stupid bride-to-be."

Zhi Min snorted in disbelief, but Jie Ke did not give him a chance to voice any more objections.

"Besides, they have all our money. They are happy and couldn't care less about me."

"Not the ones who left early. Not the ones who already lost everything."

Jie Ke started to shrug but then thought better of it. "Then they have already left." Zhi Min began to argue, but Jie Ke held up his hand. "Peace, Zhi Min. Go watch over your sister." Then, before he fell over from the pain caused by the gesture, Evelyn arrived and slipped a shoulder under his arm.

Zhi Min hesitated, but family loyalty won out. With a curt nod, he went to stand by his sister.

"You are an idiot," Evelyn hissed into Jie Ke's ear.

"So are you," he hissed back. He gasped as she wrapped an arm around his chest. "Don't squeeze too hard."

"It would serve you right if I did," she answered. "Come on. It isn't far."

But it *was* far. With a thousand and one people looking at them the entire way. Most of them jeered, though good-naturedly, their attention thankfully centered on him and not her. "There you go, Chinaman. Ye fought well, but we got ye in the end!" Or "Not looking so proud now, are ye, foreigner?" He didn't answer except to wave them off.

Only one man—older, and relatively poor—was truly angry. He'd lost his coins early but stayed around to watch. And now, as Zhi Min had predicted, he was furious.

"Ought to have a go at ye meself," he groused. "Damn unfair, with that chopping and throwing." It was a lie. There were no rules in this English fighting ring. Any blow was allowed, whether with foot, fist, or open hand. But the man wasn't in a mood to listen to reason.

Jie Ke tensed, quickly assessing his options. The man was older but still powerful. A field laborer, by the looks of him. Jie Ke could easily avoid any of the man's punches, but he wasn't so sure he could keep Evelyn out of it. Especially as she straightened to defend him. Did the woman have no sense at all?

Jie Ke spoke up before she could. "Cain't beat an Essex man, can I?" he said loudly. "Been winning all across England, but can't beat a man from Essex."

"That's right!"

"And don'tcha forget it!" called a few of the straggling revelers.

Then a Good Samaritan clapped the angry, pinch-faced man on the shoulder. "Aw, don't be that way, Marty! Come on. I'll buy you a pint with me winnings. It's only fair, since it might be your coin I got in the first place!"

Laughter erupted, and then the group wandered off. Jie Ke released a sigh of relief as he slumped back down. He did not want to fight anymore. Ever. In his life.

Except, of course, he knew that was a lie. He would be at peace now—for a few days even—but then the anger would come back. The need to feel powerful and in control would resurface. It always did. It always *had* since his first day at the temple. Even beaten and bruised, sometimes with broken bones, Jie Ke always wanted to leap up and get back into fighting. He had trained for days on end to fight. He had breathed, slept, and eaten fighting. It was the only way to keep the questions at bay and to keep the anger from consuming him from within.

The only reason he was crippled now was because of Evelyn, because he had stopped to save her reputation. How ridiculous was that? He wasn't even married to her yet, and she was already causing him agony.

"How could you be so completely stupid?" he hissed to her as they once again started moving forward.

"I? I was not the one who was too stupid to leave the ring before I got myself killed."

Did she not understand what he had done for her? That he could have fought his way back, that he had done so dozens of times? Of course not. She did not understand such sports. "The only way out of the ring is to lose," he snapped. "Or to beat all comers. That would have taken many more hours."

She turned slightly, having to double-step as she adjusted to the uneven grass. "So you lost? Just because you were tired?"

Was there ever a stupider woman? "I lost because you did

not belong here! Do you know what happens when the crowd loses everything? When every groat is in *our* pockets?"

"But—"

"We throw coins into the air and run, Evelyn. Some pursue us, yes, and others are hurt as they dive for the coins we have thrown behind."

She blinked at him, only now beginning to understand. "But you cannot possibly—"

"If we are not fast enough or if there are too many, we have to fight. It is brutal and ugly. People come at us with picks or clubs."

"No," she whispered.

"Yes. That is why Zhi Min does not fight. So he can fight at the end of the day when I am too tired or too slow. But mostly, we run."

She abruptly straightened. "You would have gone straight back to my house? You would have brought an angry mob down on us!"

He shook his head. "We usually run to the nearest pub and buy drinks for everyone. Mei Li hides half our winnings. The rest goes into getting all as drunk as possible. Then, when they are too drunk to fight, we run fast and far." He sighed. "I had planned to keep enough to pay for my clothing."

"And now you don't even have that, do you? You don't have a single groat!" She reached out to touch his face and winced. "And you are a mess. Lord, we'll never hide what you've done. All of London will know of the fighting Chinaman earl!"

"The Dragon Earl," he murmured. "Fighters from the Xi Lin temple are called dragons."

"I doubt the gossips in London care," she said with a sniff.

Nor did he. He didn't care if his name was printed in the London broadsides. But she obviously did, and that made things complicated as well as difficult. "Let us get home first.

As I recall, a man can get into all sorts of difficulties without anyone thinking less of him. A woman, however . . ."

Her lips flattened into a long straight line, and he knew he needn't finish his sentence. Just as well, because he thought he saw her horse ahead. He would play the gallant and allow her to sit on the beast. She would likely insist he take it. Given the state of his ribs, he wasn't sure if that would be a blessing or a curse.

They were almost at the horse. The field had emptied rapidly. Behind them, the stands were already being replaced back against the smithy. Very soon no sign of the day's activity would remain. And here they were alone as, blessedly, they made it to the horse and tree. He turned and leaned back against the tree trunk, closing his eyes as he tried to steady his breath.

"How bad is it?" she whispered.

He allowed pain to wash through him and held back his whimper. "I can breathe. I can walk. If someone sees you, I can fight." He hoped that last part wasn't a lie.

"No one has noticed me at all," she returned. "Did you truly do this because . . . because . . ."

"Of you?" Should he lie to spare her feelings? He wasn't that chivalrous. "Yes, I did."

"Well, that was stupid," she snapped. "No one noticed me at all."

"That isn't quite true, Miss Stanton," came a low voice from behind them. "Not quite true at all."

Chapter Thirteen

Evelyn spun, her heart in her throat. There, blocking her escape, stood Christopher and his friend, the pug-faced man. This was the man who had spoken, but her gaze was held by Christopher's, and by his tight, dark expression.

Her fiancé's fury was not the explosive kind that his father displayed. Chris held himself tightly reined, his mind working furiously on God only knew what to remedy the situation. He was nothing if not brilliant in social situations. Even as he glared at her, he shifted his body to block her from others' view.

"Chris—" she began, not knowing exactly what she could say that would explain things.

"I had not thought you so utterly stupid," he snapped.

She bristled, spine straightening. "I told you I would come. You are only angry because I am not the person you thought I was."

"Truer words have never been spoken." He folded his arms across his chest. "You will come with me now. I will escort you home. And we will pray that no one else figures out your foolishness."

She frowned at him. "I have a horse and a way home. You are doing nothing but bringing attention to me." Then she lifted her chin and turned her back on him, her eyes going to Jie Ke as he watched their byplay with hooded eyes. "Are you well enough to mount?"

"Actually," interrupted the pug-faced man, "I have a carriage nearby. Perhaps that would be the better conveyance." When she paused, he bowed politely. "Mr. Marcus Osborne, at your service."

She smiled and barely restrained herself from a curtsy.

"Excellent idea, Marcus," Christopher interrupted. Then he glared hard at Jie Ke. "Can you walk?"

"I can walk. I can do much more than walk." Jie Ke's smile was slow in coming, and it barely concealed a wealth of unspoken menace as he pushed away from the tree.

"Er, yes, well," said Osborne. "It is this way." He gestured, his expression warming as he began to speak. "I have to say that I have never seen anyone fight as you do. That was incredible. I heard about you, you know. Have a valet who writes to his brother out in Dover. Heard tell of a fighting Chinese monk that stole everyone's money. I didn't believe him, of course, but he swore his brother wouldn't lie."

Their little group began to walk. In truth, it was the most awkward situation imaginable. Evelyn wanted to lead her horse, since it was the easiest way to put distance between herself and Christopher. If she walked behind the men she could also watch for any signs of weakness or injury from Jie Ke. Also it made everything appear just as it ought, with the "boy" relegated to minding the horse while the men talked.

But Christopher would have none of it. He grabbed the reins from her and pressed them into Marcus's reluctant grip. It wasn't as nice for the poor mare, because Marcus kept talking the whole time, speaking about fighting techniques and the like while making big gestures that jerked the horse's mouth to and fro.

Then Christopher tried to trap her between himself and the horse. It was the most protected position, of course, but she had come all this way by herself, and really didn't feel the need for him to shield her in such a way. Unfortunately, there was nothing she could do to force him away.

She had just resigned herself to this unwanted protection when Jie Ke glanced back at her. "Perhaps you would prefer to ride home alone," he said softly. "You should be safe enough."

"And what would you know of a woman's safety?" Christopher shot back. "Anything could happen to her!"

"While riding a good horse over lands I've known since I was a child?" Evelyn shot back. "Don't be ridiculous."

"You are dressed—"

"As I often dress when I wish to be anonymous."

"Do not for one moment think that this is an adequate disguise!"

Evelyn huffed, growing more furious by the second. It didn't help that she knew Christopher was right. Her disguise was hardly foolproof. But in all truth, there had been little real danger. Just social danger, and that perhaps was the root of the problem. "You believe my reputation is ruined," she said softly.

"Damn right, woman!" Christopher practically bellowed.

"Hush!" inserted Marcus, glancing around. "Really, old chap, such bickering does us no good at all."

Evelyn turned to the man, considering him for the first time. He was the man brought to expose Jie Ke for a fraud, but . . . "You have never seen anyone fight like that before, have you? You said so just a moment ago."

"Never!" he returned, slipping right back into his earlier exuberance, and turned to Jie Ke. "Except for that last fight, I thought you were unbeatable. Thought it too easy at the end, I must say. There were a few things you might have done there that could have broken the attack. Thought you would have, but you just seemed too dazed."

Jie Ke gave a wan smile. "I was too tired. I got myself caught and was just too—"

"He saw *me*," Evelyn said.

"Eh?" returned Marcus.

Christopher didn't comment, but his gaze turned diamond sharp.

"He saw me," Evelyn repeated. "Then, he purposely lost."

"You don't say!" Marcus breathed, his gaze narrowing on Jie Ke. "How peculiar."

The silence stretched awkwardly as they continued to make their way to where a row of carriages were lined up on the nearby road. One by one they were pulling off, so only a few remained. They pushed toward one of the most lavish.

"Lost all your money, then, didn't you?" inserted Marcus. "Did you have any reserve? Or did you bet it all?"

"Everything," Evelyn said while guilt ate at her. He had lost everything just to protect her.

"Will take you a while to build up betting capital, I'd expect," Marcus continued. "Unless of course you were looking for a backer, someone to sponsor you into the larger fights. That's where the real money waits."

Jie Ke lifted his chin, his voice excruciatingly dry. "I am Jacob Cato, Earl of Warhaven. I hardly think I need a backer. And I believe my parents would be appalled if they knew I was fighting in a major event."

Christopher snorted. "Didn't stop you from cutting a swath through England on your way here."

Jie Ke shrugged. "I cannot spend every moment pleasing the ancestors. Some things must be done for myself, and some for simple necessity." His gaze caught Evelyn's and held. He was trying to deliver a message to her, some unspoken meaning behind his words. But she didn't understand, and a moment later Marcus inserted himself between them.

"Right here, old chap. Do you need help to climb in?"

Jie Ke didn't answer Marcus. Instead, his gaze found hers again. "Do you join us?" he asked. "Or do you ride?"

She glanced sideways at Christopher, whose countenance appeared thunderous at the suggestion. Then she frowned. "Will you be all right?" She doubted Christopher would harm Jie Ke. He might be furious, but he certainly wasn't murderous. She hoped.

Both men answered—Christopher and Jie Ke—both taking offense. "Of course!"

She smiled, startled for a brief moment by the identical response by these two vastly different men. "Then I shall ride."

"Evelyn!" Christopher snapped, but she shook her head.

"I will cover ground more quickly than you. This way I can make sure that all is prepared at home." She looked worriedly at Jie Ke's swollen face. "Will you require a doctor?"

He shook his head. "Zhi Min knows the best remedies for broken bones."

She gasped. "Truly? Oh my." She had not realized there were broken bones. He had been walking as if in pain, but—

Jie Ke grinned. "I am merely teasing. Nothing so dramatic. Zhi Min, however, will indeed know just what to do."

Evelyn nodded, vastly relieved. Then she turned to Marcus, who was watching Jie Ke with narrowed eyes. "Please stay at our home for the night, sir. It is much too late to travel back to London now."

Marcus blinked. "Why, I don't mind if I do. Are you sure you have room? Christopher said the house was full up."

"Lord and Lady Greenfield left this morning. I shall have their chamber prepared for you." She smiled warmly, then hopped up onto the mare before Christopher thought to stop her. Or perhaps speed was not the issue, because when she looked down, he had the reins still gripped tightly in his hands.

"Your behavior is quite beyond the pale, Evelyn. I cannot understand what you are thinking," he murmured.

She looked down on him. Her eyebrows arched, and she spoke in her most countesslike tone. "My behavior does not require your understanding." Then she jerked the reins out of his hand. "I shall see you at home directly."

She had time for one last look at Jie Ke. Her worry must have shone in her eyes, because he smiled reassuringly at her. "Go. I will be fine," he said.

She had little choice now; she had just made a point of

riding. Before she could double-think herself again, she kicked the horse and was away.

One thought followed her as she rode. It was a simple thought, one that she had ruminated on before, but never with such anxiety. Just what did men do when away from the constraints of women and polite company? Especially men who seemed to be mortal enemies.

Jie Ke climbed into the carriage with a muffled groan. His entire body ached from the beating he'd just received. And it was nothing compared to what he knew was coming. Fortunately, his cousin wouldn't attack with fists. The man used words to destroy. As a child he'd used his words to devastating effect on servants and other children alike. Jie Ke shuddered to think what was coming from the adult Christopher.

Fortunately, Jie Ke had learned a few defenses of his own. Still, he tried to forestall the coming confrontation by closing his eyes and pretending to sleep. That never worked with Zhi Min, but perhaps Christopher was more polite.

Or less observant. "Evelyn tells me you intend to foreswear the title."

Jie Ke didn't respond.

"Don't pretend to sleep. I shall be obliged to punch you in the ribs if you continue."

Jie Ke sighed. Christopher had always been a smart child. And rarely polite. "That would be cruel. I am already injured."

"You have ruined my wedding, claimed my birthright, and are trying to seduce my bride. A few blows to the ribs are the least that you deserve."

"Unless I am the earl. Then that was my wedding, you were the interloper, and Evelyn is her own person to give as she wills." Jie Ke finally opened his eyes. "What do you want, Chris?"

His cousin did not answer for a moment, his eyes narrowing with hard anger. Beside them, Marcus shifted but did not speak. He clearly had no wish to be in the carriage during a family spat. Christopher displayed great trust in him to allow such a conversation in his presence.

"I rather think it's what you want that is important," Christopher finally drawled. "What will it take to make you disappear forever?"

Jie Ke stared at his cousin while a war went on inside him. Jie Ke the Monk wanted nothing more than to leave this wretched country forever. He longed for the serenity of his temple home. Jacob the Man wanted something entirely different: a woman, a house, a life he was only now beginning to remember.

The carriage bounced over a rut, jarring his ribs, and Jacob gasped at the pain. It cut through his thoughts, stripping away everything but agony. He stayed in that place for a moment, knowing nothing but torment. Even his names—Jie Ke and Jacob—were burned away. And when the pain receded, when he could draw breath again, he opened his eyes and saw Marcus.

Marcus had a pleasant face with a nose broken too many times and eyes narrowed in concern. Jacob smiled to ease the man's worry, but then the inevitable questions began. Was this the man who'd had his family killed? Was this the person who casually ordered his father gutted like a fish?

He closed his eyes, not wanting to think like that again. At least in China, he knew the bandits were dead. He had seen to that. And so in China, he felt safe. In China, he felt in control. But here? In England, every man he met had him wondering: Is this the man? Should I kill this man?

A man at peace inside is always the better fighter. Zhi Min's words echoed in his head. *You enjoy the fight, Jie Ke. Why? Do you know why you are so very angry?*

"Because I still want them dead," Jie Ke answered.

"What?" Christopher's voice was sharp and tight.

Jacob the Man looked at his cousin and felt rage boil through him. This was the man who had stolen his life, planned to wed his woman and take his title. This was his cousin whom he could kill with a single blow from his open hand. How easy it would be!

Do you know why you are so very angry?

Zhi Min's words brought sanity and some measure of control. No answers, just a monk's sanity. He didn't really want to kill his cousin. And Christopher's death would solve nothing. So he tucked his fury away. Piece by piece, he buried it deep inside until Jie Ke the Monk stepped to the fore.

"I have a bargain for you," Jie Ke said, though Jacob the Man screamed with fury. "I came back to England for one true reason. I told myself it was because of grandmother. I said I was only here because the abbot ordered it. I said many things, but the truth only now becomes clear."

Christopher's lips twisted in a disdainful grimace. "Money?"

"Revenge. Justice. You choose."

Christopher's eyes widened in shock. "You hate me that much? For what?"

Jacob the Man howled at his cousin's stupidity. How could he not understand? How could he not see? But, of course, how could anyone see? Even Jie Ke had suppressed his bloodlust, channeled it into other things, fought hard to hide it from everyone, including himself. And so he calmly leaned forward despite the pain in his ribs and he began to explain.

"Someone murdered my family," he said. "Someone paid men to track our party and then kill the Earl of Warhaven and his family. Find out who, and I will give you whatever is mine to give."

His cousin controlled his reaction, but Jacob was watching closely. Chris's gaze froze in place and his breath stopped before he leaned back and waved with a casual gesture. "I thought bandits killed your family."

"It is your family, too," Jacob reminded him. "And it was bandits. But they were paid by someone to slaughter everyone in our party."

"Really? What makes you say that?"

Jacob turned away, forcing himself to look into the past. How ironic that he had to search for his monk's calm—he had to be Jie Ke—in order to speak of something so very unmonastic as revenge.

"I was with Zhi Min when the attack occurred," he said softly. "His father was our guide, and Zhi Min and I were close in age. We became friends." He swallowed, guilt and anger churning inside him. "We weren't supposed to be away from the caravan, but we were boys and very near what was reputed to be a haunted hill. We sneaked out to see a ghost. We came back to find . . ." His throat closed. He couldn't breathe.

"Bandits," Chris said, his voice flat. "Bandits killing everyone." His tone wasn't unkind, but there was enough audible disbelief that Jie Ke's anger surged.

"Not everyone at first," Jie Ke snapped. "The men were slaughtered. Zhi Min lost his father at the same time I did." He forced a breath into his lungs. The air seemed to burn as it went in, but he was able to keep talking. "We heard the screams. Up on that stupid hill, we heard the screams. At first we thought it was ghosts. Zhi Min realized the truth first. He knew about bandits and killing. I had never even heard men die before."

They were rounding a corner leading up to the manor. Jie Ke hadn't noticed where they were, but Christopher apparently did. With a grimace, he abruptly rapped on the ceiling and pushed open the trap.

"Take a tour though the countryside," he ordered the driver. "I'll tell you when to turn around." Then he sat back down in silence. Like a tree awaiting the storm, he seemed calm, proud, and unshakable.

Jie Ke forced himself to continue. He owed his parents this much. "It happened so fast. The women were the only ones left by the time I got there. I wanted . . . I tried . . ." He shrugged. "Zhi Min is a few years older than I am. He dropped me to the ground and held his arm over my mouth. He said if I made a sound, we would die for sure." He blinked, then turned his head away, pretending to find interest in something out the window.

"What of the women?" Chris pushed, his tone hard.

"I didn't understand their language. It was in a Chinese country dialect that I didn't have a hope of following. But Zhi Min heard. He said they were paid to slaughter everyone."

Beside him, Marcus huffed. "But that means nothing! You didn't even understand their language. To take the word of a boy, a mere—"

Jie Ke swung back, fury blazing through his body. "You doubt the word of a Xi Lin monk?"

"We doubt that my uncle's family was a victim of anything but bad luck and . . ." Christopher's words trailed away.

"And stupidity," Jie Ke finished for him. Or perhaps at this moment, he should think of himself as Jacob—as a son, not a monk. "I remember the words your father bellowed before we left England for China. I remember Uncle Frank said we would all die at the hands of bandits or worse if Papa took us."

Christopher's gaze did not waver. "How unfortunate that it was true."

"Not misfortune. Planned and paid for by someone in England."

"Oh, I say!" inserted Marcus. "That is going well beyond the pale, to accuse—"

"They were going to rape the women," Jie Ke pushed out. "They had my mother . . . She was stretched out, and her clothes . . ." He could not say this aloud. He had never said it aloud.

"Yes, well, that happens sometimes with bandits," Marcus said softly. "No need to go into detail."

Jie Ke shook his head. "Their leader stopped them. I didn't understand the words, but Zhi Min . . . he told me later. The leader said they were paid to kill, not rape. No rape. And so he did it right then. A knife across her throat. Marie was next. Then all the rest. No rapes, just swift and brutal death."

Jie Ke had to close his eyes then. He couldn't breathe, couldn't think. The sounds echoed in his head and clogged up his nose and throat. His tears were long since dried up, and yet sometimes emotions hovered on the edge of his calm. If he allowed himself to step even an inch outside of his monk's calm, he would scream and never stop.

He barely heard Christopher's words at first. His cousin spoke neutrally with the expected denials Jie Ke had no inclination to hear. But Chris had a way of speaking that required one to listen.

"We shall assume what you say is true, that you are Jacob and that these bandits were paid to attack the caravan. There is no evidence that someone in England could arrange such a thing. Good God, they were bandits! Brigands have their own laws."

Jie Ke didn't open his eyes. Confession was better done in darkness. "When I was old enough, I left the temple for a while. I found the bandits. The leader was already dead, but there were others. Every one of them said the same thing: there had been no plans to attack the caravan. Zhi Min's father had already paid the right fees to ensure safe passage. Bad business to go back on deals with a local like that."

"So why did they?"

Jie Ke looked up, the memory stark in his mind. "Because they were paid to. In English gold."

"You saw this gold? Some accompanying note? You talked with this bandit leader?"

Jie Ke shook his head, his gaze seeking his cousin's. "I saw nothing of the payment. It was long gone. But I verified everything I could in China. The money came from England. Someone here paid a fortune to have us killed."

Marcus snorted. "It's too far-fetched. The only one with motive would be your father, Chris. He may be a damned pig at times, but that hardly makes him a murderer."

Jacob roared inside, but Jie Ke was in control of the moment and remained absolute in his silence and his calm. The burn from his bruised ribs helped in this matter. Meanwhile, Christopher and his friend continued to talk.

"There are others capable of murder," Chris finally said, his voice low. "Not all the estate went with the title. My uncle had business dealings and the like, plus a mistress. She was a well-traveled gel, if I recall. French or some such. Claimed she'd been to China." There was a pause while he peered at Jacob, his expression as blank as that of any Xi Lin monk. "You want me to drag her before you? Let you question her in a big dramatic event and thereby add more sympathy to your cause?"

Jie Ke stared hard at his cousin and realized that right here was the reason for his journey back to England. Not for his ancestors, not because of the abbot's orders, but to do this.

"Swear to me, Chris. Swear on . . ." What would be most important to his cousin? "Swear on Evelyn's life that you will pursue the crime against my family—your aunt and uncle. Swear that you will find the one responsible and mete out justice. Swear this and I will leave. Tomorrow, if need be."

Christopher did not react, but Marcus did. He leaned forward, his eyes narrow. "Quite the thing to swear upon his fiancée's life. What if he does not find the culprit? What if there is none? What if you are wrong about the whole damned thing?"

"I am not wrong!" he bellowed. He was Jacob now, all fury and anger and pain.

"My cousin Jacob would never hand this task over to another man." Christopher's voice was hard and bracing. It was enough for Jie Ke to tuck his spoiled, angry childhood away.

"Jacob had his revenge," he said softly. "In China, I did what I had to do. Or so I thought. But it is time for me to pass the task to you now, if you will take it."

"Why?"

Jie Ke looked at his cousin, but his thoughts were turned inward. How did he explain this choice to a virtual stranger? "Do you know what it is to live with hatred? To look into every man's eyes and wonder: Is this the man who killed my family?" He held up his hands. "Show me that man and I will kill him before he draws his next breath. But I cannot find him. This is England, and I don't even know how to look." He swallowed, thinking of his rages, of his need to fight when the fear became too great or the question in his head pressed too hard. "The search is destroying me."

Christopher took his time answering. His gaze was hard and unforgiving, but there was thought behind the anger. "And if I don't agree?"

He shrugged. "Then I cannot leave England. We will continue as we are. The lawyers squabble while we dally in Evelyn's home."

Jie Ke took a breath and nearly warned the man, almost said that Evelyn was nearly lost to him, but Jacob would not allow it. The angry possessive boy he had been still wanted to claim something of his former life. That something was Evelyn, and he would not give his rival any advantage with her.

"I should have gone to Gretna Green," Christopher groused to no one in particular.

"And I should not have gone to China."

Christopher's eyes narrowed. "You really don't want it, do you? The money, your country, a home here—you want to throw it all away to eat with sticks and wear that ridiculous robe."

"What would you give for peace in your heart? For your mind to be quiet and your soul to have wings to touch the divine?"

Christopher straightened in his seat. "I have peace and all that! I know who I am!"

Jie Ke forced himself to bow. He ducked his head in all humility and tried to speak from the heart. "Then you are truly blessed."

Marcus snorted. "You are mad."

Jie Ke had no response to that. And besides, what the friend thought was of no consequence.

Christopher grimaced. "You have told me everything? What of the bandits? Do you know their names, where they came from? Did any of them speak English? The tiniest detail could change everything."

Jie Ke nodded. "I will tell you everything I know. Zhi Min as well."

"And then you will leave?"

Would he? Could he leave Evelyn behind? Yes. He had to. What had passed between them was only an interlude, a moment in the moonlight for them both. Even if he could give up his life at the monastery, he could not ask such a thing of her—to travel to China. He knew he could not ask her to give up everything she loved, just as he knew he could not give up the new homeland he had acquired.

"I will leave the very next morning," he swore.

"Then I will do everything in my power to find the murderer who slaughtered my uncle's family."

Jie Ke nodded, truly feeling a jolt of respect for his cousin. It didn't matter that Christopher couldn't bring himself to admit that Jie Ke was indeed Jacob; his choice of wording in that respect had been very careful. But no, it didn't matter—the burden had shifted. Jacob's responsibilities to his ancestors had been passed to one who would follow through. The relief and the peace that came from that decision was like waking from a nightmare. For the first time since he was ten years old, he felt like he could draw a breath free from guilt. The anger remained, but it was fading. The seething fury boiled less fiercely. Did he dare hope that it would soon recede altogether? It could. It would, especially once he was back in China.

In short, Jacob was finally done in England. Jie Ke was now free to return to the temple and take a monk's vows. All that was left was to tell Zhi Min. And Evelyn.

And with that thought, his pain redoubled. His ribs screamed with agony. And Jie Ke knew that Jacob was not fully buried yet.

"What do you mean, no?" Jie Ke demanded of Zhi Min. He had made his second official request. He'd been so confident, he'd even packed their meager belongings. "Do you not understand what I did? I have foresworn Jacob's justice! That is what the abbot wanted of me. I know this! That was his purpose behind this task. I needed to give up Jacob's thirst for revenge." His hands were trembling, his legs weak. Though his ribs burned, he had come to Zhi Min in supplication on his knees. All had been done correctly.

"There is one with whom you have not yet reconciled," Zhi Min said. For all that his voice was gentle, his tone was implacable.

"Evelyn does not require my guidance!" he snapped, stunned by how furious he felt. The anger roared through him not because he said the words, but because they were true. "Evelyn needs a marriage bed. Christopher will be able to give her everything she wants."

Zhi Min nodded, neither arguing nor disagreeing. In fact, Jie Ke had no clue as to what his friend was thinking.

"What do you want of me?" he bellowed.

Zhi Min didn't answer. That was a trick learned very young at the monastery: to be silent while the student ranted and wailed. In time, the answer always appeared.

Except, it did not appear. Jie Ke had no inkling of what his friend expected. So he pressed his forehead to the ground and whispered, "Help me."

Zhi Min sighed. "There is one person here that remembers you as a boy. One person who loves you without condition. She more than anyone needs the peace only you can bring."

His grandmother. Jie Ke did not speak. He did not breathe either, but his body shook. It trembled with the strain of what Zhi Min demanded. "I have been with her," he finally whispered. "I spent the day dancing to her tune with tailor and assistant." His voice gained strength as he spoke, and he pushed up so that he faced his friend. "And servant and tea and everything! I have no need to sit with my grandmother!"

It was no use. Zhi Min had declared the task. If Jie Ke wanted to leave for China, he would have to make peace with his grandmother. He supposed it wouldn't be hard to have tea with the woman.

He sneezed.

He supposed he could sit and have tea. . . .

He sneezed again, and pain ripped through his consciousness from his ribs.

The tea would not be so bad. . . .

He sneezed even more. The fit was so harsh, the pain so acute, that he rolled onto his side. Still, the sneezing continued.

Four more sneezes, and darkness began to eat at his vision. Jie Ke lunged for that darkness, embracing it completely. One last sneeze tumbled him into unconsciousness.

Chapter Fourteen

Evelyn forced her heart to quiet. Jie Ke was settled in his room with Zhi Min and their odd servant to help him. She had tried to talk to him. She wanted to see for herself that he was all right. He was quieter than ever. Perhaps he was enacting some Chinese monastic ritual against pain, but despite his swollen face and tender ribs, he seemed almost serene.

Their gazes connected only once. She had been hovering in his doorway, watching as Zhi Min helped him settle on the bed. Jie Ke had groaned and looked up at her. Their eyes met and she felt him stroke her face from across the room. Her lips tingled and her cheeks flushed. She had sprung forward to go to his bedside, but Zhi Min blocked her. And then Jie Ke had spoken. One sentence, but she would remember it for the rest of her life.

"Go talk to your husband."

He had obviously meant Christopher. It was the first he had ever *not* claimed her as his own, and the devastation drove deep into her soul. Her knees had gone weak, and she'd had to grip the wall for support. The servant had seen her problem, had been kind in his support, but he still gently—firmly—steered her out the door. And Evelyn had not had the strength to resist.

Moments later she was gasping for breath outside. She might have banged on Jie Ke's shut door then. She might have thrown herself at the wooden barrier and screamed her defiance. She didn't even know where her fury came from except that she would not be denied his . . . what? Nightly diversions? Erotic adventures?

What was he to her? And what right did she have to demand his attention when his body was broken?

She had no answers to her own questions. What she did have was a house full of guests who would report her odd behavior to everyone in England. She had seen that Jie Ke was settled; nothing more was required of a hostess. She should now move on, go downstairs, attend any one of the myriad duties that demanded her attention. Her mother could not be everywhere. It was up to Evelyn to see to the rest.

With one last look at Jie Ke's door, she turned to do just that. She would see to her responsibilities. But her mind would not conform. Jie Ke had relinquished her to Christopher.

That was all to the good, wasn't it? No! A thousand times no! She wanted to choose her future. She wanted to pick the man who would grace her bed and father her children. She did not want to be thrown over when she was just beginning to know the man beneath the saffron robe.

But it had all been a fantasy anyway, hadn't it? Nighttime explorations with an exotic monk were all well and good, but there was no future in it. She was to be a countess. And Christopher was right, Jie Ke would never be allowed into the hallowed British peerage. Not if there was any way to keep him excluded.

She frowned and stopped halfway down the stairs. The men had taken an awfully long time coming to the manor. She had assumed it was because carriages and foot traffic clogged the road, but that really wasn't likely. Even in the worst crush, this was still the country. They should have been here long before they had finally arrived. In her relief at seeing Jie Ke alive, she had forgotten how worried she'd been over their unexpected delay.

But now she remembered, and she wondered what exactly Christopher had said to him to make Jie Ke renounce his claim. She started moving again, her destination clear. She even had an excuse as she rounded the base of the stairs. A footman was carrying a tea tray into the near parlor. She stopped him with an impatient wave.

"Are Viscount Cato and Mr. Osborne in there?"

"No, miss, they're in the library. This tray is for Mrs. Whitsun and daughters."

Oh yes, the demands of the gossipmongers. "Get them another one, please. I shall be taking this one." And with that, she lifted the tea tray out of his arms. He was startled, of course, and would likely speak of it to everyone belowstairs, but Evelyn couldn't be bothered with that. "And send Maddie in to entertain the Misses Whitsun, please. Tell her I expressly requested it of her. Tell her I am begging as her sister." And with that, she turned and headed for the library.

Christopher was there, just as the footman had indicated. He sat and stared into the cold grate, a glass of untouched brandy in his hand. Mr. Osborne sat beside him, his eyes narrowed, his face tight with concern. But neither spoke a word, and she stood in the hallway as long as possible in the hopes of overhearing something.

No luck. And the tea tray was terribly heavy. So in the end, she had to breeze in and set the thing between the two men. The small table was not designed for so large a tray, but she was not going to let so silly a thing deter her. "Good afternoon, gentleman," she said airily. "I have brought some tea, but I see you have found your own refreshments."

They occupied the wingback chairs set around the fireplace. It was an area designed only for two, as it was usually just her brother and her father who used the room. But Evelyn refused to be excluded. While the men were hastily scrambling to their feet, she grabbed a wooden rocking chair and awkwardly brought it around to join them.

Naturally, they were too polite to question her mad behavior. Their gentlemen's code required that they indulge her intrusion by taking the chair from her hands and shifting their own chairs back to accommodate. But that was as far as their chivalry went. Once all was settled, with her sipping tea—and trying not to spill it—in the rocking chair, they stared at her, she looked at them, and awkward silence reigned.

"You took a long time to return from the—"

"I would not mention where you were," Christopher interrupted in the hardest tone she'd ever heard from him. "Though I am impressed by your current appearance. Quite lovely, actually," he said in a backhanded compliment. "No one noticed your absence?"

"No one ever notices my absence unless something goes undone. I am often at one crofter's hut or another's. Between the servants and my mother, no one pays the least mind—"

"You have never been under this much scrutiny before," he said with a scowl. "And it is not going to get any easier when you become a—"

"A countess. Yes, I know. Your mother has been most clear on this point. You both have."

"Well, she would know better than any of us."

"What she knows is beyond anyone's knowledge, Christopher, as she has been closeted in her room since our wedding day!"

They all subsided into a glaring silence. Marcus shifted awkwardly in his seat, obviously uncomfortable with what sounded perilously close to a married couple's squabble. In fact, a moment later the poor man pushed to his feet.

"I'm for a bit of a rest. An eventful day and all that."

Evelyn stood as well, guilt making her take his hand warmly. "I am so sorry that you have been party to all this ugliness. Truly, you must stay a few more days and see that I really can be a delightful hostess."

His smile warmed to such a degree that his face took on a surprising beauty. "Nonsense! You have been a delightful hostess and"—he leaned forward to add in a low whisper—"I know quite a few ladies who attend the fights. Contact me next time, and I shall match you up with them. Much less scandalous, and a good deal safer."

She smiled her thanks, but he had already glanced over her shoulder to Christopher. "We'll talk later, if you wish, about that other business."

Christopher nodded. "My thanks, Marcus, for everything."

The men shook hands warmly, and Marcus departed. That left Evelyn alone with Chris, the awkwardness growing until she could hold back her suspicions no longer.

"What other business, Chris? Is it about Jie Ke?"

He looked at her for a long moment, then his gaze slid away, down to the cold fire grate. "Everything is going to be fine, Evelyn. He is leaving soon. He has renounced his claim to the title."

"He has?" Evelyn narrowed her eyes. Something didn't feel right. If any of this were true, then Christopher would be celebrating. Right now, he appeared more like he was contemplating a funeral. "When did all this happen?"

"He will tell the solicitors when he leaves here. Then we can be married as soon as my father returns to say all is settled."

Evelyn folded her arms. Her belly was churning with anxiety. "Why? Why would he suddenly change his mind?"

Christopher glanced up. "You are the one who said he was merely playacting. That he would renounce everything when he convinced that other fellow that . . ." He waved his hand in the general direction of the monks' bedroom.

"That he was fit to become a monk," she finished for him.

"There! See, you have it then. Apparently, he has done everything he needed to do."

She shook her head. "There is more to it, Christopher. I can feel it. What aren't you telling me?"

He said nothing as he took a long sip of his brandy. After he swallowed, he swirled the dark liquid in his glass, his gaze following the movement of the drink. "I want to be an earl," he finally said. "Don't you want to be a countess?"

"Of course," she answered. The words came out automatically, much too fast for her mind to stop. She had said it so often that only now, a breath after she'd answered, did she wonder if it were still true.

"Do you know my mother has not stopped crying since I returned her money to her," he said abruptly.

Evelyn blinked. "What?"

Christopher frowned at her as if Evelyn were the one who had just abruptly hopped topics. "My mother. She refused the money and begged me on her knees to reconsider." Horror filled his expression. "On her knees."

She blinked, stunned by the image. "Begged you to what? Take me to Scotland?"

He nodded. "Gretna Green is lovely this time of year. That's what she said. That Gretna Green was lovely, a wonderful place to honeymoon." He looked hard at Evelyn. "Why do you think she is so determined to see us wed?"

Evelyn shook her head. "I don't know. I suppose because she thinks we will be happy together."

"Bah!" he said as he set down his brandy with a heavy clink. For a moment she feared the glass would break, but it held strong. "She is afraid that all your money will go to that monk."

Evelyn sighed. "He is not a monk yet. This whole situation is so that he can become one, remember? A dragon monk."

Christopher waved her comment aside. "She is afraid that I will lose the title. She is afraid that everything I have worked and studied and planned for will be wiped away."

"But that is foolish!" Evelyn returned. "Not all the land goes with the title. It can't all be entailed."

He shrugged. "Enough is. And without your dower land . . ." He shook his head.

Evelyn leaned forward, trying to understand what had

upset him so. "I thought you said they will not recognize him as an earl, that no one wants a saffron-robed monk as an earl."

Christopher nodded, then pushed out of his seat. "Yes, yes, that is all true," he said almost absently. "But we are speaking of my mother and what *she* believes."

"What she believes," Evelyn echoed, her mind churning fiercely to no avail. "Why is that important?"

"Do you recall our wedding day?"

"Vividly," she said.

"Mama was crying almost from the start."

Evelyn took a moment to think back. Yes, she did believe that Christopher was right. She couldn't remember a moment of that entire aborted service when the countess hadn't been sobbing. But that meant nothing. "Most mothers cry at weddings. My mother started sniffling a week before last."

He nodded. "True, true. Did you know she is dear friends with Mrs. Grayson?"

"The solicitor's wife? Elder or middle? The young one—the one who came to the wedding with Jie Ke—he's not married, is he?"

"Hm? No, Tom's not married. I refer to the middle Mrs. Grayson. She and Mama were schoolmates before the marriages put them in vastly different strata. But mother kept the friendship nonetheless."

"Very good of her. Marriage should not eliminate friendships, no matter how large the gulf." And how very odd it was, too, since the countess had not kept her friendship with Evelyn's mother.

The silence stretched, and Evelyn had the distinct feeling that she was missing something very important. Unfortunately, Christopher was making her guess.

"Christopher—"

"Do you recall what the elder Mr. Grayson said? He was angry at the younger one. He said that if his grandson had simply waited a day, we would have been wed. That you would have been out of the middle of this."

"But we knew that already." Evelyn stood, hating to stare up at Chris while he paced before her; at least this way she could see him eye to eye. "Jie Ke and Zhi Min were in London weeks ago."

"But they were delayed."

She nodded. "By the elder Mr. Grayson."

"Why?"

She threw up her hands in disgust. "So that we could be wed! I do not approve of Mr. Grayson's choice in delaying Jie Ke, but he was acting out of kindness. He didn't wish to see us in exactly the situation we are in: unable to wed, unable to continue our lives until all this mess is sorted out."

"Or maybe he knew."

She blinked. "Knew what?"

"Maybe he and mother have reason to believe that Jie Ke's claim is true. That he really is Jacob."

"I thought you didn't believe it. You said he is a charlatan."

Christopher merely shrugged and reached for his brandy. "I don't know what I believe, Evie. I swear to the Lord on high that I understand none of this." And that frightened him. She could see it in the way his hand trembled on the glass. His shoulders were tight and his eyes kept sliding past her to the cold fire grate.

"What do you fear, Chris?" she asked. She took a step forward, but he held himself too aloof. "Do you think that I will marry Jie Ke and you will be left with nothing?"

He shook his head. "I have money and land. Even without you, I won't starve. Neither will my parents or brothers. We will have enough." He released a short laugh. "My father won't think it's enough, but it will be. I will see to it."

She heard the resolution in his tone. He would care for his family. Then she abruptly gasped, realizing something, her hands flying to her throat in shock. "You *want* to run to

Gretna Green! You are worried enough that you want to finish it!"

He blinked, abruptly startled out of his reverie. "What? No! I'll not wed you like that. It would be an insult to us both."

She pulled back, startled that she had read him so incorrectly. "Then what is it?"

"I want to know the truth," he said softly.

"Which truth?" she pressed. "What are you talking about?"

He abruptly lifted his chin, and she saw he had made a decision. "I want to know what my mother knows," he said firmly. Then he bowed to her. "If you will excuse me, Evie?"

"Oh, no!" she cried. "You cannot imagine that I will be left behind—"

"Evie." He abruptly closed the distance between them. Taking her hands, he pulled her close for a kiss. She thought he would take her lips then, that they would touch as . . . well, that they would kiss as lovers. He didn't. Instead, he touched his mouth to her forehead, then wrapped his arms around her waist. It was a warm place to stand, filled with tender understanding in a brotherly kind of way.

"Chris . . ." She tried to push him back, but he held her even tighter.

"You must understand, Evie, this is a matter of family. My family."

This time she pushed hard enough that he was forced to release her. "I thought I was part of your family."

He smiled and stroked her cheek. "Of course you are. Or you will be. But this . . ." He shook his head. "Let me talk to my mother alone."

She saw desperation in his eyes, and also fear. He tried to mask it, but she had spent much of her childhood with him. She had watched and learned his moods since the countess first began grooming Evelyn to be a titled lady. "I know your mother. I have likely spent more time with her in the last few years than you have. I can read her moods better than you."

"True enough," he said, but she could see he wasn't swayed. "But this is something between mother and son, Evelyn. Please, I ask that you respect that."

She didn't want to listen. He was hiding something from her, and she hated it. If they were ever to have a happy marriage, he could not—

"I haven't spoken to you yet about this afternoon's activities," he said.

She lifted her head, her spirit abruptly singing. Was she about to learn what had happened in the carriage this afternoon—what had changed between Jie Ke and Christopher?

"I understand now how important it must have been for you to go to the fight. I don't agree with it, but I should have realized how desperately you wanted to be there."

As quickly as her spirit has rose, it now plummeted into her toes. "I did nothing wrong, Christopher."

"You were reckless and stupid."

She winced at the one word guaranteed to set her teeth on edge. "I am not stupid, Christopher. I—"

"But," he continued, "you only acted in such a manner because I forbade it. I should not have done that."

She didn't know how to respond. Did she agree that he shouldn't have forbidden her to go? Or did she feel outrage because he clearly thought he had the right to determine her actions? And while she was deciding how to respond, he swept the opportunity away.

"You proved to me that you are a strong woman, Evie. That you will go your own way, despite my say-so."

She smiled. He did understand! "So let me go with you. Let me—"

"You will find that I am much more understanding in the future," he said.

She grimaced. "The *future*," she echoed. "That means you will try to stop me now?"

He nodded. "Yes, Evie, and I cannot simply order you away from my mother's chamber. You have already proven how ineffective my decrees can be."

She winced. He sounded like a disappointed tutor. "Christopher—"

"Instead, I am begging you, Evie. Let me do this alone. Respect my relationship with my mother. There are things that should remain between a mother and her son."

When he put it like that, how could she refuse? How could she deny him the very independence that she herself craved? She was still deciding how to respond when he kissed her again, this time on her cheek.

"I knew you were a good girl. Never fear, it will all be over soon enough." And with that, he turned around and walked quickly from the room.

Chapter Fifteen 🐉

Evelyn meant to demand answers. If not from Christopher, then from Jie Ke. Or Zhi Min, since Jie Ke was probably sleeping. Or, hell, from Marcus. Somebody! But she'd barely put a foot on the lowest stair when her mother found her. Something Lord Greenfield had mentioned before he left was bothering her, something about the character of a woman who allowed bizarre monks to reside in her home. It was ridiculous, of course, but Mama was anxious about it. And then there was the question of dinner with an extra person at table. Mr. Osborne put their number at nine, and that was rather awkward. Should they invite an extra woman? If so, who? Or should they ask Maddie not to attend? But that would destroy the male/female ratio. The questions were endless, the distractions becoming more annoying by the second. Meanwhile, time began to slip away.

An hour later, Christopher still had not come down from his mother's room. Then his mother had sent word that she would not attend dinner. And Christopher, apparently, had left, because his horse was no longer in the stable. Evelyn didn't bother to suppress her huff of annoyance at that news. Finally, she'd had to endure an excruciating meal filled with inanities of conversation followed by yet more time spent on the most ridiculous matters.

After dinner, Evelyn was with the ladies in the parlor before the men joined them. She abruptly stood up. "Please excuse me," she said in a not-so-proper voice. "I've had quite a tiring day." Then she suffered through at least ten minutes of sympathetic good nights before she finally escaped the parlor.

Upstairs, she hesitated, staring down the hallway to Jie Ke's room. Much to her surprise, the door opened and his servant stepped out. She'd never gotten the poor boy's name. Apparently, he kept to himself and never spoke to anyone unless it was absolutely necessary.

She crossed to him. "Is everything all right? I mean, are your masters well?"

The boy looked up at her, his eyes very wide, his mouth very feminine. And for a moment Evelyn could only stare at the very alien-looking almond eyes and the sweet upsweep of the boy's cheeks. This boy who was . . .

"My God," she whispered, stunned that she hadn't noticed before what was so obvious. "You're a girl."

The servant blinked, then dipped her head in a respectful bow.

"But . . ." Evelyn began, only to let the word fade away. As soon as she had the questions, the answers came to her without thought. Why did a girl travel dressed as a boy? Safety, most likely, and freedom of movement. A host of advantages leapt into Evelyn's mind. What wonderful things this girl must have seen! Posing as a male servant, she must have been able to go everywhere!

"Apprentice monk Jie Ke sleeps," the girl said softly. "Monk Zhi Min walks outdoors. I seek dinner."

"I will send a tray up for you, if you like."

The girl smiled and bowed. Evelyn assumed that meant yes.

"And Jie Ke—how are his injuries?"

"His body heals. His mind, though, is troubled. His return to England is not at all what he expected or wanted."

Evelyn took a step forward. "But what did he want? What did he expect?"

The girl shook her head, then leaned forward to speak in a

low whisper. "Men are foolish. He thought he could come back to England and not remember. Naturally, every night it grows harder." The girl raised her hands in disgust. "How can he return to his home and not remember it? Foolishness."

Evelyn would have asked more, but someone was coming up the stairs. The girl glanced nervously around Evelyn's shoulder then bowed. "I must return to the room, mistress."

"Yes, of course." Evelyn glanced back toward the stairs. "I'll send that tray up, but could you tell me . . ." She turned back. The girl was already gone, the door to Jie Ke's room slipping shut.

Evelyn sighed. She could pursue the girl, but why? The things she wanted to know weren't available to anyone but Jie Ke himself. She wanted to know what he was thinking, what he was feeling. And most especially, what he really wanted.

She sent a servant for the tray and then returned to her room, intending to undress for bed. Instead, she grabbed her sturdiest men's attire. She had just buttoned on her pants and was raising her leg to adjust the cuffs when it struck her: She'd always thought that being a countess was a *good* thing. After all, everyone envied her future title. Throughout her Season, all the other girls had been scheming and praying and hoping for a title like "Countess" or "Viscountess," or even "Baroness." She'd been assured one.

And yet every moment of every day had been flogged and bound by those two words: future countess. Her every action, movement, and thought had been defined by her future title. When had she ceased being Evelyn and become a future countess? Very young, she wagered. Very, very young indeed.

With sudden resolve, she pulled out her men's shirt. She was *not* a future countess tonight. For the moment, she was simply Evelyn, and she would wear what she pleased. Maddie did it all the time and no one ever thought anything of it. Of course, Maddie wasn't going to be a future coun—

Evelyn cut off the thought. Those two words were hereby

banned for the night. She would have to watch her thoughts very carefully, but she could do it, for once. She could, and she would.

With that vow firmly in mind, she donned a jacket and boots that would be well suited for her purposes this night. Moments later she slipped outside. She meant to wander. She meant to go to her places to think—but that was what the future countess would do. Tonight, where would *Evelyn* go?

She found herself at the most unusual place ever, a location she had never before visited. She'd thought that in her time as lady of the manor she had visited every hut, every home, and every building in her little county. But here was one that she had never seen: Gladys's little cottage.

She'd known where the kitchen servant lived, of course. But Gladys spoke to her daily at the manor. All her information about the village and its people was delivered at the manor. And since the woman never got sick, Evelyn had never had cause to come here until now. Now, when she had no legitimate reason at all to be here.

Thankfully, there was a light burning inside. Without more than an internal nudge, she knocked and, within moments, the door was pulled wide.

"Miss Stanton! Why, miss, whatever has happened?"

"Nothing, Gladys. Nothing at all. I merely . . ."

"Wished a bite to eat outside of all that mess, eh?"

Evelyn blinked. Perhaps Gladys knew as much about her mistress as she did about the rest of the village.

"Well, come in! Come in! Ain't as fancy as you're used to, but I know you've seen worse." She stepped back, and Evelyn was ushered into a small cottage with a cheery fire and a large dinner table. A very large table. It was plain, scarred wood, and it dwarfed the main room.

"I was just about to make some stew. The babe's been fussing for his mama, but I got him settled right and tight there."

Evelyn turned and was startled to see a little cradle tucked between a rocking chair and the fire. "Whose babe?" she asked as she walked close.

"Stu and Martha's. Colicky and the like. I thought I'd take the child for a bit. Let Martha get some sleep until she's feeling better. Course, Martha won't eat the stew, not with her stomach feeling twitchy." Gladys grinned at the sleeping infant. "Like mama, like baby, eh, little one?" She walked back into her kitchen. "But Stu loves my stew. Oh! Funny that. Stu likes stew!" She grinned. "Any road, Stu will eat it and be right grateful. 'Sides, then he'll fix my back window shutter. Won't latch properly, and I never did have a good hand at that."

Evelyn let the words flow over her as she knelt by the baby. She wanted to touch the boy, but didn't dare wake him. She had heard tales of colicky babies and what a blessing it was to get them finally to sleep. But children were all so beautiful when they slept. She wondered if she would ever set hers down once she had a child. Or if she would spend her days simply staring at it in her arms until it was old enough to demand to be let loose into the world.

"Swing the pot over the fire, will you please, miss?"

She did as she was bidden, then she turned to face her servant. "Gladys, will you call me Evie, please? I think a middle of the night visit calls for that, don't you?" It took an act of will to say those words. The separation between a future countess and her servants was well ingrained. But she made the decision and it felt good.

Gladys wasn't so sure. She pursed her lips and folded her arms. "Ain't right, you know, miss. Me acting so familiar and all."

"Ain't right, you know, Gladys, for you to be cooking for another woman's husband, but you're doing it."

The woman's eyes flew open wide. "But that ain't the way of it at all! I'm just helpin' is all."

Evelyn didn't answer. She simply did as she had seen others

do when visiting: she crossed to the kitchen and pulled down the tea tin plus teapot and cups. Whenever she had visited a crofter before, she had been served such things. Other women were allowed to assist in the cooking, but not a future countess. But this time she was just plain Evie. And so she pulled down the tea tin.

"Miss, now don't be doing—"

"Shhh!" she interrupted. "You'll wake the babe."

Again the woman just stood and stared, her lips pursed, her hands on her hips. "You're right twitchy tonight, miss. Them lot have twisted your mind all up and around."

Evelyn smiled. "Maybe. Maybe not." Then, before the woman could do more but harrumph, Evie distracted her with a question. "Gladys, is that your cradle? It's lovely!"

"Ah, well, it was the cradle I was reared in, that is. And a right many babes have slept there since." She glanced sideways, answering the unspoken question. "But not my own. No, miss, I ain't never had my own."

She took the tea tin from Evelyn's hand, measured out a goodly portion of leaves into the pot, then took it to the kettle over the fire. It was only then that Evelyn noticed there was no stove in this quaint cottage.

"I should see about getting you a stove, Gladys. It would be much easier—"

"Don't you fret about that, Evie," the woman snapped. "This is how my mama cooked, and it's right tight fer me. If I want stove cooking, I'll come to your house. In my home, this is how it's done."

Evelyn's smile grew wider. She had managed to break through the social barrier enough to be scolded. And called Evie! "Of course, you're quite right." Her smile faded as she looked about the cozy little house. There was a corner for children overflowing with toys piled rather haphazardly into a crate. The huge table, of course, was the center for eating and talking, but another nook remained by the fire with the rocking chair and cradle. All in all, it was a welcoming house, quite serviceable for one or for a dozen.

"You're right about a lot of things, Gladys," she commented softly as she dropped herself onto the bench by the table. "You're right about who is sick and who needs a basket. About who hurt himself in a tumble, and who fixes shutters the best."

"What else is there for an old maid to do but mind the whole village?" Gladys answered easily. She set the tea to steeping before standing awkwardly by the table, her gaze sliding back to the pile of vegetables she'd been chopping.

"Oh, please," Evelyn said, "you must go back to fixin the stew. Stu must have it, you know, or your shutter won't latch ever again!"

"I don't know 'bout that, miss," the woman said as she crossed back to her pile of vegetables. "There's a few others I could ask."

Evie nodded, her thoughts twisting her world upside down again. "Of course there are," she murmured. "You know, I have always been taught that *I* make sure all the people on my land are cared for. That is the burden of being a fut—" She didn't want to say the two awful words tonight. "A landowner. But the truth is that I don't know anything of what goes on in the village."

"That's not true, miss! You've cared for us right well."

"No, Gladys," she replied softly. "*You* have. I mean, I only know that Stu hurt himself because you told me. If a woman goes into labor or a babe goes colicky, someone tells me."

"And how would you know elsewise? You, a fine lady in your house. You have no cause to be living down here with the likes of us."

"But that's just the point," Evelyn responded, struggling with her thoughts. "I have merely provided the food baskets you ask for or the money for a surgeon. You are the one who knows what needs to be. I listen to you."

"Now don't be silly—"

"Do not lie to me," Evelyn interrupted. "Please, I want to hear the truth."

Once again the woman pursed her lips in thought, though her hands continued to work without pause. She cut up the vegetables and threw them into the pot, and when she turned to Evelyn her gaze was unerringly direct.

"All right, Evie, if you want the truth tonight, I shall tell it. You are an important piece of this village, and no mistake. Money ain't so small a thing, and many's the lady who wouldn't think to give at all, much less as much as you and your mama do."

Evelyn nodded. She knew all this, but what she hadn't realized was that it was Gladys who managed it all, who was the true force behind keeping everything running. "I've come to believe that even if I were a pinchpenny London shrew, you would still find a way to get a basket for Nan and stew for Stu."

"Miss—" Gladys began, but Evelyn waved her to silence.

"Teach me, Gladys."

"Miss?"

Evelyn pushed up from her chair and came to the woman's side. "I have stove-cooked before. All our cooks have taught me something, ever since I was a child." She tossed a broken carrot piece into the pot. "But I have never learned this type of cooking."

"Ain't no reason to," Gladys said.

"Yes, actually, there is," Evelyn returned. A mad idea had begun to form in her mind.

Gladys frowned a moment, staring at her oddly, but in the end she shrugged. "There ain't no magic in it," she said. "Just a few special secrets I learned from my mama."

Evelyn grinned. "I would be honored to learn them."

Gladys nodded. "But you must swear not to tell Jilly. She's been trying ever so long to learn."

"I swear!" Evie replied, her hand in the air. And they spent the next hour or so working side by side.

Evelyn learned a great deal more than she'd ever imagined, and not just about cooking. It was well past midnight—long after the baby had awaked, then was rocked back to sleep— when they finally sat down to a fresh pot of tea. And in that moment, she finally asked what she already knew to be true.

"Gladys, if I were to disappear, if I set Mama or Maddie to my duties at the manor . . ."

"Hmmm?" Gladys said as she gently tucked the babe back into the cradle.

"Would there be any change at all in the village?"

"There's always change, miss."

Evelyn nodded. "Yes, yes, of course there is. But would anything important change?"

Gladys answered with a shrug. Fortunately, after hours of learning from the woman tonight, Evelyn understood the gesture.

"That's what I thought," she finally said. And she didn't know whether to be happy or sad about it. She had a place here and responsibilities, but she was much less important than she had once wanted to believe. If she left it all to Maddie tomorrow, there would be little difference in the short term.

Of course, she wasn't so sure about the years stretching ahead into the future.

She shrugged, only distantly realizing the gesture echoed Gladys's. Who could tell what would happen in tomorrow's tomorrow? She stood up from the table, feeling the ache of an hour hunched over the stewpot. "Thank you, Gladys. I shall treasure this night always." Then she left the house, wrapping her jacket tight about her shoulders.

She didn't go home, though she was tired in a way she hadn't felt in a long time. She walked to the dark rise and smiled when she saw the flash of saffron in the dim moonlight. Jie Ke was waiting for her.

Chapter Sixteen

She was coming. Jie Ke stood staring out at the darkness, and he heard her. More important, he felt her approach. He glanced to the side without moving.

Evelyn walked up the rise, her lantern shining before her. The wind played with her hair and she tried to brush it out of her face. She was always trying to be neat, he thought with a smile. And as always, her inner nature betrayed her. The moment she smoothed a lock behind her ear, three more escaped to dance about her face.

"Shouldn't you be sleeping?" she asked as she topped the rise.

"I've slept all I could," he answered honestly. "I think the English moonlight calls me. As do you."

Her lips curled into a smile at the notion, and he felt an odd surge of pleasure that he could amuse her. "Would that it were true, Jie Ke," she said, "but I have no power over you. In moonlight or otherwise."

He shrugged. "Maybe not, but I wanted to see you anyway. And this want . . ." His lips quirked into a half smile. "It is very strong." He looked at her then, allowing his desire to fill him. He kept it under control, did not even move. But he looked, and he knew she felt him near her. Her skin blushed a rosy red, and her lips parted in invitation. Her nipples tightened, and her gaze dropped to see what wind and fabric outlined on his body.

However, he was not ready to bed her. He *wanted* to bed her. His body was already rock hard with a need strong enough to bring him out of his sickbed to stand in this freezing wind, and she would be able to see that. But he liked speaking with her, too. And once he touched her, there would be no time or thought for anything else. So he turned away from her, gingerly settling down on the grass. But sitting hurt his ribs too much, and so he was forced to ease backwards until he lay flat, like an offering before her.

She followed his motion, sitting down on the ground. In her English pants, she should have seemed masculine, but her every motion was poetic and feminine. She sat as though she were in a skirt, her feet curled to one side and tucked demurely against her.

"Does it hurt very much?" she asked.

He shook his head. "Zhi Min is an excellent healer and I have suffered much worse." He touched the skin near his eye. "The swelling is nearly gone."

They remained that way for a while, he on his back, staring at the sky, and she beside him. She was watching him closely. He could feel the heat of her attention, but he didn't move. It was a strange and wonderful experience to be the center of such focused study. It teased at the back of his mind and gave him much quiet joy.

"What are you thinking?" she asked. "Sometimes I think I know, but other times—like now—you are a summer storm on a mountain: power, energy, lightning, but so far away that I can't even imagine the whole of it."

He turned to stare at her. "I was thinking of you."

She flushed and once again tried, and failed, to smooth the hair out of her eyes. "And what do you think about me?"

Should he tell her the truth? Propriety didn't matter. The words spilled out whether he wished it or not. "That I should be resting, but I am here to see you. That I should have fought through the rest of the afternoon, but I didn't . . . for you. That I have told Chris that I am leaving tomorrow, but that I cannot."

"Because of me?"

"I . . ." He sighed. "I thought it was only because I have to visit with Grandmother. But if that is so, then why am I out here when my ribs ache and my face hurts?"

"Why?" she repeated. Her voice was so quiet that the wind nearly took it away. But he heard.

"I think it is because you make me less afraid." He glanced at her, nervous at her reaction. She looked . . . baffled.

"You are afraid? Of what?"

Her shock was rather flattering. "Why do *you* think I'm afraid?"

"Don't answer a question with a question," she returned. "It's rude."

He blinked, then his lips curved in a rueful smile. "Yes, I always hated that from my teachers. Very well, why am I afraid?" He tilted his head and looked at the sky. "I think I have been afraid so very long that I no longer recognize it. Or I don't until the feeling eases—around you."

"But why?" she gasped. "You're so powerful."

He laughed, wishing it were true. "Powerful? Yes, I can usually best a man in a fair fight. Even in an unfair fight." He shook his head. "But fear is rarely reasonable." He glanced at her. "Isn't there something that terrifies you?"

"Spiders," she said. "Oh God, how I hate spiders."

He smiled. He liked that she had so simple a weakness. It made it easier to confess his own. "Is that a reasonable fear?"

She shook her head. "Not according to my sister. I know I'm many times their size. But still . . ." She shuddered. "I *hate* them."

"I learned to fight so well because I was afraid. I practiced so hard." He closed his eyes, remembering the hours upon hours of sweat, of kicks and punches, attacks and defenses. Every day until dusk or until he collapsed in exhaustion.

"It didn't help, did it?"

His eyes popped open and he stared at her. Had she read his mind?

"Just as I know I can step on a spider and I'll be fine," she said, "or get a shovel for the really big ones. It doesn't matter, I'm still afraid." She glanced uneasily around the clearing.

"I promise to kill any spider I see," he said with a grin. And then, to distract her fear, he added a bargain. "But you must take care of the snakes."

She smiled, and the tension around her shoulders eased. "What about the rats?"

"Hmmm." He frowned up at the sky, liking this nonsensical banter. It reminded him of better times long ago. "We shall have to bargain on the rats. Or perhaps work together to defeat them."

She tilted her head. "You are not very gallant, you know. Most men would swear to defend me from all foes, both four and eight legged."

He twisted his head to look at her. "Do you wish for me to swear such a thing?"

"No," she said after a moment. "No, I don't. I like that you don't act as if I'm helpless."

He shifted onto his side, grimacing as he moved. "I would try, you know," he said honestly. "Even against the snakes, I would try to protect you."

He watched her flush. She knew what he swore. She knew that he felt it deep inside, and that pleased her. Then she poked him in the shoulder, lightening the mood with a tease. "No 'trying,' Jie Ke. You swore to take care of all spiders. I will hold you to that."

He allowed her to push him flat onto the ground. He wanted to pull her over with him, but now was not the time. Not yet. "Spiders, yes," he said, struggling to keep his tone light. "But I make no promises regarding rats."

She laughed, and the sound lifted light and free into the

darkness. But a moment later, he knew she was thinking something else. Without even looking at her, he knew her mood had sobered and she would push for a deeper knowledge of something. Of *him*. He closed his eyes, praying that she held off in that search for a little bit more time. She was a relentless force, and he could deny her nothing. He knew that if she asked, he would tell her.

"Jie Ke, what did you and Christopher discuss in the carriage?"

Yes, he had been afraid she would ask that. "I gave up my revenge to him."

She started. Clearly, she hadn't expected that. In truth, he himself was still shocked by it. But the decision felt right.

"I . . . um . . . I don't . . ." She swallowed. "What revenge?"

He smiled, trying to distract her. "I like it when I fluster you. Your cheeks go pink and your nose wrinkles."

"It does not!" She popped her hand to her nose to smooth it down. "And you're avoiding the question."

He was. He looked at her, studying the subtleties in the way she carried herself, in the casual way she tugged at her hair and lifted her face to the wind, and he avoided it further. "Something is different about you tonight."

She looked at him, then abruptly flopped over onto her side, propping her head with her hand. "I've decided I'm just Evie tonight. Not an FC at all."

"FC?"

"Future countess. Tonight, I can be as inappropriate as I like."

He arched a brow at her. "I didn't think you had a problem with that before."

She shrugged, but underneath that gesture he caught a simmering sexuality, a wildness that slipped out more freely than ever. "Maybe. At least not with you." Then she grinned. "And we were speaking of you. What revenge?"

He grew still. Not quiet, just still. He didn't want to tell her, didn't want to sully her image of him. And yet, no one asked such direct questions. At the temple and often throughout China, things were stated obliquely unless spoken in the language of fists. And so when Evelyn asked a direct question, he found himself powerless to answer in any other way but directly. "My parents were murdered."

"I know. By bandits."

He nodded. "Yes, bandits, but someone paid them. Someone English."

She started upright. "No!"

"Yes."

She dropped back onto her elbows and frowned as if thinking very deeply. "You know this, and you 'gave up that revenge' to Christopher? What does that mean?"

He grimaced, but his gaze remained on her. "Have you ever done something you thought would help, but ended up not doing anything at all? Or ended up making things worse?"

She wrinkled her nose. "All the time."

He arched an eyebrow in query, but she shook her head.

"We can speak of my mistakes later." She raised her eyebrows at him. She had the most expressive face. "We are talking about you."

"I have never told anyone this," he realized. "Not even Zhi Min."

She waited in silence, not pushing, merely waiting. And in her silence, he found the strength to continue.

"I killed them all, Evie. Every single one. I found the bandits that murdered my family. Some I interrogated, some I just killed. But they all died, and all by my hand."

He spoke without inflection, but inside, his entire body trembled from the force of what he confessed. He tried to move his hand, but found himself too weak to control the shakes. Better not to move at all.

"I have lived a life of fear. When I was ten, I watched them slaughter my family, and I was terrified. I was taken to a temple in China—an English boy alone in China." He closed his eyes. "Lord, the fear ate at me night and day. But then I saw them learning how to fight, and I thought that if I could fight like that then I would not be afraid anymore." He looked to the dark sky because he could not bear keeping his eyes closed any longer. "The fighting I saw was different from English fighting," he said. "I thought it the most powerful thing I'd ever seen."

"I noticed," she said softly. "It *is* very powerful. It was . . . You are very good."

"I am one of the best now," he said without arrogance. "I made sure of it. But it didn't lessen my fear. The bandits were still out there, you see. I thought—I feared—they would find out I was still alive. I thought if they were dead, then I wouldn't be afraid anymore."

"Jie Ke—" she began.

"No!" he snapped. Didn't she understand? "I wasn't a monk then. I was Jacob. Just a frightened boy named Jacob."

Her lips curved into a tiny smile. "You know they're the same person, right? That you are both Jacob and Jie Ke?"

He arched his brow back at her. "Is that right, Just Evie, and you are not the future countess?"

She laughed softly and without rancor. "Point taken. So, tonight you are Jacob."

He nodded. "I was Jacob all the time then, a frightened boy who could fight like a demon."

"How did you find them?" she asked. "The bandits, I mean."

"It's not really that hard. Monks—even novice monks— are revered in China. People tell us things. Not me, because I am white, but my friends. I learned where the bandits lived. With a few questions, I learned how they played, where they worked, what they did. I made it a point to know."

"But you were just a boy!"

"I thought my life depended on knowing." He shrugged.

"Besides, this bandit band wasn't cunning. They ruled by intimidation. I was not the only one who watched them carefully or wished them dead."

"So you killed them," she said. He couldn't find any condemnation in her tone. "That doesn't sound so bad. The murderers were murdered. Justice, right?"

He could tell she didn't understand—how could she? She was a pampered flower of England. Yet he still tried to explain. "That's what I thought, too. Justice. Until I was the perpetrator." He shifted, pushing up onto one elbow and asking a sudden question. "Had you ever kissed a man before?"

She blinked, obviously startled. "Are you avoiding—"

"No, no," he said. "I'm trying to explain. Before me, had you ever kissed a man?"

"Um . . . yes," she said, and he was annoyed by the sudden flash of jealousy that cut through his thoughts.

"Who?" he demanded.

"Christopher, of course. And others. There was a stolen kiss beneath the mistletoe every now and then from other gentlemen." She flashed a girlish smile at him. "I had a Season in London, you know. I flirted and kissed a few then as well."

He shifted until he rose above her, though he still sat. His position pulled at his ribs, but he wanted to know. "What about . . . what we've done? Have you—"

"No!" she said, her face heating in embarrassment. Then she pushed up as well, coming to kneel before him. "Why? What difference does it make?"

He forcibly reined back the possessive fury churning within him. He didn't want her with anyone else.

"Jie Ke?"

He clenched his teeth and ordered his thoughts. He had been trying to explain . . . *Oh yes.* "The kissing and other . . ." He cut off his words. "You thought about it, didn't you? You've dreamed about your wedding night. About—"

She nodded. "Yes, I've thought about it." Her blush deepened. "I've thought about it a lot."

He reached out and grabbed her hand, not pulling her closer—though the potential was there. And where they touched, her tiny hand so fragile in his, he burned with a fierce hunger.

"Was the reality anything like what happened? What we did?"

She shook her head. "More," she whispered, and he had to fight the roar of satisfaction inside him. "It was what I had thought and more."

"For me as well," he said softly. "I know what to do with a woman. Boys in a temple . . . we talk about it a great deal. And once or twice, there was a woman who wanted to see what . . . what a white man was capable of."

"Jie Ke—"

"But with you it was different. It was more, and it was . . . I have not stopped thinking about you since the moment I first saw you in the church."

He looked at her, and she looked back. She wet her lips, and he could not help but stare. He wanted to kiss her. His lips ached with the need. But she held herself apart, and he could not bear to force her.

"How does this relate to your revenge?" she whispered.

He flinched and would have rolled backwards again, but she held him still by their gripped hands. "That, too, was more than I expected," he said. "I cannot tell you everything it feels like to kill a man, to watch his blood gush, to smell that scent." He took a shallow breath against the pain in his chest. "The bowels let loose, and there are . . . sounds of death, too. Things that I did not expect."

"It must have been awful," she whispered.

"I kept thinking that it would get better, that it would become easier or different. That eventually I would feel better." He looked at their joined hands. He gripped her so tightly, and yet she did not break. She did not even flinch. "Each death was different, and some were easier than others. But always . . ." He shook his head. How to explain? "The fear remained."

Evelyn held herself still, her eyes wide and her breath so sweet and steady before him. He focused on that, on her sitting here with him. He had no other thought but her.

"You were still afraid?" she asked. "Even after they died?"

"Terrified." He took a gulping breath, and his grip did not relax.

She frowned. "I suppose if you're sure that it was someone from England, that might be a source of fear. But . . ."

"I lived in fear for so long, it became a habit. But added to that fear was guilt and blood." He raised his gaze to hers. "Jacob is a killer." He swallowed. "*I* am a killer."

She raised their joined hands and pressed a kiss to his knuckles. "Is that why you want to be a monk? Is that why you don't want to be Jacob? Because Jie Ke is gentle?"

"Gentle?" He looked up at her, vaguely insulted, vaguely amused. He'd worked all his life to be a man who struck terror into the hearts of others, and she saw him as gentle?

"Er . . ." she began. "I mean as tough as you are, you seem, um, kind. But I guess all monks are kind."

He frowned, still thrown by her remark. "Being a monk is . . . is a serenity of the soul. It is a peace that radiates from the heart and surrounds everything and everyone. It's like being—"

"Forgiven," she said softly. "You want to be forgiven."

He jerked backwards. "What?"

"That's why you want to be a monk. You think a monk feels forgiven."

He didn't know how to respond to that. "Of course I want to feel forgiven. I killed people!"

"You killed thieves and murderers," she stressed. "Was there a court of law that could be appealed to? Was there another way?"

He shook his head, but honesty forced him to admit the truth. "They had the entire area cowed for many, many miles. The viceroy took their bribes, and there was no other law beyond him. Perhaps if I had gone to Peking."

"As a white man? Would it have worked?"

"No." He wanted to stomp away in his frustration, and yet he could not let go of her hands. He wanted to take her into his soul. "They were terrorizing the area, Evie. They were brutal, cruel men. They deserved to die!"

"So you meted out justice, and yet you still feel guilty."

He knew what he had done was justice, and yet it ate at him. The memories burned in his heart and soul. "I cannot find peace. No matter how I try, I cannot feel it except when I am with you."

"Because you feel guilty," she stressed. "But not about the bandits. Not about stopping cruel, brutal murderers." She shifted on her knees as she tried to pull him closer. "You were raised to be an earl, Jacob. If there's one thing about being an earl—or a countess—it's a responsibility that weighs on the soul. You have people to care for, whole families dependent upon you. Chris feels it too."

He pushed back, not wanting to think about his cousin.

"And when you fail in that responsibility . . ." She took a breath. "Whenever I fail, I feel guilty. Reasonable or not, I feel like I failed. And I want—I need—to be forgiven. Does that make sense to you?"

He shook his head. "I didn't forget to fix some peasant's roof, Evie. I killed people!" Why didn't she understand?

"You killed people who deserved to die. That's not where your guilt comes from."

"Of course it does!" he cried. But then he frowned, wondering if her words could hold some truth.

"You failed to save your parents. So in an attempt to atone for that, you killed their murderers. But that doesn't bring your parents back."

"I know!" he snapped, then immediately regretted it. She was biting her lip, obviously trying to explain. He wanted to touch her, wanted to soothe away the frown line between her eyes, but there was so much emotion churning inside him that he couldn't move a muscle.

"I have never killed anyone," she finally said, "but I have seen death. Loved ones, hated enemies, people claimed quickly or slowly. I began seeing death in my youngest years. It's part of being a future countess."

"It's not the same—" he began.

"Of course it isn't, but the guilt is. It makes no sense, but someone always feels guilty, for not giving enough, for not helping at the right time, or seeing, or . . ." She pressed her lips to his hand. "It seems there is always guilt, and no matter what the person does to atone, it never helps. You tried to atone for not helping your parents. You killed their murderers, but justice isn't forgiveness. You need to be forgiven."

"I wasn't there for my father. But I saw my mother. My sister. I saw," he whispered.

"Which makes the guilt more real, more powerful, more . . . terrifying." She leaned forward and cupped his cheek. "Jacob, that's why you're still afraid."

"I'm *not* afraid," he said, and he tried to make it the truth. "I have given up my revenge to Christopher. He will find whoever is responsible. He will pass judgment." He clutched her wrist, holding her hand still against his face. "I gave it all to him."

"And did that help?"

"Yes!" Justice would be done in England as it had been done in China.

"And you are no longer afraid."

He swallowed, ashamed to feel a tear slip down his cheek. Was he afraid still? Had he ever felt safe?

"Release the fear, Jacob," she said. She pressed a kiss into his lips. "No one is going to touch you now. You have been safe for almost two decades."

"I can't," he whispered, stunned to feel terror slipping into his veins.

She stroked her mouth against his again. Another kiss, and then another. "Are you afraid now?"

"No," he whispered. "Not when I am with you. Never with you." He pulled back to look more directly into her eyes. "Why is that, Evie? How can *you* keep my fear at bay?"

She smiled. "Because I forgive you." She pressed her lips into his hands. First one palm and then the other. "I forgive you for being a child who couldn't save his parents or his sister. I forgive you for being angry at the monks who took you in, and for nevertheless learning their ways because you were too young to run."

"How do you know that?" he whispered, awed by her words.

She looked up, a smile on her face. "You think I've never seen angry boys?" She cupped his cheek, and he closed his eyes to feel the touch of her hand. "You are forgiven, Jacob. There was nothing you could do to change what happened."

"I killed," he whispered, "and it made everything worse."

"It added to the guilt," she agreed. "So, now you wish to become a monk to atone."

He shook his head, though he meant yes, and he wasn't able to look her in the eye. "They have peace, Evie. Like you cannot imagine. The monks have a serenity that builds from the inside out."

"You don't need to be a monk, Jacob. You are forgiven. Be at peace now."

He let the words shiver through him. More important, he felt a benediction in her touch. She caressed his cheek and pressed her lips to his forehead. She raised his face to hers and stroked her forgiveness into his mouth. He drank her generosity. He breathed in her sweetness. And with every whisper, every touch, every blessing, he craved more.

"I cannot release you, Evie," he whispered. "I need you too much."

"I didn't ask to be released."

He jerked back enough to look her in the eye. She didn't understand. "I cannot give you up," he said, trying to explain, his voice hoarse. "You quiet the noise in my head, Evie. You make me feel—"

"You are forgiven," she repeated.

Her words sealed her fate. He took her mouth, he took her forgiveness, he wanted to take her. He framed her face with his hands and lowered her to the ground. He tried to be tender and careful. He wanted to be all the things she thought he was, but he couldn't. Not in this moment. Right now he felt a need much more compelling. She was his, and he could not stop.

Chapter Seventeen

At last. That was all Evelyn could think as Jie Ke pushed her down into the grass. They had been building to this forever and now, finally, the moment had arrived. She understood it was a bad choice. She knew that whatever emotions she felt now, in the morning she would once again be a future countess and would regret her loss of virginity.

And yet, she wouldn't stop herself. She had wanted this for so long. And she wanted it with him and for the silliest of reasons: because he allowed and even wanted her to choose her own path. Of all the people in her life, he was the one who allowed her to choose what she wanted. Every touch, every caress between them, had been at her instigation, because of her desire. Every interaction had been without pressure for her to act in one way or another. Even when she had gone to his fight, he had acted to protect her, had forcefully pointed out her errors in judgment, but there had been no suggestion of punishment or desire to orchestrate her actions. In short, Jie Ke asked where Christopher told. He advised, Christopher decreed.

That was attractive enough, but Jie Ke did one more thing that made her heart shudder with love: he did not revile her for any of her choices. He looked at her with such need, such worship, that she felt cherished. He made her feel perfect even when she knew she was not. In truth, she strove desperately to deserve such adoration, especially since she wanted him just as deeply as he seemed to need her. She ached to soothe the frightened boy he was, and she hungered to embrace the man he'd become.

So when he pressed her down to the ground, she went easily, loving the power in his body, the weight of his legs and the grip of his hands. She reached up to touch his face, letting her fingertips slide over his beard-roughened skin and the hard edge of his jaw. He was clenching his teeth, and his eyes seemed to burn in the darkness. He was so fierce, and yet he said *she* made *him* less afraid.

"I understand nothing about you," she whispered as she stroked his skin. "You are so different."

He leaned close and his cheek brushed across hers. His lungs expanded as he inhaled, and his chest trembled against her. He was holding himself apart, giving her time to think, to understand. She pulled back just enough to look into the dark hollows of his eyes.

"Yes," she said clearly. Then she soared upward enough to take his mouth, to claim her kiss, to brand him with herself. A fierce joy burned through her. She couldn't tell whether it came from inside her or from him, but it exploded like lightning in the chambers of her soul.

His kiss dominated her. Though she had initiated it, he quickly took control. Her mouth opened beneath his assault and his tongue swept inside. He touched, he stroked, and he owned. Her mouth burned wherever he touched, and her breath became his. She felt his hands on her shirt, tugging at the fabric, and she arched into him. Her own hands slid down his body to grab his robes. The garment moved easily as she pulled it aside, but there was so much fabric! Not so her shirt. She soon felt cool night air on her chest even though her corset still restricted her.

"Lie down," she ordered, pushing at him.

He didn't answer. His hands were on the corset, pushing at

the stays, trying to unhook her. He would succeed soon, but she had no interest in waiting.

"Lie back!" she said, and she pushed at his chest. She hadn't intended to hurt him, but he gasped in pain. Cracked ribs, she remembered. He rolled backward, his breath shallow. She leaned down over him, dropping her apology onto his lips. "Even with your hurt ribs, you could break me in a second, couldn't you?"

He frowned, obviously not wanting to answer.

"Couldn't you?" she demanded.

"Yes. There are ways."

"And if I asked, would you teach me how? Would you show me how to defend myself even with hurt ribs?"

He nodded slowly. "It is not generally taught to women. The training is hard enough for a man."

"But if I asked—"

"I would teach you." He arched his brow, a flash of vulnerability in his eyes. "I do not think I could refuse you anything."

She laughed. She did not know why his words made her heart so free. Perhaps because most everyone in her life thought to protect her, to keep her safe. *Don't go to the fight, it's dangerous. Don't wander too far away. Don't dance in a storm.* Only Jie Ke would give her the tools to make herself safe.

As if he understood her thoughts, his expression grew sober. "Do not think you will be safe. Fighting is only a tool, just like anything else. It will not—"

"The point is," she said as she leaned down to kiss him, "that you do not limit me. I cannot tell you how amazing that is." Her words faded away as she abruptly straightened and released the hooks on her corset. She took a deep breath, lifting her breasts to the moonlight as she tossed the thing aside.

He reached for her, both his hands rising to hold her breasts. She leaned forward, letting him stroke and shape them. God, it felt so good. His fingers flowed across her skin, her nipples tightened as he rolled them, and fire burst from breast to groin only to sizzle right back up. It felt so wonderful, and his hands were so large. Oh, she could kneel like this forever, if only he would continue to touch her like this.

He urged her higher on his body, closer to him. She went easily, her legs trembling and weak until her breasts were just above his mouth. When he at last took her nipple with his tongue, she moaned in sheer delight. She reveled in the wetness of each stroke, the long, pulling draw that curled deep into her belly. Sensation built upon sensation as she trembled above him.

With one hand, she fumbled with the buttons on her trousers. Though her breath was shortening, her thoughts stuttering into incoherence, she was able to push all her clothing down. A simple shift of her hips, and all slipped to just above her knees.

Her bottom was exposed to the air and the sudden shift in temperature added to the delight. Her groin tightened in reaction, and her internal fire blazed white-hot. But it was too awkward, it was too . . . She pulled away, her breasts aching with the loss. She shifted quickly to kick out of the trousers. She had left her stockings on when she'd changed, and so the thick knit warmed her legs even as the ribbon teased against her inner thighs.

She looked over at Jie Ke, who was spread out like a present before her, but she was impatient with the wrapping. She grabbed his middle robe, bunched the fabric in her fists and tossed it aside. Soon a blanket of saffron lay on the ground. His underrobe was pale and almost gray. She stripped the downy, soft fabric aside with only the most casual appreciation of its texture.

He was naked, his organ large and thrusting up between narrow hips and corded thighs. His body was beautiful, but it barely registered. Her gaze had shifted up to his face. Before, she had thought of his muscles and his physique. Tonight, she looked in his eyes and saw his desire.

She watched his nostrils flare and his mouth tighten. She saw his eyes darken as he rose up from the ground. The motion was smooth, the glory of his body only a small portion of the power in the image. She could not stop him now even if she wanted. She had already said yes, and he was rising up to take her.

Her breath caught in her throat. His hand slipped between her knees, skimming upward over stocking and ribbon. She barely had time to tense before his hand found upper thigh and then more intimate flesh. He stroked into her from below as he pushed her down from above. He rolled her easily onto his robes and followed her to settle on his knees between her thighs.

One finger thrust inside her, sliding in and out with a sharp push. She gasped and arched, tightening her legs around his knees. He thrust two fingers inside her, but it wasn't enough and she whimpered. Then he withdrew in a long lingering stroke that pushed a knuckle right where she most wanted it.

"Oh!" she gasped. "Do that again!"

He did. He thrust with two fingers, deep, then followed this with a smooth pull that rolled higher and harder. Her belly tightened, her back arched, and she began to gasp in time to his strokes.

Again he thrust. Her legs widened further. She dug her heels into his back. And when he pulled his hand away, she released a soft keen of need. The sensations collided in her body, building in a way that was familiar and yet so much more. She grabbed onto his shoulders, but they were too broad for her to grip. So she slid her hands lower, onto his arms, and she pulled on his biceps, raising herself up higher to him.

Her weight unbalanced him. His arm shifted. His last thrust was pulled away, and his hand shifted, drawing upward until he braced himself on his elbows. She felt his organ pushing slowly against her, but he didn't thrust inside. He pushed himself upward, not inside but *against* that place, and it made her shudder with delight.

He groaned against her ear, a low rumble that echoed the booming thunder of her heart. The tension was nearly unbearable. She wanted more. She wanted *him*. "Jie Ke," she gasped. "Jacob! Oh please, do it now!"

He thrust. She felt the flex of his belly and the sudden tightness in his biceps. But that was nothing compared to the sudden fullness of him inside her. Pain flashed through her mind, and she cried out in shock. Her back was arched and her body frozen. She had known this would happen, but she had forgotten. And besides, this was not as she'd imagined.

The pain had been a shock—like the sudden splash of icy water. It froze everything. And yet, he was there, warming her, easing her, being here with her. And he, too, was more than she'd expected. Large. Hard. Thick.

He began to slide out of her. He eased away, slipped backwards, drawing her belly down and—

In. He thrust in again, hard and powerful. She felt a flash of delight from that other place higher up. And this time as he drew out, slowly pulling back, she arched to follow. She pressed her groin forward to catch the angle again.

In. Ripples of his movement shivered up her spine. Oh, yes! But the force of his thrust pushed her away when she wanted him deeper. So she tightened her legs, gripping him close. He gasped against her ear. She looked into his eyes. His face was in shadow, his eyes dark pools, but she saw him. Not physically—all was in shadow. But she knew he looked at her. She felt his gaze on her face as deeply penetrating as his organ, and knowing he was watching her, she found bliss.

An ecstatic eternity later, Evelyn opened her eyes. A bug was crawling up her arm. She didn't want to wake, much less move, but it was cold here, lying naked on the lumpy ground. Jie Ke was a delightful source of heat, and she snuggled backwards into his arms. He tightened them around her and she smiled even as she brushed irritably at the insect on her arm.

The wind blew across her body and she shivered. Lord, it was cold. She reached out and tugged the robe off the ground, flicking it so that it dropped across her hips and legs. It helped cut the wind, but the dust that came with it made her sneeze. Then Jie Ke grunted because she must have jerked at his ribs—and damn, but her feet were freezing!

She pushed away from him, hating to leave the warm haven of his arms, but she had to get dressed. She sneezed again, more violently this time. She hated the dust! Where had she set her corset? She squinted in the moonlight. There it was. She stood slowly, trying not to jostle Jie Ke. She moved gingerly, surprised to feel the strain of sore muscles, the wetness in places that weren't normally wet. Perhaps when she got back to the manor, she would order a bath—a hot one, first thing in the morning.

Is that what married women did? She wondered. A hot bath, or at least a full cleaning with cloth and water? Did they do it after every time?

She picked up her corset and shook out the dirt. She couldn't see if it was truly stained, not in the dark. If so, she would have to throw it out. She hated the feel of the grit that rubbed between corset and skin. She knew her sister Maddie was constantly complaining about getting raw patches because she could not keep her clothes clean, and Evelyn didn't want that.

She wrapped the corset around herself, welcoming the covering against the wind. When she and Jacob were married, they could lounge in bed all day. She wouldn't even—

Evelyn froze, her mind in sudden turmoil. She hadn't just thought . . . She couldn't possibly think . . . She wasn't really going to marry . . .

She swallowed and looked behind her at Jacob. He was

stretched out on his back, his mouth slightly open in sleep. He was obviously cold—his nipples were tight, his skin was puckered with goose bumps—and yet he slept without difficulty. She pulled on her shirt and pants, then knelt beside him to look.

He was undeniably beautiful. His muscles were lean and long, his torso broad in just the right way. Even the hair on his skin seemed sleek to her, like the fur covering of a stunning wild animal. She could have sat and stared at him for hours, watching the way he moved and slept.

Or she could have if she weren't so cold. If it weren't the middle of the night and she had no responsibilities in the morning. Or if she didn't wish to be in a warm house with a bright fire and a thick cup of hot chocolate. Obviously, Jacob was used to this kind of weather. He had traveled here from China, often on foot. Sleeping outdoors was part and parcel of his life. But not hers.

He wanted to be a monk—she wondered if that meant a celibate monk—in China, of all places. He fought like a demon and had killed people. The things he did and said were so alien, even if they fascinated her. Who thought of "giving over" his revenge? She still had no idea what that meant.

The inner workings of his mind were yet another fascination. She could spend her entire life trying to understand the complicated man lying before her and still have more to explore. And yet, did she want to?

The thoughts she had been trying to hold at bay—the regret at her loss of virginity, the knowledge that she had a family who expected her to act in a certain way, the fiancé she had just betrayed—all crowded into her mind. She had thought they would wait until morning, prayed that she could have one night of bliss.

Well, it had been blissful, and now . . . She sighed as she gently covered Jacob in his robe, not knowing what to think. She closed her eyes and tried to think of Christopher, but within moments her mind slipped and replaced him with the image of Jacob. She saw how he looked at her that first night after he had—after *they* had—begun their sexual explorations. He had resettled her clothing, then stood. She remembered his words so clearly.

To see the truth with clarity, and to search for a better answer. That is what it means to be a monk.

He had told her right then who he was. He had said what he wanted and how he struggled every day to grow into a better man.

She realized now that she had fallen in love with him at that very moment. What man worked so hard against his own frailties? No one she had met. Even Christopher, whom she adored, focused more on his strengths, on maximizing his accomplishments without regard to . . . to . . . well, to anyone else, including herself.

But Jacob was different. And now that she knew more of his past, of what he had suffered in China, she was even more impressed. Add to that his encouragement for her to explore her life—it was her own life, he said, her choices were her own—and her heart could not fail to follow. She was becoming more because of Jie Ke. And the shared sexuality was only a small part. She would never have dared see a fight before, would never have thought to visit Gladys, would never even have imagined a different role for herself than what had been presented to her. But now she had.

Jie Ke was an impressive, admirable man. And he'd made her into a woman who could grow into something equally amazing—not a countess, but something more. And that something more was something she'd never thought possible. In less that a week, she'd become a woman who could learn from Gladys, who could attend pugilistic matches without shame, who could challenge the world on her own terms. Who knew what was possible in her future?

And therein lay the conflict. Her spirit yearned to become

more, to grow, to explore, to be a woman in ways that she'd never imagined. But she wanted to do so from the comfort of a warm bed in a house with servants who would do her bidding. She was a revered member of her little community, and her status would only increase when she became a countess. She would host balls and create opportunities for intellectual discourse, for political change, for art and society and civilization. That was no small thing, and she had been groomed from birth for such a life.

But that was a life with Christopher, not Jie Ke. It was the life she knew. It was categorically not a life following a monk on his travels back to China. And yet, as she sat there, watching the wind ripple through the fabric of Jie Ke's robes, tears began to slip from her eyes. Her heart swelled when she looked at him. Her body tightened in lust, and love seemed to expand out of her to surround and infuse him. She *loved* him. Oh God, she truly loved Jie Ke. She loved how he made her feel. She loved who she became—or had the chance of becoming—when she was with him. She loved everything about their time together. And yet . . .

"I can't," she whispered, horrified to realize that she was so small a person. "I just can't give up everything I've ever known."

Would that she had realized this an hour ago. Would that she had come face-to-face with the knowledge of her cowardice long before she had walked up the rise and into his arms. Before she had betrayed Christopher. How was she ever to explain this? How was she ever to look at her own children and say, "Grow strong, my children, and fly free because I was too frightened to do it myself."

She tried to choke back a sob but failed. Jie Ke stirred, opening his eyes and focusing on her with sudden clarity. She tried to hide her sorrow, wiping at her cheeks, but he saw. He understood. And true to his nature, he didn't bluster or demand an answer. He merely rose slowly to a sitting position before her.

"Evelyn?"

She touched him. How could she not? He was even more beautiful when he looked at her like that. He waited for her to speak, giving her his complete and total attention. What man would ever listen to her like this again?

"I'm so sorry," she whispered.

"I . . . um . . . Shouldn't I be apologizing to you?" he asked.

She shook her head. "I don't regret it. I don't regret any of it!"

He stroked his hand across her cheek. "It doesn't look that way to me."

She turned her face, pressing her lips into his palm. "I love you," she said. She thought she spoke too quietly for him to hear, but she felt the shock go through his entire body. His hand jerked against her skin and then abruptly stilled.

"I'm so sorry," she repeated, louder this time. "It's so stupid. You haven't even asked. In fact, you've even said you don't want me, so it doesn't matter." She pressed a last kiss into his hand, then pushed to her feet. "Which is for the best. I can't marry you. I have to be with Christopher." Her voice broke on her fiancé's name. She didn't want Christopher. More important, she didn't want to be so small a person as to need the security and comfort and wealth of his position. "I wanted . . . I thought I wanted to be so much more, but I'm . . . I'm not strong enough. I'm just not." She held her head up for a moment, looked into his eyes. He was staring back at her, obviously confused. He was giving her all his attention, but that didn't mean she made any sense to him.

It didn't matter, anyway. She'd made her decision. She pushed to her feet, wanting desperately to stay with him. She hovered there a moment before him, praying he'd say something. Maybe if he said the right thing, if he did the right thing, she would find the strength. Wouldn't he please make everything right?

He said nothing. How could he? He was still half asleep, he didn't understand what she was thinking, and there was no solution. She knew that, and yet she still hoped.

"Tell me," he said. "Evie, tell me how to help."

"You can't," she confessed. "I want you to, but there's nothing you can do."

Feeling like the worst kind of fool, she leaned down and kissed him on the mouth. She poured everything into that kiss—her love, her regret, the future she wished she could have—and then, as his fingers tightened on her shoulders and her breaths shortened with desire, she ripped herself away. She didn't stop running until she'd made it back into her toasty warm bedroom and curled sobbing beneath her down coverlet.

Chapter Eighteen

"Out of bed, lazy slug."

"I can't breathe," Jie Ke lied. "Don't make me move." Zhi Min wouldn't be fooled. He never was, but the long silence gave Jie Ke hope.

"You breathed well enough last night."

Jie Ke kept his eyes resolutely shut. It was hard enough lying to his friend like this; he'd never get away with it if he looked Zhi Min in the eye. "I was stupid last night." That was certainly true. "Today I confess to it, so let the idiot die in peace."

"You aren't dying."

Jie Ke opened his eyes. For a brief moment, he let his despair show. "Yes, I am."

His friend watched him closely. Jie Ke had intended to roll away, but he couldn't. Not when Zhi Min *became* a monk of the Xi Lin order. It was a transition that few could see and fewer still understood, but Jie Ke had seen it in others and was mesmerized as it happened to his friend. He watched Zhi Min become more than himself. His body faded from sight and a glowing orb of light replaced him. Zhi Min became power in its purest form, channeled, directed, and so perfect as to bring tears to Jie Ke's eyes. That was what it meant to be a Xi Lin monk, and it was what he had wanted for himself for so long.

Yet right now, it seemed so meaningless. *I love you. I have to be with Christopher.*

He closed his eyes and rolled away, turning his back on Zhi Min. "I hurt too much," he said to the wall.

"That is the first truth you have said this day."

Jie Ke resolutely kept his eyes shut, and in time Zhi Min left him alone. Unfortunately, being alone was not as wonderful as he had thought. His body was indeed exhausted, but his mind would not quiet. He kept reliving every moment with Evie—every breath, every kiss, every shared secret.

Nothing has changed, he told himself. He had come to England as his last task before becoming a full monk. He'd never intended to remain here, never intended to do anything more than kiss his grandmother hello and then turn back to China. All the rest had simply been for show so that Zhi Min would see he had done what his parents would have wanted, attempted to regain his title and marry the woman betrothed to him.

That was all, and it was over and done. Or it was nearly over, since he had yet to make peace with his grandmother. But that could be accomplished soon enough, and then it would be time to go home. Evelyn had made her choice—she had chosen his cousin Christopher—and so everything had worked out as was intended. He could become a full monk now. All he needed to do was speak with his grandmother.

He pulled the blanket over his face. When that didn't work, he made himself some of Zhi Min's tea for pain. Moments later, unconsciousness crept black and ugly over his thoughts.

He welcomed it with a smile.

"Wake up! Your grandmother awaits you."

Jie Ke braced himself without moving. He knew Zhi Min would kick the bed when he didn't respond. Next would come a smack to the head. Then the final insult, a bucket of cold water—but that was at the temple where pallets dried quickly in the sun. Here, he would likely be—

Splash! Icy water hit hard and full, stealing his breath and freezing him to his bones. He burst upright with a sputtering gasp. Zhi Min stood in front of him, eyes hard.

"I am done playing in this freezing country with you, English boy."

"Zhi Min!"

"Shut up! I left you to sulk for a full day. I lied to your family and your grandmother, saying you were too ill to move—"

"It wasn't a lie."

"But you have not come to your senses. So now I must force you, apprentice monk. Present yourself to your grandmother and be done with this farce."

Jie Ke frowned. His head ached, his breath was foul, and now his sheets stank. Or perhaps they already had. A full day and night in bed had not helped him any. Neither, apparently, had it helped his friend.

"What disrupted *your* serenity?" he groused as he pushed aside the sodden sheet.

"My serenity is fine."

"Dragon monks don't lie."

Zhi Min glared at him. "You do."

"I am not a full monk."

"Nor will you ever be if you don't finish this. Today."

Jie Ke stopped. He had been searching for a dry corner of the sheet to use as a towel, but he paused now to look at his friend. Something in Zhi Min's tone of voice was different. He narrowed his eyes.

"What aren't you saying?" he asked.

Zhi Min curled his lip and turned away. It was the most emotion the man had displayed since becoming a full monk.

Jie Ke grabbed his arm and pulled him back around. "What aren't you telling me?" he demanded again.

Zhi Min frowned. "Ever since you entered the temple grounds you have wished to be me."

"That's not true!"

"It *is* true," Zhi Min snapped back. "You wanted parents,

and my mother cared for you. You saw me fight and you wanted to learn."

"Of course I did—"

"Shut up, idiot, and listen!"

Jie Ke reared back. Never, even the night before Zhi Min's initiation, had Zhi Min ever been so rude to anyone. To hear it now was beyond shocking. Jie Ke closed his mouth.

"Good. Now hear me, white man. You wanted my mother, you wanted to fight, and then you wanted to be a monk. . . ."

When his friend didn't continue, Jie Ke threw up his hands. "That is the normal progression, isn't it? To see, to learn, to want more?"

Zhi Min poked a hard finger into Jie Ke's chest. "Who are you, white man? Do not look to me for your answer. Do not think, 'I want *that*.' Think, 'Who am I?' Then you will be what you were meant to be, not someone else's dream you are chasing."

Jie Ke stood slowly, coming to face his friend eye to eye. "I was meant to be a monk." He said it clearly and firmly. He spoke with all the conviction in his heart, and he believed it.

But as he spoke, he heard, *I am meant to be with Christopher.*

Zhi Min looked him in the eyes. Jie Ke knew he was being weighed and judged and measured. "Be sure, Jie Ke," his friend said. "It is not the only path. It is not an easy path—"

"I am sure."

Zhi Min sighed. "Very well then. Make peace with your grandmother and we will leave." He said it like a death knell, as if Jie Ke had just chosen to die. What was wrong with his friend that he spoke so full of sorrow? But Jie Ke got no further than an indrawn breath to question before Zhi Min held up his hand.

"I have told you, do not look to me for your answers. I have none." And with that, Zhi Min stomped out of the room.

His clothes were choking him. High collars, stiff fabrics, and the constant pinch of new shoes—Jie Ke remembered disliking this as a boy, and he despised it now. But he was sitting in a carriage with his grandmother and Evelyn on the way to Nana's home. It wasn't far from Evelyn's manor, but the road was pitted and the horses slow, which meant an eternity in these terrible clothes. Plus he remembered how she used to scold him when he fidgeted, so he sat still and tried not to breathe for fear of another sneezing fit. Powder and starch— who wore such irritants? Certainly not Evelyn, who was sitting beside him, her body stiff, her manner so reserved as to make her seem like a cold statue.

He knew how to unfreeze her. He knew where to touch her and what to whisper into her skin to make her warm up to him. But that had been a different time and a different place, and she had made her choice. He simply had to survive this day and then he could leave all of England behind.

"You needn't have come," he said to her stiff profile. "I'm sure grandmother and I would have rubbed along quite well without—"

"I insisted, Jacob," his grandmother inserted. "A husband and wife should get to know one another without others interfering and gossiping. This was the perfect opportunity—"

"Please, Lady Warhaven," Evelyn interrupted. "Please don't say such things. You know that . . . that Jie Ke and I will not marry. He wishes to go back to China, you know."

"China!" the old woman said with a gasp. "But the earl must remain here. In England."

Jie Ke smiled at his grandmother, remembering a different argument long ago. She had lost then, too. "My father went to China despite your protests. And you must know that they will not give me the title back. My cousin Christopher will make an excellent earl, someday."

"Christopher will make good whatever he does," she answered with a sniff. "We are speaking of you and your rights."

He opened his mouth to respond, though he had no idea

what he intended to say. Sneezes came out instead, a whole
slew of them, and by the time he caught his breath, they had
arrived at his grandmother's home.

The family estate at Warhaven was huge and depressing. The
stone and mortar edifice had once set his boyish heart beating
with excitement. It was perfect for a child who wanted to live
out pretend battles of knights and dragons, sieges and heroism.
Looking at it now, he well understood why Uncle Frank and
his family chose to live in the London residence instead. This
place was dark, old, and probably freezing cold in the best of
weather. Yet this was where his grandparents had lived for as
long as he could remember, and this was where he had spent a
great deal of his childhood.

"Come along, come along," his grandmother said as she
disembarked from the carriage. "I sent word ahead. Cook
will have prepared a luncheon." She turned and gave him a
wink. "Banbury buns, Jacob, just for you."

Evelyn descended next, her movements as graceful as ever
as she took the footman's hand and stepped out onto the
gravel path. She smiled as she went, the expression as unconscious as it was beautiful. The servant blushed. Jacob felt his
lip curve in a sneer as he stepped out of the vehicle. Then he
pulled up short, his breath frozen in his chest.

He looked up to see the sweeping entrance of the Tudor
mansion. His gaze skimmed the wide open doorway, the very
English proliferation of chimneys and the patterned red
brick. But what he saw instead was in his mind: a walkway
covered in icy snow. He remembered wading knee-high
through it while his nanny tried to call him back. He had
climbed every tree here, front and back. The old oak on the
west side had been his favorite.

"Jacob, Jacob! Come inside!"

He blinked, coming out of his reverie, but not completely.
It was as though he waded through air suddenly thick with
half-felt emotions and clogging thoughts. He desperately

wanted to leave, but he forced himself to remain, to walk slowly and enter the house of his childhood.

A butler bowed to him, extending a hand to take his hat and gloves. Jie Ke peeled them off gratefully and slowed his pace as he extended them. "I know you," he murmured.

The man smiled and gently lifted the gloves and hat away. "Yes, my lord."

Jie Ke focused on the bones of the man's face, the bristly brown hair, the crinkles at the sides of his eyes. None of it was perfectly familiar, and yet . . . Then the butler turned slightly as he set aside the hat, and Jie Ke saw a dark patch of skin, a birthmark that extended from the ear and down beneath the collar of his clothing.

"Egan the footman. I used to call you Egan, but you were really—"

"Edgar, my lord."

"Yes. Edgar. You used to play soldiers with me." Jie Ke blinked and frowned. "You're butler now. Congratulations."

"Thank you, my lord. Tea has been laid out in the near parlor."

He paused a moment, his gaze traveling down the dark interior hallway. He hated the near parlor. Why did he hate the near parlor? He looked at his grandmother, who stood watching him closely. Evelyn did, too, though her face was averted.

"The near parlor is where I poured sugar down your back," he said to her, remembering.

She looked up, obviously startled. "Yes," she said softly.

"Grandfather caned me after that. He knew and beat me for it." He glanced at the parlor door. "That's why I hate that room."

Grandmother's eyes widened. "Oh, well, we don't have to go in there, then. We can eat in the library—"

He shook his head. "No, I deserved it." He started walking forward, but again the air felt almost too thick for him to move. "Besides, every room in this house will have memories." His gaze shifted up the stairs. The nursery was there. He glanced back to Edgar. "Are my soldiers still up there?"

The older man grinned. "Bottom shelf of the bookcase."

"Just as if I never left them," Jie Ke said with a smile. He'd never cleaned or picked up his toys until China. Well, in China, he hadn't really had any toys to pick up.

Steeling his spine, he crossed into the near parlor. Nothing had changed, except that the rug had faded over time and the settee fabric had been replaced—though it remained the same soft blue color that his grandmother favored. The fireplace mantel appeared more cluttered, and . . .

"May I go upstairs?" Had those words come out of his mouth? He could barely breathe, so thick was the air. And yet, he was pulled to see more, to remember more.

"Of course," his grandmother answered.

Evelyn said nothing as she stepped out of his way. He would have to pass by her to leave the room. She was pale today, the rosy flush to her face changed to a dull whitish brown. But she was alive, she was beautiful, and she had absolutely nothing to do with the memories that were crowding around him now.

"Come with me," he said as he passed her. And then, acting on impulse, he grabbed her hand, quickly intertwining their fingers. She gasped, startled, and made to pull away, but he held her fast. And when their gazes met, he lifted her hand toward his chest. "Please walk with me. I breathe better when you're with me."

It was the truth, though he didn't understand why. Neither did she, and she glanced nervously at his grandmother.

"Go on, dear. My bones are too old to go up and down the stairs like that. I'll just wait here."

He could see that Evelyn was going to object. The propriety of the situation was clearly dubious, but he didn't care. "I am leaving tomorrow morning," he whispered. "Please, just walk with me."

Her eyes lifted to meet his. They were crystal clear and blue, even in this rather dark house. He met her gaze and held it, and was soon lost in her eyes, focusing on the widening of her pupils and the shifting blue striations. If he thought only of that—of the beauty of round, blue eyes so like his own—then he could breathe again.

Evelyn never actually agreed aloud to walk with him, but they moved as one. They took two steps back into the hallway together, and then he had to break eye contact. He could not mount the stairs while staring at her.

"What is up there that you want to see?" she asked.

"I don't know," he answered. "Perhaps I am only delaying breaking Grandmother's heart." He glanced back into the parlor. "She will not accept that I have to leave. She thinks this is my home."

"Isn't it? Do you really want to return to that foreign place? What waits for you there that can compare to all of this?" She gestured as she spoke, pointing out the stately English home he'd once loved. "Even if you never regain the title, there is still land and wealth and English society. Your grandmother . . ."

He wasn't listening. The moment she had gestured to the house, his attention was once again caught by the stairway. He began climbing, their entwined hands dragging slightly behind him. He slowed a bit so that she could keep pace, but he did not release her. And she dutifully walked with him.

The nursery was to the right, but he couldn't even see the doorway. He saw instead his memories: chasing his sister down the hall; crashing into a hallway table and breaking one of the legs; rolling a ball down the long expanse and trying to knock flat a wall of soldiers at the opposite end.

He pushed through the nursery door just as he had as a child, with force and complete disregard for the wall behind. He was much stronger now than he'd been at ten. The door banged hard against the plaster and he winced. Then he wrinkled his nose. The smell of the nursery was wrong. He smelled dust and dry rot.

"My sister painted," he murmured. There was no scent of charcoal or watercolors. No brushes or wet fabric. "She painted on clothing—muslins first, but then velvet and even silk." His gaze went to the corner where the light danced through dust motes. His sister's brushes were there, neatly lined up on a desk, her sketch papers stacked beside them.

A chill entered his body, and he shivered. Evelyn tightened her grip in question, but he shook his head. He couldn't speak, but he could hold her as his lifeline. She was beside him as he turned to leave. As a reflex, he whistled, two notes—one high, one low—calling a dog that was long since dead. But he had always whistled like that before leaving the nursery, and so he did it now. Then he froze. Of everything he had missed after leaving England, his dog had been the hardest to lose.

He stared at the empty spot before the fire. "Zeus always slept there," he murmured. Then he swallowed and looked away, once again finding Evelyn's gaze. Blue eyes, so like his own. "Why do I have to remember this?" he asked.

"Because it is yours—your memory, your heritage."

Blue eyes like his own. "Do *you* want me to stay in England? Do you want me to be with you?"

Her gaze dropped away. Her blue eyes were shielded from him.

"I am too Chinese for you." He laughed. "And I am too English for the Chinese."

"That's not the reason," she answered. He thought she was lying, but she raised her eyes, her gaze skittering between him and the door and back. "What you want, where we would go—I would leave everything behind."

"Not if I lived here in England."

He watched hope spark in her eyes. A flash of desire appeared, so strong that her hand spasmed inside his. "Could you do that, Jie Ke? Could you stay in this place?"

"No." The word came out in a kind of panic. He could not stay here. He couldn't bear it. And he couldn't give up all that he had worked so hard for in China. "I am a monk," he said firmly. He looked about the room, seeing it for what it was, not what it once had been. "These memories hold no power over me," he lied. Then he walked out of the room, intending to go downstairs.

He ended up somewhere different. Instead of downstairs, he found himself in the opposite wing of the house, in front of what once had been his parents' two bedrooms. For Mama: lilac and white, with ruffles everywhere. Browns and gold, dark wood and a high bed for Papa. Jie Ke stood in the doorways—one room after the other—and felt the heavy battering of memory.

The smell of snuff had faded. Similarly, his mother's perfume was gone. Dust and old furniture polish were the scents that lingered. And yet he could still hear his father's booming laugh and his mother's chiding voice echoing down the hall. Tea. He remembered his mother drank tea up here in her bedroom.

"Are you all right?" Evelyn's words were a soft whisper, but they somehow drowned out the echoes of time.

He nodded. "The Chinese believe in ghosts. They believe the ancestors follow and protect their descendants or haunt those who don't honor them."

She stared at him. "But you don't feel them."

"No," he agreed. "I thought they would linger here. I thought I would feel them, but . . ." He shrugged. "They are just an echo. A memory that is already fading."

He took a deep breath, feeling his chest ease for the first time in days, perhaps months. "One last ghost to lay to rest," he said, gesturing to his grandfather's room. "Ready?"

She nodded, though he could see regret in her eyes. It warmed his heart that she didn't want his last tie to England to disappear. But she had chosen Christopher, he reminded himself, and so he turned away from her. But he did not release her hand.

His grandfather's room wasn't dusty. The room was aired, but the smell of pipe tobacco was still strong, plus the remains of a fire dead a week or more now.

"Your grandmother must still come in here," Evelyn said. And with her words he caught an echo of the dowager countess's powder.

"Yes, she must," he agreed. Then he wandered deeper into the room. "My grandfather was a stern man," he murmured. "He had no understanding of my father's passions. A dog, toy soldiers—these things he understood. But my father's love of plants? Of exploration into foreign climes to sketch bizarre people and things?"

"He didn't approve of your father?"

"Not in the least. He called Uncle Frank a boor at times, but at least Uncle Frank 'knew what it meant to be English.'"

She smiled, recognizing his description of the current earl. "Sheep, wheat, and local politics—what more could a proper Englishman care about?"

He tightened his grip on her hand. "I never really understood either of them. Why did my grandfather have to limit the world to England? And why did my father care so much about pictures of foreign birds? Back then, I wasn't sure why we were setting off to China. . . ."

She tilted her head. "And now?"

He frowned back at her. "Now? Now, nothing. They are both dead and their thoughts are even fainter than their memories."

He turned to leave the room, but she held him back by their joined hands. She stood there and looked at him, her eyes widening as if she saw something for the first time.

"What?" he asked.

"I see now why the abbot made you come back here."

He pulled away, startled. "What?"

"You are a lost boy, cut adrift from everything you once were."

He gaped at her. She might as well have been speaking Greek. He had no true comprehension of her words.

She waved at the room with her free hand. "Your family is dust, and they mean nothing to you. Your home is an echo to you—your grandmother makes you sneeze. You push me to discover who I am, what I want, and yet you are like a blank slate. It's like you have no past and no future, so you might as well become a monk."

Fire burned through his mind, bringing pain with it. "You know nothing of what I want or who I am," he growled.

"Nothing at all," she agreed. "Because you don't know either. Isn't that what the abbot said—that you have to remember who you are?"

He spluttered, looking for the words to fight her, but his mind had splintered open with pain. A headache threatened. He hadn't had one like this since that first day at the church, but now he longed for a bucket of ice water.

"I see it so clearly," she murmured. "You said it that first night. The path of a monk is to see the truth with clarity and to search for another answer when one fails." She stepped closer to him, pulled herself directly in front of him to see into his eyes. "This is the truth you have failed to see, Jie Ke. That you are blank until you remember *this*."

"But I remember all of this! It just means nothing!"

She looked at him sadly, and the compassion in her eyes cut him all the way to the bone. "I have lived all my life as a 'future countess.' Until you, that label occupied my every waking and sleeping thought." She brought his hand to her mouth, pressing her lips against his knuckles. "It was maddening, it was overwhelming, and most of all, it erased everything I could have been long before I even had a chance to discover what I wanted to be. Jacob, my past was . . ." She shrugged. "It is so much more than nothing."

He pulled his hand out of hers, a fury rising from deep within him. "That is your choice, Evelyn, to be saddled with your past. It is most certainly not mine."

She threw up her hands. "That's the whole point! Where one comes from is not a choice. It *exists*. And until you acknowledge the past, you can't progress to the future."

"You are being foolish!" he snapped and whirled away. He didn't see where he was going. The pain in his head impinged too much on his vision. He had thought he was moving to the bedroom door. Instead, he ducked through the connecting hallway to his grandmother's room.

He recognized the error immediately. Her huge dressing table loomed before him as he stumbled forward. He saw his face in her mirror: pale, as white as the ghost man the Chinese peasants labeled him. The sight made him shake, and pain lanced once again through his head.

He tried to focus elsewhere. He blinked at the array of bottles and perfumes. Feminine frippery, his grandfather used to say, yet his sister had been fascinated. He reached out to touch a tin. The lid was askew, and he could push it back down. He thought of nothing else but that. Replace the lid for his grandmother. Push the top back down.

But Evelyn had followed him. She didn't speak, or if she did, he couldn't hear. But he felt her. She touched his back at just the wrong moment. He jumped and his hand slipped off the tin. The lid clattered on the table and the tin tipped with the force of his reaction. The powder flew up. It had been filled with Grandmother's white powder, which now perfumed the air and whitened everything—the table, the air, and him. In his reflection, he saw himself covered in the stuff.

And in that moment, he remembered.

Chapter Nineteen

Powdered. Mama's face was white and perfect, just as she liked it. The monks had insisted that he help prepare the bodies. Jacob hadn't done anything. The orange-robed brothers did all the work, but he'd been in the room. He'd seen. He'd smelled. And like the earl he had become upon his father's death, he hadn't vomited.

His parents looked almost nice. With the blood and mud gone, Mama's face didn't even *need* powder. It was white and perfect, just as she liked it.

Jie Ke turned away, knowing she would never see his cowardice, but there was nowhere to turn. Papa was to the left, Maria to the right, and Mama in the center. There were other bodies, too. Other people the abbot insisted he visit: porters, servants, the monk guide. He saw them all as he walked body to body with the abbot. And every one of the corpses was powder white, even the ones whose skin was normally colored like mud. Their eyes were slightly open, their bodies stretched out as if dozing.

Zhi Min's mother had joined them for part of the walk, her Chinese words flowing out of her like turbulent water. She had held his hand for a while and patted his cheek, but then her duties had called her away. Jacob had been left with the abbot and all those bodies.

He endured a rough night on a pallet, bad dreams with screaming people and knives and blood. So much blood. Then early morning prayers. Even at that time he'd understood the rhythms of the temple, though it would be many weeks before he adopted them as his own. And after prayers . . . the burning.

The abbot tried to explain it to him, but Jacob's Chinese was deplorable. Even with pictures drawn in the dirt he hadn't understood. Bodies in a crematorium with smoke rising meant nothing to him. The English buried their dead. He hadn't understood until he saw them carry the body of a porter inside the building, and still it had taken a moment to comprehend that his parents and sister had gone in first. That they had all been burned inside.

None of it felt real. He had expected to accompany his family back to England. He had held on to that. It would be his first act as an earl. He would travel with them all the way back to England.

But then he'd felt the powder: ash. White ash was everywhere—in the air, on his clothes, in his nostrils.

His parents and sister had burned first. Out of respect to their status, the title he kept repeating over and over, his family had been burned first, and now they were gone. There was nothing to take back to England. Even the ash was mixed in with everyone else's, and the air was thick with it.

Jacob screamed and ran for the crematorium. He desperately needed to recover what little of them was left. He ripped past the women, tore through the line of praying monks, and neared the workers with the other bodies. He was an earl, he screamed, they had to listen to him. He was an earl! He had to bring his family back to England!

He couldn't breathe. The ash was everywhere, a thick cloud that choked off breath. He nearly made it to the door. The heat was unbearable, flowing in waves over his body, bringing pain to every inch of skin.

Then pain exploded along his temple. He'd learned later that the abbot had struck him. He had caught Jacob with a kick to the temple, and only that swift action had kept him from running into the oven with his family.

He'd woken an hour later and had begun screaming with his first breath.

He realized now that he'd never stopped.

Evelyn held Jie Ke. He was screaming and clawing at his face. She tried to pull his hands down, but he was too strong. Servants poured into the room, quickly followed by the dowager countess and . . . and the Reverend Smythe-Jones?

"Help me hold him down," she cried. He would claw bloody streaks in his face soon if she didn't prevent it. Except, just as the Reverend stepped close, Jacob shifted. He was still screaming, but his voice had cut out. The only sound that emerged from his open mouth was a high keening. His hands stopped working at his face to pull tight to his chest, and he curled against her. His face buried against her breast and he rocked.

"What happened?" his grandmother asked.

Evelyn had no answers. "He fell and knocked over that powder," she said. She didn't mention the way he had looked at himself in the mirror as if he'd stared at death itself.

"It's everywhere," added the reverend, brushing ineffectively at the dressing table.

Evelyn came to a quick decision. "Please, Reverend," she said. "Please go find his friend Zhi Min and bring him here. As discreetly as possible," she added with a wince. There was nothing discreet about anything that involved the reverend, but at least he wouldn't be here gathering more fodder for gossip.

The man nodded sagely. "Excellent notion. I'll go straightaway." Then he left without fanfare.

The dowager countess meanwhile dispatched her servants for water and a washcloth. If they could do nothing else, Evelyn supposed, they could clean the powder away. Once all the servants had been dispatched, the elderly woman knelt in front of her. "Tell me it all," she ordered sternly. "What happened?"

Evelyn looked down and stroked Jie Ke's hair back off his brow. His body still shook in her arms, but he no longer seemed to be screaming. At least, not on the outside. He had the look of a man who had been living a nightmare all his life—or, more likely, since that awful massacre two decades earlier.

"He remembered something, I think," she finally said.

"That awful place," his grandmother snapped. "I told his father over and over that he had no business taking the family out there. No business at all." She wiped at her eyes, then placed a hand on her grandson's shoulder. "What that boy must have seen." She abruptly straightened. "But that's all over now. He is back in England where he belongs."

"I don't think so," Evelyn murmured, finally giving voice to something she was only now beginning to understand. "That's what we were arguing about before." She tightened her hold on him. Jie Ke wasn't aware of her, obviously still trapped in his own nightmare, but it gave her comfort to cradle him in her arms. "He's not really English anymore."

"Well, he's certainly not Chinese!" the woman snapped.

Evelyn nodded. "That's the problem, I think. He doesn't really know who he is. An earl without a title, a monk who isn't fully . . . ordained." She didn't know the real word for what he wanted, but that would have to do. She leaned down and pressed her lips to his temple. "Jacob or Jie Ke," she murmured. "I don't care who you are. Just come back." She pressed her cheek to his. "Come back to me, please."

The world was white ash as fine as the powder they put on their faces. Jacob stood in the middle of a blank landscape. One moment he thought he saw the rolling hills of England. The next, he saw the ornate roof tiles of the temple. But then the wind blew powder in his eyes and he saw nothing.

The landscape flattened, buried beneath the weight of all that powder. If there was sound, it was deadened. If there was scent, it was lost. Nothing existed here except for him. And he had been alone here for such a long, long time.

A ripple shifted through the landscape. Like a circle on a pond of white, he saw the world change, a tiny fraction of movement until it was gone again. He found himself staring at the ground, focusing hard. Would it come again? Would he see the movement again?

There! Life. Where there was movement, there was life. Or so he told himself. And he was so tired of sitting with the dead. But where was it?

Beneath the surface! Something—someone—was below the ash. Someone was struggling there to breathe, to get out, to . . .

He had no tool with which to dig, so he dropped to his knees and began shoving aside dust with his hands. Until now, he hadn't wanted to touch the stuff. He had hated the feel of it in his hair, the taste of it in his mouth, but not now. Now, someone's life was at stake. So he dug even as he sneezed and coughed and gasped.

The rippling continued, more obvious now that he was digging. "Can you hear me?" he screamed. "Are you there?"

He heard an answer. More important, he felt a response, but he couldn't make sense of it. His only choice was to keep digging as hard and as fast as possible. And the deeper he went, the more the landscape changed.

First came the mounds of debris. Like charred bodies in gruesome display, they grew around him. It made no sense that ash and dust could form such ugly skeletons, but there they were, and he paused a moment to stare.

They were his parents, he realized, and his sister. He looked at them and mourned, but they were gone and someone was alive beneath. So he turned away from them and dug, and the landscape changed again.

The winds blew hot and dry like the summers in China. The ash whispered away, but the ground remained brown and parched. His mouth ached for something to drink. To the side, a lake of cool water appeared. He heard the splash of boys at play and turned to see cranes stepping delicately through the water, searching for fish. He straightened, feeling bizarrely unsettled by the sight. Water, play—and Zhi Min was smiling at him from his place of contemplation just beyond the near rushes.

"Come help me!" he screamed to his friend. "Here! Under here!"

Zhi Min didn't respond except to wave. He was too far away to hear, and Jacob would not waste the time to run to get him. His only hope was that Zhi Min would see him digging and come help. So he dived back into the hole he'd created and continued to dig.

It was quiet here, the air cool, and the smell of rich black dirt invaded his nostrils. Sheep, horse, even dog smells filled the air. England, he realized with a slight laugh. He'd dug all the way to England, but where was the person beneath? Where was the movement?

He stilled, listening hard. He heard his own heartbeat. He felt a warmth surround him. He felt filthy and exhausted, and grimaced at the bitter taste in his mouth. But where was the person beneath?

He would have to do it. He would have to plunge himself all the way into this deepest, darkest pit he had dug. Only down there could he find the soul beneath the grime.

He took a breath. He looked up to see the gray sky that was so familiar. He heard the laughter of the children and the echoing gong of the temple. Then he straightened his spine—he was an earl after all and would show courage—and dove.

He opened his eyes in his grandmother's bedroom and saw Evelyn, so beautiful and so perfect, with her arms wrapped around him. He blinked, trying to separate fact from fantasy. Had he been dreaming? It had seemed so real.

"Jacob? Jie Ke?" she said, her hand stroking his temple.

Evie, he thought. He hadn't breath to say her name. Evie was real. Her chest pressed tight against his, heart pounding, was real. Her arms supporting his head, her hands stroking his face, and her eyes—so blue, like his own—these things were real. She was real.

Surging up, he kissed her. And in that moment, two things happened. First, the world righted itself. His mind focused on his senses: his lips pressed to hers, the scent of her skin, and the sound of her gasp just before she kissed him back as deeply and as possessively as he'd taken her.

Second, came chaos. The room exploded with the sound of people and exclamations and Zhi Min speaking in his most formal tone: "So be it. I will miss you at the temple, my brother."

Jacob tore himself away from Evelyn and forced his gaze to find that of his best friend. They looked at each other without words, communicating as they had often done in their morning sparring matches, with a flick of an eye or the twitch of a hand. Today there was nothing more than a nod . . . but it was enough.

Jacob would not be accepted at the temple, he now knew. He had never been right for a monastic life, and his place was here with Evelyn. It always had been. The message was understood and accepted by both men, and it felt so desperately right to Jie Ke. Or it did until Evelyn suddenly shoved him backwards and away.

He didn't fall. He had regained too much strength to fall flat on the ground, but he hadn't the power to keep her at his side. She pulled back from him, her eyes leaping between him and Zhi Min . . . and then to Christopher, who was just outside the door.

"No," she gasped. "No, you don't understand," she said to the room at large. "He belongs in China. He's not an Englishman anymore."

"Don't be ridiculous," his grandmother exclaimed happily. "Of course he is! He's the earl!"

Chapter Twenty

Evelyn could not bear to look at Jie Ke. The pain in his eyes overwhelmed her. It made her want to help him—to dare anything—if only the agony in his eyes faded. It made her want to be bold, but she couldn't do that. So she turned her gaze aside.

Yet she didn't release him. They were still touching—his arm was across her lap, her hands on his shoulders. She held him, she knew him, and she wondered if life would ever return to some level of normalcy.

In that instant, Christopher pushed into the room. He shouldered his way in, his gaze cutting across the tableau before him. Evelyn knew what he saw: his fiancée holding his cousin and rival. The shock at her final betrayal was stark on his face, but it swiftly shifted to an angry glower. It was an expression she had seen more and more of in the last few days.

"What's the meaning of this?" he demanded.

"Calm yourself, Christopher," she said smoothly. How easily she slipped into her intended role of future countess. "Jacob fell. I was merely helping him up." It was a thinly veiled lie. Anyone with eyes could see that she was doing a great deal more than helping Jacob stand. In fact, at the moment, she was holding on to him like a child with a favorite toy. Or a woman protecting a lover.

"I am well enough now," Jacob said softly. He slowly, stiffly, disentangled himself from her. It was no more than she deserved. She had just disavowed him, and yet the pain of it cut through her heart so deeply that she momentarily lost her breath. And in that gasping pain, she lost her grip on him.

Jacob rolled away, gaining his feet in one smooth motion. She watched him stand, noting that there was no hesitation in the movement, no sign of injury either physical or mental. In fact, he seemed more directed, more focused than she'd ever seen him.

"So, you have it all," Jacob said softly. "My title, money, even my bride."

Christopher stepped more fully into the room, his eyes narrowing, his hands tightening into fists. "I have nothing that is not rightfully mine."

Jacob laughed, the sound bitter and angry. "You still deny it? You still can look me in the eye and pretend that I am not Jacob? I am your cousin. We once were friends!"

Christopher shook his head. "You are a liar and a fraud. You have done nothing but confirm that opinion."

"You are blind, Christopher. A fool who sees nothing but what he is told to see." Then Jie Ke glanced over at Evelyn. She had been slowly gaining her feet, but his gaze froze her in place—not because it was cold or angry, but because it was filled with admiration and love. "Enjoy her while you can, cousin," he said softly. "She has taken the first steps to becoming her true self. She will not be ruled by your emptiness for much longer."

The blow was struck too fast for her to see. One moment, Jacob was looking at her with such tenderness, the next, his face was slammed aside and his blood splattered her clothing. She cried out in alarm, instinctively stepping forward to steady Jacob, but he didn't need her. Instead, his bloodied lips split into a slow grin.

"Are we to fight then, Chris? Do you think she will be impressed and choose—"

More blows flew at him, but this time Chris aimed for Jie

Ke's injured ribs. Jie Ke blocked them, his arms as fast as his attacker's, but she knew how the effort cost him. Though no blow connected, the force of each impact echoed in the room.

"You have no right to even look at her!" Chris bellowed. "She is mine!"

Jie Ke laughed at that, though the sound was strained. "Do you truly believe you can own anything, much less Evelyn?"

The words clearly enraged Chris. He attacked with a fury that seemed to explode through the room. Jie Ke was hard-pressed. The room was narrow and filled with furniture, not to mention the people who crowded forward, all speaking at once.

Evelyn didn't hear any of them. All she saw was the steady rain of fists from Chris. All she heard was the echoing smack as Jie Ke blocked blow after blow. Jie Ke's breath was becoming more labored, and she saw grimaces of pain flash through his features.

"Stop it!" she said, her voice becoming more commanding with each word. "Christopher, he's hurt. Stop this now!"

No effect. If anything, Christopher attacked with more ferocity.

"You are losing her," Jie Ke said. "She already sees you for a lout!"

"You're taunting him!" Evelyn cried. "What the hell are you thinking?"

Jie Ke didn't answer, for the fight got uglier. At first there had been controlled and forceful blows, steadily blocked. Now Christopher attacked with a wild anger, and Jie Ke fought back with equal ferocity. Blow after blow was exchanged, with neither man gaining ground. Except, something was different. Evelyn had seen Jie Ke fight. Not only the time in the ring, but the morning before with Zhi Min—not to mention when he had single-handedly held off Christopher, Chris's brothers, and the reverend. Why wasn't he finishing this travesty?

She stepped closer, seeing the mounting darkness in both men's faces. "Stop it!" she cried again. "Jie Ke, end this now!"

Timing her interference as best she could, she tried to reach into the fight. Both men flinched away with hardly a break in their rhythm. She wasn't touched, but neither did she change anything.

"Damn it, Jacob! End this!"

"See him," he grunted between blows. "See him clearly."

She looked at Christopher and saw the vicious anger that poured out of her onetime fiancé. But the same primal fury surrounded Jie Ke as well. She had always known he had this darkness in him, but never had she seen it so clearly displayed. It was there—raw and ugly—and he still didn't end the fight.

Only one person could end this, and it obviously wasn't either of the two men. With a muttered curse, Evelyn gathered her skirts and dove forward. It was ridiculously stupid, like stepping in the middle of a dogfight, but she knew it would work. Both men loved her, and she would see them stop fighting each other.

She tensed, expecting the blows that were sure to land. She'd leapt toward their fists, thinking to knock them both aside. She managed in beautiful style, spinning both men aside while her arm took the brunt of the impact.

Jie Ke was sure-footed. As she pushed in, he'd spun around, moving with her momentum so that she fell forward and he didn't lose position or footing. Christopher was not so skilled. She'd shoved his left arm aside, but the right shot forward. He'd been aiming at Jie Ke's face, but now his fist headed straight for her.

Jie Ke was faster. While she fell to the ground between them, Jie Ke caught Christopher's fist in his open palm.

"Are you mad?" screamed the reverend from the side.

"Furious!" she snapped. Her two suitors stood frozen above her, their eyes narrowed, their bodies taut with leashed fury. She glared at them both, then quickly made her decision. She slowly, deliberately stood up between the two men. Then she planted both palms on their chests and pushed outward.

They didn't move, and with a grimace of disgust, she pulled back, curling her fingers like daggers, then she shoved, nails first and with all her strength, against their chests.

This time they moved backwards, though perhaps they were only humoring her. Each man kept his gaze locked on the other.

"Are you both idiots? Do you think this impresses me?"

She could hardly believe that these two men were fighting over her. In some ways it was the stuff of every girl's romantic dreams, but right now it wholly disgusted her.

"I love you both!" she cried. "Do you think I want to see you kill each other? Bloody hell, how stupid are you?"

Christopher flinched, his fist twitching in Jie Ke's grip. "You love *him*?"

Jie Ke didn't say anything, but she saw hope spark in his eyes. She shook her head to clear it, putting a hand on each man's extended arm and pushing them apart. Eventually fist and palm separated, and both men dropped their hands.

"You are like two little boys fighting over a toy," she growled. She turned to Christopher. "Where have you been? Two days ago you went to speak to your mother. The next thing I know you are gone without a word. Where did you go? And why are you back? Why are you here?"

Christopher blanched and then glanced at the other people in the room. "Perhaps this is best discussed elsewhere."

She snorted. "You didn't think about the other people when you burst in here." She stepped forward, trying to feel what she once had for this man. She took his hands and held them up. "Can you not be honest with me?"

He looked down at her, his lips tight and his fingers strong. "This is a *family* discussion," he stressed.

She nodded, her suspicions confirmed. "So you know now. You know he is the true earl."

His gaze jumped from her to Jie Ke and then back. She could see the panic in his eyes, and a terror that went all the way through his body. "I know no such thing," he said stiffly. "But we can certainly discuss the possibility at a more seemly time."

She touched his face, the truth at last clear to her. "Does England only breed cowards?" she murmured, thinking of herself as much as him.

His eyes widened and his head jerked so that he looked away from her. "You go too far!" he growled.

She blinked, her thoughts coming back to the present. "I didn't mean you, Chris. Not really. I meant me." She shook her head. "Jie Ke says that monks see the truth with clarity. And they search for a better answer when one fails." She sighed. "I am not a future countess," she said finally. "Not like you want. I think I pretended for so long that I didn't believe I could be anything else." She lifted her chin, feeling strength come with the movement. "But I *can* be something else. I can find a better answer."

She started to turn away from him, but Christopher grabbed her arm, holding her still. "Find a better answer? What does that even mean, Evie? You think I've failed you?"

She looked him in the eye, recalled every moment that they had shared, every touch, every secret. "We are too much alike, Chris. And because of that, I think we have failed each other. I'm so sorry that I didn't understand this earlier. And sorrier too for the way I have hurt you." She pulled her arm free and turned away, relieved to realize that she would never marry him. No matter what happened in the future, Christopher was now in her past. He must have understood as well because she heard him back away.

Which left Jie Ke. Or Jacob. She smiled at him, but her hands shook. He reached for her.

"Does that mean I am your other answer?" he asked.

"No," she said softly. She turned and her chest ached to see the pain and fear fill his eyes. "You have just this hour re-membered your past. How can you know what you want?"

"As you have just discovered yourself," he responded. She felt the tremors coursing through his body. "But I know my answers lie with you, Evelyn. The question is: what do you think of me?"

She hesitated. For all that she wanted to commit herself body and soul to this man, she was still terribly afraid. She knew so little of the world outside of England. How would she survive it?

"Do you remember the last time I saw you as a child?" he asked.

She frowned, thrown by his strange question. "When you put sugar down my back."

"No, there was one more time, but perhaps you don't re-member. We were both very young."

She shook her head. "No. There was no other time—"

"Do you remember a boy in the rain? A child that threw mud at you and chased you through the thunderstorm? We played tag and laughed when the thunder rumbled down at us."

She gasped, the memory so clear in her mind. "That was you? You were my faery boy?"

Around them, the others listened with rapt attention. Eve-lyn didn't care. Let them hear it all. He was the boy from that night!

"I never wanted to go to China, you know," he said. "So the night before we left, I ran away. I was going to show my father that I could live on my own without him."

Evelyn pressed a hand to her mouth, but she could not hold back the words. "It was a summer storm and it was so hot in my room. I had to get outside. In just my shift, I ran outside and giggled when I was soaked to the skin." Her whole body lightened at the memory. "I felt so free."

"That is how I remember you. Wild, spinning in the rain, laughing as if you had so much joy—"

"My body couldn't contain it all," she finished for him. "That was you?"

"Whenever it got bad in China, whenever I was lonely or frightened or hurting so bad I could barely breathe—I would remember that night in England and . . ."

"You would think of me?"

"I would hate you, Evelyn. I was stuck in a hot, dry foreign land while you were here in the wet, the wild, and the green. And you were so very free." His eyes looked vulnerable. She could not stop herself from stepping closer to him, from touching his face.

"You. My faery boy was you."

"And you were Miss Evelyn Stanton who was a stuffy priss by day—"

"And a wild child at night." She closed her eyes and remembered how wonderful she'd felt. Cold, wet, covered in mud, and yet so happy that the memory had become her secret delight—a treat she pulled out and held tight whenever she felt too restricted.

"Were you afraid then?" he asked.

"Of course not. The world was so marvelous a place. How could anyone be afraid?" She bit her lip as a fierce longing rushed through her. "But I was a child. I knew nothing."

"All of us know nothing," he said. "We are as vulnerable now as we were as children. It is only the illusion of name and title—"

"House and servants? They are very real."

He nodded. "They help. But at what cost, Evelyn? Who do you want to be: a countess locked inside her home with servants and people to shield you against the world? Or that child set free in the elements?"

The child. She wanted to be the child again, so ready to embrace the world even when it was wet, cold, and dirty.

"I love you," she said, hearing the weight of those words and the power of saying such things aloud. "But I do not know that I can be so free during the day. I do not know how."

"I will help you," he said. Then he kissed her. One moment they were touching hand to hand, the next, she was in his arms and all else faded away. He stroked her mouth in awe, and she opened her lips to his in offering. And as he plundered and possessed her physically, her soul slipped inside him.

Within seconds, she felt as if the two of them had become one body and soul. It was amazing, frightening, and wholly wonderful. She didn't know it was possible to marry a man with just a kiss, but that was what the moment felt like. And as they separated, she saw the same stunned awe reflected in his eyes.

Into this moment of perfection, Jacob's grandmother abruptly dragged in the Reverend Smythe-Jones. "I told you!" she crowed. "I told you they would end up together. Now marry them right now!"

"But—"

"Legalities be damned," she snapped.

"Lady Warhaven!"

"I will make sure all the proper notices and the like are covered, and that the current contract is dissolved," she said with all the force in her frail body—and a stern look at Christopher. "Now do God's will!"

Other voices exploded in the room, a cacophony of objections and complications and noise. Evelyn ignored them all, her eyes still held by Jie Ke's.

"I will have to go back to China," he said softly. "I need to talk to the abbot. There are still things I need to understand."

She nodded, already committed to the travel. But then she sobered. "You cannot become a monk now, can you?"

He shook his head, but his smile grew. He said, "I think the abbot always knew that." They both glanced sideways at Zhi Min, only to discover that the man had already left.

"Where did he go?" Evelyn asked.

Jie Ke shrugged. "I don't know. I think he had his own task to complete here in England. He never said for sure, but I think he has gone to complete it." Then Jie Ke's gaze shifted again, this time to where Christopher stood watching, body stiff and angry. If he weren't boxed in on all sides, then Evelyn was sure her ex-fiancé would have left by now. Fortunately he was trapped, so he could hear what Jacob was now saying.

"I renounce my claim to the title," Jie Ke said. "When you inherit, have it with my blessing."

That silenced the room completely . . . for about ten seconds. And then the objections began—first from his grandmother and then, surprisingly, from Christopher himself.

"Don't be a fool!" they all cried.

Evelyn silenced them with a raised hand. "No, he's right. Christopher, you already told me that it would never go through. And besides . . ." She smiled at Jie Ke. "He doesn't know how to be an earl. Not as you do. Let him choose his own path. Let *us* choose our own paths." Then she turned to the Reverend Smythe-Jones. "Marry us, please. We will need my dowry for the long trip to China." She looked to Christopher. "Will you be steward of my family's land? It's what our fathers really wanted, anyway, our estates combined."

Christopher's expression shifted, emotions tightening his features so that she couldn't even begin to read them. In the end he spoke, his tone low and dignified just as a future earl's should be. "Our estates *won't* be combined, and this is not what *I* wanted." He ground this teeth together as he glared at Jie Ke. He turned back to Evelyn as he sketched her the briefest of bows. "But I will do as you wish. I will look after your people and land."

She had to be content with that. She wanted to apologize to him, she wanted to see the anger and pain fade from his eyes, but that was no longer possible, she knew. She could only thank him as graciously as possible and pray he would eventually forgive her.

Then the Reverend Smythe-Jones cleared his throat so that it echoed in the room. Evelyn nearly laughed. Here, finally, was her wedding. She stood in Lady Warhaven's bedchamber with Christopher and a score of servants in attendance. Not the ceremony of a future countess, not really appropriate in any sense of the word. But then Jie Ke spoke, and his voice held such clarity and truth that his words echoed through her soul.

"I love you, Evelyn Stanton," he said. "I will honor you, cherish you, and protect you with everything I am. Thank you, my love, for choosing to stand by my side for the rest of our lives."

It wasn't the traditional vow, but she knew these were words that she would remember forever. The reverend, of course, insisted on the traditional vows, which Jacob dutifully spoke. Then it was her turn, and she spoke from the heart.

"I love you, Jacob Jie Ke Cato. I will follow you to the ends of the earth and will try not to complain too much. Thank you, my heart, for helping me to become better than I was and for staying by my side as I discover so much more."

More usual words came later, as did the kiss and the wedding night. And for the first time in Evelyn's life, the future stretched before her in unexplored majesty. She was terrified, and yet she couldn't wait to begin. With Jacob by her side, she could do anything.

"Are you sure?" she asked late that night. They were lying naked next to one another, their legs still entwined.

"About what?" He was stroking lazy circles across her back that made her toes curl in delight.

"Your title. Your life here in England." She pushed up to look him in the eye. "You were the earl. Do you really want to give all that up?"

"Do you?"

She nodded, absolutely sure. "I'm afraid, but . . . I never

thought it possible, but there is so much more to the world than being a countess. So much more than England." The very idea seemed amazing, and yet the truth of it rang in her soul.

"I was never trained to be an earl," he said. "My father hated it—all the responsibilities and duties made him cringe."

Evie smiled. She understood that better than anyone. "But you could learn."

"I don't want to learn." He pushed up on his elbow, his expression so open that she was momentarily stunned by the beauty of him. "I don't know what will happen at the temple." He grinned. "And before you ask: Yes, if I must choose between you and a holy path then I will choose you. I *have* chosen you."

She released a breath she didn't even realize she'd been holding.

"I may simply want to live near the temple or, perhaps, if I can, begin a whole new one closer to home."

"I could still see my family sometimes?"

He grinned and dropped a kiss on her nose. "Of course. I would not cut you off from them completely."

"I would endure it, if you asked. My life is with you."

He shook his head. "Your life is your own. I am simply happy that you share it with me."

"What about your family—your parents and sister? Can you . . ." *How to ask this?*

"Can I really give up my revenge?"

She stared at him. If *her* family had been murdered, the anger would run so deep and dark—

"I walked that path a decade ago, Evelyn. The anger only made my soul more empty." He took a deep breath and searched her face. "Christopher will see that justice is done, won't he? I believe he will. He must."

Evie nodded. "Of course. He is the most honorable man I know."

"Then holding on to my hatred will serve no one."

She blinked away the tears in her eyes and wondered how she had found so different and yet so perfect a man. "I think my future is going to be much more than I could ever have imagined. I think you are going to show me . . ." She took a deep breath, her imagination failing.

"You are going to be amazing," he breathed. "I cannot wait to see what you choose to become."

She kissed him then. There was such love between them that she could not stop herself from expressing it in the most elemental of ways. He matched her excitement and her joy. And when he thrust himself inside her, their eyes met in a moment of total unity.

"I love you," they said to one another. England was forgotten. The universe lay before them and within their two hearts.

"Everything I want is right here," she said.

"You are my world," he replied, his voice filled with awe. "I love you."

Their life and their future of unexplored wonder had begun.

EMILY BRYAN

"An author to watch."
—Michelle Buonfiglio, LifetimeTV.com

BURIED TREASURE

All it took was a flick of the wrist. A deft touch of his sword point and Drake the Dragon bared her bound breasts. Then with the heat of his hands along her skin, he bared her soul. All the wantonness Jacquelyn had denied herself as a famous courtesan's daughter, all the desire she'd held in her heart while running Lord Gabriel Drake's estate flooded through her at his touch. Not that she could let a bloody pirate know it.

Gabriel may have left his seafaring days behind, but his urge to plunder was stronger than ever. Especially if it involved full, ripe lips and a warm, soft body. Unfortunately, he needed Jacquelyn's help, not her maidenhead, to learn how to behave properly toward a lady so he could marry and produce an heir. Yet Mistress Jack was the only woman he wanted, no matter what her heritage. And everyone knows what a pirate wants, a pirate takes....

Pleasuring the Pirate

ISBN 13: 978-0-8439-6133-1

Alissa Johnson

"A joyous book from a bright star." —Kathe Robin, *RT BOOKreviews*

As Luck Would Have It

A WOMAN OF THE WORLD...

After years of wild adventures overseas, Miss Sophie Everton is in no hurry to return home to the boring strictures of the ton. But she's determined to reclaim her family's fortune—even if she has to become a spy for the Prince Regent to do it.

A MAN ON A MISSION...

Before she can get her first assignment, she lands right in the lap of the dark and dashing Duke of Rockeforte. She's faced hungry tigers that didn't look nearly as predatory. Somehow the blasted man manages to foil her at every turn—and make her pulse thrum with something more than just the thrill of danger.

AND THE FICKLE FINGER OF FATE

To make a true love match, they'll have to learn to trust in each other...and, of course, a little bit of luck.

Available October 2008!   ISBN 13: 978-0-8439-6155-3

To order a book or to request a catalog call:
1-800-481-9191
This book is also available at your local bookstore, or you can check out our Web site **www.dorchesterpub.com** where you can look up your favorite authors, read excerpts, or glance at our discussion forum to see what people have to say about your favorite books.

✁ ☐ **YES!**

Sign me up for the Historical Romance Book Club and
send my FREE BOOKS! If I choose to stay in the club, I will
pay only $8.50* each month, a savings of $6.48!

NAME: _____

ADDRESS: _____

TELEPHONE: _____

EMAIL: _____

☐ I want to pay by credit card.

☐ **VISA**   ☐ **MasterCard.**   ☐ **DISCOVER**

ACCOUNT #: _____

EXPIRATION DATE: _____

SIGNATURE: _____

Mail this page along with $2.00 shipping and handling to:
Historical Romance Book Club
PO Box 6640
Wayne, PA 19087
Or fax (must include credit card information) to:
610-995-9274

You can also sign up online at **www.dorchesterpub.com**.
*Plus $2.00 for shipping. Offer open to residents of the U.S. and Canada only. Canadian
residents please call 1-800-481-9191 for pricing information.
If under 18, a parent or guardian must sign. Terms, prices and conditions subject to
change. Subscription subject to acceptance. Dorchester Publishing reserves the right to
reject any order or cancel any subscription.